CW00555616

the GIRLs GUIDE TO GETTING HITCHED

Also By Sophie Hart:

The Girl's Guide to Falling in Love
(previously published as The Beginner's Guide to the Birds and the Bees).

the GIRL'S GUIDE TO GETTING HITCHED

SOPHIE HART

bookouture

Published by Bookouture

An imprint of StoryFire Ltd.
23 Sussex Road, Ickenham, UB10 8PN
United Kingdom

www.bookouture.com

ISBN: 978-1-910751-22-0

CHAPTER 1

'My mother says I didn't open my eyes for eight days after I was born, but when I did, the first thing I saw was an engagement ring. I was hooked' –
Elizabeth Taylor

Julia Crawford was lying in bed with her husband, Nick, his body spooned around hers as they snuggled down beneath the duvet. It was a Sunday morning in early October, and neither of them had anywhere to be or anything to do, so they were snoozing lazily, enjoying the rare lie-in.

Julia sighed contentedly, as she stretched out her legs so that their feet were touching. Her head was nestled in the crook of Nick's arm, her honey-blonde hair splayed across the cream pillowcases. Nick wrapped his arm around her waist, softly caressing her bare stomach where her T-shirt had ridden up. Then his fingers moved lower, sliding beneath her sleep shorts and over the curve of her hip, suggestively stroking the soft skin of her thigh. Julia giggled as Nick pressed closer, his stubble-peppered chin resting in the hollow of her shoulder, his breath warm against her neck.

'Mmm, I know what I feel like right now,' he murmured.

'What's that?' Julia teased, with a pretty good idea of just what exactly he had in mind.

'See if you can guess. I'll give you some clues.'

Julia squirmed delightedly as Nick nuzzled her neck, little butterfly kisses running across the top of her back, his teeth gently nibbling her earlobe. Her breath grew quicker, and she wriggled round until she was nose-to-nose with her husband.

'Morning you,' she murmured, staring at him lovingly. Nick was undoubtedly an attractive man, in his mid-thirties, with thick, dark hair dotted with occasional strands of grey. His bright blue eyes sparkled as he looked back at his wife, and when he spoke his voice was low and husky.

'Morning you too.' He leaned in for a kiss, as Julia slid one leg between his, their bodies moving closer. Nick's hands began to roam, and Julia let out a sigh of pleasure… before bolting upright so fast she almost elbowed Nick in the face.

'What was that?' she asked anxiously.

'Huh? I didn't hear anything.'

'I thought…' Julia stared hard at the baby monitor, and then the noise came again. This time it was unmistakeable: a hic-coughing cry that turned into a full-on wail within seconds. Julia was instantly up and out of bed, cramming her feet into her slippers and pulling on her dressing gown, as Nick fell back against the pillows with a frustrated sigh.

'There we are… It's okay, Jack…' Julia murmured sooth-ingly, as she dashed across the hall to the baby's room, reaching into the crib and picking up her crying son. 'Mummy's here.' She held him close, rocking him softly from side to side, but his cries only became louder. 'Are you hungry, hmm? Is that what it is?'

Cradling his tiny body against her, Julia carefully carried six-month-old Jack out of his nursery and down the stairs, settling herself on the living room sofa where the support cushion was arranged. She slipped open her dressing gown and Jack began to feed, his cries stopping immediately, as Julia sank back against the sofa and watched him.

She didn't think she'd ever get over the wonder of simply staring at her son; how adorable and perfect he looked, and how incredible it was that she and Nick had created this little person together. Jack had a bundle of dark hair, just like his daddy, and everyone said the two of them looked so much alike; Jack's strong nose and dimpled chin were the spit of Nick. But Jack definitely had her eyes, Julia mused. They were green and almond-shaped and currently half-closed as he fed contentedly, making little snuffling noises. This tiny bundle had utterly transformed her and Nick's lives, and it seemed impossible to remember a time before he'd been around, when they'd been an incomplete twosome and not a blissful little family of three.

It was hard to believe that a couple of years ago, Julia had been worried that she might not even be able to *have* children. She and Nick had been trying for a baby for months, to no avail, and it had taken a serious toll on their relationship. The two of them had stopped communicating, and Julia could freely admit that she'd gone a little bit crazy back then, obsessed with getting pregnant to the exclusion of everything else. Nick had barely been able to walk through the door without Julia jumping on top of him and trying to remove his trousers, and while that sounded great in theory, the reality had left Nick feeling – in his own words – like little more than a sperm donor. He'd been constantly exhausted as he tried to keep up with Julia's insatiable demands, and for a while all the two of them did was argue, both of them becoming increasingly unhappy.

Things had got so bad that they'd been to see a sex therapist, at Nick's suggestion. Julia had refused at first, but in the end she'd had to acknowledge that the sessions with their counsellor, Annie, had really helped. Therapy hadn't been anything like she'd expected and, after a few bumps in the road, Julia and Nick had fallen in love with each other all over again. Ironically, it was when they'd mutually agreed to take the focus *off* trying for a baby that she'd finally fallen pregnant.

Upstairs, Julia heard Nick stir: the creak of the bed as he climbed out; the heavy footsteps as he padded across the landing; the gush of the shower a few moments later. Outside, a gust of wind whipped up a whirl of rust-coloured leaves from the back lawn, hurling them against the window before they dropped to the ground. The big rowan tree was bent almost double by the force of the breeze, and Julia felt grateful to be warm and cosy inside, protected from the chilly autumn weather.

Yes, she was a very lucky woman, Julia reflected, with her nice house and handsome husband and adorable baby. So why did she feel as though something was missing? A nagging sensation that one piece of the puzzle wasn't in place yet?

Over the last few weeks, Julia had begun to feel what could best be described as... restless. Of course, she adored being a stay-at-home mum, being with Jack 24/7 and administering to his every need, but recently she'd started to get the sense that she needed to do something for herself again. To rediscover her own identity, and spend time pursuing something that didn't involve cleaning mashed banana off the walls or singing endless rounds of 'Old MacDonald'.

Before Jack was born, Julia had been building up her business as an events planner, and her company had been going from strength to strength. She'd started off small, organising birthday parties and weddings for friends at a discounted rate, but word had spread quickly, and her last job before going on maternity leave had been to organise a gala dinner for the Norfolk Chamber of Commerce. It had been a magnificent event, with men in black tie, women in glamorous ballgowns, and a sumptuous meal of poached quail's eggs followed by roast sirloin of beef, before mingling and dancing to a twenty-piece orchestra. The night had been a triumph, and the Lord Mayor himself had congratulated Julia on what a fantastic job she'd done. After the bustle and excitement of dealing with VIP guests and overseeing a team of fifty, it was quite an adjustment for Julia to spend her days changing dirty nappies and wiping up vomit.

'I'll make a start on breakfast,' Nick called, sticking his head around the living room door and smiling at the tender scene in front of him. He was freshly showered and dressed in jogging bottoms and a long-sleeved top, his dark hair still damp. 'What do you fancy?'

'Anything,' Julia replied, trying to stifle a yawn. 'Surprise me.'

'Will do.' Nick gave a smart salute before disappearing into the kitchen.

Julia peered down at Jack still nestled against her. He seemed to have stopped feeding, fully awake now as he looked up at her, his eyes bright and alert.

Gently, Julia moved him off her breast, covering herself with her dressing gown and draping a muslin over her shoulder as she began to wind him. Noticing her mobile phone on the coffee table in front of her, she reached for it, scrolling through her emails with one hand as she patted Jack on the back with the other. There was the usual spam – a mid-season sale at Debenhams, offers on spa breaks from Groupon – then she noticed one from a woman called Valerie Cunningham, with the subject line: 'Wedding Planner Required'.

Intrigued, Julia clicked on it and began to read:

Dear Ms Crawford,

My name is Valerie Cunningham, and I am looking for an events planner to assist with the organisation of the forthcoming nuptials of my son, Jonathan, in July of next year. Your name has been recommended to me by Mary Moorhouse, President of the Norfolk Chamber of Commerce and a very dear friend of mine. I hold her opinion in high regard and believe you may be the right person for this very important task.

If you would like to discuss this further, please contact me at your earliest opportunity so that we can arrange a meeting and discuss my requirements. My phone number is below.

Kind regards,

Valerie Cunningham (Mrs)

Julia blinked twice, trying to take in what she'd just read. Baby Jack let out a little hiccough then settled back down, as Julia hastily re-read the email.

Already, she could feel tingles of excitement sweeping through her, a sense of anticipation replacing the usual feeling of exhaustion. Her heart began to beat faster as her eyes swept over the screen once more, picking out the key words: *forthcoming nuptials... recommended to me by Mary Moorhouse... please contact me...*

Nick strolled through carrying two plates of scrambled egg on toast, and Julia turned to him, her eyes shining.

'Hey, what's got into you?' he asked, immediately sensing the shift in her mood. 'I've never seen you so excited about breakfast before.'

'I've had an email,' Julia explained, the words tumbling out as she stood up and moved across the room to sit Jack in his bouncer. 'From a woman called Valerie Cunningham, asking me about organising her son's wedding next July. Apparently she got my name from Mary Moorhouse – you know, after I did the Chamber of Commerce event.'

'Fantastic.' Nick looked genuinely pleased as he attacked his eggs with gusto. 'It's a great opportunity for you.'

'Do you think so?' Julia wondered, suddenly feeling doubtful. 'I mean, it's not definite yet. I'd still have to meet her and go through everything. *Discuss her requirements*, as she said. But… Well, am I even ready to go back to work? We hadn't planned for me to start back this early, and…' She gazed down at her son who was gurgling happily, mesmerised by the blue elephant hanging from his rocker. 'And what would we do about Jack?'

'Don't worry about that for now,' Nick insisted. 'We'll make it work if you want to do it.'

Julia smiled gratefully at him, her mind already scrolling through potential venues and useful contacts. She recalled the excitement and exhilaration she used to get from her job, the satisfaction when everything was finally complete and the client was thrilled with the finished result. She thought about what it would be like to dress up in smart clothes once again – not just the pyjamas and dressing gown she seemed to live in nowadays – and get out of the house and meet new people, dealing with all the challenges her profession could throw at her. She loved Jack absolutely and unconditionally, but perhaps it was time to do something for herself again.

'At least meet with this Valerie woman,' Nick suggested. 'You don't have to decide anything until then.'

'And you really wouldn't mind?' Julia pressed. 'I mean, if I was working again, it might make things different around here. I wouldn't be at home all the time like I am now, and we'd have to work something out with the childcare. It wouldn't be easy, and I don't want us to go back to how we were before.'

Julia didn't have to spell out what she meant – both of them could instantly recall the time before Jack was conceived, when all they seemed to do was bicker and sulk. Back then, Nick had started spending longer at work in an attempt to avoid the strained atmosphere at home, leading to him becoming a little too close to a female colleague, and Julia had struggled to forgive him for the indiscretion. They'd managed to put the incident behind them, but it was a situation neither of them wanted to repeat.

When Nick finally spoke his voice was gentle, his eyes warm as he looked at his wife. Yes, Julia might have dark circles under her eyes, her blonde hair hastily pulled back in a scruffy ponytail, and as far as he could tell she'd been wearing the same T-shirt for a week, but she was still gorgeous; still the woman he married; still *his* Julia. They'd been through their ups and downs, but come through it stronger than ever. 'Do whatever makes you happy,' Nick told her honestly. 'I'll support you all the way.'

Julia stared back at him, a smile slowly spreading across her tired features at the prospect of tackling a new venture and getting her business back on track. She leaned over to Nick, kissing him softly. 'Thank you. I'm a very lucky woman.'

'And don't you forget it,' Nick replied with a wink. 'Now eat your breakfast,' he admonished her, as he pulled her down onto his lap and she let out a squeal. 'It's getting cold.'

CHAPTER 2

'Grow old along with me! The best is yet to be' –
Robert Browning

The first strains of Wagner's 'Bridal Chorus' creaked into life on the organ in the old country church, and the expectant congregation turned around in their seats, every eye focused on the ornate door through which the bride would make her entrance.

Outside, on a brilliant, summer, sun-dappled afternoon, a beautiful young woman stood beside her father, aware that these were her final few moments as Miss Deborah Barlow. In approximately thirty minutes' time, she would be Mrs Stephen Reid, and the happiest woman on earth.

Debbie turned to look at her six bridesmaids, resplendent in peach silk. Her six-year-old niece looked cute as a button as she skipped around excitedly, a basket of flower petals hung over one arm, as Debbie's best friend, Angela, gave her an enthusiastic thumbs up. Debbie turned back to her father, his face glowing with pride, and the two of them linked arms before stepping forward and walking reverentially into the church.

There were gasps as the assembled friends and relatives caught their first view of the blushing bride, her Auntie Jean hastily tugging a handkerchief from her clutch bag to wipe away a stray tear. And at the far end of the aisle stood Debbie's beloved fiancé, Stevie. He was gazing at her as though he was the luckiest man alive, and Debbie knew without a doubt that she was marrying the right man for her.

A radiant smile lit up her face as their eyes locked, and the congregation exhaled in a collective 'aaah'. Debbie looked utterly beautiful, her dark, wavy hair pinned up to reveal her long, elegant neck, and showing off her cheekbones to perfection. Her shimmering dress fitted her slender figure as though she'd been born to wear it, the strapless style highlighting her toned arms and defined collarbone, whilst the corset-style bodice sculpted her tiny waist before dropping to the floor in layer after layer of white organza. Debbie knew that she'd never looked more incredible in her whole life, and she beamed round at her family and friends, taking in their smiles and tears, acknowledging the envious glances at her perfect size ten figure…

Then Debbie opened her eyes and the image faded. The hot summer's day disappeared and the quaint old church was no more. Instead, Debbie found herself standing in her messy bedroom, with the tatty old curtains and the bed sheets that needed washing. Her dog, Scamp, a scruffy Yorkie-cross she'd got from a rescue centre, was lying on the duvet staring at her curiously.

As Debbie gazed into the wardrobe mirror in front of her, her heart sank. The stunning wedding dress had vanished and, in its place, Debbie was wearing only her saggy old bra and greying knickers; a Cinderella in cheap lingerie after the clock had struck midnight.

Nor was Debbie's body the goddess-like vision she'd been imagining. Biting her bottom lip unhappily, she took in the way her wobbly stomach hung over the waistband of her panties, the way her thighs were rippled with cellulite and rubbed together when she moved. As she held up her arms to give them an experimental shake, flaps of loose skin – the dreaded bingo wings – quivered like blancmange.

Although she knew it was un-feminist to admit it, Debbie hated her body. Oh, it was fine for all the women's magazines to say you should be happy whatever size or shape you were – then hypocritically fill their pages with image after image of body-beautiful specimens – but Debbie just couldn't seem to find the love for her thick ankles or double chin.

Whilst all her friends looked great in strappy little tops and skinny jeans, Debbie covered up in baggy trousers and shapeless jumpers. Fluctuating between a size eighteen and twenty, depending on where she shopped, Debbie was hardly the biggest woman on the planet, but there were days when she felt like an elephant amongst her slim, toned friends, with their neat little bosoms and impossible-to-achieve thigh-gaps.

The front door banged and Debbie jumped, realising Stevie was home from work. Panic-stricken, she lunged for her jogging bottoms and frantically pulled them on, as Scamp leapt off the bed and bolted downstairs, barking in welcome.

'Hello, Scamp. Hello, boy! Debs, you around?'

'Upstairs,' she called back, trying to keep the panic out of her voice, as she yanked open the chest of drawers and grabbed a clean sweater. She knew it was ridiculous, but she suddenly hated the thought of Stevie looking at her body, despite the fact he'd seen it hundreds of times before.

Wrestling frantically with the jumper, she heard Stevie bound up the stairs, and seconds later he was pushing open the bedroom door, the dog following at his heels.

'Aha, what do we have here?' he grinned, his eyes lighting up as he took in the sight of his semi-naked fiancée. Stevie was twenty-seven, the same age as Debbie, and worked as a trainee surveyor. He had a shock of red hair that had made him the target of endless teasing in his school days, but which he now embraced, and he was far from skinny himself, with a cute little paunch that Debbie loved to squeeze.

Right now, Debbie looked horrified, her face flaming as she tried to cover herself with the jumper she hadn't had time to put on. Even though she was exactly the same size as she had been when Stevie left for work that morning, she suddenly felt hugely self-conscious, all too aware of every lump and bump.

'That's exactly the sight I want to see when I get home from a long, hard day,' Stevie continued, reaching out for her.

Debbie flinched and backed away, almost tripping over the corner of the bed in her haste to get away from him.

Stevie frowned. 'What's the matter? Where's my welcome kiss?'

Debbie looked back at him, her dark eyes anxious. Reluctantly, she stepped towards him, holding the jumper tightly against her as she stretched up to peck him on the lips.

'That's better.' Stevie wrapped his arms around her, but as Debbie felt his hands settle on the hated back fat pushing out from underneath her bra, she squirmed away uncomfortably.

'What?' Stevie demanded. 'What's the matter?' He looked hurt, and Debbie winced guiltily.

'It's nothing.'

'It must be something! Have I done something wrong?'

'No, of course not.'

How could Debbie explain what the problem really was? She didn't want Stevie thinking it was *his* fault but, equally, she really didn't want a conversation about how much she loathed her body shape right now. 'It's… Oh, it doesn't matter. It's fine.'

'Really?' Stevie looked doubtful, but Debbie nodded insistently. 'Good. Come here then.' He opened up his arms, and Debbie looked at them uncertainly.

'I'll just put this on,' she stalled, holding up the jumper.

'No, don't do that,' Stevie protested. 'I like you all naked.'

'Well I *don't*.' The words slipped out before Debbie had a chance to censor them.

Stevie sighed, suddenly understanding why she was being so cold towards him. 'Is that what this is about, Debs? You know that doesn't matter to me. I love you, no matter what you look li-… no matter what,' he finished awkwardly.

Debbie didn't reply. The two of them stood in silence, the jumper still held protectively over her chest, like a defensive shield.

'Debs, you know I think you're gorgeous,' Stevie tried again, his voice soft. 'Always have, always will. I just wish you could see that.' Gently, he took hold of her hands, attempting to prise the sweater from her, but Debbie clung on determinedly.

'Do you know what I'd really like?' Stevie murmured, changing tack. Debbie looked back at him questioningly, as he reached into his trouser pocket and pulled out his phone. 'I'd love to take a photo of you, just like you are now. All sexy in your bra, with your hair curling around your face, and that amazing cleavage…'

Debbie recoiled in shock. 'Is that a joke?'

'No! Why wouldn't I want a photo of my gorgeous fiancée?' Stevie said honestly, unable to understand Debbie's outrage. 'It'd stay private obviously – just for you and me. Something for me to look at when I'm at work, to cheer me up when I think about the wonderful woman who's waiting at home for me. Who's going to be my wife next year.'

'No way. Absolutely no way.' Debbie was appalled at the suggestion. 'What if one of your mates saw it? I'd never hear the end of it. Besides, they'd probably wonder why you had a picture of a beached whale on your phone…'

She choked back a sob as she fled from the room. Stevie tried to stop her as she ran past, but she pushed him off.

'Leave me alone!'

Debbie raced down the stairs and into the living room, finally able to pull on the oversized black sweater she'd been clutching all this time. It felt warm and soft, cosy like a blanket, and she was instantly more relaxed. Throwing herself down on the L-shaped sofa, Debbie listened for a moment, her heart beating fast as she wondered whether Stevie would follow her. She heard the creak of the floorboards as he moved around the bedroom then crossed the landing to the bathroom, and Debbie realised he'd decided not to come after her. She could hardly blame him, she thought, furious at herself. She'd been feeling insecure and taken her mood out on him when it really wasn't his fault. Even Scamp had stayed upstairs, clearly taking Stevie's side in the argument.

Almost without thinking, Debbie got up off the sofa and drifted through to the kitchen, automatically opening the cupboard and reaching for the biscuit tin. Suddenly she realised what she was doing and stopped short, dropping the custard cream she'd picked out and slamming the lid back on with a satisfying crash.

For a moment she simply stood there, her breath coming fast, her eyes glazed, as she hung onto the tin like a drowning man to a life raft.

'You okay, Debs?'

She hadn't heard Stevie come into the room and she jumped as he spoke, whirling round to face him. Taking in the worried look on his face, she forced a smile then put the biscuit tin back in the cupboard.

'Fine,' she assured him, busying herself with taking ingredients out of the fridge for the lasagne she planned to cook tonight. 'Totally fine. Look, I'm really sorry about earlier. I don't know what came over me.'

'Come here, silly,' Stevie sighed, as Debbie put down a family-sized block of cheese and crossed the kitchen, falling into his arms without hesitation. Stevie stroked the top of her head, smoothing down the silky hair that smelt of fruity conditioner, before planting a kiss on her forehead.

'I love you, Debbie. You know that, don't you?'

'Yeah,' she nodded, as she nestled against his chest, the size and smell of him reassuringly familiar. At five feet eleven, he was a few inches taller than she was, and his body felt solid and protective. 'I love you too. Sorry for being a numpty – I was just having a moment.'

Stevie's chest vibrated as he laughed, her head bouncing against the soft cotton of his T-shirt. 'Listen, I've got an idea.'

'Oh no, not another one,' Debbie groaned. 'Does it involve a camera-phone and me taking my clothes off?'

Stevie chuckled. 'Not this time. Although I'm still up for it if you are?'

Debbie glared at him, narrowing her eyes.

'That'll be a no, then. Seriously though, I was thinking, why don't we grab a takeaway tonight, save you cooking? My shout. Indian, maybe? I've been craving tandoori chicken all afternoon, with a peshwari naan and some onion bhajis. Mmmm,' Stevie was practically dribbling. Even Scamp was licking his chops, as he stared up at the two of them, a low whine escaping from him. 'What do you reckon?'

Debbie hesitated. Her mouth was watering at the thought of a creamy korma, accompanied by poppadoms dipped liberally in sweet mango chutney.

'Yeah, go on th—' she began, but something stopped her. Suddenly the vision of a takeaway feast was replaced with the daydream she'd had earlier; the perfect size ten wedding dress, and how incredible she'd looked in it.

She wanted it to be more than just a daydream.

She wanted it to be reality.

'You know what?' Debbie began slowly. 'I don't know if I *do* feel like ordering out. How about I whip us up a stir-fry instead? I've got everything I need in the fridge, and it won't take long.'

'Sure,' Stevie shrugged, a little gutted to be giving up his Indian, but ready to agree to anything if it got his fiancée back in a good mood. 'Do you need a hand with anything?'

'No, it's fine. You go put your feet up,' Debbie insisted, putting the cheddar and beef back in the fridge and bringing out carrots, peppers, onions and courgettes.

'If you say so,' Stevie grinned, stealing another kiss before heading through to the living room and turning on the TV.

Debbie quickly got to work, a growing pile of colourful veggies soon appearing on the chopping board in front of her. As she sliced and diced, she felt a growing sense of excitement, a certainty that she'd never experienced before. She *could* do this! She *could* lose weight! Other people did it all the time, so why shouldn't she?

Oh, she'd tried to diet in the past, but never got very far. Debbie's regimes usually consisted of living on soups and juices for a day or two, becoming increasingly hungry and bad-tempered, before finally cracking in dramatic style. Craving fat and carbs, she would binge on macaroni cheese and chips, litres of fizzy drink and whole tubs of ice cream with chocolate sauce.

Food was used as a reward when she'd done something good; as a treat when she was miserable; as a pick-me-up when she was tired. But now it was time for her to take control, Debbie vowed, thinking once again of her ideal wedding dress. All she needed was a little motivation and a lot of willpower.

Debbie drizzled a miniscule amount of oil into a wok, throwing in two sliced chicken breasts, then adding garlic, chilli and ginger.

'Smells delicious,' Stevie called through appreciatively.

Debbie smiled to herself, thinking of his reaction when he saw his new, slimline fiancée in just a few months' time. She would definitely buy herself some sexy underwear to show off her hot body; maybe she'd even let Stevie take that picture he'd been asking for!

Yeah, thought Debbie, feeling another surge of excitement. This time she was going to do it. She was going to lose weight, shape up, and nothing – not even red velvet cupcakes or deep-pan four-cheese pizza – was going to stand in her way.

CHAPTER 3

*'It is a truth universally acknowledged, that a single man in possession of good fortune, must be in want of a wife' – **Jane Austen, Pride and Prejudice***

'Wow,' Julia murmured under her breath, as the iron gates in front of her slowly swung open. She drove through them onto the sweeping gravel driveway, feeling a little self-conscious in her ageing Renault Clio as she pulled up beside a veritable fleet of enormous 4x4s and sleek Jaguars, the massive vehicles dwarfing her own tiny one.

The house itself was just as impressive. The address on Eaton Road was one of the most prestigious in Norwich, and Julia had been prepared for something big, but this was practically a mansion. An Arts and Crafts-style house, built in faded red-brick with mullioned windows, it boasted lush green lawns and even a small, stone water fountain, bubbling away.

Julia stepped out of the car, breathing deeply and telling herself that she'd be fine. This was her first potential job since having a baby, and to say she wasn't feeling on top of her game right now would be an understatement. Her emotions were all over the place, on account of having to leave Jack for a couple of hours, and she couldn't help but remember the uncertain look on Nick's face as he'd waved her off. Jack had been wriggling and fidgeting in Nick's arms, his face reddening and on the verge of a tantrum.

'Maybe I should reschedule?' Julia had wondered unhappily.

'We'll be fine,' Nick had told her, sounding less than convinced. 'Good luck!'

'You too,' Julia had replied, her stomach churning uncomfortably.

Right now, standing outside the huge house with its imposing facade, Julia felt a million miles away from the calm, competent professional she was hoping to portray.

She quickly glanced down at her sensible black trousers and navy-blue blouse, checking that they weren't covered in apple puree or porridge or… something worse. She was convinced that the outfit was frumpy and unflattering. It didn't help that her boobs were straining against the buttons of the blouse, occasionally offering a peek at the sturdy white nursing bra below; she was still breastfeeding, and hadn't yet gone back down to her pre-pregnancy cup size.

'Ah, you must be Julia. I'm Valerie. Do come in.'

The front door had opened to reveal a woman who was even more intimidating than the house she lived in. She appeared to be in her late fifties, and was immaculately groomed, with her light grey hair swept back in an elegant chignon. Her make-up was neat yet subtle, and she wore a cream pussy-bow blouse with a tweed pencil skirt and low-heeled brown court shoes.

As someone who'd spent the last six months in flannelette pyjamas and fluffy slippers, Julia could only admire her dedication to looking good.

'Yes, I'm Julia Crawford,' she smiled, recovering herself as she extended a hand. 'It's very nice to meet you.'

But Valerie was already marching off down the corridor, and Julia hurried to keep up with her, her eyes darting round at the beautiful wooden staircase and the oil paintings on the walls. Her feet sank into the pristine cream carpet as they walked, and they passed endless corridors leading off to who-knew-where in this enormous house.

'You have a beautiful home,' Julia said, as she finally caught up.

'Thank you,' Valerie replied graciously, turning left into what Julia assumed must be the sitting room. It looked like a reception room at Buckingham Palace, with its elegant furniture and antique grandfather clock. There were heavy draped curtains hung at the long windows, and as Julia glanced outside she could see through to the large back garden, with its well-maintained flower beds and leafy shrubs. Even the trees hadn't dared to spoil the perfection of the scene by dropping their leaves. Valerie probably had a gardener who rushed out to pick them up as soon as they fell, thought Julia, stifling a mildly hysterical giggle.

'Aimee, don't just stand there like a spare part, go and get us all some tea,' Valerie snapped at a young woman Julia hadn't noticed. She was in her early twenties, with dark blonde hair cut in a flattering bob, and she flashed a brief, nervous smile at Julia before hurrying out of the room.

'Now,' Valerie turned to Julia with a flourish. '*This* is my son, Jonathan. Isn't he handsome?' she purred, beaming at him.

Jonathan rolled his eyes indulgently, but seemed to revel in his mother's attention.

'Pleased to meet you,' he said, standing up from the damask couch to shake Julia's hand. He *was* very good looking, Julia noted; tall, with dark hair, bright blue eyes, and flashing white teeth. There was an air of confidence about him too, as though he was used to getting his own way.

'So you're the groom-to-be,' Julia grinned. 'Congratulations.'

'Thank you. I'm a very lucky man.'

'And will your fiancée be joining us?'

'Yes, she'll be along shortly,' Valerie cut in, taking a seat on the sofa beside her son, and indicating that Julia should take one of the armchairs alongside. 'Now, I've already impressed upon you – I hope – the importance of this wedding,' Valerie began seriously, as Julia nodded. 'Jonathan is my only son – my only child, in fact – and he's incredibly special to me, so this has to be a memorable and, indeed, magnificent occasion. Nothing vulgar, of course.'

'No, of course not,' Julia agreed, as she opened her pad and began to make notes. She wrote the words 'ONLY SON' in capitals, then added 'NOT VULGAR' and underlined it.

'This wedding is going to be the highlight of the summer social calendar, and I need to ensure that everything goes without a hitch. I've heard very good things from Mary Moorhouse about the work you did for the Chamber of Commerce gala, and I hope you live up to your reputation.'

'Thank you, I'm flattered,' Julia replied, unsure how to take Valerie's comments and deciding to give her the benefit of the doubt. 'Do you have any dates in mind?'

'We're looking at the first Saturday in July.'

'And have you approached any venues? I should warn you that places can get booked up years in advance, and ten months is an extremely tight timeframe for an event on this scale.'

'I have a few possibilities in mind,' Valerie explained, and Julia noticed how neatly she was sitting, with her knees and ankles together, her posture rigidly upright. 'I'm sure that with the right incentive, we'll be able to have the venue – and indeed caterers, orchestra, florist, and anything else this wedding might require – of our choice. Money is *not* an object,' she finished, with a slight hint of a smile.

Julia was about to reply when Aimee came back into the room. She was carrying a tray on which she'd balanced a teapot, teacups and saucers, a milk jug and a sugar bowl, all in the same floral-patterned china. She set it down nervously in the centre of the Louis IV-style coffee table, and began pouring out the tea.

'Would you like milk and sugar?' she asked Julia, in a soft voice.

'Just milk, please,' Julia smiled at her, wondering what it must be like to have staff. The house was immaculate, and Julia very much doubted that Valerie ever got down on her hands and knees to scrub the skirting boards or disinfect the toilet. She wondered if this girl was some sort of live-in housekeeper.

'No biscuits?' Valerie burst out sharply. 'Where are your manners, Aimee? Well, I suppose you're not to know, are you? There's a Marks and Spencer's selection in the pantry, go and get those. And for heaven's sake, don't just bring the box through. Arrange them nicely on a plate first.'

'Yes. Sorry,' Aimee apologised, her cheeks flaming red as she scurried off. Julia felt bad for her – the girl had looked mortified – but when she glanced across at Valerie she merely shook her head and tutted disapprovingly.

Jonathan evidently felt bad too, as he leaned across to his mother and commented, 'You know, you really shouldn't be so hard on her. She's trying her best.'

'She's got to learn,' Valerie shot back, without a trace of remorse. 'It's a very valuable skill, being able to hostess and run a household. Now, where was I?'

'We were talking about venues,' Julia reminded her, keen to get the conversation back on track and steer Valerie away from the deficiencies of her housekeeper.

'Ah, yes. Now, we went to look at Hambledon Hall, didn't we Jonathan?' Valerie was all charm once more, as she reached across to pat her son on the knee. 'And that really was beautiful. But the ante-rooms were very cramped, and there were no hand towels in the bathroom – just those noisy dryers, which I find very inappropriate. Wellington Lodge was charming, but they only served Lanson champagne.' Valerie pulled a face.

'How many guests are you thinking of having?' asked Julia, underlining 'NO LANSON' in her pad, as Aimee walked back into the room, a selection of chocolate biscuits arranged in a fan shape on a bone-china plate. She set them down in front of Julia and then, to Julia's astonishment, Aimee poured a cup of tea for herself and went to sit on the sofa, on the other side of Jonathan.

Perhaps Valerie was more lenient than Julia had imagined, if she was happy to fraternise with 'the help' in this way. It was Saturday after all, so perhaps once Aimee's duties were completed she was allowed to sit with Valerie and her son.

Of course, Julia realised suddenly. Aimee would most likely play a key role in helping out with the wedding, so no wonder Valerie wanted her to sit in on the meeting. She was probably some kind of personal assistant, rather than a domestic housekeeper.

'I think we're looking at around two-fifty. Possibly three hundred,' Valerie said airily. 'Of course, we have an extensive network of friends and acquaintances, then there are all Jonathan's business contacts, not to mention everyone from the club. How many from your side?' she asked, her voice dropping several degrees, as she turned away from Julia back towards her son.

'Not very many,' Aimee replied in that same, soft voice. 'I only have a small family, so there won't be many relatives. I have a few school friends that I'd like to invite.'

'Hmm,' Valerie's lips pursed into a tight pucker. 'We'll see if we can fit them in. There might be some room towards the back.'

As Julia looked on in confusion, Jonathan stretched his arm languidly, draping it around Aimee's shoulders and giving her a little squeeze.

'Of course we'll find room,' he assured her. 'We've got to have… what's her name? Rachel, that's it. We've got to have her there, haven't we?'

'I had thought she could be one of my bridesmaids,' Aimee offered shyly.

'Whatever makes you happy, darling. Of course that's fine, isn't it, Mother?'

'I suppose,' Valerie replied coldly.

'Thank you, Jon,' Aimee beamed, snuggling up against him.

Julia was growing more incredulous by the second. *Aimee* was Jonathan's fiancée? Aimee, who she'd mistaken for some kind of hired help – whose future mother-in-law *treated* her like some kind of hired help – was actually the bride-to-be?

'So *you're* the future Mrs Cunningham,' Julia burst out, unable to help herself.

'Yes, I am,' Aimee confirmed, with a tinkling laugh, as she gazed up at her fiancé.

'I told you I was a lucky man,' Jonathan grinned. 'Isn't she incredible?'

'You both look so happy together,' Julia told them. 'And what a gorgeous engagement ring,' she gushed, suddenly noticing it for the first time and leaning over to take a closer look as Aimee stretched out her hand. 'It's very unusual. Is it a ruby?'

'In a pavé diamond setting,' Aimee nodded. 'I have to confess, it's far bigger than anything I would have chosen. I'm terrified of losing it.'

'No need to sound so ungrateful, dear,' Valerie interjected. 'It's a family heirloom,' she informed Julia, her face once again a picture of disapproval. 'And Jonathan has clearly decided that Aimee is the right person to give it to.'

'Of course she is, Mother,' Jonathan laughed easily.

Valerie picked a piece of lint from her skirt, brushing it onto the carpet. 'Well, at least it's heavily insured.'

'It really is a beautiful ring,' Julia cut in hastily. Valerie's displeasure hung heavily in the room, a black thundercloud looming threateningly on the horizon. 'And Aimee, do you have any thoughts about what you'd like for your wedding day? I'm sure you have lots of ideas.'

'Oh, if it was up to me, I'd probably have a very small, intimate wedding. Just me and Jon – maybe on a beach somewhere tropical…'

Julia glanced across at Valerie and saw her turn positively pale at the thought.

'But I'm happy to go with whatever Jon wants. And Mrs Cunningham is so good at organising. She has ideas for things I'd never even have thought of.'

'Well, we have to make sure that everything's appropriate, don't we?' Valerie smiled tightly. 'That the day is elegant and sophisticated, with a real sense of class. And some people are just better at this kind of thing than others.'

Her words lingered in the air, a thinly veiled insult, and Julia waited for Aimee to spit back a reply, or for Jonathan to defend his fiancée against his mother's obvious barbs. But no one spoke. The only sound was the chink of china as Valerie placed her teacup back down on its saucer.

Julia swallowed, wondering whether she really wanted this commission at all. She could be back at home now, cuddling with Jack, watching him smile and gurgle as she played with the furry caterpillar toy that never failed to make him squeal with delight; not here in this strained atmosphere, wondering whether she could ever meet Valerie's impossibly exacting standards…

But no, she was being silly, Julia reassured herself. It was merely nerves at being a working woman once again and getting back into the swing of things. She'd dealt with bigger events than a simple *wedding*, and come up against bigger divas than the demanding Valerie. Besides, Aimee seemed like an absolute sweetheart, and Julia felt sure that as the wedding drew closer, Valerie would take a step back and let Aimee have her say. After all, how bad could the woman possibly be?

Shaking her head to dispel any negative thoughts, Julia opened her notebook to a fresh page, and turned to Aimee with a beaming smile. 'So,' she asked brightly. 'Have you started shopping for your dress yet?'

CHAPTER 4

*'Hollywood brides keep the bouquets and throw
away the grooms'* – **Groucho Marx**

'That's *my* T-shirt, give it here!'

'Not until you give me back my lip gloss. It's Benefit, it cost a fortune.'

'I haven't got your stupid lip gloss. You probably lent it to one of your stupid friends.'

'You're such a liar! I know you took it out of my school bag. Give it back or I'll punch you.'

'I'd like to see you try…'

Gill closed her eyes, trying to block out the sounds of fighting coming from upstairs. She'd just got herself settled in the living room with a cup of tea and a copy of *Blushing Brides* magazine, but she should have known that five minutes of peace and quiet in her chaotic household was going to be impossible. She turned to the first page, but barely had a chance to take in the contents when there was the sharp sound of a slap, followed by an outraged yell.

Gill threw down the magazine and jumped up from the sofa, taking the stairs two at a time.

'What's going on here?' she demanded, as she burst into the room that her thirteen-year-old daughter, Kelly, shared with her soon-to-be stepsister, twelve-year-old Paige. Posters of boy bands were plastered over every spare inch of wall space, whilst the floor was a sea of discarded clothes. Hair straighteners, tongs, and half a dozen bottles of glossing spray jostled for space on the vanity table, alongside perfume and jewellery and abandoned school books.

The two girls barely looked up at Gill, her eyes blazing, her hands planted firmly on her hips. She was a formidable woman in her early forties – stocky, with a large bosom, her hair cropped short and dyed a vivid shade of aubergine – but her daughters paid little attention.

'She took my lip gloss,' Kelly screeched, at the same time as Paige yelled:

'She never lets me borrow anything, she's such a mean cow.'

'Don't call your sister a cow.'

'She's not my sister! And you're not my mum. I should have known you'd take her side, you always do,' Paige stropped, flinging herself down on her bed, tears springing to her eyes.

'Paige, that's not true. Kelly, can't you let her borrow it? Just a little bit to try?'

'Mum, that's not fair,' Kelly retorted, with a terrifyingly teenage roll of the eyeballs. 'Just because she doesn't have nice stuff doesn't mean she can borrow mine. She shouldn't even be wearing lip gloss, she's only a kid.'

'I'm, like, nine months younger than you.'

'Yeah, and you still don't have any tits.'

'Oh here, have it back,' Paige yelled, flinging the lip gloss with venom. 'I didn't want to wear it anyway, you selfish bitch. I'll probably catch herpes from it.'

'Paige, language!' Gill was shocked.

'I don't care. I hate you.'

Gill inhaled sharply, stung by Paige's words. She knew the situation was difficult for her – well, it was difficult for all of them – but she didn't deserve to be spoken to like that.

'Paige, you can't—' Gill began, when a riot of shouting erupted from the next bedroom.

'Yes! I killed him! I totally beat you, you loser.'

'Yeah, but only 'cos you cheated. You never normally win.'

'I didn't cheat! How could I cheat? You're just mad 'cos I totally smashed your score.'

'Boys, please,' Gill snapped, poking her head around the door to where her nine-year-old twins, Freddy and Finlay, were furiously bashing at their PS3 controllers.

'Sorry, Mum,' both of them replied in unison, neither looking up from the screen where round two of *Street Battle* had just started.

Four-year-old Sammy was sitting on a beanbag watching them, half-heartedly playing with a plastic dinosaur. When he saw Gill, he jumped up and ran over to her, twining himself around her legs like a cat. She reached down to stroke his soft, sandy-coloured hair, and he stared up at her with hopeful eyes.

'I'm hungry. Can I have some peanut butter?'

Gill smiled. 'Okay. Let's go make some snacks.'

He wandered happily out of the room, Gill following behind him. Then he sat down at the top of the stairs, slowly bumping his way down every step.

'Sammy,' Gill said warningly, as she eyed the threadbare carpet in the centre of the stairs. 'Do it properly, please. On your feet.'

Sam swivelled round, flashing her an adorable smile, before continuing to bump-bump-bump all the way down to the bottom where he waited for Gill, taking her hand and leading her through to the kitchen.

'So, peanut butter,' Gill said brightly, as she pulled the almost-empty jar out of the cupboard and opened the breadbin. 'Do you want banana on it too?'

Sam thought for a moment, his dark eyes serious, before he nodded decisively, hitching up his trousers, which were starting to slide down.

Gill quickly made the sandwich, cutting it into four then pouring Sam a glass of blackcurrant squash. She carried it all through to the living room where he climbed up onto the sofa beside her, balancing the plate on his knee.

'What's that?' he asked through a mouthful of bread, spotting Gill's magazine.

'It's full of pretty dresses. Wedding dresses. Do you want to help me choose one?'

Sam reached for it, leaving smeary banana fingerprints on the glossy pages.

'Pretty,' he commented. 'Like Princess Elsa.'

Gill laughed. 'Yes, like Elsa from *Frozen*. Although I'm not sure I'm going to look quite like that,' she said ruefully, looking down at her distinctly un-Disney-princess-like figure.

Sam took another bite of his sandwich and chewed it thoughtfully.

'Are you my mummy now?' he asked.

Gill took a breath, the question catching her off guard. 'No,' she began carefully. 'Not exactly. You've already got a mummy, remember?'

Sam frowned, so Gill stood up and walked over to the dresser, rifling through the top drawer and pulling out a photo. It was a holiday snap, taken in what looked like a bar or restaurant in some hot Mediterranean country, and it showed an attractive young woman with curly blonde hair and a deep tan wearing a vivid pink bandeau top. She was smiling at the camera, and in her arms she held a mousy-haired child, less than a year old. He was wedged on her hip, looking away from the camera at something that had caught his attention.

'That's your mummy. Do you remember?' Gill asked softly, brushing the crumbs from Sam's cheek.

He stared at the photo in silence.

'And who's that, do you know?' Gill prompted, pointing at the young boy in the picture.

'A baby,' Sam replied confidently, as Gill smiled.

'It *is* a baby, but it's *you*. It's you when you were a baby, with your mummy.'

Sam stared up at Gill, wide-eyed with disbelief. Then suddenly he seemed to lose all interest in the photo. Cramming the last of the sandwich into his mouth, he climbed down from the sofa and announced, 'I'm going to play with Freddy and Finlay.'

Moments later, Gill heard the pounding of his feet as he ran up the stairs, followed by the blare of computer games as he pushed open the door to the twins' room.

Gill was deep in thought as she replaced the photo in the drawer, taking one last look at the woman – whose name was Tina – before firmly closing it. She found herself wondering what it would be like to have your own child forget about you. How you could go off and leave your babies without a backward glance, then get on with living your life as though nothing had happened. To Gill, the idea was inconceivable.

She carried Sam's plate through to the kitchen, brushing off the crumbs and quickly rinsing it, before heading back to the living room where her tea was rapidly cooling. Sitting down, she picked up her magazine, and had barely raised the mug of tea to her lips when Kelly wandered in.

'What's wrong with you?' Gill asked cheerfully, noting her pouting lips and sullen expression.

Kelly shrugged, managing to convey frustration and anger and apathy all in one movement. Gill was reminded once again of how terrifyingly teenage her daughter had already become.

'Come and tell me all about it,' Gill offered, putting down her tea and patting the space beside her that Sam had just vacated.

Kelly flopped down on the tired brown sofa, letting out an enormous sigh. Gill waited patiently for her to speak.

'It's not fair!' Kelly burst out finally. 'Why do I have to share a bedroom with Paige? She's so annoying, and she always steals my stuff. I thought I'd lost my Jack Wills hoody, then I found it stashed in her wardrobe. She reckoned it had got there "*accidentally*".' Kelly put air quotes around the word.

'I know it's hard sometimes, but there's no other option.'

'Why can't we get a bigger house? I bet it wouldn't cost that much more.'

'It'd cost more than we could afford.'

'But I'm the eldest,' Kelly pressed on, with flawless logic. 'I should have my own room, not Sam. Why does he need to be on his own? He's only a little kid.'

'We've been through this. Obviously the twins can share a room, and it makes sense for you and Paige to share.'

'Why can't Paige share with Sam?' Kelly was kicking the sofa with her heels in a slow rhythm. 'They're brother and sister after all.'

'Yes, but Paige is twelve and Sam is only four. It wouldn't be… appropriate. If you two could learn to get along, I'm sure you'd love it.'

Kelly frowned, looking at Gill as though she'd just suggested going on a hot date with Nigel Farage. 'That's not happening, Mum.'

This time it was Gill's turn to shrug with frustration. She reached for her tea again, and Kelly caught sight of the magazine curving over the sofa arm.

'What's that?' she asked, giving an exaggerated yawn as she saw the title. 'Oh, wedding stuff. You're still planning on doing that then?'

Gill couldn't hide her amusement. 'Yes, we are still planning on doing that. Do you want to help me out? Maybe give me your opinion on some dresses?'

'No, not really.' Reluctantly, Kelly took the magazine her mother was proffering, listlessly flicking through. 'That one's okay I suppose,' she offered, pointing out a very simple dress, with a lightly jewelled bodice and plain skirt. 'But seriously, Mum, you're going to look ridiculous.'

Gill's eyebrows shot up in surprise.

'I mean, you're not some skinny twenty-five-year-old model, like in the photos,' Kelly went on. 'You've already been married once anyway. What's the point in doing it again? There's no guarantee you've made the right decision this time around either.'

Gill took a deep breath, biting back a dozen snappy retorts that were on the tip of her tongue. 'Like Mike says,' she replied calmly, 'when we're married, we'll all be a proper family.'

Kelly snorted.

'I do wish you'd make more of an effort. Besides, you'll get to be a bridesmaid. Aren't you looking forward to that?'

'Little kids get to be bridesmaids,' Kelly remarked witheringly. 'I'm too old for that. It'll just be embarrassing.'

'What'll be embarrassing?'

The two of them turned to see Mike standing in the doorway. He was thirty-eight, five years younger than Gill, and he was well built, with a pleasant face and a balding head that he shaved. His hands were covered in oil, from where he'd been tinkering with his motorbike out in the garage.

'Nothing,' Kelly muttered.

'Right, nothing,' he grinned, catching Gill's eye. She flashed him a look of exasperation. 'And what are you up to today?' he asked, directing the question at Kelly.

Kelly gave an enormous sigh, dragging herself off the sofa as though it required superhuman effort. 'Like you'd care,' was her parting shot, as she sloped out of the door.

Mike looked at Gill, disappointment written across his face. 'Something I said?'

'Give her time. She'll come round.'

'It's been almost two years. How much more time does she need?'

Gill said nothing, and Mike came to sit down beside her, catching sight of *Blushing Brides*.

'How's the planning coming along? Found anything yet?'

'Sometimes I think this wedding'll never happen,' Gill sighed. 'I barely get five minutes to myself in this house, let alone time to sit down and think about the venue and the guests and the food and the flowers and all of the endless stuff that goes into planning a wedding. Chair covers! Who knew that naked chairs were frowned upon and you need to hire things to dress them up in? And with a colour theme too.'

Mike smiled, leaning across to peck her on the lips. 'Don't stress about it. Let's just do something small, like we agreed. We're hardly Kim Kardashian and Kanye West.'

'But even something small takes planning,' Gill wailed.

'Okay then, let's elope. You and me, Gretna Green, next Saturday.'

'With five kids in tow?'

'Nah, we can leave them at home. They can fend for themselves for a weekend.'

Gill blanched. 'Can you imagine? It'd be like *Lord of the Flies*. We wouldn't have a house left to come back to.'

'Which would solve the bedroom issue,' Mike pointed out. 'No one would have a room, so there'd be no arguing. We could just camp out in the garden, tell the girls to pretend they're at a music festival. They'd love it.'

Gill burst out laughing, as Mike leaned across and kissed her once again. He might not be the richest or most handsome man out there, but he was steady, dependable, faithful – exactly what Gill needed.

'Now, how about I wash this muck off my hands and make us both a nice cup of tea,' Mike suggested, getting to his feet. 'If I forage really hard, I might be able to find us some biscuits too.'

Gill looked across at the mug of cold tea sitting on the side table, realising that with all the comings and goings she'd never had time to drink it.

'That,' she said with a grateful smile, 'sounds absolutely perfect.'

CHAPTER 5

'Marriage is not a word but a sentence'
– Oscar Wilde

'So have you decided whether or not you're going to do it?' Nick asked, watching as Julia carefully placed Jack down on their bed. He rolled onto his back and kicked his legs joyously, apparently fascinated by the sight of his toes.

'I think so.' Julia crinkled her nose, mulling it over. 'I might as well, right? I've been looking for something like this to get me out of the house – not that I don't love being with Jack,' she added hastily, laughing as she pretended to cover his ears. 'But you know what I mean. Something to give me a sense of self again.

'And Aimee seems really sweet,' Julia chattered away, as she pulled a pair of brightly coloured patterned leggings out of the wardrobe and tugged them on. She turned round to view her bottom in the mirror, frowning at her reflection. 'Plus how bad can Valerie be? I'm sure she'll lighten up once I get to know her.'

'A mother-of-the-groom-zilla? You've never dealt with one of those before. And your arse looks amazing, by the way.'

Julia flushed, realising what he'd just said. 'I don't think so, somehow. It's still very much recovering from being pregnant and practically horizontal for the past six months. But tonight's Zumba class is going to sort all that out. This too,' she added, patting her bare stomach below her industrial-strength sports bra. 'Not that it'll ever be the same again.' Julia cast a rueful glance at her newly created stretch marks and out-of-shape abs.

'Mmm, it all looks good to me,' Nick raised his eyebrows suggestively, as he leaned across to give her love handles a playful squeeze.

Julia slapped his hands away. 'Hey, stop that! There are children present,' she teased, glancing over at Jack who now seemed to be attempting to swallow his foot whole. Julia pulled on an exercise vest then bent her head to fuss over the baby, tickling his cheeks and blowing bubbles on his belly until he was laughing uncontrollably.

'Uh oh, I think it might be nappy change time,' Julia grimaced, as the unmistakeable smell hit her nostrils. 'I'll leave that one to Daddy, I think. I don't want to be late.'

Nick looked horrified. 'You're leaving already? Can't you just change him quickly before you go?'

'No! You're on your own with this one, buster, I've got to dash. Now, you know where his blanket and the spare nappies are. I've left milk in the fridge – it just needs warming through, but don't forget to check the temperature on your wrist. Try and make sure he drinks at least three-quarters, and he should go down without a problem. And don't forget to bring his giraffe to bed with him or else—'

'I do know how to look after my own son,' Nick snapped irritably, cutting her off.

Julia looked up in alarm, startled by his tone.

'I know you do, I wasn't saying…' She trailed off and tried again. 'Look, this is the first time I've left him at bed time, that's all. I can't help but worry.'

Nick ran a hand through his hair, and Julia noticed how tired he looked.

'I know,' Nick nodded. 'But we'll be fine.'

'Sure?'

'Yes.' Nick sounded exasperated. 'You get off and enjoy yourself.'

Julia turned towards the door then paused. 'It's just for an hour. Ninety minutes, max.'

'Like I said, we'll be fine.'

Julia hesitated, looking from Nick to Jack and back again. 'Well, I'll see you both later.' She smiled weakly as she blew them both kisses, trying to shake off the unexpected swell of anxiety. With one final glance at her husband and baby son, she jogged down the stairs and out of the front door.

—

Debbie was standing nervously in the corridor of St Agnes' church hall, pulling her top down self-consciously, and trying to ignore the feelings of nausea that clawed at her stomach.

She was convinced that she looked hideous. In black Lycra leggings and an oversized T-shirt that didn't quite provide the coverage she'd been hoping for, Debbie felt that all her flaws were on display for the entire world to see. The tight, unflattering outfit seemed to have been designed to emphasise all the parts of her body she was most insecure about.

For a brief moment, Debbie considered not going in to the class at all. No one had seen her yet; all she had to do was turn around and go back outside, jump in the car and drive home. It was that simple.

But then she would feel like even more of a failure than she already did, Debbie realised, and she was determined to go through with this.

Not even Stevie knew what she was planning – she'd deliberately chosen a night when he was working late so she could sneak out of the house and attend the Zumba class in secret. Not because she thought he'd make fun of her or anything, but because this was something she wanted to do by herself. *For* herself.

Summoning her courage, Debbie pulled open the heavy wooden door and walked into the room. Then almost walked straight back out again.

It seemed to be full of women chatting and laughing together as though they'd known one another for years. The wooden floors and exercise equipment piled up in corners brought back long-buried memories of humiliating PE classes in school, and Debbie immediately felt like an outsider; the unpopular, overweight kid that no one wanted on their team.

She stood awkwardly for a moment, fighting the urge to flee.

'Hello! Are you here for the Zumba?' A woman approached her with a wave, smiling cheerfully. She was in her mid-forties, with dyed black hair tied up in a high ponytail.

Debbie nodded gratefully. 'Yes. Yes, I am.'

'Great! No need to be nervous, we're a friendly bunch. I'm Maggie, by the way.'

'Debbie.'

'Nice to meet you, Debbie! Now,' Maggie continued, taking her by the arm and steering her into the centre of the room. 'Have you ever done Zumba before?'

'It's my first time,' Debbie confessed.

'Not to worry, you'll soon pick it up. It's a lot of fun,' Maggie winked. 'Is there anything medical I need to know about? Sprains, breaks, old injuries, heart conditions?'

'Not really. I haven't exercised for a while – well, ages in fact – so I might be a bit out of shape.'

'That's fine, just go at your own pace. Usually if I go onto something more advanced, I'll show you all a more basic routine you can stick to, if you're not feeling ready to step it up just yet.'

'Thanks,' Debbie smiled, as Maggie skipped off to greet another new arrival.

Finding herself alone once again, Debbie glanced around, catching the eye of a young, blonde woman, who looked equally unsure of herself. The two of them smiled at one another, recognising the similarity of their situation, although Debbie secretly wondered what the woman was doing there. She was slim and pretty, with a figure Debbie would kill for. She couldn't have been more than a size twelve at most, so why did she need to come to an exercise class?

A burst of music blasted out from the sound system in the corner, abruptly cutting short Debbie's musings. It was Latin, with fast flamenco guitar over an insistent hip hop beat. Debbie's hips began to move involuntarily, a grin breaking across her face.

'Okay everybody,' Maggie called over the music, as she took up her position in front of the group. 'Let's Zumba! So we're going to start with a little side step – side to side, just like this, that's right. Swing your arms, loosen your shoulders, and feel the rhythm!'

Debbie giggled. Maggie's enthusiasm was unmistakeable, and so far this was easy. Stepping from side to side she could manage!

'So now we're going to add in a little forward movement with a hip roll. That's it, Ellie, just like that. Oh, I forgot to mention,' Maggie continued, without breaking her stride. 'You may have noticed that we have two newbies tonight, so please say hello to Julia and Debbie.'

Debbie felt her cheeks flame, turning redder than she already was, as everyone turned to stare. They all waved hello and smiled, as Debbie nodded back, realising that the blonde woman beside her was the other newcomer, Julia.

'Fabulous, now let's get those arms involved,' cried Maggie, as she began twirling her wrists in time with the music. 'And shake that booty!'

Debbie followed her lead, uncertainly at first as she tried to get her arms, legs and booty moving in unison, but soon she was doing what she hoped was a reasonable approximation of Maggie's expert movements, and it felt surprisingly good. It was as though she was doing a proper dance routine, like a Pussycat Doll or a Spice Girl, and the thought made Debbie want to giggle.

'Imagine you're in a smoky little South American bar, up close and personal with a handsome Argentine gaucho!' Maggie called out, with a sensual sweep of her hips that caused another ripple of laughter to run through the group.

Then the music changed, to a slightly quicker salsa track, and Debbie had to concentrate for a moment before finding her groove. But Maggie's moves were easy to follow, and the Latin music made it impossible not to get caught up in the rhythms.

As Maggie added in an extra, more complicated step, Debbie caught sight of her reflection in the full-length mirrors opposite. She looked a sight – red-faced and sweaty, with her dark hair escaping from the rough ponytail she'd pulled it back into – but Debbie found that for once she wasn't bothered. The person in the mirror looked joyful, carefree. It didn't matter about her appearance; she was having a brilliant time!

Debbie certainly wasn't the biggest in the class either. There were about thirty women altogether, of all different shapes and sizes, including one lady who looked about seventy and who was as thin as a rake; the bones of her arms and shoulders protruded like a spindly bird, but she was shaking her body like a born Latina. If she could do it, then so could Debbie!

The class passed in a blur of music and dancing and, before Debbie knew it, the hour was nearly up and Maggie was starting the cool-down session. Debbie was almost sorry that it was over; the endorphins were whizzing around her body, giving her a buzz that she hadn't felt for a very long time.

'Well done to all of you, great class,' Maggie praised them, as the group burst into spontaneous applause.

They slowly began to disperse, moving to grab their bags and coats, saying goodbye to friends and promising one another that they'd be back next week. As Debbie headed across to get her handbag, she found herself next to Julia again. The two women grinned at one another, eyes sparkling from the intense workout.

'So did you enjoy it?' Julia asked brightly, as she pulled on a zip-up hoody then took a long drink from a bottle of water.

'I did actually. Much more than I expected to. I'm trying to lose weight, you see,' Debbie admitted, unexpectedly finding that her guard was down and she was happy to talk about it.

'Yeah, me too,' Julia replied, as the two of them began walking out of the room together. 'It's so bloody hard, isn't it?'

Debbie was genuinely shocked. 'But… but you don't need to!'

'You haven't seen what's under here,' Julia joked, gesturing to her jacket. 'Seriously, I had a baby just over six months ago, and it's not a pretty sight. This is the first time I've exercised in months.'

'Oh, congratulations! On the baby, not the exercising,' Debbie added hastily, as Julia laughed. 'What did you have?'

'A boy, called Jack.'

'Aw, that's lovely,' Debbie gushed. 'I love kids.'

'Do you have any?'

'No, not yet. But I work in a nursery. It hasn't put me off, surprisingly.'

'Which nursery? I might be looking for one soon. I'm thinking of going back to work so I'll need to find somewhere to take Jack when my husband's at work. It wouldn't be full time for now – just the occasional afternoon here and there.'

'Well we could definitely do that,' Debbie insisted as the two women strolled along the road, faces glowing in the chilly night air. The cold was a welcome relief after the hot and sweaty hall. 'I work at Two Trees, do you know it? It's just off the high street, near the Scout Hut.'

'That's really close to me! I'm at the other side of the main road, near the big Tesco,' Julia exclaimed, as they reached her Renault Clio and she stopped walking.

'Obviously it comes highly recommended,' Debbie grinned. 'But it really is a lovely place. They've got great facilities, and it was all completely refurb'd last year, so everything's fresh and new.'

'Sounds perfect, I'll definitely check it out. So will I see you back here next week?'

Debbie thought about it, a smile slowly breaking across her face. 'Yeah. You will.'

She waved as Julia got into the car and drove off, then marched briskly down the street to find her own vehicle. In spite of her aching limbs and sweaty body, Debbie meant what she'd said to Julia. She'd had far more fun than she'd expected tonight, and in just a few short days she could already feel that her body was changing. She'd been sticking to her diet – well, with the occasional slip-up; she was only human after all – and already her clothes felt looser, her stomach seemed flatter, and the feeling spurred her on, determined to complete the challenge that she'd set herself.

As she walked along, Debbie found herself drifting back to the familiar daydream that was now her daily motivation: her as a slim, beautiful bride, walking down the aisle to gasps of astonishment and Stevie's adoring face. She wanted it so badly; it felt so close that she could almost touch it.

This time, Debbie was determined not to fail.

CHAPTER 6

*'The trouble with some women is that they get all
excited about nothing – and then marry him'* – **Cher**

Aimee stepped out of her sporty little convertible Mercedes,
which she'd parked next to Jon's gleaming white Porsche, acutely
aware of how out of place both vehicles looked beside the ageing
Fords and rusty Peugeots in the staff car park. Jon's was in the
executive space, where '*Reserved for Director*' had been painted
onto the tarmac, and Aimee's was in one of the VIP visitor spac-
es alongside.

The Mercedes had been a present from Jon on her last birthday, when she'd turned twenty-three. There was no way Aimee
could have afforded to buy it for herself. If the truth be told, she
felt somewhat self-conscious in the showy convertible, with its
personalised number plate and shining alloy wheels. She'd tried
to decline the present, suggesting something more low-key, but
Jon had insisted that she keep it. All of her friends thought she
was crazy; if her rich, older boyfriend wanted to buy her a brand
new Mercedes, it would be madness to refuse.

Aimee stepped out of the car and clicked the button for the
central locking, then smoothed down her clothes where they'd
creased during the journey. She was wearing a cream turtle-
neck jumper, with a short black skirt, black tights and high-

heeled boots, her moss-green woollen coat thrown over the top. The outfit was perhaps smarter than she might ordinarily have chosen, but Jon loved it when she looked feminine and well-groomed, so she'd made the effort for him.

The building she'd just pulled up to was the headquarters of Cunningham Haulage, a small, single-storey structure situated on a twenty-acre site north-east of Norfolk. Scores of the company lorries, in their familiar orange and blue, were parked up outside, and beyond them Aimee could see the vast warehouses used for storing goods before they were delivered to their destinations. It wasn't the most glamorous of businesses but, according to Jon, it was extremely profitable.

As Aimee walked towards the building's entrance, she could hear two men talking, although she couldn't see where they were.

'Well I think he's an arsehole,' one of them said. 'Rumour is he's going to stop buying milk for teas and coffees, says we have to bring in our own. Some cost-cutting malarkey. Next he'll be charging us to use the lav.'

'You're joking! His old man would never have stood for that.'

'No, he was a good 'un, God rest his soul.'

The two men strolled out from behind the industrial-sized wheelie bins, dropping their cigarettes on the ground and stubbing them out before noticing Aimee. She recognised one of them immediately: Rob Mitchell, who'd been in her class at secondary school. The difference between their situations now couldn't have been more stark.

'All right Aimee?' he called.

'Good thanks, Rob. You?'

He shrugged. 'Same shit, different day.'

Aimee smiled at the two men, and carried on walking.

'Who's that?' the older man asked, once she was safely out of earshot.

'Don't you know? That's Cunningham's missus.'

'Shit! Do you think she heard us?'

'Dunno. Guess we'll find out tomorrow if we've still got jobs!'

The older man laughed. 'Still, bit of all right, isn't she? He's done well for himself.'

'*She's* done well for herself, more like. Grew up on the Larkman estate, now she's acting like Lady Muck, driving round in a bloody Mercedes!'

Aimee was long gone by now, and hadn't heard the exchange, as she pushed open the glass door and walked into the reception. It was sparse and functional, with a couple of chairs and a basic reception desk, livened up with a potted aspidistra.

Irene, the homely receptionist, was on the phone, but smiled when Aimee walked in and pointed down the corridor, indicating that Aimee should go ahead.

Aimee flashed her a smile in return – she liked the friendly, no-nonsense Irene, who'd been with the company almost since it was founded – and strolled towards Jon's office, her heels clicking on the lino floor. Knocking lightly on the door, she pushed it open and walked in.

'Darling!' Jon jumped up from his desk and rushed round to greet her. 'What are you doing here? Is something wrong?'

'No, nothing's wrong,' Aimee reassured him, reaching up to kiss him. His skin was smooth, and he smelt of expensive cologne. She couldn't help but notice how handsome he looked in his crisp white shirt and suit trousers, one button of his collar casually undone, indicating that he was winding down for the day. 'I just got a little… bored, I suppose,' she admitted. 'So I thought I'd get dressed up, take a drive out and come and see you.'

Jon took her face in his hands, stroking the delicate skin of her cheeks. His blue eyes pierced hers. 'What have I told you before about that? You should give Mother a call, she'd find something to keep you occupied. She's always running here and there, with her committees and her charity work.'

Aimee smiled weakly. 'Oh, she always seems so busy. I don't like to bother her.'

'Of course you're not bothering her, darling. You're family now.' Jon planted another little kiss on the tip of her nose. 'Don't get me wrong, I'm delighted you've come to see me. You look gorgeous today. Totally edible.' He licked his lips wolfishly, his hands finding their way beneath her coat and running over the contours of her body. 'Delicious.'

'Oh, and I also came over to tell you that Julia Crawford called this morning,' Aimee remembered, giggling as she pulled away from him.

'Who?'

'Julia. You know, the wedding planner we met last weekend. She's going to take the job, isn't that great? I really liked her.'

Jon nodded, as he went to sit back down in the swivel chair behind his desk. Aimee took the chair on the other side, feeling strangely like she was in an interview.

'Mother wasn't really sure about her, although she'd heard very good things. But if you want her, my little cupcake, then you shall have her.'

'Thanks, Jon. I think she'll be perfect. We were brainstorming ideas for the wedding, and she came up with some really good ones. Did you know you can get married in one of the old windmills on the Broads? The ceremony would be tiny, but then you can put a marquee up in the grounds and have as many people as you want at the reception. Or there's a rowing club right on the water at Wroxham. It's such a pretty location.'

Jo wrinkled his nose. 'I'm not sure. What's the capacity?'

'It can hold up to eighty max, which I think would be fine. We did originally say that we wanted a small wedding, and it seems to be growing out of all proportion. I don't even know half the people coming.' Aimee laughed lightly, but she was telling the truth.

'Sweetheart, I know we initially said something small, but this wedding is so important to Mother,' Jon said, patting his knee and indicating that Aimee should come round to his side of the desk. She did as she'd been told, sitting lightly in his lap and wrapping her arms around his shoulders. 'I'm her only son – her only child. And it's especially important now that my father's not here any more.'

Automatically, both of them looked up at the photograph of Nigel Cunningham that was mounted above the door. It was a head-and-shoulders shot, taken in the same office in which they were now sitting, with Nigel looking smart in a tailored suit, every inch the successful businessman. He was less handsome than Jon, with a jowly face and a thatch of grey hair, but he smiled proudly at the camera, satisfied with what he'd achieved in life.

Clustered on Jon's desk were three smaller frames: one of Nigel standing outside his first business premises, beaming beside a brand new fleet of Cunningham Haulage HGVs. The second was a photo of Jon's parents on their wedding day, with Valerie looking younger and happier than Aimee could ever have imagined her being, in a simple tea-length dress and modest veil. Finally, there was a picture of Aimee herself; she was grinning broadly, a vision of happiness, in a shot that had been taken on a wild night out when she and Jon had first got together.

'But it's *our* wedding,' Aimee murmured, twining her hands through his hair.

'Yes, but Mother *is* paying for it.'

'Not all of it,' Aimee bristled. 'My parents are paying for my dress, and some other things too.'

Jon raised his eyebrows dismissively.

'And they'd be able to do more if the wedding was smaller,' Aimee continued, warming to her theme. Her mother worked part-time in the local Spar, whilst her father was a bricklayer and his income depended on what work was available. 'They can't afford two hundred chair covers, or pearl-encrusted, handmade invitations, or whatever else your mother's decided is absolutely essential.'

'I just want our wedding day to be the most special day of your life,' Jonathan murmured, as he began to nuzzle her neck. 'You deserve it. Haven't I always given you the best of everything?'

Aimee couldn't argue with him on that point. It was true. Jon had always spoiled her.

She thought back to when they'd first met, just over two years ago; she'd been twenty-one years old and drifting through life without any real idea of what she wanted to do. She'd fallen into an admin job for a company that rented out printers and photocopiers – a temp role that had become permanent somewhere along the line – and she was working in a bar a couple of nights a week for extra cash. She was still living at home, blowing all her wages on partying at the weekend and saving up for Ibiza in the summer.

Jon had come into the bar where she worked, and seemed instantly smitten. Aimee wasn't in the habit of giving out her phone number to customers, but he'd been so persistent, so charming, that she'd finally given in. It was no exaggeration to say that he'd pursued her, and the attention had been both overwhelming and flattering.

Aimee had never dated anyone like Jon before. Her previous boyfriends had all been content with a few cans of beer in front of Netflix, or a night out at Nando's if it was a special occasion, but Jon was different. He took her to some of the best restaurants in the city, to the theatre, to Paris on Valentine's Day. And he bought her presents: flowers, jewellery, a book she'd mentioned she'd wanted to read, or tickets to a film she wanted to see, and Aimee had fallen head over heels.

Her friends were stunned, commenting that she'd really landed on her feet by dating a handsome, loaded guy like Jon. But for Aimee, it genuinely wasn't about the money. She'd never been a materialistic kind of girl, one who needed the latest handbag or a wardrobe full of designer outfits. She loved spending time with Jon and learning what he had to teach her. Six years older than her, and from a considerably different background, Jon had far more life experience than the sheltered Aimee, and she was in awe of his worldliness and confidence.

Before long, she'd given up her bar job to spend her evenings with him, and when Aimee came home from work one day, complaining of feeling unappreciated and undervalued, Jon suggested she resign. They were already living together in his flat near Eaton Park, so he would cover the mortgage and the bills, plus give her a small allowance to treat herself. The temptation to walk into work and tell her boss where to shove it was at that moment stronger than Aimee's desire for independence and, after a brief hesitation, Aimee had accepted Jon's offer.

Then just over six months ago, Nigel Cunningham had died of a heart attack, leaving Jon to take over the family business. Jon had been working there since he was eighteen, and had been his father's second-in-command, but heading up the firm was a whole different ballgame. He'd experienced moments of doubt, moments of insecurity, all wrapped up in a heady package of grief, and Aimee had been there for him every step of the way.

Nigel's death had left Jon thinking about his own mortality, and his instinct was to marry Aimee and start a family as soon as possible. He wanted to create a legacy, his own little piece of immortality. Nigel Cunningham had left big shoes to fill, and Jon was very aware of that.

'Let's not fight,' Jon whispered, as his hand began stroking Aimee's knee, his fingers drifting up beneath her skirt and sliding between her thighs. 'I tell you what, I've got some spare time before the accountant comes at four…'

Aimee giggled and glanced up at the clock. It was 3.30pm.

'So how about I lock the door, tell Irene to hold my calls…'

Aimee caught her breath as his fingers moved higher, and she leaned in to kiss him urgently. 'I think that sounds like an excellent idea…'

CHAPTER 7

*'Marriage is a wonderful invention; but then again, so
is a bicycle repair kit'* – **Billy Connolly**

'The wheels on the bus go round and round, all day long…'

Sitting cross-legged on the floor, as she clapped her hands
and mimed the actions, Debbie looked round at the smiling
group of toddlers in front of her. There were thirty of them altogether, boys and girls all aged between two and five years old,
some cuddling furry toys, others kneeling up excitedly as they
sang along with the familiar words. It was a pleasure to see.

'The wipers on the bus go swish, swish, swish…'

The room they were in was brightly decorated, filled with toys
and games and bookshelves crammed with copies of *The Gruf-
falo* and *The Very Hungry Caterpillar.* One wall showed a display
of enormous paper leaves, messily painted by the children in
shades of orange, brown, red, and, in one case, a distinctly un-
autumnal pink. Paper pumpkins, decorated with faces drawn in
black felt tip, hung from the ceiling, while sandpits and trikes
had been pushed to the edge of the room to create the commu-
nal singing space in the centre.

'The mummies on the bus go chatter, chatter, chatter, all day
long.'

When the song came to an end, everyone burst into applause.

'Okay, lunch time,' Debbie's colleague, Angela, called out, causing another excited outburst and a near-stampede as the little ones scrambled to their feet and made their way through to the dining hall, shepherded by the staff.

Two Trees Nursery was housed in a sprawling Victorian property, with the front parlours being used as the main play-room and dining room, whilst the back boasted a large kitchen and staff rest room. Upstairs was a separate baby room for the younger children, and there was a big stretch of garden out the back, where the kids could play out when the weather was fine.

'Can I have a yoghurt?' asked three-year-old Mia, who stared up at Debbie with big blue eyes as she toddled along beside her.

'As long as you eat your lunch,' Debbie smiled. 'And as long as you say please.'

'Pleeeeease,' Mia sang, as she skipped off to find a seat.

There were four circular wooden tables, with kid-sized blue plastic chairs arranged around them, and Debbie and the other staff quickly got the children settled, eating their sandwiches and fruit. As Debbie finished pouring out glasses of squash, Angela sidled up to her, a mischievous grin on her face. She was tall and athletic looking, with mid-length copper-coloured hair and a cute freckled face. The two of them had worked together for three years now, and were best friends.

'I'm going to do a McDonald's run when the kids go down for their nap. What do you fancy? Large Big Mac meal with a strawberry milkshake?' Angela wiggled her eyebrows enticingly.

Debbie's eyes lit up in anticipation. She was on the verge of saying, 'Hell, yeah!' when suddenly she caught herself.

'Not for me, thanks,' she replied, with a supreme effort of will. 'I've actually brought something in today.'

'You made a packed lunch? Are you trying to save money for the wedding or something? I can get it if you want, my treat.'

'No, it's fine,' Debbie insisted, thinking of the homemade chicken salad sitting in a Tupperware box in the fridge, and desperately trying to convince herself that she wanted it more than a cheeseburger. 'I'm on a bit of a health kick, actually. Sort of a diet thing – you know, for the wedding.'

'Oh, you've got loads of time 'til then. You're not getting married 'til the middle of next year.'

'I know, but I'm really trying this time. Luke, eat your crisps properly,' Debbie called to a little boy who was grinding his cheese puffs into a fine dust on his plate. 'I even went to Zumba class the other night.'

'Did you? You never told me. I'd have come with you.'

Debbie shrugged, looking a little guilty. 'I wanted to go by myself, see if I liked it.'

'And did you?'

'Yeah, more than I expected to. It was good fun. I'm planning to go again on Thursday, so you can come with me then if you want.'

Angela looked at her admiringly. 'You're really serious about this, aren't you?'

Debbie nodded eagerly. 'I think I've had an epiphany. Honestly, Ange, I'm tired of being this size. I'm tired of getting insulted by strangers, and never being able to buy clothes from Topshop because they don't make them to fit women like me. I'm sick of hiding my body from Stevie because I'm so ashamed of it, and of only having S-E-X with the lights off.' She lowered her voice, aware of the children nearby. 'Being married will be a new chapter in my life, and I don't want to start that chapter like *this*,' she finished, gesturing in frustration at her stomach and thighs.

'I'm not sure *I* want a Big Mac now,' Angela joked. 'After your inspiring speech, I feel like I should be going out and running a marathon instead.'

'Don't be daft. Just because *I'm* eating rabbit food doesn't mean *you* have to. Maybe I'll even steal some fries.'

Angela shook her head. 'No, I won't let you! You sound so committed, I don't want you to break it for the sake of a few chips. Ah, now I get why you didn't have a KitKat at break time.'

Debbie nodded, feeling caught out. 'Do you think I'm being stupid?'

'No, I think you're amazing. I wish I had your willpower.'

'Well, we'll see how long I stick to it. I'll probably crack in a couple of days, just like every other time I've tried to lose weight, and by next week I'll be stuffing my face with chocolate, eating all the burgers you can throw at me.'

'You know what you need to do?' Angela said thoughtfully, as she bent down to help Luke peel his banana. 'You need an incentive scheme – it worked for my friend Clare. Every time you lose, say, half a stone, you treat yourself to something nice. Maybe getting your nails done, or buying a new outfit.'

'Not looking like a heifer on my wedding day is a pretty big incentive in itself.'

Angela rolled her eyes. 'You do *not* look like a heifer. But if you *are* determined to do this, then it's something to think about. You could buy yourself some new lingerie, give Stevie a treat too.'

'Maybe it would be nice to remind him what I look like with the lights *on*,' Debbie agreed, remembering back to the evening that had kick-started this latest diet, when she'd hidden her body from her fiancé and been horrified when he'd tried to snap a photo of her. Suddenly, her eyes widened, sparkling naughtily. 'Ooh, I just had a brilliant idea!'

'From the look on your face, I'm not sure I want to know.'

'That's probably for the best,' Debbie giggled, her mind racing. 'I need to look into this, find out if it's possible. Let's just say that Stevie will be a very happy boy if I manage to pull this off.'

'As the actress said to the bishop,' Angela sniggered.

'We should probably change the subject,' Debbie grinned, mentally filing away her idea with the promise of revisiting it later. 'So how's everything with you? How's Mitch?'

Mitch was Angela's new boyfriend. They'd been dating for a few weeks, but Angela was notorious for going through men quicker than Harry Styles went through supermodels. She was the complete opposite of Debbie, who'd only had two boyfriends before Stevie, both long-term relationships. Angela teased her that she was a serial monogamist.

Right now, she wrinkled her nose uncertainly. 'He's okay. I'm not sure whether I really like him, or if—'

They were interrupted by one of the boys getting up from his chair and coming over to Debbie, wrapping his arms around her legs.

'Sammy, you're supposed to be sitting on your chair and eating your lunch, like a good boy,' she reprimanded him.

'But I don't feel very well.'

'No? What's the matter?'

'It hurts,' he murmured listlessly, pointing to his stomach.

'You've got tummy ache?' Debbie crouched down, touching her hand to his forehead. She looked up worriedly at Angela. 'He's really warm.'

'Feel sick,' Sam said, his lower lip pouting.

'I'd better take him to the sick bay. I'll see how he goes, and maybe give Gill a call if he gets any worse.'

Angela nodded. 'Shout me if you need a hand.'

'Thanks. Come on, Sammy,' Debbie said softly, as she reached down to pick him up. He wrapped his legs around her waist, laying his head wearily on her shoulder. 'Let's go see if we can get you feeling better.'

She left the dining room and headed out into the corridor, doing a double-take as she spotted Julia standing awkwardly in the entrance hall. A BabyBjörn carrier was strapped to her body, and she was looking at the drawings on the wall. The kids had created firework pictures, bright streaks of coloured chalk on black sugar paper, with their names written neatly on white stickers in the bottom corner.

'Hey, how are you?' Debbie grinned, walking towards her.

'Oh, hi!' Julia exclaimed. 'I wondered if I'd see you here. I thought I'd take your advice and come for a look around.'

'Fantastic! And this must be Jack,' Debbie cooed, as she leaned closer to look at the sleeping baby, all bundled up in his sling.

'That's right. I'm Julia, by the way. I don't know if I properly introduced myself the other night.'

'I'm Debbie. And this is Sammy,' Debbie explained. 'He's not feeling very well, so I'm taking him to the sick room.'

'Oh no, what's wrong with you?' Julia asked, as Sammy shyly buried his face in Debbie's neck.

'He's got a tummy ache and a temperature. Just a bug, I think, but we don't want the other kids to catch it so I'll give his mum a ring. Is someone showing you round?'

'Yeah, I think Mrs Palmer – Helen? – is on her way. The receptionist lady went to find her.'

'Oh yeah, Helen's the boss. She really nice though, great to work for.'

'Good, I'll tell her you recommended me,' Julia beamed.

'So you decided to go back to work then?' Debbie asked, shifting Sammy on her hip.

'Yeah. I think it's time. I'm lucky because I freelance, so I can decide what jobs I want to do. I'm not taking on much yet, as Jack's still so small, but I'll probably need to drop him here a couple of times a week. Maybe more when I get busier in a few weeks' time.'

'What do you do?' Debbie asked curiously.

'I'm an events planner.'

'Ooh, that must be fun!'

'It can be. It's hard work, and pretty stressful at times, but it's all worth it when the party's a success and the client's happy. It's definitely an adrenaline rush when you're running round trying to bring everything together, hoping it'll all go off without a hitch.'

'Have you ever organised anything for a celebrity?'

'You mean like a post-Oscars party at Elton John's house?' Julia laughed. 'That's a bit out of my league, I'm afraid. Although I did once organise a twenty-first birthday that a couple of the *TOWIE* cast turned up to! Weddings and sweet sixteens are more my style though.'

'You do wedding planning?' Debbie asked excitedly, as Julia nodded.

'That's what this new job is. It's quite a large scale one actually, with a big budget, so there'll definitely be a lot to keep me busy. But I'm looking forward to getting stuck in.'

'I'm getting married next summer,' Debbie burst out, unable to contain herself any longer. 'I'm sure it's nothing like the wedding you're organising. Ours won't be massive – we can't afford anything extravagant.'

'Well I cater to all sorts of budgets, if you're interested. Or if you just need some advice, I'm happy to point you in the direction of good caterers, photographers, that kind of thing.'

'That would be amazing,' Debbie gushed. 'Ooh, I feel like I'm J-Lo or something, with my very own wedding planner! So how come you—'

She broke off as a woman came dashing round the corner. She was dressed smartly, but practically, in comfortable fitted trousers and a plain jumper with a shirt underneath. Her hair was dark, cut short, and she looked busy but friendly.

'I'm so sorry, I got held up on a phone call. I'm Helen Palmer.' She held out her hand.

'Julia Crawford, lovely to meet you.'

'And this must be Jack.'

'Yes, it is, although I should probably warn you that he's not always this quiet.'

Helen laughed, then looked across at Debbie. 'Is everything okay? Is something the matter with Sam?'

'He's got a sore tummy and a temperature. I was just taking him to the sick bay when I got chatting with Julia.'

Helen frowned, putting her hand to Sammy's forehead. 'He is warm, isn't he? Has someone contacted Gill?'

'I'll ask Magda to, then sit with him until she arrives.'

'Great, thanks Debbie.'

'No problem. I'll hopefully see you soon, Julia.'

'Yes, definitely. If all goes well, you could be seeing a lot more of me – and Jack – around here!'

CHAPTER 8

*'It is not a lack of love, but a lack of friendship that makes unhappy marriages' – **Friedrich Nietzsche***

'Oh, doesn't it look beautiful,' Aimee breathed, as she gazed round in awe.

The usually staid and traditional Hurlingham Manor had been transformed into a bridal Winter Wonderland. An eight-foot pine tree, beautifully trimmed in white and silver, stood majestically in front of the grand, sweeping staircase, its banisters garlanded with holly, ivy and red berries. On the other side of the marble reception area, a festive snow scene had been created, complete with frolicking deer and other woodland animals, all gathered around a traditional wooden sleigh filled with presents.

'Maybe I should switch to a winter wedding,' Aimee wondered, wide-eyed as she pictured herself swathed in white faux-fur, snow falling softly outside as she and Jon said their vows.

Valerie pursed her lips in disapproval, clearly thinking that the idea was tacky.

'I'm sure we'll get lots of inspiration here,' Julia said diplomatically, as she followed Aimee through to the Grand Ballroom.

Hurlingham Manor was holding a wedding fayre, and the space had been transformed, with dozens of stalls showcasing everything from florists to caterers, videographers to DJs. Hordes of young women were dashing around excitedly, chattering loudly to accompanying friends and family who trailed in their wake as they bounced from one booth to the next.

Aimee's mother, Pauline, was starting to get a little tearful. She was a small, round woman with ash-blonde hair and a distinct resemblance to her daughter.

'I can't believe my baby's getting married,' she sniffed, the impending wedding finally becoming real as she gazed around the room. 'And it's going to be so grand. When me and your dad got married, we didn't have anything like this,' she went on, gesturing to a stall displaying shimmering tiaras and jewelled fascinators. 'Your granny helped make my dress, then after the ceremony the George and Dragon did a lovely spread for us in their back room.'

'Yes, well, now Aimee's marrying a Cunningham, I'm sure we can do better than that,' Valerie sniffed.

There was an awkward silence, which Valerie didn't appear to notice.

'So where do you want to start?' Julia turned to Aimee. 'Anything in particular that you're looking for?'

'No, not really.' Aimee looked overwhelmed. 'There's so much to think about.'

'Don't worry, that's what I'm here for,' Julia smiled reassuringly. 'All you need to do is tell me what you like.'

'Well I like *those*,' Aimee gushed, her gaze landing on a display of table decorations. She drifted closer, examining frosted glass bowls half-filled with water, purple chrysanthemums and tea-lights floating on the surface.

'We can customise the colours to match your theme,' the stallholder explained helpfully.

'Ooh, look how pretty they are! And so unusual. I've never seen anything like that before,' marvelled Pauline.

Beside her, Valerie gave a little shudder, her face contorting into a pained expression.

'Aimee, darling, you might as well fill it with goldfish and seaweed. There's unique, and then there's a step too far. No, I think we're better sticking with a classic floral display for the centrepieces. Something like that, for example.'

Valerie moved across the aisle, pointing out a very simple arrangement of white orchids in a tall, stem vase.

'It's… nice,' Aimee tried to work up some enthusiasm.

'It's not very *you*, though, is it?' Pauline put in. 'I mean, anyone could have that at their wedding. It doesn't really say much about you, does it?'

'That's the point,' Valerie cut in icily. 'It's elegant and classic. As you say, perhaps that's not quite right for Aimee.'

Aimee flushed at the insult, and Julia gasped. Pauline opened her mouth to speak, but Aimee quickly laid a hand on her arm, her eyes flashing a message of: *Please don't say anything.*

Dutifully, Pauline closed her mouth, but she still looked furious.

'Shall we move on to stationery?' Valerie said smoothly, apparently unaware that anything was wrong.

The others tripped after her, Pauline's expression still mutinous, as Valerie cut through the crowds imperiously.

'We've got about twenty minutes until the catwalk show starts,' Julia informed them, glancing at her watch. 'So we'll need to save some things until afterwards. Apparently there's a whole area upstairs dedicated to champagne and cake tasting.'

'Mmm, that sounds fun,' Pauline grinned, smacking her lips in anticipation.

'As long as you're not planning to have one of those ghastly cupcake towers,' Valerie called over her shoulder. 'Honestly, I just don't understand the fascination with those things. It's a wedding, not a chimps' tea party. No, a beautifully iced, traditional fruit cake is what we'll be looking for.'

'But Aimee doesn't like fru—' Pauline attempted to speak, but Valerie was on a roll.

'Oh, and I should warn you, Aimee,' Valerie turned and smiled coldly at her future daughter-in-law, 'if you're thinking of having one of those awful chocolate fountains, you can think again.'

Aimee blanched, and this time Pauline couldn't contain herself. 'I thought this was Aimee and Jon's wedding,' she burst out. 'Maybe it should be about what *they* want.'

'I'm the one writing the cheques,' Valerie replied acidly. 'And I can assure you I won't be writing any for cupcake towers, chocolate fountains, Cinderella carriages or, indeed, anything I deem unfitting for the occasion. Oh, look, there's Tibby Cavendish-Grey,' she continued without missing a beat, waving across the room at a well-dressed woman in a powder-blue skirt-suit and pearls. 'Her daughter, Caroline, is marrying Henry Lennox. He's terribly ugly, but he's set to inherit an enormous estate and half a dozen regional publishing companies.'

And with that, Valerie strode away, slipping through the throng to air-kiss Tibby, as Julia, Aimee and Pauline remained rooted to the spot.

'Ooh, I can't *stand* that woman,' Pauline burst out, clenching her fists in frustration. 'Why do you let her speak to you like that, Aimee? You need to stand up for yourself.'

Aimee looked torn. 'It's not that easy. She *is* Jon's mother after all, and, like she says, she *is* paying for most of the wedding.'

Pauline's face fell, interpreting the comment as a personal dig at her. 'You know we'd help out more if we could, love. We've always got by, but there's never been a lot to spare, and then we had to buy that new boiler last month, not to mention the car's on its last legs…'

'I know, I know, I wasn't blaming you,' Aimee insisted. 'But Valerie has very strong opinions, and sometimes it's just easiest to go along with them. After all, the most important thing is that Jon and I will be married. What's one day, when we'll have the rest of our lives together?'

Pauline frowned, not looking convinced. 'What do you think?' she demanded, turning to Julia. 'I bet she's one of the worst clients you've ever had to work with.'

'I… um…' Julia's mouth flapped open and closed. 'It wouldn't be right for me to—'

'You can't ask her that!' Aimee cut in, as Julia shot her a grateful look.

'Well I think she's an absolute nightmare,' Pauline asserted. 'And you know I'm only saying what we're all thinking. But I'll keep my mouth shut for your sake, Aimee.'

'Thanks, Mum,' Aimee replied gratefully, as she spotted Valerie making her way back towards them.

'It's always so delightful to see Tibby,' Valerie announced on her return. 'Her daughter's having Alessandro Lombardi sing at her wedding – you know, the famous opera singer. Can you imagine? I really should introduce you to Caroline, she's exactly the sort of person you should be getting to know. Did I mention that she studied Fine Art at the Courtauld Institute? Delightful girl.'

'Wow,' Aimee said weakly, unsure how to respond.

'I think the catwalk is this way,' Julia interjected. 'Maybe we should head over there now to get a good seat.'

The runway area was already busy when the women arrived, and Valerie took the lead, pushing through the crowds to ensure a seat on the front row. Two young women were sitting in the centre, with two spare chairs on either side of them.

'Could you please move along,' Valerie asked them haughtily. 'We're a group of four, and we'd like to all sit together, so if you could move down that would be much appreciated.'

The two women looked at one another. Moving down would mean that their view was somewhat restricted, as they'd be partially sitting behind a pillar, but they both got up and moved without a word of protest. Aimee felt for them. It was hard to refuse anything of Valerie; she knew that herself.

Before long, 'Spring' from Vivaldi's *Four Seasons* began playing, and the first model came out onto the catwalk. She wore a strapless white gown, with a dramatic feathered skirt, and she was holding the hand of an excited little girl wearing a purple crushed-velvet bridesmaid dress. They walked to the end of the runway and struck a pose, as the second model came out in a stunning halterneck mermaid gown, shimmering with beads and sparkle. She was accompanied by a cute little pageboy, looking proud as punch in his miniature waistcoat and matching tie.

'Aw, isn't he sweet,' Pauline leaned across to murmur to Aimee. 'Your cousin Jennifer's little boy, Riley, would look gorgeous in that.'

'I like that dress,' Aimee whispered back, pointing up at the model who'd just emerged. She was wearing a striking gown with a red-and-white panelled bodice and red lacing down the back of the train. 'I've never seen one like that before.'

Valerie, who'd clearly heard the exchange, leaned across and said to Aimee in low tones, 'You're a bride, not a nineteenth-century French prostitute. Red is certainly *not* an appropriate colour for a bridal gown. Now *that's* much nicer,' she continued, as the next bride came out in a traditional gown with a demure neckline and long, lace sleeves. 'Very Duchess of Cambridge,' Valerie finished approvingly.

Aimee glanced across at Pauline, who pulled a face.

'Have you decided what's happening about Christmas yet?' Pauline murmured, as they watched one model after another walk the runway, showcasing the different styles and shapes.

Aimee swallowed, knowing that this was yet another conversation she didn't want to have. Sometimes she felt as though she was constantly trying to keep everyone else happy – Jon and Valerie and Pauline – and no one ever stopped to ask what *she* wanted to do.

'I'm not sure—' Aimee began evasively.

'Only we'd love you and Jon to come to us for Christmas lunch. Or even just a drink in the afternoon, if you can't manage that.'

'I know, Mum. Jon and I haven't really decided yet and—'

'I mean, I know you probably don't want to be bothered with me and your dad,' Pauline continued, as she watched a model in an off-the-shoulder A-line gown slink past. 'But I think Charlie's spending it with his girlfriend' – Charlie was Aimee's younger brother, who was studying geology at Birmingham University – 'and it's your last Christmas as a Nicholls, so we'd love you to spend at least part of it with us. We really want to get to know Jon better too, as we hardly ever see him.'

Aimee felt the all-too-familiar pangs of guilt sitting hollowly in the pit of her stomach. How could she explain to her mother that every time she suggested going to visit her parents, Jon came up with some excuse – he had to work, or he was tired, or they would definitely go *next* week. Or that whenever she and Jon *did* go round to visit Pauline and Ken, Jon always came away complaining about how small her parents' house was, or that he was allergic to their cat, Tinkerbell, or that her father's table manners left something to be desired, as he mopped up his leftover gravy with a slice of thick white bread.

'It's just hard,' Aimee tried. 'Especially now that Val's on her own. At least you've got Dad, but she doesn't have anyone now.' Aimee saw her mother's face drop, and hastily added, 'But we haven't made any decisions yet. I'll speak to Jon and let you know, okay?'

Pauline nodded stiffly, staring straight ahead, and Aimee could tell she was upset.

Would it always be like this, Aimee wondered? Forever trying to balance the needs of her husband and his demanding mother with trying not to offend her own parents? And what about when she and Jon had children? Then the issue would be ten times worse, with everyone fighting for priority on Christmas, birthdays, family occasions.

Aimee reached over to take her mother's hand. 'Don't worry,' she told her, with a reassuring squeeze. 'Of course we'll see you on Christmas Day. I wouldn't want it any other way.'

Mother and daughter turned back to the catwalk show, which was now reaching its grand finale. The bride was showcasing an enormous, Princess Diana-style dress, all puffed sleeves and a three-foot train. She was flanked by the little girl, wearing a mini replica of the model's gown, and the pageboy all dressed up in a dinner jacket with black bow tie. As they posed at the end of the runway, everyone applauded, with a few of the audience getting to their feet immediately and making a beeline for the most popular stalls.

Julia stood up, smoothing down her skirt and looking around at the three women. 'What do you say we head upstairs for cake and champagne?'

'Yes, please,' Aimee nodded eagerly. The way today was going, a drink was exactly what she needed.

CHAPTER 9

'There is no more lovely, friendly and charming relationship, communion or company than a good marriage' – **Martin Luther**

'Hey there, Jacky-boy, how are you? Did you have a good time?'

Jack burbled away happily as Julia covered his face with kisses, holding him close as though she hadn't seen him for days.

'He's great,' Debbie smiled reassuringly. 'He had lots of fun with us, didn't you, Jack? We played with the train set, and with the building blocks, and did some potato prints. I'd say he's just about ready for a nap now.'

'Thanks so much, Debbie. It sounds ridiculous, but I was so nervous about being away from him, even though it was only for a couple of hours.'

'No need to explain. I see it all the time, and it's perfectly understandable. It just means that the next time you bring him, you won't be quite so worried, and you can leave him a bit longer. It gets easier, honestly.'

Julia had just returned from leaving Jack at Two Trees Nursery for the very first time. She'd had an appointment with Valerie to view the final proofs for the Save the Date cards; they'd been approved, meaning Julia could instruct the designer to go ahead with the production of two hundred copies. From there, they'd be sent to the calligrapher, who would hand-write them in beautiful italic script, before they were posted out to the great and good of Norfolk society.

Julia had considered taking Jack with her to the meeting, but she wasn't sure Valerie would be particularly sympathetic if she turned up hoisting an eight-month-old on her hip, covering the precious Save the Dates with sticky fingers and drool. So she'd taken the plunge and booked him in for a two-hour trial at the nursery. He certainly looked in fine fettle, Julia thought, relieved, as she brushed his fine, dark hair out of his green eyes, which were closing sleepily.

If the truth be told, Julia had been increasingly anxious about leaving Jack since that night she'd met Debbie at Zumba. She'd returned home to find her baby son still awake and grizzling, with Nick stressed out and bad-tempered. Jack had settled down as soon as he'd seen Julia, which had only increased Nick's exasperation, and Julia couldn't help but feel a sharp pang of concern over the way father and son were struggling to bond.

'We should definitely meet up some time too,' Julia told Debbie brightly, pushing her worries out of her mind and stepping to one side as half a dozen other mothers came in to reclaim their toddlers and the corridor turned into a busy thoroughfare. 'You know, we can have a chat about your wedding, get to know each other a bit better.'

'That sounds great. How about this weekend?'

'Sure.' Julia moved politely out of the way as a large-busted woman with cropped reddy-purple hair dashed past. 'I'll text you.'

'Yeah, definitely. Anyway I'd better get on. See you soon.' The space was getting even busier, as Debbie turned to reunite parents with their children, helping the little ones to pull on their coats and scarves.

Julia gave her a final wave, then began to make her way towards the front door.

'Jules, I just remembered,' she heard Debbie shout after her. Julia turned around. 'I wanted to introduce you to Gill. Gill, this is Julia, the wedding planner I was telling you about. Gill's getting married too,' Debbie explained, indicating the purple-haired woman Julia had noticed a few moments ago.

'Well, eventually,' Gill laughed. 'If we ever find the time. Everything's always pretty manic in my house.'

'That's why I wanted you to meet Julia,' Debbie said excitedly. 'She's a professional wedding planner. She could do all of that for you.'

'I should put you on commission,' Julia joked, before turning to Gill. 'Congratulations, by the way.'

'Second time around,' Gill told her. 'Been there, done that, so it's not quite such a big deal this time. Hey, Sammy!' she exclaimed, as the little boy rushed up to her, eager to show off the snowman he'd made from a plastic cup and a ball of cotton wool. 'Clever boy, Sam. We'll put that straight on the mantelpiece when we get home.'

Sam beamed proudly, looking up at the three women.

'Is it your little boy that was poorly the other week?' Julia wondered, as she recognised Sam. 'I came to look round with Jack, and Debbie was taking him to the sick bay for a stomach ache.'

Gill nodded. 'Yeah, it was just a bug I think. The kids are always picking them up, but he's fine now, aren't you Sam?' She ruffled his hair affectionately, as he leant against her leg. 'Well, we'd better get going. It was nice to meet you, Julia, I'm sure I'll bump into you again.'

'What are you both doing now?' Debbie cut in, as something occurred to her. 'Only my shift finishes in about five minutes, once everyone's out of here, and we could all head for a coffee or something, have some wedding chat. I'm driving Stevie mad trying to get his opinion on flowers and favours, so it'd be nice to talk it over with people who understand.'

'I've got to pick the twins up from school in…' Gill looked at her phone. 'About forty minutes.'

'You've got twins as well?' Julia exclaimed.

'Yep. Not to mention twelve- and thirteen-year-old girls, who already give me as much attitude as if they were ten years older. They're not all mine though,' she explained hastily, as she saw Julia's jaw drop. 'Sammy here, and Paige, the twelve-year-old, are my fiancé's from his previous marriage.'

'I don't know how you do it.' Julia was genuinely in awe. 'I've only got one and I'm constantly shattered. How do you cope with *five*?'

'You check your sanity at the door and drink a lot of coffee,' Gill chuckled.

'Speaking of which, I'm sure you could squeeze in a quick one now, couldn't you?' Debbie pleaded. 'There's Mimi's round the corner, and they're very child-friendly. You could have a half-hour pit-stop and still be in time to collect the twins.'

Gill looked torn. 'Are you coming, Julia?'

Julia made an instant decision. 'Yeah, why not? Jack can always sleep in his buggy, and my husband won't be home for another couple of hours.'

'Go on then, you've twisted my arm,' Gill grinned, as she steered Sam towards the door.

'I'll go grab my coat,' Debbie said eagerly.

—

Ten minutes later, the women were sitting at a table in Mimi's, three coffees and a large chocolate chip cookie in front of them.

'Do you want some, Debbie?' Julia asked, as she broke off a piece and popped it in her mouth.

'No thanks,' Debbie shook her head. 'I'm sticking to the diet.'

'You've been doing brilliantly,' Julia told her admiringly. 'Honestly, I can really see the difference from that first Zumba class.'

Debbie smiled, pleased and proud. 'I've lost nearly half a stone. I mean, there's still loads to go obviously.'

'Half a stone?' Gill looked impressed, and guiltily put the cookie back down. 'I haven't even thought about losing weight for the wedding. I suppose it would be nice to, but it'll probably be a case of Mike taking me as he finds me. Sam, do you want a piece?' She held up the cookie, but Sam shook his head. He was happily playing with Maisy, a girl of his age who went to the same nursery, and whose mother was having tea with a friend a couple of tables away. Sammy and Maisy were sitting on the floor in the carpeted area, with paper and coloured pencils provided by the cafe, whilst Jack was sleeping in his pushchair beside Julia.

'So we think we've found our reception venue,' Debbie said excitedly. 'Do you know the Tythe Barn, over near South Walsham? It's a converted barn, and it's sooo pretty.'

'I've never been there, but I've seen it online, and I've heard great things about it,' Julia replied. 'Eloise, who runs it, is supposed to be lovely. Really nice and super organised.'

'She is, we met her last week. I was wondering, Julia, if you wouldn't mind coming with me to see it some time. You can let me know what you think, and I'm sure you'll have loads of great ideas for how to decorate it and stuff. We're actually getting married at the parish church in the village – it's where I grew up – so this will just be for the evening do.'

'Sure, I'd love to. Plus I'm sure you won't mind if I bring Jack with me. Not all of my clients are quite so understanding.'

'Of course not. He's always so well behaved.'

'I'm not sure about that,' Julia said doubtfully. 'You don't see him when he's grizzling in the middle of the night, refusing to go back to sleep without a feed. Anyway, what about you, Gill? Have you picked a venue?'

Gill shook her head, looking stressed. 'We've barely decided on anything. We were supposed to get married *last* summer, but we've been pushing the date back and back. At the moment we're thinking we'll have a registry office ceremony, and maybe a hotel for the reception, but it might all change still.'

'Just book somewhere, then you can't get out of it,' Debbie suggested.

'That might be the way forward. But we can't even decide on what kind of wedding we want. I mean, Mike and I would love something really simple, but then there's the kids to consider too, and they all have really different ideas. Then Kelly, my eldest, doesn't want us to get married at all, and just pours cold water on everything we suggest.'

'Oh, that's a shame,' Julia sympathised. 'Does she not get along with Mike?'

Gill shook her head. 'And it's not for lack of trying on his part. I think he's great with her – you know, he's friendly and supportive, but not trying to replace her dad. I think it's the age she's at. She's very defensive, and she argues like crazy with his daughter, Paige, who's only a few months younger.'

'And you all live together, all the time?'

Gill nodded. 'Well, Kelly and the twins go to stay with their dad, Ian, every couple of weeks, which makes the house a little more peaceful. Me and Ian have a fairly civilised relationship now – I won't be inviting him to the wedding, but I'd never stop him seeing the kids.'

'What about Mike's children?' Julia wondered, nodding towards Sam. 'Do they see their mum?'

'No, not really. She lives in Cyprus now. It's not a great situation. The whole family were on holiday there – this was back when Mike and Tina were still married, and Sammy was about nine months old. They got back from holiday, then a week later Tina announced she was leaving him and moving to Cyprus to live with some bloke. Poor Mike didn't have a clue she'd even met anyone out there.'

Julia and Debbie were staring at Gill, utterly stunned.

'She took the kids with her at first,' Gill continued. 'Apparently Mike was gutted, as you can imagine. I think he went off the rails a bit – you know, drinking, not going into work. But after a couple of months, Tina called and asked him to fly out and take the children home with him. I think they were getting in the way of her new relationship.' Gill's pursed-lipped expression showed exactly what she thought about that.

'Mike was on his own for a few months before we got together – I met him at the school gates actually, when he was picking up Paige and I was collecting Kelly. So I've been with them for about two and a half years now, and I really do feel like they're my kids too. It can be a struggle at times, especially financially, but we get by.'

There was silence around the small table. Julia was shaking her head in disbelief. 'I can't believe a mother could just abandon her children like that,' she burst out. Looking at Jack, sound asleep and vulnerable, she found it impossible to imagine ever giving him up. She'd found it hard enough leaving him for two hours that afternoon.

'Me neither,' Gill agreed, taking a sip of her coffee. 'Obviously I have to be careful what I say in front of the kids,' she continued, glancing over at Sammy. 'But I just don't get how someone could do that.'

'Have they seen her since?' Debbie wondered.

'Mike took them over to Cyprus the summer before last, but it didn't go well. Sammy didn't really understand who Tina was, and while Paige wanted to spend time with her mother, it was a bit half-hearted on Tina's part. Some days she'd spoil her rotten and they'd have an incredible time. Other days, she never showed up, and Paige naturally got really upset. It's like birthdays and Christmas – sometimes she makes an effort and sends them beautiful cards and gifts. Other years they don't hear a thing.'

'That must be so hard for them,' Julia sighed.

'They're so lucky to have you,' Debbie added, leaning across to give Gill an affectionate squeeze.

'Thanks,' Gill smiled. 'Anyway, you can see all the issues we're dealing with. And if it's like that in everyday life, imagine trying to plan a wedding with all that baggage!'

'Any tips, Julia?' Debbie asked, as she finished her cappuccino and made a mental note to be extra strict with her calories when it came to dinner that night.

'Hmm, well I've never come across a situation quite like this before,' Julia began thoughtfully, turning to Gill. 'If you and Mike aren't too bothered about where and how you get married, maybe you should get all the kids involved. You know, let them come up with ideas and help with the planning.'

Gill's eyes widened. 'I'd have a wedding day with wizards and magicians, and a One Direction tribute band, where everyone eats pizza and ice cream and I'm dressed like Elsa from *Frozen*!'

'Sounds amazing,' Debbie quipped. 'In fact, I might do that for mine.'

'Well maybe don't let them plan the entire wedding,' Julia continued. 'You and Mike can veto anything too extreme – but you could definitely get them involved.'

'Or maybe you get your small registry office ceremony, but the kids get to organise the reception,' Debbie chimed in.

'And I'd be happy to speak to them,' Julia offered. 'You know, if they wanted to plan some surprises, or find out more about venues and themes.'

Gill's forehead was creased in thought. 'That might be a good idea…' she said slowly. 'Everyone's here this weekend, so I could call a family meeting and get all the kids' suggestions and input. If we can get everyone on board, this wedding might finally happen!'

'I think it sounds perfect,' Debbie breathed, as Gill glanced at her phone and jumped up in alarm.

'Is that the time? I'm going to be late picking up the twins. Maybe I'm not a candidate for Mother of the Year after all.' She pulled on her coat and drained her coffee. 'Come on Sam, time to go now.' Sam looked up at her and his sweet face crumpled. 'Say goodbye to Maisy, we can do some more drawing when we get home. Right now, we've got to go pick up Freddy and Finlay, so get a wriggle on.'

Sam was crying loudly now, completely uncooperative as Gill zipped up his thick jacket and pulled on his mittens. Not even the remains of the giant cookie could appease him.

'Thanks for the coffee, ladies, I enjoyed it. I'll see you both soon.'

'Bye, Gill.'

'Nice to meet you.'

'She's lovely, isn't she?' Debbie grinned, as Gill walked out of the door. 'I knew you two would get on. I just hope she gets to have a great wedding. She deserves it.'

'Yeah, definitely,' Julia nodded. 'I agree that she needs to have a really special day. Leave it with me. I might have one or two ideas…'

CHAPTER 10

'Marriage is like a besieged castle; those who are on the outside wish to get in; and those who are on the inside wish to get out' – **Arabian proverb**

Julia hurried through the crowds of Christmas shoppers as they ambled along Haymarket, their arms laden with bags full of presents. The atmosphere was festive; traditional Christmas songs drifted out from shop doorways, whilst the windows were filled with gift sets and fake snow and tinsel. Against the darkening late-afternoon sky, snowmen and stars and Santas were lit brightly atop lampposts, strings of illuminated baubles crisscrossing the street.

It was freezing cold, but Julia was wrapped up cosily in her hooded parka and thick woollen scarf. She'd left Jack at Two Trees for the afternoon, and was relishing this precious 'me time', as she picked out presents for him and Nick. Julia was all too aware that this would be her son's first Christmas, and she wanted to make it as special as she possibly could – even if there was very little chance he'd remember it. Both Julia and Nick's parents were coming down from Derbyshire over the festive season, and Julia knew she'd be run off her feet, so they'd agreed to spend New Year alone, just the three of them.

Julia hastily checked her phone, aware that she was running late, and quickened her pace, finally coming across the old-fashioned little tearooms, tucked away in the backstreets. The windows were steamed up, with the promise of warmth inside. Julia pushed open the door and set the bell jangling, the delicious smell of freshly baked cakes hitting her nostrils.

She spotted who she was looking for straight away.

'Annie!' Julia cried excitedly, weaving her way through the cramped tables to where her friend was sitting.

'Julia!' Annie stood up as she saw her, and the two women hugged.

'How are you?' Julia demanded, taking a step back to look at her. 'Wow, you look great. Seriously, Annie, really amazing.'

'Thanks,' Annie smiled back, looking faintly embarrassed by all the praise.

Annie was a professional relationship therapist, and the two women had met when Julia and Nick had gone to her for counselling. Julia had struggled to fall pregnant, and their marriage had seriously suffered as a result. Surprisingly, Nick had been the one to first suggest therapy, whilst Julia had been fiercely resistant. In fact, when she thought about how rude she'd been to Annie in those first few sessions, she felt incredibly guilty. But that was all behind them now. Annie had been hugely helpful to Julia and Nick, and they'd kept in touch ever since.

'Have you had your hair done?' Julia wondered, as she shrugged off her coat and draped it over the back of her chair, trying to find room for her shopping bags in the confined space.

'Yeah, I had a little colour put in it,' Annie admitted, running her hands through her soft, shiny bob, which was now a rich mahogany colour. She was wearing a black polo neck with slim-fitting jeans and knee-length boots and, as Julia had observed, she cut a striking figure. Her skin was glowing, her eyes sparkling.

'Life's obviously treating you well,' Julia grinned.

'Yeah, everything *is* pretty good,' Annie nodded, as she flicked through the menu. 'Shall we order? I'm dying to hear all your news.'

'Mmm, let's,' Julia agreed, glancing round at the other customers, her mouth watering at the sight of clotted cream scones and delicious-looking slices of fluffy Victoria sponge. She quickly scanned the selection, and within minutes a waitress was at their table.

'What can I get you?' she smiled.

'I'll have the coffee and walnut cake, with a latte,' Annie requested.

'I'll go for the breakfast tea, with a strawberry tart, please.'

The waitress jotted down their order and walked away, as Julia sat forward in her seat and grinned at Annie. 'So, tell me all the gossip! How's Jamie?'

Jamie was Annie's boyfriend. He was a software designer, and the two of them had met when they rented offices in the same building.

Annie's face lit up once again, the faintest blush stealing over her cheeks. 'He's good,' she said bashfully. 'We're both really busy – you know he's working over near Cambridge now? But we moved in together in the summer, so that's great 'cos at least we get to fall asleep in the same bed – even if we're too tired to do anything while we're there.'

'That doesn't sound good,' Julia frowned. 'Sounds like you need to start taking some of your own advice.'

'Oh, don't worry, we always make time for that,' Annie grinned.

'So no wedding bells yet?'

'Not yet. We *have* talked about it,' Annie admitted. 'But there's no rush for now. We're just enjoying being together for the moment, and I'm getting to know Olivia.'

Olivia was Jamie's daughter from a previous relationship. It had been a shock to Annie to find out that she existed, but the two of them got on brilliantly, and Annie enjoyed spending time with her.

'Well you know where to come when he does finally pop the question,' Julia couldn't resist adding. 'I could plan an amazing wedding for you two. I can picture it already,' she sighed. 'All vintage romance, with beautiful pastel flowers and lots of pearls and lace. Or maybe something more modern, with a black and white theme and a funky band in the evening?'

'I don't exactly know that I'm a big wedding kind of girl,' Annie demurred, promising, 'But you'll definitely be my first port of call when it happens. *If* it happens.'

'It will,' Julia replied confidently, her eyes dancing.

The waitress arrived, placing the drinks and cakes on the table, and Julia and Annie tucked in.

'So how is the wedding business? You mentioned in your last email that you'd gone back to work,' Annie said, before taking a bite of her coffee and walnut cake. It crumbled on her lips, and her face dissolved into an expression of delight. 'Mmm, this is delicious.'

'Ooh, let me try a bit,' Julia grinned, leaning across to scoop up a spoonful, before offering her strawberry tart. 'Here, have some of this. Yeah, work's good. I took on one job, and before I knew it I suddenly had three on my hands. I'm not quite sure how that happened!'

'Three?' Annie exclaimed.

'Well, two of them are more small scale, and I'm doing them more as favours, just to get me back into the swing of things. The bigger one is proving to be a bit tricky.'

'Bridezilla?'

'No, the opposite. The bride's lovely. It's the mother-in-law that's the problem. Worships the ground her son walks on, and thinks nothing is good enough for him. They're having a do for three hundred people at Southwark Castle.'

'Southwark Castle? Isn't that the enormous stately home where they filmed *Pride and Prejudice*?'

'Exactly. I mean, it's beautiful, but that's not the point. And *three hundred* guests. Who has three hundred friends? Like I said, the bride's a sweetheart, and she seems mortified by all the hoopla. I think she'd have preferred something intimate and low-key, but there's no way the mother-in-law will stand for that.'

'She sounds like a nightmare!'

'She is. And I just know that the closer we get to the wedding, the worse she'll become. Honestly, if it wasn't for Aimee – the bride – I'd have thought about quitting.'

'I'm sure you can cope with it,' Annie grinned. 'I have faith in your skills. Seriously though, do you ever get time to see Jack amongst all the craziness? Or Nick for that matter?'

'Of course,' Julia's face softened. 'It's working out pretty well actually. Jack seems settled in a local nursery, and I'm only ever away for a few hours at a time. I can pretty much dictate when I want to work, so it's really convenient.'

'How is Jack? I haven't seen him since he was born. He must be huge.'

'He's nearly nine months. Here, have a look at these pictures.' Julia pulled out her iPhone, handing it across to Annie who began scrolling through.

'Oh, he's gorgeous,' she exclaimed. 'Look at those cheeks! Wow, he looks like Nick, doesn't he?'

'Everyone says that.'

'But he's got your eyes. He really is so cute. You'll have to bring him with you next time we meet up.'

'Yes, definitely. I just thought it would be easier to get the Christmas shopping done without him today.'

'I don't blame you. Did you get some good stuff?' Annie asked, leaning over to peek into the heap of bags.

'Too much,' Julia bit her lip guiltily. 'But it's Jack's first Christmas so we want to spoil him. I think I might have gone a bit overboard.'

'No such thing,' Annie assured her. 'Here, I brought a little something for him,' she continued, reaching into her bag and handing over a brightly wrapped parcel with a red bow.

'Oh Annie, you didn't have to do that.'

'It's fine. Make sure you save it until Christmas Day,' she grinned, taking the last mouthful of her cake. 'And how's everything with Nick? Are you two still making time for each other?'

'Yeeaah…' Julia said slowly, a guilty expression appearing on her face. 'It's just hard, with Jack and everything. Honestly, Annie, I never realised having a baby could be so exhausting. And then with going back to work, I'm run off my feet. Whenever I do get time to slow down all I want to do is sleep.'

Annie said nothing, taking a sip of her coffee and giving Julia a stern look.

'I know, I know,' Julia said, burying her face. 'It's just so difficult¸ this concept of "having it all" – husband, baby, career. It's really hard to juggle everything, and you constantly feel that something has to give. That you're going to drop one of the balls. Plus Nick's been kind of… distant, lately.'

'Do you think he feels pushed out? I know how easy it is for Mum to get all consumed with the new baby, and Dad ends up feeling like a spare part.'

'Maybe.' Julia wrinkled her nose thoughtfully. 'But even when I try to get him involved he never seems that interested. Granted, it's only boring stuff like changing nappies or giving Jack his feed but sometimes I get the impression he's trying to avoid it.'

'Avoiding changing dirty nappies? Sounds sensible to me,' Annie chuckled.

Julia smiled weakly. 'I know it sounds silly. I mean, I know Nick loves Jack like crazy, but it's like there's part of him that's detached somehow. It's hard to explain.'

'Maybe you need a top-up session with me?' Annie suggested, only half joking.

'It might not be a bad idea – just to keep us on track. Speaking of which, do you ever see Zoe and Simon? We keep up through Facebook, but I'm a bit out of the loop recently. Oh, and what about Linda and Ray? I used Linda's florist for quite a few events, but of course I haven't worked for a while so haven't seen her. She sent me a lovely card after Jack was born though.'

'Nice subject change,' Annie teased. But she knew that Julia was genuinely interested to find out how their mutual friends were getting on. As well as the couples' therapy sessions, Annie also ran group meetings which were much more fun and light-hearted, and could consist of anything from salsa lessons to 'Mr and Mrs' style quizzes. The sessions Nick and Julia had attended saw them riding tandem through the Norfolk countryside, and enjoying a day trip to Great Yarmouth Pleasure Beach, amongst other things, and they'd become close to some of the other couples they'd met.

'I think Linda's fully retired now,' Annie went on. 'So if you do want to use her for events it's her daughter, Rose, that's running Expressions now. Linda and Ray spend most of their time travelling, I think. Every time I do speak to them, they're about to go off on another trip. And when they're here, they're mostly with their grandkids.

'Zoe and Simon are still as crazy as ever, and crazy about each other still. I get emails from Zoe every now and again. She mentioned you last time actually, wondering if I'd heard from you.'

'I really need to get in touch with her,' Julia admitted. 'There's just been so much going on recently. We all need to meet up for a coffee – I should have asked her to come today, actually.'

'Next time,' Annie promised.

The waitress appeared, clearing away their empty cups and crumb-covered plates.

'Would you like the bill?' she asked politely.

'Yes, please,' Julia replied, reaching for her purse. She turned to Annie, 'I'd love to stay longer, but I need to get back.'

'No problem,' Annie said easily. 'It was great seeing you, Julia. We need to do this more often – if you ever get a spare minute.'

'Oh Annie, it's been so lovely to see you too,' Julia said genuinely. 'I'd forgotten how easy it was to talk to you.'

'That's my job,' Annie laughed.

'I know. And you've really made me think about Nick. I do need to start making an effort, and get him to open up to me more. I don't want us to go back to how we used to be – you know, before we came to see you.'

'You won't, I'm sure. I know you've both got a lot on your plate, and having Jack means you need to make a massive adjustment, but don't let one another drop to the bottom of your priority list. It's so easy to concentrate on work and baby, and take your relationship for granted, but that needs as much effort as everything else.'

'Yes, oh wise one,' Julia teased, getting up from the table and putting on her coat.

Annie grinned. 'Okay, lecture over. Say hi to Nick for me, and give Jack a huge cuddle.'

'Will do. Send my love to Jamie. And call me as soon as he proposes so I can start the planning.'

Annie rolled her eyes, as Julia picked up her bags, and the two women hugged warmly.

'Have a great Christmas, Annie.'

'You too, Julia. You too.'

CHAPTER 11

'Always get married in the morning. That way, if it doesn't work out, you haven't wasted a whole day' –
Mickey Rooney

Gill's house was warm and welcoming, with the gas fire blazing in the living room and the Christmas tree decorated in the corner. It smelt of cooking, and pine needles, and everywhere there was evidence of what a bustling, busy household it was, with school books and homework and Christmas cards in haphazard piles on the coffee table, toys thrown hastily into brightly coloured storage boxes, and someone's dirty gym kit bursting out of a carrier bag in the corner. Uncoiling rolls of wrapping paper, haphazard fairy lights, and five different advent calendars propped up on the mantelpiece all added to the general feeling of chaos.

The faces staring back at Julia weren't quite so warm and welcoming. Instead, they were a mixture of bemusement, disinterest, and outright hostility in one case. All five of Gill and Mike's children were lined up on the enormous L-shaped sofa that had seen better days, while Julia sat opposite on a dining room chair that Mike had brought through. She was beginning to wonder what she'd got herself into.

'Now, as I explained, we've called this family meeting today to talk about the wedding,' Gill was saying. 'We've finally booked a date for the summer – the eleventh of July, so seven months to go – and we really want it to happen so that we can all be one big happy family. But to do that, we're going to need your help.'

'I can help!' Freddy volunteered, thrusting his hand in the air as though he was in class.

'Me too,' echoed Finlay, copying the action.

'Thanks boys,' Gill smiled. 'I knew I could count on you.'

'We want *all* of you to be involved.' Mike took over. 'So we thought it'd be helpful to hear any ideas you might have. That way, we can make the wedding about all of us.'

Freddy put on his best thinking face, sticking one finger in his mouth as he concentrated.

'Can we have balloons?' Finlay asked hopefully, as he bounced against the sofa cushions. 'And a big birthday cake?'

'There'll definitely be balloons and cake,' Mike chuckled. 'Although it'll be a wedding cake, not a birthday one.'

'Father Christmas!' Sam burst out excitedly. 'Will there be Father Christmas and reindeer?'

'Not in July, Sammy,' Gill shook her head. 'He'll have gone back to the North Pole by then. It'll be too hot for him and Rudolf.'

'Hopefully,' Mike grinned. 'You can never tell with the British weather.'

'This is my friend, Julia, by the way,' Gill explained to the kids, who were eyeballing her suspiciously. 'She works as an events planner, which means it's her job to organise parties and make sure everyone has a brilliant time. She's got loads of ideas and can help you think of things, or answer any questions you might have.'

Julia took this as her cue to smile and say hi to everyone.

'That's cool,' Paige exclaimed. 'Have you ever done a party for Justin Bieber?'

'Sorry to disappoint, but no I haven't,' Julia laughed. 'If he ever comes to Norfolk, then maybe I'll get the chance.'

'Mum, is this going to take long?' Kelly sighed, perfectly nailing her bored teenager tone. 'Because I really need to wash my hair. That's not even a joke.'

'Kelly,' Gill said sharply. 'None of that attitude please, I can't cope with it today. Do *you* have any ideas for the wedding?'

'Um, call it off? What's the point at your age?'

Julia saw Gill's sharp intake of breath, and hastily cut in before Gill had a chance to speak. 'Kelly, is it?' she asked, and Kelly nodded warily. Julia could see the intrigued look on her face, as though challenging Julia to hold her interest. 'Your mum asked me to come here today because she wants to throw an amazing party after her wedding, but to do that I need to hear what all of you can come up with. So if there's anything you've seen on TV, or something at a friend's party that you liked, let me know and I'll see if I can make it happen.'

Kelly didn't reply, but raised her eyebrows appraisingly, as though considering what Julia had said.

'One of the first things we need to decide,' Gill went on, throwing Julia a grateful look, 'is what kind of wedding to have. There are all different styles you see. We probably won't get married in a church, but we could choose a registry office, or a hotel, or a country house. Maybe even somewhere unusual like a castle or a museum. But we don't have a massive budget, so no suggestions of outer space, Freddy,' she warned, as Freddy grinned.

'Mrs Barnes at school says that you should go to church because if you don't believe in God then you won't go to heaven,' Finlay spoke up.

'Mum already got married in church once, so they won't let her do it again, because she promised that the first time it would be forever but it wasn't so she lied,' Kelly finished triumphantly.

Finlay narrowed his eyes suspiciously, looking between Gill and Kelly as though trying to figure out who was right.

'It's true,' Kelly went on, scrolling through her iPad and handing it over to Finlay. 'There, see? That's a photo of when Mum married Dad. Don't they look happy?'

Gill had gone white, completely unaware that Kelly even had a copy of her wedding photo.

'Did you lie?' Finlay was wide-eyed as he stared at Gill. 'Did you lie to God?'

'Kelly,' Gill snapped, as she jumped up to grab the iPad from Finlay. 'Mike and I are getting married now, so if we could think about that wedding and not any other ones.'

'I hate Mike,' Kelly muttered under her breath, just loud enough for everyone to hear.

'Don't you dare say that,' Gill yelled furiously. 'Apologise right now, or you're grounded for a week. And don't think you're getting this back any time soon,' she added, holding up the precious iPad.

'What? That's not fair! You can't ground me for having an opinion.'

'Why are you always such a cow to my dad? He's never done anything to you,' Paige rounded on Kelly, jumping to Mike's defence.

The atmosphere was horribly uncomfortable, and Julia couldn't help but feel like an outsider, intruding on an issue that should have been kept within the family. Seeing what Gill had been dealing with made Julia want to get up and leave, to run away and not get involved. But then she had an idea.

'You know what?' she spoke up, before the argument had a chance to take hold. 'How about if I chat with the kids for a while, on my own? Gill, you and Mike can take a break, and I'll brainstorm with everyone, see what we can come up with.'

Gill looked at Julia as though she was crazy. 'Really? Are you sure?'

'Of course,' Julia smiled brightly to hide her misgivings. It felt as though she was about to be left in the lion's den with five hungry animals. 'Grab yourself a cup of tea, and we'll be out soon.'

Mike raised his eyebrows. 'Do you know what you're letting yourself in for? They're a tough crowd.'

'I'll be fine, honestly. I'll yell if I need help.'

Reluctantly, Gill stood up, fixing the children with her steeliest glare. 'Right, you lot, I want you all on your *best* behaviour for Julia. Answer everything she asks you, and no silliness or cheekiness, or else she'll come and get me immediately. Okay?'

Freddy gave an enormous nod which involved using his whole body, while Sammy shouted, 'YES!' and Finlay and Paige stated their agreement. Kelly remained ominously quiet.

'Good luck,' Gill offered, as she and Mike left the room, closing the door behind them.

Julia glanced around, trying to stay positive, as she opened her notebook and took the lid off her pen. It was like dealing with wild animals – you couldn't show your fear.

'Great, now what I thought might be a good starting place is if you all come up with ideas for the reception – you know, the big party after the wedding,' she explained, noting Freddy and Finlay's confused expressions. 'What about you, Sam?' she asked, trying to involve the youngest child. 'Where do you think Daddy and Gill should have their party?'

'Ummm…' Sam put his finger to his head to show he was thinking. 'The circus!'

'That's a brilliant suggestion,' Julia enthused. 'We could definitely have a circus-themed party, and we could have a marquee done out like a Big Top, and get jugglers and magicians.'

'And lions and helephants!' Sam squealed.

'It's elephants,' Paige corrected him, moving across the sofa and pulling him onto her lap. 'And we can't have real elephants or lions because they'd eat us.'

'Elephants wouldn't eat us, they're herbivores, which means they're vegetarians like Connie Ellison in my class,' Finlay ran on. 'But she can eat tofu. Do elephants eat tofu?' he asked wonderingly, looking up at Julia for the answer.

Julia frowned. 'I don't think so. Just grass and cabbages,' she giggled. 'Any more ideas for the party?'

'We could build a massive church out of Lego,' Freddy suggested.

'I saw on TV where a wedding couple got married in Disneyland,' Finlay cut in earnestly.

'DISNEYLAND!' Sam squealed excitedly, kicking his legs. 'Mickey Mouse and Simba and Princess Elsa and Tigger and—'

'I think they should get married abroad, on a beach,' Paige suggested dreamily, talking over her brother who was still listing his favourite animated characters. 'Then we could all have bare feet and swim with dolphins afterwards.'

'That's a lovely idea,' Julia encouraged her. 'But it's very expensive. I think they'll have to get married in this country.'

'Maybe they could get married on the beach in Cyprus,' Paige continued brightly. 'Then we could all stay with Mum and Costas and it would be really cheap.'

Kelly threw her a scornful look. 'We can't stay with your mum, when your dad is marrying *my* mum,' she retorted. 'That's just stupid.'

Paige looked stung, and Julia quickly cut in, asking Kelly whether she had any suggestions.

'No,' Kelly replied sulkily.

'Oh, I bet you have,' Julia pressed, refusing to give up. 'Your mum told me you're really clever and creative, and always get top marks in art class.'

Kelly looked torn, unsure whether or not to take the flattery, or to continue with her usual aloof style.

'I reckon they should have a festival-style wedding,' she said eventually. 'My friend Becca's sister had one. She's older than her – like, twenty-six or something – and they hired a field for the whole weekend.'

'Why would you hire a field?' Freddy looked confused. 'There'd be nothing there, except maybe some cows. Moooooooo.'

'You put things *in* the field,' Kelly told him witheringly. 'You hire, like, fairground rides and a band and food stalls, so it's like a music festival, and then everyone camps overnight.'

'Camping? That sounds cool,' Freddy brightened.

'What kind of fairground rides?' Finlay wondered.

Kelly shrugged. 'Whatever you want, I guess.'

'Bumper cars?'

'Maybe…' Kelly looked uncertainly at Julia.

'They'd probably be a bit out of budget, but you're definitely thinking along the right lines. I once organised a summer party for a big company, and they had a carousel. Or you can get smaller things like bouncy castles and bucking broncos.'

'Bouncy castle! I love bouncy castles,' Freddy screeched, standing up on the sofa and jumping up and down.

'Freddy, you heard what Mum said, sit down *now*,' Kelly told him. Surprisingly, Freddy did as he was told, and Julia shot Kelly a grateful smile. Even more surprisingly, Kelly smiled back.

'Any more ideas?' Julia wondered, as she scanned the notes in her book.

'We could eat doughnuts!'

'And go in a hot air balloon.'

'…And Woody and Buzz and Mr Tumble…'

'Get married on a boat. Or a lake. Or an island.'

'A treasure island—'

'A jungle—'

'With dinosaurs!'

'Okay, okay, I think I've got more than enough to be going on with,' Julia laughed. 'I'll probably come back and see you all in a couple of weeks, so try and think of anything else before then. If you want to do any drawings of what you imagine the wedding might look like, that would be really helpful. And if you have any amazing ideas, don't forget to tell someone, or write them down so you don't forget them.'

'But don't tell Mum or Mike because it's supposed to be a surprise,' Kelly warned them.

'That's very true,' Julia agreed, as she had a brainwave. 'Actually, Kelly, if I give you my email address, would you be able to email me if you think of anything? And everyone else, you can tell Kelly then she'll let me know. Does that work for you?'

Kelly looked surprised, but pleased. 'Yeah, sure,' she shrugged.

'Great,' Julia smiled, handing Kelly her business card then picking up her handbag. 'Thanks so much, everyone. It was great to meet you, and I'm really looking forward to working with you all. Let's give your mum and dad a wedding they'll never forget.'

CHAPTER 12

'Love, n. A temporary insanity curable by marriage'
**– *Ambrose Bierce,* The Unabridged Devil's
Dictionary**

'Merry Christmas, Mum,' Aimee beamed, as she stepped through the front door into the little terraced house and hugged Pauline tightly.

'Merry Christmas! Come in, come in, it's freezing outside. Hello, Jon, how are you, love?' Pauline squeezed past him in the narrow hallway, closing the door behind him. She went to give him a hug as he moved to kiss her on the cheek, and they ended up in an awkward embrace.

'Mmm, something smells delicious,' Aimee breathed happily, as she took off her coat and hung it over the banister at the bottom of the stairs.

'Ooh, that's a nice outfit. Very festive,' Pauline remarked. Aimee was wearing a white sweater dress with silver sparkle threaded through, and knee-length grey boots that Jon had given her that morning. 'Can I take your jacket, Jon? You are staying, aren't you?' she joked, not noticing the pained expression on his face as she threw his expensive designer coat casually over Aimee's.

'Hi Dad, happy Christmas,' Aimee called, as she went through to the living room, where her father, Ken, was sitting in his usual armchair wearing a purple party hat. The television was playing in the background, with Macaulay Culkin trying to outfox the burglars in *Home Alone*.

Ken reached for the remote control and turned down the volume, before getting up to greet his daughter and her fiancé.

'These are for you,' Jon smiled, handing over two bottle-shaped gift bags.

'Thanks very much,' Ken said, peering inside and pulling out the contents. 'Ooh, champagne, very fancy. And red wine, I like a drop of that.'

'It's a claret,' Jonathan elaborated.

'Is it now.' Ken looked blank. 'Well, that's very nice of you both, very generous. Pauline,' he called. 'Come and see what Jonathan's brought us.'

'Oh, is it present time already?' Pauline sang as she bustled back through, a tatty old apron over the lacy dress she was wearing. 'We've got a few bits for you two of course,' she smiled, bending down beneath the Christmas tree to retrieve the parcels.

Aimee felt a warm glow of nostalgia as she gazed around the room; the Christmas tree was the same one they'd used since she was a child, as were most of the baubles and the tinsel. Everything was verging on shabby but it was all infused with happy memories. The decorations Aimee and her brother, Charlie, had made at primary school hung from the tree's branches, just like they did every year, and beside the fake fir was the light-up reindeer her mum had bought in the Woolworths sale many years ago.

Aimee glanced over at Jon and saw him taking in the cards hung on lengths of red wool, tacked to the wall with drawing pins; the chipped wooden nativity by the gas fire, which was missing a wise man; the dancing Santa Claus stood on the sideboard, who sang a tinny version of 'We Wish You A Merry Christmas' when you pressed the button between his boots. The look of distaste on

Jon's face couldn't be hidden, and Aimee felt a stab of embarrassment for how homely her own parents seemed, compared with Valerie's enormous house and sophisticated tastes.

'You don't go in for a real tree then, Mrs Nicholls?' Jonathan asked, his tone scrupulously polite. Aimee's heart sank even further.

'No, not for years,' Pauline explained as she straightened up, holding two messily wrapped parcels covered in mismatched ribbon and bows. 'They drop needles everywhere, and the cat goes mad for the smell. Unless you want her spraying all over your presents, it's best to stick with the fake one,' Pauline chuckled, as she handed them across, her face pink with anticipation.

Aimee tore into her gift, giggling as she spotted the familiar Cadbury's selection box; it was a family tradition, and Pauline bought one every year for Aimee and her brother. On top of it was a pretty silk scarf in a butterfly print.

'Thanks Mum,' Aimee grinned, leaning over to hug her once again.

'You're very welcome. It's so difficult to know what to get you now you're getting older.'

'It's perfect,' Aimee smiled. She turned nervously to watch Jon open his gift, hoping that he'd accept it graciously and wouldn't cause a fuss. Her heart was racing as he carefully peeled back the paper, revealing a burgundy jewellery box. Inside was a shiny gold-plated watch with a fake-leather strap, and Aimee knew instantly that Jon would hate it.

'It's a watch,' Pauline announced, in case they hadn't realised. 'Aimee told me that yours had broken, so I thought I'd get you another one.'

'Thanks Mum, that's really thoughtful,' Aimee told her enthusiastically. Jon's old watch had been a Breitling, worth over two thousand pounds.

'If you don't like it, you can take it back and swap it. I kept the receipt. It's from Argos, so very convenient.'

'No, that won't be necessary, will it Jon?' Aimee interjected, giving her fiancé a pleading look.

'It's… just what I needed, thank you,' Jon managed through gritted teeth, looking around for somewhere to discard it. He popped it down on the mantelpiece, beside the patchwork stocking that was hanging there, and Aimee winced inwardly.

Her fiancé wasn't a snob, he really wasn't, Aimee told herself. They just came from very different worlds, with very different upbringings. And when those two worlds collided, it didn't always make for the most comfortable of occasions, Aimee realised, trying not to think about the implications this had for her wedding day.

'Oh, and we got you something else too,' Pauline continued excitedly, as she picked up an envelope from the coffee table and handed it to Aimee.

The flap was folded inside and Aimee untucked it, pulling out a card which showed two cartoon mice wrapped up in scarves and hats, sitting inside a horse-drawn sleigh. '*To a Wonderful Daughter and her Fiancé*', read the gold italic script on the front.

'Aww, that's cute,' she smiled, showing it to Jon. As Aimee opened it to read the message, she realised there was another piece of paper inside. It was a cheque for two hundred and fifty pounds.

'Towards the wedding,' Pauline beamed, as Aimee lifted it out. 'I know how expensive these things are and we thought, well, every little helps.'

'Mrs Nicholls, you really didn't have to,' Jon cut in.

'It's fine,' Pauline waved away his words. 'Ken managed to get some overtime at work, and I've been making savings here and there.'

'Honestly,' Jon insisted. 'It's really not necessary. My mother's more than able to cover the whole cost.'

Pauline looked taken aback, and Aimee's heart went out to her. 'Well, I'm sure it'll go towards something,' she said uncertainly. 'Or maybe you can use it to buy something you need for the flat.'

'We already have everything we need,' Jon told her with a smile. He was trying to be kind, but Aimee could see how this looked like a rejection of her parents' generous gesture.

'Thanks, Mum,' Aimee interjected, with a sharp look at Jon. 'It's so kind of you, and we really appreciate it. This'll cover my bouquet and the buttonholes, won't it Jon? Or maybe we can put it towards the honeymoon.'

'Yes, the honeymoon,' Jon repeated stiffly.

There was an awkward silence. Aimee played absent-mindedly with the cheque, folding it in half then folding it once again, her fingers leaving damp marks along the crease.

'Well, shall we make our way through to the kitchen?' Pauline suggested brightly. 'The turkey's ready, so I'll start dishing up. Turn the telly off, Ken.'

Ken rolled his eyes, hitting the off button on the remote before getting up from his chair and following Aimee and Jon through to the kitchen, where Pauline had extended the small table to make it large enough to seat four. Aimee's parents didn't have a separate dining room, and usually ate in the living room when they didn't have company.

Tinkerbell, the Nicholls' ageing moggy, was curled up in the centre of the table, and Pauline hastily shooed her off. Aimee saw Jon's eyes widen as he took in the trail of cat hairs she'd left behind on the tablecloth.

'Now it's going to be a bit of a squeeze,' Pauline apologised, bumping her bottom on the corner of the table as she tried to take the turkey out of the oven. Jon was hit by a blast of hot air and fanned his face irritably. 'Why don't you sit over there, love?' Pauline suggested anxiously, pointing at the chair furthest from the cooker.

'Should I open the champagne?' Jon offered, eyeing up the bottle he'd given Ken earlier.

'No, no need for that,' Ken replied. 'I've got some wine over here. Let's save the champagne for a special occasion.' He reached for a bottle that was standing on the worktop and unscrewed the cap, dividing the bottle equally between the four glasses. 'I'm not sure what this is exactly, but it was on special at the super-market. Still, down the hatch as they say. Cheers everyone.'

Ken raised his glass to an echo of, 'Cheers'.

Jonathan grimaced as he took a hesitant sip; it was all he could do not to spit it back into the glass.

'It might have been better in the fridge, Dad,' Aimee suggested tactfully, staring down at the lukewarm, acidic wine in her hand.

Ken shook his head. 'I don't like it too cold. I have sensitive teeth you see, Jonathan, and anything cold really sets them off.'

Jon didn't reply, sparking yet another uncomfortable silence.

'Sit down, everyone, sit down,' Pauline insisted, placing the last of the dishes on the table.

'Wow, Mum, you've really pushed the boat out,' Aimee ex-claimed. The table was practically groaning under the weight of all the food, and every spare inch was covered with plates and dishes. There were sprouts, carrots, parsnips in honey, roast potatoes, red cabbage, Yorkshire puddings, pigs in blankets and a vast array of sauces in their sticky, faded jars. Aimee couldn't help but think of Jon's usual insistence on having no bottles at the dinner table; he preferred that Aimee decant all of their con-diments into classic ramekin dishes, just like Valerie always did.

'So have you heard from Charlie?' Aimee asked, as Ken set about carving the turkey. Her brother was spending Christmas with his girlfriend's family in Portsmouth, but would be coming home for New Year.

'Yes, he called this morning to wish me happy Christmas. He said to say hello to you – and Jon of course,' Pauline added hastily.

'Hopefully we'll get to see him when he's back.'

'Well, I'm sure he'll be busy doing his own thing,' Jon commented. 'And besides, we've got plans for New Year.'

'Oh, have you decided what you're doing?' Pauline poured gravy over her food and tucked in.

'We're um… going with Jon's mother to her club.'

'The Lancaster Club,' Jonathan added.

'Ooh, very fancy. They'll put on a good do there.'

'It's a black tie dinner, with champagne reception and an award-winning swing band,' Jonathan explained.

'Lovely,' Pauline replied, looking somewhat blank at the concept of 'black tie'.

The meal continued with sporadic conversation, Pauline cheerily overcompensating as Jon made the occasional cutting remark that he imagined was going over their heads, but Aimee could see that her parents were taking every comment to heart.

'That really was delicious, Mrs Nicholls,' Jon said effusively, pushing his plate away as he sat back in his chair.

'She does a good roast, does your future mother-in-law,' Ken grinned.

'You can come round for a meal any time you like,' Pauline encouraged. 'You don't have to let us know, just drop in. It'd be lovely to see more of you. *Both* of you.'

Aimee felt a familiar pang of guilt, knowing that she didn't visit her parents as often as she should – Jonathan even less so.

'Jon's very busy,' Aimee said, hearing how pathetic it sounded.

'I know he is. I don't know how you do it, running that big company,' Pauline marvelled, and Aimee again felt bad, hating the way her mother felt the need to grovel to her fiancé.

'Well, it's great to know that I've got Aimee to come home to,' Jon smiled, putting his arm around her.

'Aw, isn't that nice,' Pauline cooed, as she stood up to clear the plates. Aimee got up to help, but Pauline waved her away. 'It's fine, you sit down and relax. It's Christmas! Now, Jon, this was always our Aimee's favourite dessert when she was younger, so I thought it'd be nice to get it out today.'

Pauline moved to the worktop and took out four bowls, filling them up and carrying them across to the table with a flourish.

Jon looked down at the dessert that had been placed in front of him – vanilla flavoured ice cream decorated with chocolate fingers and drizzled in strawberry sauce – and exhaled loudly, shaking his head. 'I'm stuffed, thanks, Mrs Nicholls.'

Pauline's face dropped. 'You don't want any?'

'I couldn't eat another bite. And to be honest, we really need to get going soon. My mother's expecting us.'

'But you've only just eaten!'

'I know, I hate to rush off, but now that Mother's on her own I don't like to leave her for too long. Especially not at Christmas.'

'Oh, I didn't think of that. Yes, it must be a very difficult time of year. You're such a considerate son, Jonathan.'

Jon stood up, pushing his chair under the table with a scraping sound. He hit the cat with the chair leg, and Tinkerbell slunk off with a yowl. 'Well, we really must be off. Thanks so much for everything. Pauline, Ken.' Jon kissed Aimee's mother on the cheek and shook hands with her father.

Aimee followed in his wake, wondering what the sudden rush was all about, but not wanting to question him in front of her parents. She hastily pulled on her coat and hugged her mum. 'I'll call you tonight, okay?'

Jon was practically sprinting down the driveway and Aimee hurried to catch up with him, sliding into the Porsche where he revved the engine and pulled away at speed.

'Whew, thank God that's over, right?' he said with a little laugh, glancing across at Aimee.

'What do you mean?'

'Oh Aimee, I know they're your parents, but I honestly couldn't take another minute. That ice cream concoction was the last straw. And what did your dad look like in that hat? You can tell I love you very much if I'm willing to put up with your family,' Jon chuckled. 'Don't worry, we'll be at Mum's in ten minutes tops,' he continued, nodding at the empty roads. 'I need to get some decent champagne down me, get rid of the taste of that vinegar your father served.'

Aimee felt as though she'd been slapped in the face, stunned by Jon's damning critique of her parents. They drove in silence, with Aimee too upset to speak, her mind reeling as she tried to take in everything he'd just said. Jon didn't seem to notice, humming along to the Christmas carols that were on the radio, tapping his fingers on the steering wheel.

It was only as they swept into the driveway of Valerie's house that Aimee realised Jon had never picked up his gift. He'd left the watch on the mantelpiece at her parents' house, half-hidden behind a glittery candle display.

Aimee looked across at her fiancé, at the firm set of his jaw, his handsome face and immaculate designer clothing, and couldn't help wondering whether he'd be callous enough to do something like that deliberately.

CHAPTER 13

'Never go to bed mad. Stay up and fight'
– Phyllis Diller

Debbie squinted through half-closed eyes, holding her breath as she looked down at the chipped pink polish on her toenails. Between her feet, the electronic dial of the scales flickered back and forth, before finally coming to rest.

'Three pounds!' she squealed indignantly. 'I've put on three pounds overnight! How did that happen?'

'Well, it *was* Christmas Day,' Stevie replied reasonably. 'You're supposed to indulge.' He was lying in bed, shirtless and bundled up in the purple duvet, as he called out to Debbie who was in the bathroom. She stormed back through, tying her dressing gown tightly around the middle, a furious look on her face.

'It's not fair. I take my eye off the ball for *one day*, and *that* happens.'

'Never mind, it's just a blip. Come back to bed.'

'Hmph,' replied Debbie, unimpressed, as she crawled back in beside him. Stevie wrapped an arm around her and she snuggled against him, enjoying his warmth, as Scamp dived onto the bed, settling down by their feet.

'It was a festive one off,' Stevie assured her. 'Don't worry about it.'

'Hmph,' Debbie said again, unconvinced. Although, now that she thought about it, she really had given herself free rein to eat whatever she wanted yesterday. She'd started in the morning with a glass of Buck's Fizz and two croissants spread liberally with butter and strawberry jam, then demolished half a box of Ferrero Rocher as soon as she'd unwrapped them. There'd been a full roast dinner with all the trimmings when they'd visited Stevie's mum and dad for lunch, before moving on to her own parents' in the evening who'd produced an enormous cheeseboard, with crackers and bread. She'd ended the night with a cheeky Baileys or three, and gone to bed feeling stuffed to the gills.

'I think I know a way to burn off some of those calories,' Stevie murmured naughtily, leaning over to run a hand along her thigh.

'Me too,' Debbie replied, kissing him. 'How about we have a long, hot, sweaty… Boxing Day walk?'

'Huh? That's not exactly what I had in mind.'

'Why not?' Debbie sat up excitedly, getting carried away by the idea. 'We could drive out to the Broads. It'd be so romantic, strolling by the water, and Scamp would love it. Plus we'd be burning calories and getting fit.'

'I thought all those healthy resolutions didn't start until the New Year?'

But Debbie refused to be put off. 'No time like the present.' She bounded out of bed and began getting dressed, pulling on an old pair of jeans and layering up beneath a thick jumper. 'I want to grab a quick breakfast before we go, otherwise I'll be starving. Do you want me to do you a fry-up?'

Stevie looked torn. 'What are you having?'

'Special K with skimmed milk.'

'You know what? I'll have that too.'

Debbie's eyebrows shot up in surprise. 'Really? You don't have to.'

'No, no it's fine,' Stevie said quickly, before he changed his mind. 'I want to support you. I'm really proud of how well you're doing, Debs.'

Debbie stopped mid-change, surprised at how honest he was being. Her fiancé wasn't the kind of man to gush about his feelings, so for him to say he was proud of her was a big admission. Dropping her socks on the floor, Debbie crawled back across the bed towards him, giving him a long, loving kiss. 'Thanks, babe. I really appreciate it.'

'Good,' Stevie grinned, kissing her back. 'Now let's get going before I change my mind.'

—

The two of them tumbled out of the car an hour later at Berney Marshes, Scamp jumping out of the boot excitedly and immediately haring off after a group of pigeons. It was one of those deliciously cold and clear winter days, when the sun is bright and the fresh air brings the colour to your cheeks. Debbie was wrapped up cosily, wearing a fleecy jacket and her spotty Wellington boots. She'd tied her hair in two long Pocahontas-style plaits, and was wearing a bobble hat with matching scarf.

'It's a gorgeous day, isn't it,' she sighed, tucking her arm through Stevie's as the two of them set off walking, Scamp running around their feet, snuffling at bushes and tree trunks.

'Not bad at all,' Stevie agreed cheerily. 'As long as we get back in time for the football.'

Debbie rolled her eyes. 'Oh, I meant to tell you, I spoke to your mum yesterday and she said she'd be more than happy to make the wedding cake, so that's brilliant. It means we can save a bit on the budget. I can't believe how much some people charge, just to make a cake!'

Stevie nodded in agreement.

'So everything's coming together nicely. Julia's been amazing, getting us a great deal on the caterers and the florist. You've got the photographer sorted, right?'

'Right.'

'And I *still* need to make a final decision on a dress. Everyone keeps telling me I'm leaving it really late, but I want to lose a bit more weight first, then I'll get more of an idea of how it will fit.'

'Uh huh,' was Stevie's contribution, as he took her hand in his. They were strolling along the muddy path beside the water, the fields stretching away in the distance, and the trees bare and bleak against the winter sky. A group of ducks paddled by, and Scamp watched them longingly, whilst a heron stood at a safe distance, half-hidden in the long grass at the side of the marsh.

'Have you had any thoughts about the honeymoon?' Debbie wondered. 'It might be worth booking in the New Year, as they always have some great offers. January sales and all that.'

Stevie shrugged non-committally. 'I don't mind. Where d'you fancy?'

'Well, I've been thinking…'

'I thought you might have been,' Stevie grinned, as Debbie stuck her tongue out at him.

'Look, one of us has got to do some planning, or else this wedding's never going to happen. Anyway, I think it'd be nice to go somewhere warm, but not too far flung. I don't think the budget will stretch to the Caribbean or the Maldives,' she sighed wistfully. 'But there are some really nice places in Greece. Santorini's gorgeous, and so romantic. Look.'

Debbie pulled out her phone, opening up a page she'd clearly been looking at earlier. It showed a perfect little village with whitewashed houses and domed roofs, against a stunning backdrop of blue Aegean sea.

'Very pretty,' Stevie commented admiringly. 'I wouldn't mind being there right now.'

'Mmm, me too,' Debbie agreed, as she put her head down and sunk deeper into her scarf, trying to keep out the chill blowing off the North Sea and across the Norfolk countryside.

'If you don't fancy that, there are loads of cheap deals to Egypt, and some lovely looking hotels along the Red Sea. You can go snorkelling, and camel trekking…'

'And is that what you want to do on our honeymoon?' Stevie teased.

'Maybe. If I get bored of you I can always ride off into the desert and join a harem,' Debbie shot back.

'That won't happen,' Stevie asserted confidently. 'You won't get bored of me. I plan to keep you *very* entertained during our honeymoon.'

'Ooh, promises, promises,' Debbie giggled. 'I'll remember to pack my handcuffs. Oh, I was looking at Dubai too,' she suddenly remembered. 'Although we probably shouldn't pack the handcuffs if we go there. But Angela's friend Clare went and she said it was amazing. Loads of shopping and nice restaurants, and a fantastic water park.'

'Water park?' That got Stevie's attention.

'Yeah. Actually, I was browsing bikinis online the other day,' Debbie confessed. 'I saw this really pretty aquamarine one, with ruffles around the bust and along the top of the bikini bottoms.'

'Bikinis?' Stevie was looking at her thoughtfully. 'You know, I don't think I've ever seen you wear a bikini. Even when we went to Majorca, you had a swimsuit and a cover-up thingy.'

Debbie flushed, unable to keep the proud smile off her face. 'I know. But now I've started losing weight, I thought "why not"?'

'How much weight are you actually planning to lose?'

'I don't know really. As much as I can.' Debbie hesitated for a moment, wondering whether or not to confide in him. 'I'd love to get down to a size ten.' Her confession came out in a rushed whisper; she felt giddy with excitement at having said it out loud.

'Size ten? There'll be nothing left of you. I won't recognise the girl walking down the aisle towards me.' Stevie laughed, but he was clearly disconcerted.

Debbie felt a wave of anger pulse through her chest at the way he was reacting. Why wasn't he happy for her? Didn't he understand how hard she was working? That all the Zumba classes and salads and the saying no to KitKats were as much for him as they were for her?

'That's the point, Stevie,' she snapped back. 'I *want* to look different. I don't want to look like a big pile of blubber on my wedding day.'

'But I *like* the way you look,' Stevie insisted. 'I love *you*, and it doesn't matter what size you are. Besides, you'll always be a big girl, won't you, Debs?'

Debbie stopped walking. She dropped his hand, staring at him in disbelief. And once the disbelief had passed, the anger kicked in. 'What did you say?'

'I just meant…' A look of panic flashed across Stevie's face and he began speaking quickly, trying to extricate himself from the hole he'd started digging. 'You know, you've never been small the whole time I've known you. And size ten is just… well, I like you as you are, and there's no need to…' He was floundering now, terrified by Debbie's expression.

'You don't think I can do this, do you?'

'It's not that, Debs, it's just that—'

'Or you don't *want* me to do it, is that it? Is this all you think I am?' Debbie waved her hands in the air, gesturing at her body. 'You think this is me forever now? Chubby and miserable, not capable of wearing tight dresses or sexy bikinis?'

'I didn't say—'

But Debbie was on a roll. 'I thought you'd be supportive. I thought that *you*, out of everyone, would be the one person who'd understand and try to help me out.'

'I *do*. I *am*,' Stevie gabbled helplessly. 'Why do you think I came out with you today, and ate Special K for breakfast? It's to help *you*, Debs.'

Debbie flashed him an exceptionally withering look, a look that could have turned lesser men to stone. 'Oh thanks, Stevie. Thank you so much. Could you *be* any more patronising?'

'But… I…' Stevie's mouth flapped open and closed uselessly. He was desperate to make the situation better, but everything he said seemed to unintentionally make it worse. Just as he was trying to decide what to do for the best, Debbie let out a scream of frustration, then turned on her heel and began stomping back towards the car, Scamp chasing at her heels.

'Debs, wait.' Stevie rolled his eyes upwards towards the heavens, pleading for divine intervention, then set off at a jog after his furious fiancée. 'Debbie, *please*.'

Debbie's mouth was set in a tight line, her expression furious. By the time they'd got back to the car, at twice the speed it had taken them to walk away from it, the two of them still weren't speaking. Debbie stood mutinously outside the passenger door, her arms folded across her chest as she waited for Stevie to unlock it. Instead, he came round to her side and attempted to take her hands. She snatched them away angrily.

'Debbie,' Stevie sounded annoyed now. 'I'm not getting in the car until we've resolved this.'

'Fine. Give me the keys and I'll drive home. You can stay here as long as you like.'

'That's not what I meant. And I didn't mean what I said earlier, you must know that.'

'Sounds like you're saying a lot of things you don't mean today. Are you sure you really want to marry me, or was that something you accidentally said as well?'

A flicker of a smile broke across Stevie's face, amused at how petulant his fiancée was being. At least she was speaking to him now – even if it was to insult him.

'I absolutely definitely want to marry you. And I hope you want to marry me too, even if I do say stupid, ridiculous things that come out all wrong sometimes.'

Debbie stayed quiet, but Stevie could see that she was starting to thaw.

'Now it's absolutely freezing out here, so if we're done with all this exercise business I'd love it if we could get in the car and go home. Or else I'll drive home, and you can walk, which, admittedly, would burn a lot of calories.'

Debbie couldn't help it; she let out a little giggle. Scamp jumped up at her, his tail wagging furiously as he covered her jeans in muddy paw prints.

'And if you get in the car with me now,' Stevie added, taking advantage of the distraction to move closer and slip his arms around her waist, 'I'll treat you to a fruit smoothie on the way home.'

'Done,' Debbie smiled, wrapping her arms around him, as he kissed her. 'But you do know that what you said was stupid, right? And that this is something I'm really self-conscious and insecure about?'

'I know, I know.' Stevie was nodding away like the Churchill dog. 'And I'm really sorry. Of course I believe you can do it. You can do anything you want to. You're amazing like that.'

'Yes. Yes, I am,' Debbie joked. 'Keep up with the flattery and I might think about forgiving you.'

'That's my girl,' Stevie winked.

CHAPTER 14

'Before marriage, a girl has to make love to a man to hold him. After marriage, she has to hold him to make love to him' – **Marilyn Monroe**

'You can go out if you want, I really don't mind,' Julia insisted.

'Don't be silly, we agreed we'd spend tonight together. Our first New Year as a new family.'

'Well Jack'll be sound asleep by midnight, and to be honest I probably will be too, so if you want to head out for a drink then don't let me stop you.'

Nick put down his phone with a sigh. It was New Year's Eve and a group of his friends were hitting the local pub, texting him to encourage him to come along. Most of them were married with kids, like himself, so it wasn't going to be a wild night, but Nick and Julia had already decided to spend the evening at home. Besides, despite Julia's protestations that he was fine to go out with the boys, Nick knew that she would hate it if he *did* actually leave her home alone for a night on the town.

'Maybe I should have invited people round,' Julia was fretting. 'We could have done that instead – had a civilised dinner party, or nibbles and drinks, or something. We could have invited Debbie and Stevie, and Annie and Jamie, and maybe Sara and Anthony from your work, they're always good fun.'

'But we didn't and we haven't,' Nick told her softly, coming to sit beside her on the sofa. 'It'll be just the two – well, three – of us.'

Inadvertently, they both looked over to where Jack was sitting on his play mat, trying to cram a stacking cup into his mouth with one hand, whilst smacking a sturdy rattle against his fire engine with the other. He looked impossibly cute, dressed in blue cord trousers and a blue and white sailor-style jumper.

'Can you believe that this time last year we didn't even have Jack?' Julia marvelled, as Nick shook his head.

'I genuinely can't remember what life was like before him. Did we really used to do things like go out to restaurants and have weekends away and, oh, I don't know, sleep?'

Julia laughed. 'Doesn't it make you feel old, though? I mean, all over the country people are getting ready for their big night out, doing their hair and make-up and putting on their party frocks. And we're going to stay in and probably pass out before we even see the fireworks on the news.'

'I guess we *are* old now. Old, married and past it.'

'Great.' Julia's tone was sarcastic.

'Of course, it doesn't have to be that way. We could let our hair down, go wild…' Nick leapt to his feet, turning up the volume on the television where a compilation of the biggest hits of the year was playing. As a Taylor Swift song kicked in, Nick took Julia's hands and pulled her to her feet.

'What are you doing?' she shrieked, as Nick held her close and began to dance, spinning her round and dipping her backwards. On the floor, Jack stopped what he was doing and stared in astonishment, breaking out into a wide smile that showed off his two tiny front teeth.

'Recapturing our youth,' Nick winked, as he slowly brought a breathless Julia upright and kissed her softly.

Julia smiled up at him, thinking how handsome her husband looked. Like a fine wine, he got better with age: the salt and pepper hair; the crinkles around the eyes; the craggy features. She kissed him again, realising how long it was since they'd had a really passionate smooch – not simply a peck on the lips when one of them left the house.

Nick's hands began to roam, finding their way under the layers of clothing Julia was wearing. As he touched her belly, she instinctively flinched, feeling self-conscious.

'No, Nick,' she snapped, more harshly than she'd intended.

'What's the matter?' he protested, looking hurt as he pulled away. 'It feels like so long since I've touched you, Jules.'

'I'm just not feeling my best, that's all. My stomach's still flabby, and I'm all out of shape.'

'I thought that's what the Zumba classes were for?'

'Yeah, but it's about how I feel, and I'm not quite there yet.'

'Well I hope you get there soon,' Nick muttered under his breath, unable to hide his frustration.

'And what's that supposed to mean?'

'You know what it's supposed to mean. It been ages since we… you know.'

Julia glared at him. 'No, I don't. Why don't you spell it out, Nick.'

'Okay, then. It's been ages since we had sex. Weeks in fact.'

'Oh, well excuse me for having an eight-month-old to look after and three weddings to organise, not to mention trying to keep this house clean and have your dinner on the table when you come in from work. Now you want me to be swinging from the chandeliers every night too. Why don't you just replace me with a Stepford wife and have done with it?'

Julia was instantly on the defensive. The problem was that, like all comments that really got under your skin, it had the ring of truth to it, and Julia knew that was the real reason she'd got so angry. She was well aware that her and Nick's sex life had dwindled to practically zero; she could count on the fingers of one hand the number of times they'd actually got it on since Jack was born.

Nick rolled his eyes. 'You're such a drama queen, Jules. That's not what I said at all. Just once in a blue moon would be appreciated.'

'I can't seem to get it right, can I? First there's too much sex, then not enough. Make your mind up, Goldilocks.'

Nick laughed hollowly at the insult, knowing exactly what Julia was referring to. It had taken a long time to get pregnant with Jack, and Julia had become almost obsessive in her desire for a baby. She'd been jumping on Nick every chance that she got, leaving him exhausted and irritable. That was the reason they'd gone to see Annie for counselling.

'All I'm saying is that it would be nice to know I'm on your priority list somewhere. You know, after the baby, and the Royal Wedding' – which was how Nick jokingly referred to Aimee and Jon's upcoming nuptials – 'and all the other weddings you seem to be organising "as a favour", and the Zumba classes and God knows what else. You know, once you've finished with all that, it would be great to spend a little quality time together if you can fit me in.'

'Exactly!' Julia threw both hands in the air to emphasise the point. 'I feel like I'm constantly juggling all these different things, trying to keep the plates spinning without them crashing to the ground, and sooner or later I'm going to mess up. I can't please everyone all of the time, Nick, something's got to give. And all *you* have to do is go to work every day, while the rest of your life is sorted out for you.'

'Well I apologise for trying to keep a roof over our heads and food on the table, just so you can run around having coffee with your friends and organising their weddings free of charge. I'd love to sit around watching daytime TV, popping out occasionally to look at country houses, but unfortunately I can't because I have a proper bloody job.'

Nick's voice was growing louder with every word, and he looked furious. Julia stood open-mouthed, equally as angry at what he'd just said. She knew that this row had been coming for a while – both of them had felt it creeping up – but New Year's Eve was incredibly bad timing.

'Don't you *dare*—' she began, incensed and gearing up for a rant, but at that moment Jack began to wail. 'Now look what you've done,' Julia snapped. Instinctively, she went to pick him up, but then stopped herself. 'Why don't *you* see to your son for a change?'

There was a moment's hesitation on Nick's part, then he stomped across the room, bending down to Jack. Jack began to scream even louder, holding out his arms towards Julia.

'Oh great, he won't even let me get near him,' Nick stropped, looking at Julia as though it was her fault, while Jack's howling reached unprecedented levels. 'For Christ's sake, can't you shut him up? He clearly prefers you anyway.'

Julia stared at Nick in astonishment, anger and confusion written across her face, hardly able to believe what he'd just said. 'Fine, I'll see to him,' she retorted, pushing past her husband and scooping Jack up into her arms where he immediately quietened down. 'It's time for his bath anyway. Why don't you put your feet up, you must be exhausted from having the last two weeks off work. Don't worry about me, I'll do everything else, as usual.'

With that parting shot, she marched angrily out of the room, running up the stairs and into the bathroom with Jack. As she filled the tub with shallow water and poured in baby bubbles, Julia could feel her heart pounding, her mind racing.

Once again, things seemed to be going wrong between her and Nick, and she couldn't quite put her finger on why. They were bickering and sniping at one another, each concerned with their own point of view and neither taking into account the other's feelings.

Did Nick resent Jack? she wondered unhappily, as she undressed her grizzling son and lowered him gently into the bath, scooping water over his fine, dark hair while he kicked and spluttered. Was Nick feeling pushed out and neglected, like Annie had suggested?

Perhaps the two of them needed some time alone together, to reconnect and ease the pressure. After all, a new baby with its accompanying stress and lack of sleep could put a strain on even the strongest of marriages.

Over the past few months, Julia and Nick had managed to have a handful of nights out, when Debbie had been kind enough to babysit. Their parents both lived a three-hour drive away in Derby, but Debbie was becoming a good friend to Julia, and she was great with Jack, who seemed to love being looked after by his honorary Auntie Debs.

On one occasion, Nick and Julia had dragged themselves to the local pub, but found they were too exhausted to stay out late, and the fun of getting drunk was tempered by the fact they knew they would have to be up at the crack of dawn to deal with their crying son. They'd headed home at half past nine, surprising Debbie who was shocked to see them so early, and even told them off for not making the most of their free night.

Another time, they'd gone to the cinema to see the latest Daniel Craig movie, and Julia had fallen asleep after twenty minutes, the darkness and warmth of the cinema enticing her eyelids to close and catch up on some much needed rest. On balance, it just seemed easier to stay at home.

Julia lifted Jack out of the water, wrapping him in a hooded blanket and holding him close as she carried him through to his room. He smelt delicious, that freshly washed new baby scent, so pure and clean. She dried him carefully, tickling his tummy and marvelling at his tiny fingers and toes, at the little changes that took place every day. He was growing so quickly, and the time seemed to be flying by.

In the routine that was now so familiar to her, Julia slathered Sudocrem over Jack's chubby little bottom then put a fresh nappy on him, dressing him in a red starry sleepsuit and placing him in his cot while she went down to the kitchen to warm some milk. As she cradled Jack in her arms and fed him, his eyes slowly closing as he began to doze, Julia noticed with a pang how much he looked like Nick, with his dark brows and the dimple in his chin.

Of course bringing up a baby was tough, especially combined with all the other challenges life threw at you, but she and Nick were so lucky to have one another, Julia realised. This was just a bump in the road, and they would get back on track soon, as long as both of them made an effort.

She tucked Jack's blanket around him and turned on the nightlight, giving him a final goodnight kiss before heading back downstairs. She felt much calmer now, ready to apologise and make up with Nick.

Walking into the living room, Julia saw that Nick had opened a bottle of red wine and poured out two glasses. He'd filled the fancy porcelain serving dishes they'd received as a wedding present with olives, Kettle Chips and cheese straws, and arranged them on the coffee table. He smiled tentatively when he saw her, trying to work out if she was still mad with him.

'Drinks and nibbles,' he said casually. 'We didn't need to invite anyone round after all.'

'Thanks, darling,' Julia smiled, taking the glass of wine he was holding out like a peace offering. 'I'm sorry for getting angry.'

'Me too. I want us to have a nice, relaxing evening tonight. Not to go into the New Year fighting.'

'Sounds perfect,' Julia replied, taking a long swallow of the warming, peppery wine. She clinked her glass against his. 'To the Crawfords.'

'The Crawfords,' Nick repeated, as he took a sip then exhaled deeply, the stresses of the day finally melting away. 'Did Jack get off okay?'

'Yeah. He loved his bath, then he looked ready to pass out when I put him down.'

Both of them were silent for a moment, lost in their own thoughts. Julia wondered whether or not to bring up everything that was troubling her – the way she and Nick were fighting, Nick's reluctance to bond with Jack – but before she had a chance, the sound of loud snoring came from the baby monitor. They both burst out laughing, relieving the tension.

'Out like a light,' Nick smiled.

'Just like his dad.'

Julia leaned across to kiss him, deciding to put aside her anxieties for now. Tonight really wasn't the time to discuss them.

Nick was gazing at her adoringly. 'I love you, Jules.'

'I love you too. I really am sorry about earlier.'

'Me too. You know I didn't mean—'

The moment was interrupted by a series of loud noises from outside, bangs and whizzes and squeals exploding in the distance. Nick strode across to the rear window, pulling open the curtains.

'Fireworks already?' Julia wondered.

'They must be letting them off early, over near the park,' Nick replied, wrapping his arm around her as she came to stand beside him.

Julia let her body mould into his, sipping on the delicious red wine as they watched the shimmering display, brilliant bursts of gold and red and silver. She knew that the situation with Nick was far from resolved, but for now they'd made a truce, and that was a good start. As the dazzling fireworks exploded high in the night sky, Julia made a silent wish that next year would bring everything that was most important in life – health, happiness and joy for the whole family.

CHAPTER 15

*'I love being married. It's so great to find that one special
person you want to annoy for the rest of your life'*
– Rita Rudner

'How do I look?'

Aimee pirouetted on her heels as she walked down the corridor towards Jon, her A-line skirt flaring out as she span. She'd teamed it with a smart black top and mid-height court shoes, and she looked fresh and perfectly groomed, her eyes sparkling nervously in anticipation of his reaction.

Jon assessed her critically as he swirled the ice cubes in his pre-prandial gin and tonic. He was standing in their sleek, open-plan kitchen, and was impeccably dressed in a dark grey suit and crisp white shirt that Aimee had ironed earlier that day. 'Yeah, it's… fine.'

Aimee's face fell. 'Fine?'

'Well, obviously you look beautiful. You always do…' Jon tried to inject a little more enthusiasm into his voice.

'But?'

'But there's something…' He stood back, half-closing his eyes in thought. 'What about that navy dress? You know, the fitted one with the square neckline? No, even better,' Jon clicked his fingers as the thought struck him. 'The red lace one you wore for my birthday?'

'Really?' Aimee frowned. 'You don't think that's a little over the top?'

'We want to knock Huddlestone dead, don't we?'

Aimee stood uncertainly for a moment, before turning round and heading back towards the bedroom. 'Okay then, I'll get changed.'

'Make it quick,' Jon called after her. 'We need to leave in five.'

In the bedroom, Aimee hastily kicked off her shoes, rifling through the hangers in her wardrobe until she found the dress Jon had suggested. Pulling it out, she eyed it dubiously. It was definitely on the slutty side, with its low-cut front and less-than-generous hemline. Fine for date night at a cocktail bar, less appropriate for a Wednesday evening client dinner.

Oh well, Aimee thought, trying to dismiss her concerns. If Jon thought it was okay, then who was she to argue?

She quickly got ready, wincing at her reflection as she tried to simultaneously pull up the front of the dress and pull down the bottom. The clinging fabric left little to the imagination, but it was too late to worry about that now. She rooted around for her favourite pair of nude heels, the ones with the bow on the back, then grabbed her bag and tottered back through to Jon.

His jaw practically hit the floor when he saw her, his eyebrows raising so high they almost hit his hairline.

'Wow, you look incredible,' he told her, pulling her in for a kiss, his hands roaming over her body. 'You feel pretty incredible too.'

'Jon, you'll mess up my make-up,' Aimee flushed, detangling herself from him and smoothing down her hair.

Jon's gaze travelled over her one final time before he switched into professional mode, straightening his tie and shrugging on his heavy wool overcoat. As he checked his appearance in the mirror by the front door, he said casually, 'You know tonight's important for me, don't you? Don't mess it up.'

Aimee was startled by his tone, struck by the unfamiliar coldness in his voice. For a second, she was thrown, but then he turned to her with a bright smile, reaching for her hand.

'Ready? Good, let's go.'

Aimee put the incident out of her mind, and obediently followed Jon out of the door.

—

'So then I said to him, I don't care if you have to swim, make sure you get to Rotterdam by seven or I'll dock you a week's salary!'

Malcolm Huddlestone roared with laughter, and Aimee dutifully chuckled at Jon's anecdote, before taking a fortifying sip of red wine. She saw Malcolm glance slyly across at her, his eyes lingering a little too long on her cleavage, and Aimee found herself wishing she'd brought a wrap to cover up.

Malcolm Huddlestone was a Yorkshireman by birth, but had settled in Norfolk and was now the biggest independent bathroom furniture retailer in the East of England – a fact he'd already mentioned six times, and they'd barely even finished their starters. He was in his early sixties, with a florid complexion and a wiry grey moustache, flecked with strands of ginger.

Tonight's dinner, Jon had explained to Aimee, was all about schmoozing. Huddlestone had used Cunningham Haulage for almost ten years, having built up a solid working relationship with Jon's father, Nigel, but he was showing signs of jumping ship now that the company was in Jon's hands.

'We've got to take him out, throw some money at him, make him feel like a king for an evening, and that'll secure us another decade of his business,' Jon had told Aimee on the way to the restaurant. 'You see, the thing about business, Aimee, is that it's all about people. People deal with people, and if you can get that bit right then the money follows.'

Right now, Jon was speaking effusively about his plans for the business, and Huddlestone was listening and nodding, interjecting with the occasional comment. Aimee watched the two men as they conversed, Jon trying to flatter and impress, as the older man enjoyed his fawning. If Aimee was being honest, she found the whole scenario somewhat cringeworthy, but she knew that tonight was a big deal for Jon and she wanted to play her part.

As the waiter approached to refill their wine glasses, Aimee became aware of someone watching her, and turned her head to see Malcolm's wife, Janette, glance disapprovingly at her exposed cleavage before quickly looking away. For the umpteenth time that evening, Aimee found herself wondering why on earth Jon had insisted that she wear this revealing outfit.

Janette herself was wearing a classic little black dress in a forgiving fabric, with brightly coloured costume jewellery and a quilted Chanel clutch bag. She was approximately thirty years older than Aimee, and her ash-blonde hair was cut into a bob and styled in soft waves.

'It's a lovely restaurant, isn't it?' Aimee said brightly, leaning across to speak to her. She knew she had to put her reservations out of her mind and make an effort; Jon was always telling her how important it was to get the wife on side at these corporate dinners.

'Wives always have so much influence over their husbands' opinions,' he'd winked at her.

'Yes, the food's delicious,' Janette smiled graciously. 'They've completely refurbished the place since we were last here. Ah, here come the main courses.'

The waiter brought out a chunky rib-eye steak for Malcolm and a rack of lamb for Jon, whilst Aimee and Janette had both opted for the seafood risotto.

'And what do you do for a living?' Janette asked Aimee, as she speared a prawn and popped it in her mouth.

'Oh,' Aimee looked embarrassed. 'I don't… Well, I don't actually work at the moment. I used to be an admin assistant but… it wasn't for me.'

'I'm surprised. I thought all you young ones were career women now.' Janette smiled, but there was no malice in the comment.

'I… Well, I never really figured out what I wanted to do, I suppose,' Aimee said apologetically, although that wasn't strictly true. She realised she felt embarrassed about not having a job, and hated the idea that this woman might think she was a gold digger. 'I'd like to be a teacher,' Aimee confided, surprising herself with the announcement. 'I'm thinking about pursuing that.'

'Oh, that's a wonderful profession, you should definitely look into it. Our eldest son, Neil, teaches maths in a secondary school near Cambridge.'

'Really? I'm not great at maths, but I'd love to teach English. Jon and I are getting married in the summer, but once the wedding's out of the way I'll have more time to look into it.'

'Yes, Malcolm mentioned that you were engaged. Congratulations! Oh, and what a beautiful ring,' Janette exclaimed, taking hold of Aimee's hand for a closer look.

'Thank you. It was Jon's grandmother's.'

'It's stunning.'

'Look at the ladies there,' Malcolm bellowed across the table. 'Getting on like a house on fire.'

Aimee smiled sweetly, noticing that he had a piece of rocket stuck between his teeth. She caught Jon's eye and he gave a small nod of approval, a sign that she was doing well.

'I was just congratulating Aimee on your engagement,' Janette told Jon.

'Yes, I'm a very lucky man,' Jon returned warmly.

'I'll say,' Malcolm chipped in, with a slight leer in Aimee's direction. 'But just you wait until that ring's on your finger and she's got you locked down. It all changes then,' he guffawed loudly.

'And Aimee was telling me about her plans to enter the teaching profession, after you're married,' Janette continued. She smiled expectantly at Jon, but Aimee caught something – confusion? displeasure? – flash across his features, and instantly felt her stomach tense.

She knew it was ridiculous, but she wished Janette had never said anything. More accurately, Aimee wished *she* had never said anything to Janette in the first place, and wondered why she had. Probably out of a desire not to come across as vacuous and directionless, Aimee realised. She didn't want to spend the rest of her life living off Jon's money, and she didn't want anyone else to assume that was her intention either.

The problem was that Aimee got the very strong impression Jon wasn't in favour of her career plans; she'd tried to raise the topic with him once or twice and he'd instantly shut the conversation down.

'Was she now?' Jon replied tightly, not taking his eyes off Aimee. She looked down uncomfortably, pushing her rice around her plate. 'Well, I've just been sharing my vision for the future of Cunningham Haulage with your very knowledgeable husband,' Jon changed the subject seamlessly. Only Aimee, who was an expert at reading Jon's body language, could tell he was annoyed. The slight puckering of his lips gave it away, the tension along his jaw line.

'I recently placed an order for twenty new vehicles, and I want us to be the biggest carrier of furniture and white goods in the East of England area,' Jon announced proudly, following his words with a slug of wine. 'We currently have one hundred and fifty trailers in our fleet, but I plan to double that in eighteen months. I also intend to introduce refrigerated vehicles, so we can carry palletised food for retail, and train a specialist team for hazardous assignments – chemicals, waste, that kind of thing.'

Jon was on a roll, waxing lyrical about his aspirations for the business, his goals and targets for the coming months.

'Goodness. What an ambitious young couple you are,' Janette commented, smiling at Aimee once again.

Aimee stayed silent as Jon continued to talk, outlining his plans to build half a dozen new warehouses, and describing how his site was the best placed in the region for access to Norwich Airport.

'Obviously the way my father built up the business from scratch was impressive, but now it's time to take that to the next level, and I'm the only man who can do that. We're really branching out from the foundations that Dad laid. His business acumen was sound, but limited, and I have the vision he lacked,' Jon boasted, the alcohol making him breathtakingly arrogant.

'It's all well and good being ambitious,' Malcolm cut in, waving his steak knife recklessly in the air. 'But you have to make sure you're not overreaching yourself. Your old man specialised in consumer goods. He knew his market like the back of his hand, and he built up a loyal customer base with that knowledge. Beware of spreading yourself too thinly.'

'Of course, of course, you're absolutely right, Malcolm,' Jon backtracked, but Aimee knew that Jon hadn't changed his opinion in the slightest; he was simply savvy enough to know that he should show deference to his long-term client. After all, the real aim of tonight was to retain Huddlestone's business, not to detail Jon's expansion plans and polish his ego.

'And what does your fiancée think?' Malcolm asked, grinning across the table at Aimee. 'Surely you're not going to want to be slaving away at your desk all the hours God sends when you've got a pretty little thing like that waiting at home for you?'

'Oh, I'll always make time for Aimee,' Jon smiled.

Aimee attempted to smile back, but she wasn't sure that she liked being discussed as though she was merely some pet or plaything.

'What do you think of his ideas?' Malcolm pressed, his speech beginning to slur. 'You think they're good?'

Aimee hesitated, not expecting to be asked for her opinion. 'Of course I'll support Jon, whatever he decides to do,' she replied, realising that she sounded like the loyal wife of a disgraced politician at a press conference.

'Ha, I bet you don't care, as long as you keep getting that diamond jewellery and those designer dresses, eh?' Malcolm chuckled. 'You're all the same, you women.'

Aimee's cheeks flamed, and she felt a sudden surge of anger towards this boorish, presumptuous man. She inhaled sharply, dropping her napkin on the table as she jumped to her feet.

'Do excuse me, I need to visit the bathroom.' She flashed a brilliant smile before quickly walking away, feeling everyone's eyes on her as she left.

—

Later that evening, they wished the Huddlestones good night and left the restaurant, crossing the car park to Jon's Porsche.

'Do you want me to drive?' Aimee asked. Her fiancé was clearly over the limit, but he strode purposefully round to the driver's side, glaring at Aimee as he slid into the car.

The atmosphere on the way home was unbearably tense. Aimee's hands gripped the leather of the seat rests so tightly that her knuckles turned white as Jon drove far too fast, haring along the dark country lanes and taking corners at speed.

'What's the matter?' Aimee asked eventually, her voice cracking with nerves.

Jon glowered beneath his dark brows. 'Do I have to spell it out?'

Aimee swallowed. She didn't know what would enrage him more – to stay silent, or to speak.

'Were you deliberately trying to ruin this evening for me?' Jon demanded angrily, slamming his foot down on the brake so that the tyres screeched.

'Of course not, what do you mean?'

'You made me look an absolute idiot tonight. It'll be a miracle if Huddlestone renews his contract with us. Do you know how many thousands of pounds' worth of business you might have cost me?'

Aimee's mouth fell open in shock. 'I don't understand! What did I—'

'You think he didn't notice how rude you were being to him? With your smart alec comments and your fake little smiles? And then you start boring his wife with some ridiculous notion about becoming a teacher. I mean, where the hell did that come from? We were there to talk about *my* business, not your little pipe dream.'

Aimee blinked away tears, her face growing hot. 'I'm sorry Jon, I didn't realise—'

'Don't I give you everything, hmm? Are you not satisfied enough with your life with me that you're running around telling people you need something more? You just had to try and make tonight all about *you*, didn't you? Rubbishing my business plans, talking about yourself, with your breasts practically out on the table.'

'But you told me to wear...' Aimee began, and then closed her mouth, knowing it was pointless to protest when Jon was in this kind of mood. He was being cruel and irrational and nothing she could say would make a difference.

Instead, Aimee turned away from him, resting her forehead against the cool glass of the window, a thick lump forming in her throat. Blindly, she stared out at the starry night sky, letting the salty tears roll freely down her cheeks.

CHAPTER 16

'If I get married, I want to be very married'
– Audrey Hepburn

'Oh, Debbie, you look absolutely beautiful,' Julia gushed. She'd attended dozens of wedding dress fittings over the past few years, but the transformation from excited fiancée to blushing bride never failed to move her.

'Do you think so?' Debbie tugged self-consciously at the dress, smoothing down the fabric over her stomach, before pulling at the cap sleeves in an effort to hide her hated bingo wings. She turned from side to side in front of the mirror, trying to find a flattering angle.

'It's gorgeous. *You're* gorgeous. Here, have a sip of this, you've hardly touched it.'

Debbie eyed the champagne warily. 'I don't know if I should drink it. Isn't it full of calories?'

'No, it's full of bubbles and fun,' Julia giggled. 'Seriously though, champagne is one of the lowest calorie alcoholic drinks out there.' She spoke confidently, although she wasn't sure whether or not that was true. She was fairly sure she'd read it in a magazine once… 'There's less calories in this than a bunch of grapes.'

'Isn't it made of grapes?' Debbie wondered doubtfully.

'Mmm hmm,' Julia said slowly, trying to bluff her way out of it. 'Something to do with science. During the fermenting process. I think the alcohol kills off the calories…'

'Maybe later,' Debbie replied, staring sadly at her reflection. Across the shop, another young woman was trying on a dress, and Debbie turned round to look at her. They were roughly the same age, but the other woman was slender as a reed, with a handspan waist and a figure so small that she'd had to be clipped into the dress she was trying. It was an incredible one-shoulder creation in tulle and organza, and an assistant was currently fussing around her, arranging the long train to show it off to its best advantage.

'She looks stunning,' Debbie murmured.

'*You* look stunning,' Julia assured her, knowing exactly what Debbie was thinking.

Debbie was about to reply when the assistant came hurrying over. She was tall and thin, dressed all in black, with sharp features and dyed auburn hair swept up in a French twist.

'And what do you think of this one, madam?'

Debbie wrinkled her nose, looking down at the tight-fitting mermaid skirt. 'I don't think it's the one.' She drifted over to the other gowns, rail after rail of exquisite dresses all waiting to be plucked from their hangers and worn and loved. There was no denying that they were incredible, but Debbie wasn't having her fairy-tale moment, feeling far too self-conscious about her appearance.

If only she'd been able to lose a little more weight, Debbie thought desperately. She'd already lost a stone and a half, meaning that she could fit comfortably into a size sixteen, but there were still at least another couple of stones to go before she hit her target. Julia had warned her that suppliers could take months to make and ship her dress, and that was before any alterations took place, so reluctantly Debbie had agreed to come shopping today. But the reflection in the mirror wasn't what she wanted to see.

'Do you have anything like that?' Debbie asked, pointing at a dress on a mannequin. It had a deep V neckline and a flattering full skirt. 'But maybe in satin, with a little bit of sparkle?'

The assistant frowned. 'I think something like this would be more flattering, madam,' she said, pulling out a lace monstrosity. 'It has the full-length sleeves, to cover your arms, and the ruching here around your waist distracts from any extra pounds.'

Debbie froze, feeling her cheeks flame at the way the assistant was drawing attention to everything she hated about herself. She felt horribly embarrassed and willed herself not to cry, hot tears prickling behind her eyes.

'Do you like that dress, Debs?' Julia asked her gently.

Still unable to speak, Debbie shook her head.

'No, we won't be trying that one,' Julia told the assistant firmly. 'Like Debbie said, we're looking for something in satin, with a little bit of sparkle.'

The assistant gave a petulant shrug before turning back to the rails, making a big show of pulling out dresses then tutting loudly before putting them back again.

'I like this one,' Debbie volunteered, holding up a halterneck gown with a beaded bodice and diamanté sash.

But the assistant was already shaking her head. 'No, we only have the size eight sample in that one.'

'Oh.' Debbie's voice was barely more than a whisper.

'But what we can do with, um, larger ladies, is this,' the assistant pushed on tactlessly, as she grabbed the dress and looped the halterneck over Debbie's head like an apron. The dress dangled uselessly in front of her, flapping about as she moved. 'There,' the woman said, with false brightness. 'What do you think?'

Mortified, Debbie glanced across at Julia. 'Um… I'm not really…'

'That's ridiculous,' Julia spoke up. 'It's impossible to get a sense of how the dress will fit just from hanging it around her neck.'

'Well I don't see what else we can do,' the assistant replied tartly. 'If she can't fit in the gown, this is the best you're going to get.'

'It's fine,' Debbie interjected hastily, not wanting Julia to get into an argument. 'I'll try and find something else.'

'How about this one?' the assistant suggested, pulling another dress from the rail. 'It's a similar style, but with straps instead of a halterneck, and it's much bigger – size twelve.'

'That won't fit me either,' Debbie swallowed, wondering when her dream day had turned into a complete nightmare. This woman could give Simon Cowell a lesson in humiliating put-downs.

'Well it probably won't fasten up but it will give you an idea. Why don't you try it?' she said forcefully, whipping back the changing room curtain and practically pushing Debbie inside. 'Go on.'

Debbie felt cornered. Reluctantly, she headed into the cubicle and unhooked the last dress from where it still hung around her neck. The sales assistant followed her inside, roughly unlacing the dress Debbie was currently wearing and manhandling her out of it. Debbie's face burned with humiliation as she stood there in her bra and knickers, all too aware of the fact that her thighs were dimpled, her breasts enormous, and her skin strangely mottled in the unflattering changing room light. She couldn't help but wonder what the assistant thought of her, certain she must be judging every inch of Debbie's overweight, imperfect body.

Neither of them spoke as the woman wrestled her into the size twelve dress. It was clearly far too small; the tiny cups barely covered Debbie's nipples, whilst the back was wide open, exposing her skin to the cold air.

'Go and show your friend then.'

The remark was supposed to be encouraging, but to Debbie it sounded almost menacing. Taking a deep breath, she pulled back the curtain and stepped into the showroom. Julia took one look at Debbie's face and saw instantly that she felt thoroughly miserable in the ill-fitting gown.

'This is stupid!' Julia burst out. 'Don't you have any dresses in other sizes? You know, for anyone who's not a model?'

'We can only stock a small range of samples,' the assistant replied patronisingly. 'And the majority of brides-to-be who visit True Bridal are between a size eight and a size twelve. I'm aware that may seem small to you, but most women try to slim down before their wedding.'

'I *am* slimming down,' Debbie insisted, unable to hide the frustration in her voice. 'There's still almost six months to go before I get married, and I'm going to be much smaller.'

'In our experience, the size a bride is when she comes in for her first consultation is more or less the size she actually is on her wedding day. Despite their best intentions, very few women drop more than six or seven pounds in the lead up to the big day, so there's a downward shift of no more than one dress size. We tend to find,' the assistant smiled coldly, 'that if a woman wanted to lose weight, she would have already done so.'

'She's already lost twenty pounds,' Julia retorted, immediately coming to Debbie's defence. 'I'd say that's pretty good willpower, wouldn't you? And if she's done that in three months, imagine what she can do in another six.'

The assistant arched an eyebrow. 'Of course, it's your choice, but we don't recommend ordering a dress more than one – or two at the absolute maximum – sizes smaller than you are currently. It's simply not realistic.'

The other customers were turning round to look, hearing raised voices and wondering what the commotion was. Debbie could see them staring at her and felt horribly self-conscious, crossing her arms over her chest and wishing that her body wasn't so exposed. She could feel the dress digging into her skin, and knew that her back must be bulging out for everyone to see, rolls of fat rippling beneath her bra.

'Don't worry,' Julia smiled sweetly at the assistant. 'We won't be ordering anything from here anyway so you won't have to worry. Debbie, shall we leave?'

With a mutinous glare at the assistant, Debbie marched back into the changing room and gratefully tore off the too-small dress. It felt blissful to slide back into her stretchy jeans and oversized jumper, and she emerged with the first genuine smile Julia had seen since they'd entered the shop.

They left with their heads held high, the freezing January wind hitting them as they stepped onto the pavement.

'What a bitch!' Julia exclaimed, unable to hold back any longer, and furious on Debbie's behalf. 'I'm so sorry for taking you there, Debs.' True Bridal was relatively new, and had opened while Julia was on maternity leave.

'Don't be silly, it's not your fault. I wanted to try it. I guess you can't take any of your other clients there now.'

'I wouldn't *want* to take anyone there. I like my clients to have an enjoyable experience when they're shopping for their wedding dress. Honestly, women like that shouldn't be allowed near brides,' Julia ranted. 'It's supposed to be one of the highlights of your entire life, and it's like she deliberately wanted to spoil the whole thing.'

'She was nice to the other girl,' Debbie pointed out, thinking how the assistant had kowtowed to the slim blonde in the one-shoulder dress.

'Hmm…' Julia muttered darkly.

The two women walked on, coming out of the narrow lanes around Pottergate and emerging opposite the medieval splendour of the Guildhall.

'So where do you want to go next?' Julia wondered. 'We've got a while before our appointment at Millie's Bridal, but they might be able to squeeze us in early.'

Debbie shrugged despondently. 'I don't mind.'

Julia watched her for a moment; her head was bowed as she trudged along, no sign of her usual exuberance.

'Are you okay?' Julia asked worriedly. 'Don't let that silly cow upset you.'

Thoughts were swirling in Debbie's head, all of her demons and self-confidence issues coming to the fore. 'She's right though, isn't she?'

'What? No, she's not. She's prejudiced and stupid.'

Debbie smiled weakly. 'It's sweet of you, Jules, but I'm just fooling myself. I'm never going to be thin, am I? I need to accept it.'

'What are you talking about? You've done brilliantly! You've already lost twenty pounds, and you look amazing. Even on your face, I can see the way your cheekbones and jaw line are really well defined, and—'

'D'you know what Stevie said to me the other week?' Debbie interrupted. 'He said, "You'll always be a big girl, Debs." We had a massive row at the time but, thinking about it now, he was right.'

'No, he wasn't.' Julia sounded exasperated.

'For the last three days I've lived on nothing but green juice and cabbage soup, because I knew I had this appointment to-day. And when I got on the scale this morning, I'd *put on* two pounds. How is that fair? I didn't even have any chocolate cake at work for Angela's birthday, and it made absolutely no difference.'

'You had a bad week, it happens. Maybe it was hormones or something. The most important thing is that you're still losing weight overall.'

But Debbie wasn't listening. 'Seriously, what's the bloody point? I'm bad-tempered and miserable and *starving* and I *still* look like a fat cow. I mean—' She broke off suddenly, seeming transfixed by something in the distance. When she finally spoke, her voice was all distant and dreamy. 'How much time did you say we had before the appointment at Millie's?'

'About an hour. Why?' Julia frowned, following Debbie's gaze to a branch of Little Italy pizzeria. 'Oh, no. No, I'm not letting you, Debs. Debbie!' she screeched, as her friend suddenly made a break for it, bolting across the road with an ecstatic expression on her face. She was already seated at a table and perusing the menu by the time Julia caught up with her.

'No, Debbie, don't do it! You've been doing so well, this will spoil everything.'

'Having the occasional break from your diet is a great morale booster,' Debbie parroted, without looking up from the list of starters. 'Humans need fat in their diet, as well as protein and carbs.'

'But—'

Before Julia could reply, a smartly dressed waiter appeared with a smile.

'Ladies, can I help you?'

'Yes,' Debbie said immediately, her eyes glittering brightly. She appeared to have been seized by some kind of mania. 'I'll have the dough balls to start, followed by the biggest pizza you have, with everything on it, and a side of cheesy garlic bread. And for dessert, I'll have the chocolate fudge cake.'

'Will that be with cream, or ice cream, madam?'

'Both.'

'Excellent choice. And to drink…?'

'An enormous glass of full-fat Coke.' Debbie handed the menu back to the waiter with a beaming smile which he returned, not seeming in the least bit fazed.

'And for you, madam?' He turned to Julia.

Julia bit her lip, looking down at the menu then back across at her friend. Debbie was still grinning widely in anticipation of the feast that was to come, and Julia hesitated, unsure what to do.

'Oh, sod it!' She threw her hands up in defeat, then burst out laughing. 'I'll have bruschetta to start, followed by the calzone, and pencil me in for a tiramisu if I've got room,' she giggled. 'Well, if you can't beat them, join them. Right?'

'Right,' Debbie agreed happily, as she reached for a bread-stick.

CHAPTER 17

'Why does a woman work ten years to change a man, then complain he's not the man she married?' –
Barbra Streisand

'No, Kelly, I've said you can't do it.'

'But whhhhyy, Mum?' Kelly's whining made her sound more like a three-year-old than a thirteen-year-old.

'We've been through this. There are all kinds of dangerous things – dangerous *people* – out there on the internet, and I don't want you taking that kind of risk.'

'But I'm on the internet every day, Mum. You're happy enough to let me research a school project on there, so why can't I start my own blog?'

'Kelly…' Gill rubbed her hand tiredly across her eyes. They were in the kitchen, and Kelly had just got in from school; she was still wearing her uniform, with her shirt untucked and her skirt hitched up. There were smudges of kohl-pencil around her eyes, a classic sign of teenage rebellion – Gill was sure she hadn't been wearing it when she'd left to catch the bus that morning.

'It's different, okay? Using the computer to search for infor-mation is a whole other matter to putting your entire life out there. It means anyone can just log on and read about what you're up to.'

'Duh! That's, like, the whole point of a blog.'

'Don't get smart with me, Kelly. I'm not in the mood.'

'Mum, I'm not stupid, okay? I'm not going to start putting topless pictures on there, or my address and phone number. I just think it'd be something fun and creative for me to do. Loads of my friends do it. Liana writes one about her dancing, and puts up pictures from the competitions she does, and photos of her trophies, and tons of people read it.'

'Well good for Liana.'

'You can even make a career out of it,' Kelly wheedled. 'Some people earn loads of money, and companies send them free stuff, like designer clothes and make-up samples.'

'I know it *seems* innocent enough, but it's my job to look after you, and I'm really not comfortable with it.'

'I should have just done it without telling you,' Kelly threatened. 'Maybe I still will.'

'Kelly,' Gill finally snapped. 'I said no, and that's final.'

'God, why do you have to ruin everything for me?'

At that moment, the back door opened and Mike came in, home from work. He immediately picked up on the tense atmosphere, looking nervously from Gill to Kelly as he took in their angry expressions and furious body language. It was clear that some kind of stand-off had just been taking place.

'All right?' he asked casually, dropping his bag by the back door and coming over to give Gill a peck on the lips.

Kelly looked away, making a revolted face.

'What's going on here then? What are we talking about?'

'Kelly wants to start a blog,' Gill explained, her tone making it clear exactly what she thought of the idea. 'You know, give away every last detail of her private life on the internet so any old nutter can track her down, or random perverts start chatting to her online.'

Kelly threw up her hands in exasperation. 'It's not going to be like that! You're not listening to me.'

'Just drop it, Kelly. How many times do I have to tell you you're not doing it?'

'Now hang on a minute, let's not be too hasty,' Mike interjected, as he took off his jacket and hung it over the back of a kitchen chair. Gill and Kelly's heads snapped up, both looking at him in surprise.

'A lot of the kids these days are into it, aren't they? What's the name of the girl I was reading about in the paper? She made a fortune from putting videos online just doing her hair and chatting about her day. Got a book deal from it and everything. What is it they call it? V Logging?'

'Vlogging,' Kelly corrected him sullenly. 'It's video blogging, and it's exactly what I'm talking about. It wouldn't all be recorded though – I'd be writing some posts too, so it'd help me with my English.'

'Don't you need lots of fancy equipment?' Mike wondered doubtfully. 'A microphone and a camera and all that malarkey?'

Kelly shook her head vigorously. 'No, I can do it all on my iPad, it's really easy. I can even get a free hosting site, so it wouldn't cost anything at all. Look,' she carried on, encouraged by Mike's reaction, as she picked up the iPad she'd left on the kitchen table and switched it to video mode. 'Say something,' she demanded, aiming it at Mike.

'Um…' Mike gave an awkward wave. 'Hello, my name's Mike.'

'Lame, but never mind,' Kelly muttered, as she quickly jabbed at the screen a handful of times, then turned it round to show him the finished article. She'd put a neon filter on the short video and played it on a loop, once at normal speed and then slowed right down. A dance track played in the background and, at the end, the word '*Mike!*' was scribbled across the screen by an invisible hand. 'All I'd need to do now is upload it,' Kelly explained. 'Easy.'

'That's amazing,' Mike marvelled. 'Gill, have you seen this?'

He turned to look at her, but the expression on her face was as though she'd been sucking lemons.

'That's not the point, Mike,' she said tartly. 'The point *is* that she shouldn't be putting everything online for any Tom, Dick or Harry to watch.'

'Aw, where's the harm, Gill?' Mike shrugged. 'I can't see that it's a big deal.'

Gill's jaw dropped. 'You can't see that it's a…'

She trailed off as she realised that Kelly was watching them, her eyes shining, a triumphant look on her face. She was obviously thrilled that Mike was taking her side – and that he and Gill were arguing.

'You know what, we'll discuss this later,' Gill said, clearly still fuming. She yanked open the fridge and began pulling out ingredients for their evening meal, slamming them down on the worktop. 'Kelly, go upstairs and start your homework. I'll call you when dinner's ready.'

For once Kelly didn't protest, still revelling in the upset she'd caused, as she turned on her heel and trotted smugly out of the room.

Mike cleared his throat awkwardly, sensing that he was in trouble. Gill ignored him as she bustled around the kitchen, chopping carrots in a faintly terrifying manner.

'Gill, I didn't mean—'

'I said later,' Gill snapped, in a tone that left no room for disagreement.

'Right,' Mike nodded timidly, deciding to make himself scarce as he headed upstairs to shower.

—

Later that evening, Gill and Mike were lying in bed together, the bedside light still on as they settled down for the night. They were both feeling exhausted, as usual, after another hectic day of work and running around after five kids. The atmosphere between them had slowly returned to normal, but their earlier fight was still troubling Gill.

'Mike, I don't want to start an argument or anything, but I really don't appreciate the way you took Kelly's side tonight when we were talking about that blog business.'

Mike frowned. 'But I agree with her. I think it'd be a great thing for Kelly to do.'

'Yes, but I'd already told her no, she wasn't doing it. And then it completely undermines me when you waltz in and openly disagree. Now she'll never shut up about it.'

'I can't win, can I?' Mike was trying to keep his tone light, but Gill could tell that he was getting annoyed. 'If I back you up, Kelly hates me, and then you tell me to make more of an effort with her. If I happen to agree with her, and say so, you want me to take your side regardless of what I actually think.'

'It's just…' Gill paused, trying to find the right words. 'I genuinely don't think this blogging thing is a good idea. She's only thirteen, and she wants to put her life out there for anyone to read about. You hear horror stories every day on the news. I mean, what about trolls? What about online grooming?'

'She's a sensible kid, Gill, as much as it pains me to say it. She's not going to be hanging around in chat rooms, talking to creepy old men pretending to be school kids. She just wants to express herself, put up pictures of the new clothes she's bought, or write about what she saw at the cinema with her mates.'

Gill looked at him wryly. 'When did you get to be such an expert on the habits of teenage girls?'

'I've practically got one myself, remember. Paige'll be there in a few months.'

'And would you let Paige write a blog?'

'If she was Kelly's age then yes, if she wanted to.'

Gill snorted disbelievingly. 'We'll see.'

'Look,' Mike shifted over in bed, pulling her closer to him. 'Think about it. Maybe a little bit of compromise is what we need. Kelly's growing up, and no matter how badly you want to, you can't protect her from everything any more. Plus, the chances are she's going to start this blog anyway, whatever we say.'

'That's what she threatened to do.'

'Exactly. So how about we get involved and embrace it? That way, we can at least keep an eye on what she's doing.'

Gill hesitated. As much as she hated to admit it, Mike had a point, but she wasn't quite ready to concede that yet.

'I'll sleep on it,' she relented, leaning over to switch off the light, then cuddling up to Mike's solid, reassuring bulk.

———

It was the usual early morning chaos in the Skinner/Marshall household, with everyone rushing around getting ready for their day. Gill was shouting at the twins to get their packed lunches out of the fridge and organise their school bags, as Kelly helped herself to cereal with a splash of the almond milk she'd specially requested *'because that's what the top models drink'*.

She hadn't said a word to Gill so far, and Gill wasn't sure whether it was the standard teenage lack of communication in the morning, or whether Kelly was sulking and refusing to speak to her mother.

Gill helped Sammy with his Coco Pops, putting on his apron and getting him settled at the table, then sat down opposite Kelly.

'So Mike and I were talking last night…'

'Congratulations,' Kelly grunted, without looking up from her bowl.

'We were talking about your blog,' Gill pressed on, determined not to be put off by her daughter's snarky attitude.

At this, Kelly looked a little more interested. Her spoon froze for a second in mid-air, and she didn't reply, waiting for Gill to continue speaking.

'He reminded me of how sensible you are, and how responsible, and we decided that perhaps you could start a blog after all.'

'Really?' Kelly squealed, all thoughts of breakfast forgotten as she looked up in excitement.

'Yes. There'd have to be certain conditions, of course. We'd want to know the website address, so we could take a look if we wanted and make sure we approve of what you're putting on there.'

Kelly rolled her eyes. 'I'm not going to be posting bikini selfies or anything. It'll be fashion tips, and book reviews, and maybe some make-up tutorials or something.'

'Great. All the same, we'd feel more comfortable if we could take a look from time to time. And it's absolutely forbidden to meet up with anyone who speaks to you on there, okay? No matter who they say they are, or however much you've got in common, you *do not* arrange to meet them.'

'I wouldn't do that anyway, Mum!'

'Good. Well, we can talk more about it later. I just thought I'd let you know what we'd decided.'

'Sure. I'll have a think about it too. See if I accept your conditions,' Kelly added cheekily, getting up from the table and rinsing out her bowl.

Just then, Mike walked into the kitchen with Freddy and Finlay in tow. He prepared himself for the usual scowl from his soon-to-be stepdaughter, but there was nothing. She passed by him without comment, but when she reached the doorway, she abruptly turned back.

'Hey, Mike.' She regarded him levelly, her body language neutral. 'What do you think sounds best? Kelly's Place or The Kelly Edition?'

'For what?' Mike frowned.

'For my blog, duh!'

A faint hint of a smile stole across Mike's face as he crossed his arms thoughtfully, considering the question. 'I like Kelly's Place. Or maybe even Kelly's World?'

Kelly nodded coolly, her expression giving nothing away. 'Right. See you both later.'

'Bye, Kel. Love you,' Gill called out.

Seconds later, they heard the front door bang. Gill looked across at Mike, her eyebrows raised in astonishment.

'Well, well, well,' she commented wryly. 'Wonders will never cease.'

CHAPTER 18

'Wives are young men's mistresses, companions for middle age, and old men's nurses' – **Francis Bacon**

'This was such a good idea, Julia,' Debbie beamed, as she picked up her glass of prosecco and took a sip of the delicious, bubbling liquid. 'Tonight's going to be a brilliant night, I can just tell.'

'I hope so,' Julia smiled. 'You look incredible, by the way. Gorgeous outfit.'

Debbie was wearing a faux-leather pencil skirt with a sheer black shirt and knee-length boots, her long, dark hair styled in soft ringlets. 'Thanks,' she replied, her eyes sparkling. 'I feel pretty good actually. Can you believe this skirt's a size sixteen and it's actually gaping round the waist?'

'Amazing!'

'I only bought it the other week as well. I'm having to rein myself in 'cos I keep wanting to spend the wedding budget on new clothes.'

'You've got to treat yourself now and again,' Julia insisted. 'I love your necklace too, Gill.'

'Oh, do you like it? Kelly helped me pick it out. I didn't want to look too overdressed, but I wasn't sure what to wear. Honestly, you've no idea how long it is since I've had a night out,' she giggled. 'The kids were stunned when they heard I was hitting the town.'

'What's the name of the other girl that's coming?' Debbie wondered, turning to Julia.

'Aimee.'

'And she's one of your clients?'

'That's right. She's getting married at the beginning of July – the weekend after you.'

'Is she nice?' Debbie fretted, as Julia laughed.

'Of course, she's absolutely lovely. I wouldn't have invited her otherwise.'

In a flash of inspiration earlier that week, Julia had decided to organise a get-together for the three brides-to-be. Not only were they all outgoing, friendly women who she thought it would be fun to spend more time with, it would also be a great opportunity for them to talk weddings to their hearts' content, and do a little bridal bonding. Julia also had a sneaking suspicion that it might be good for Aimee to get away from Jon and Valerie for a night, so she could let her hair down and relax a little.

'Oh, here she is now,' Julia beamed, standing up and waving as Aimee walked towards them.

She looked pretty and fashionable in a tailored black jumpsuit and cropped jacket, which perfectly showed off her slender frame. She'd teamed it with high-heeled ankle boots, and the giant ruby and diamond ring dazzled on her left hand.

'Hi,' Aimee said shyly, kissing Julia on the cheek as she waved at the other two women.

'Aimee, this is Debbie and Gill,' Julia introduced them, as Aimee sat down on the empty bar stool around the high table. 'Can I get you a glass of prosecco?'

'Thanks, I'd love one.'

Inside Aimee's bag, her phone vibrated and she reached for it. She read the text and frowned.

'Everything okay?' Julia asked.

'Fine. It's Jon. He's just dropped me off outside, and apparently he's going to wait up so he can come and pick me up when we're done.'

'Aw, that's sweet,' Debbie sighed. 'My fiancé left me to get the bus.'

'Hmm,' Aimee replied uncertainly. 'I told Jon I didn't mind getting a taxi home, but he insisted on driving me. He can be a little overprotective sometimes.' She pushed her phone back into the depths of her bag, as though by doing that she could push Jon to the back of her mind, and Julia smiled at her sympathetically.

'What's Jon got planned for this evening?' she asked. 'How's he going to entertain himself when you're not there?'

'He's got a pile of paperwork that he's brought home with him. And I left out the menu for the Chinese takeaway, so at least he won't starve,' Aimee giggled.

'Well I'm so pleased you made it out tonight,' Julia said genuinely, as she filled Aimee's glass and topped up everyone else. 'And I'd like to propose a toast. To weddings, and the happiest day of your lives.'

'And to Julia,' Debbie added with a grin. 'For making all the weddings possible.'

'To weddings, and to Julia,' the others echoed, laughing.

'So where are you getting married, Aimee?' Debbie asked, looking at her with interest.

'Oh… um… Southwark Castle,' Aimee explained, looking more than a little embarrassed at the revelation.

Debbie's mouth fell open. 'Southwark Ca— … You mean that huge place? That massive stately home, with the gardens and the peacocks?'

Aimee's nodded, her cheeks flaming.

'How many guests are you having?'

'About three hundred…'

'*Three hundred!?*'

'That's why I need Julia,' Aimee tried to joke.

'Although I get the impression it's not exactly what you'd have chosen, if it was all down to you,' Julia smiled, coming to Aimee's defence.

'No, that's true,' Aimee agreed. 'I don't even know half the people who are coming – seriously!' she insisted, taking in Debbie's incredulous look. 'I'd have been happy with something small, but it's all turned into a bit of spectacle.'

'Is that something your fiancé's chosen then?' Gill wondered.

Aimee locked eyes with Julia, and the two of them shared a look. 'No, his mother,' Aimee explained, trying to keep her tone neutral. 'She has rather strong opinions and as she's paying for, well, practically the whole thing, this seems to entitle her to get her own way, regardless of what Jon and I want.'

The words came out in an angry rush, and Julia stared at her in surprise. She'd never seen Aimee quite so heated before when talking about Valerie; perhaps she was finally getting ready to fight back.

'But that's terrible,' Gill burst out, outraged on Aimee's behalf. 'It's *your* wedding, not hers. What does your fiancé say about it?'

'I think he finds it easiest to go along with her. He keeps saying, "What's one day when we'll have the rest of our lives together?" Anyway…' Aimee looked discomfited, feeling all eyes on her. 'That's enough about me. Debbie, what's your big day going to be like?'

Debbie leapt eagerly into a detailed explanation of her wedding plans, and the conversation flowed as easily as the prosecco.

Aimee offered to go and get another bottle when the first one ran dry, and as she climbed down from the stool, she realised that she was feeling tipsy and happy, hugely enjoying the company of the other women. It had been a long time since she'd had a girly night out like this, and it felt so good to be able to open up and vent some of her frustration.

She hardly seemed to see her old friends these days, Aimee thought with a pang. Everyone was so busy with their own lives, with their jobs and partners and babies. She couldn't wait to catch up with them all at her hen party in a few weeks' time.

'So, Julia, what's the secret to a happy marriage?' Gill wondered. 'I clearly didn't get it right the first time, so any tips would be much appreciated!'

'Oh, I really don't think I'm the right person to ask,' Julia waved away her suggestion.

'Come on, you and Nick are the perfect couple,' Debbie sighed. 'You look like the cheerleader and football captain from some American movie, and then you have such a gorgeous little baby, *plus* you balance all of that with running your own business…'

'Well I'm glad it *looks* that way,' Julia smiled. 'Because it certainly doesn't feel like it. Honestly, my life seems constantly manic, with me never having enough time for anything. If I'm busy with a job, then I feel bad because I'm neglecting Jack. If I'm spending time with Jack, I often feel that Nick gets the short straw… I wonder how they're both getting on tonight, actually,' she said anxiously, taking her phone out of her bag and checking it. No messages or missed calls.

'They'll be fine,' Debbie assured her. 'Jack couldn't be in safer hands than with his dad, could he?'

'Yeah, I know. I've just been worrying lately that… Well, I don't know how to explain it, but it's like there's a distance between Nick and Jack. As though they haven't properly bonded yet. Nick goes through the motions, but if he can get out of spending time with Jack, he usually does.'

'He's probably feeling a bit overwhelmed,' Gill tried to reassure her. 'Having your first baby is such a massive change in your life, and I think mothers naturally adapt a lot quicker. You have to, because you're the one feeding the baby and doing the majority of the work usually. Dads tend to sit back and bask in the reflected glory, while you're running round behind the scenes. That's my experience anyway.'

'Yeah, maybe…' Julia didn't sound convinced.

'Talk to Nick, if you're really bothered about it,' Aimee suggested sensibly. 'I'm sure he'll set your mind at rest, and you'll realise you've been worrying about nothing.'

'Yeah, Nick's great,' Debbie chimed in. 'I mean, I've only met him a handful of times but he seems like a lovely guy, and I'm sure he wouldn't want you fretting about this.'

'Thanks ladies,' Julia smiled. 'It's so nice to talk it through with someone.'

'And if you ever want time away, I don't mind having Jack,' Debbie continued. 'I don't just mean for an evening here and there – although I'm totally happy to do that, you know I am. I'm talking about a whole weekend, a couple of nights in a nice hotel, so you can get a real break.'

'Really?' The idea was surprisingly tempting.

'Of course. I'd love to do it,' Debbie grinned, draining her glass and realising they'd got through yet another bottle. 'More prosecco!' she called out, slipping off her bar stool and pulling her purse out of her bag. 'I'll get this one.'

'Thanks Debbie,' Aimee smiled shyly, as Debbie disappeared into the tightly knit crowd. It was Friday night in central Norwich, and the bar was rapidly filling up with revellers eager to start the weekend.

'And how's everything with you?' Julia asked, turning to Gill.

Gill gave a wry smile, replying, 'Madness, as ever.'

'Gill's got five children,' Julia explained to Aimee, whose eyebrows shot up in astonishment.

'*Five?* How do you cope?'

'I'm not sure I do,' Gill laughed. 'They're not all mine by the way – three of them are, and then Mike, my husband-to-be, has two children from his previous marriage. We're the ultimate blended family.'

'Are they all behaving themselves?' Julia asked, as Gill gave her an incredulous look.

'No. It's carnage, as usual. Although Kelly and the twins have gone to their dad's tonight so Mike doesn't have too much to cope with. Kelly's been a nightmare this week.'

'Why?'

'She's been desperate to start a blog.' Gill rolled her eyes.

'Oh, that sounds like a great idea,' Aimee spoke up innocently. 'There are some brilliant ones on the net – really funny and creative.'

'You sound like Mike,' Gill told her. 'I'm not quite so keen on the idea, I have to confess. But we've agreed that she can do it for now, as long as—'

Gill broke off as Debbie appeared beside her; she looked flustered, with spots of colour high on her cheeks. She plonked the ice bucket down unceremoniously on the table, hastily pouring herself a glass of fizz and downing three-quarters of it. The others watched her in astonishment.

'Is everything okay, Debs?'

Debbie glanced up guiltily, her eyes wide.

'I think I just got chatted up,' she confessed, looking mortified as she glanced from one woman to another then drained the remainder of her glass.

'You *think* you did?' Gill asked, unable to stifle a giggle. 'You're not sure?'

Debbie shook her head.

'What happened? Don't worry, it's not a bad thing,' Julia reassured her, as Debbie began to talk.

'I can't even remember the last time I got chatted up. I don't know if it's ever actually happened. Not properly, anyway. I was at the bar, waiting to buy this,' she gestured at the bottle. 'It was really busy so I was squeezed in between two men, and one of them started chatting to me…' Her face flushed as she recalled it all over again.

'What did he say?' Aimee asked, looking intrigued.

'Nothing much, just general chit-chat. He was asking who I was out with, and where we going later and I… I sortofendedup-givinghimmynumber.' The words came out in a mumbled rush.

'What was that last bit?' Gill frowned.

'I said, I sort of ended up giving him my number,' Debbie whispered, looking as though she was about to be sick.

There was a moment of silence, then Julia suddenly burst out laughing.

'Don't laugh, it's not funny!' Debbie protested hotly.

But Julia couldn't stop, wiping away a tear as she asked, 'What on earth did you do that for, Debs?'

'I don't know! I panicked. He asked me and I couldn't think of a way to say no. It felt rude not to, so I just gave it to him.'

'You gave him your number because you were being polite? Only you, Debs.'

'Why didn't you give him a fake one?' Gill chuckled.

'I would have done if I'd thought of it! I was under pressure. My mind went blank.'

'Was he hot?' Julia asked cheekily.

Debbie went even redder. 'No! Well, maybe, yes. A bit.'

'Didn't he see your ring?' Aimee wondered, nodding at the vintage diamond band on Debbie's left hand.

'I never thought of that. He can't have done, can he?'

'Some men'll try it on, regardless,' Gill muttered darkly.

'Oh no, what must he think of me?' Debbie wailed.

'Don't worry about it,' Julia smiled. 'I told you you were looking hot tonight, and this just proves it.'

'Yes, but I didn't want this to happen!'

'Maybe it's something you need to get used to, now you're all slim and sexy. You'll be beating them off with a stick.'

'Oh stop it, don't be ridiculous.'

'Perhaps you should start practising your turn-down lines – you know, how to say "no" when a man who's not your fiancé asks for your phone number,' Gill teased.

'Aaaargh,' Debbie squealed, burying her face in her hands. 'I'm such an idiot!'

'Aw, bless you,' Gill laughed, leaning across to squeeze her hand.

'You know what you need?' Julia was grinning across the table at her.

'My head examining?' Debbie wailed.

'Nope. More prosecco,' Julia called out gleefully, refilling everyone's glass.

The women cheered, and Debbie gratefully took a long gulp, hoping it might erase the memory of giving her number to some complete stranger in a busy bar.

And if all else failed, there was always tequila.

CHAPTER 19

'Husbands are like fires. They go out if unattended'
– Zsa Zsa Gabor

'Ohhh, this is the life,' Julia groaned, as she sank deeper into the enormous claw-foot bath, overflowing with bubbles. Nick, seated behind her, wrapped his arms around her and she closed her eyes blissfully as she leaned against him, enjoying the feel of his—

Damn, had she remembered to put Raffy the giraffe in Jack's bag? He couldn't sleep without it and… Yes, yes, she had, Julia realised, relaxing once more. She distinctly recalled putting it in the side zip compartment, along with half a dozen muslins, just in case.

Julia lay back again, resting her head on Nick's soapy chest. Lazily, she let her fingers run over his thighs, tracing little designs on his skin with the soapy water.

'Would madam like more champagne?' Nick murmured into her ear, as he reached out and refilled their glasses from the bottle in the silver stand beside them.

'Mmm, delicious,' Julia smiled, as the two of them clinked glasses and she took a sip of fizz.

She gazed dreamily out of the window across the room; it was dark now, but she could see the curve of a crescent moon and lights in the distance illuminating the little town of Windermere. Just outside their hotel lay the blackness of the lake, with bare trees dotting its shoreline, and beyond that lurked the shadowy mountains. They were beautiful in their bleakness, thickly layered with snow at this time of year.

'It's so thoughtful of you to bring me here,' sighed Julia. After Debbie had agreed to look after Jack for the weekend, Nick had seized the opportunity, and told Julia to leave all the planning to him. He'd booked the same hotel in the Lake District where they'd gone for their first ever mini-break, all those years ago.

'I know. Aren't I a good husband?' Nick beamed. 'Full of romantic gestures.'

'Okay, Casanova,' Julia laughed. Then a thought struck her and she sat up so quickly she almost spilt her champagne. 'Damn, did I tell Debbie that Jack might have a peanut allergy?' She span round to look at Nick, her face filled with panic.

'Yes,' he assured her. 'Yes, you did. This is Debbie remember, she's always looking after Jack. She knows his routine.'

'But that's during the day,' Julia protested. 'We've never left him overnight before.'

'He'll be fine,' Nick insisted softly, encouraging Julia to lie back down. 'It's completely natural to be worried, but we knew it was going to be like this, and he couldn't be in better hands.'

'I know,' Julia agreed. 'It just feels so strange. I mean, what if he takes his first steps this weekend? He's been getting so close to walking by himself, and I'd never forgive myself if I missed it. I told you he almost said "car" the other day, didn't I? Or maybe it was "cat". What if he starts saying whole sentences and we're not there to hear them?' Julia was growing hysterical.

'If he starts chattering away at ten months old then he's clearly a genius and we need to get back immediately,' Nick chuckled. 'But short of him reciting Shakespeare, I reckon we're not missing out on anything much. Let's just think about us, shall we? Just for one weekend.' His voice was low, and he began nuzzling at Julia's neck, nibbling at her earlobe. She gave a throaty laugh, tilting her head up to kiss him, long and deep.

'It's been a long time since you've kissed me like that,' Nick grinned, as they finally came up for air. 'I'd almost forgotten what it was like.'

'Here's another reminder,' Julia purred, shifting her whole body around so that the water went sloshing over the side of the tub, bubbles landing in wet, white mounds on the floor. Neither of them noticed the mess as they reached for one other, discovering places they hadn't explored for a very long time.

'So, what do you say to making another baby?' Nick growled, raising his eyebrows suggestively.

'Er, no thanks, I've got enough on with one for now. But I *am* happy to practise…'

Julia smirked as she went to kiss him and Nick reached for her, pulling her closer. Suddenly she sat bolt upright, wriggling out of his grasp.

'What now?' Nick asked in exasperation. 'Yes, Jack has his special blanket, and we've packed enough nappies to see him through until he's old enough to vote, and Debbie knows not to let him play with matches, or—'

'Shush, Nick!' Julia snapped, as she cocked her head to one side, listening intently. 'I'm sure that's my phone ringing – I left it in my bag.'

'It'll be a wrong number, or a PPI call.'

'What if it's not? What if something's happened to Jack?'

Julia was up and out of the bath in seconds, her eyes wide with fear. She pulled an enormous fluffy towel off the heated rail, hastily wrapping it round her as she ran through to the bedroom, her feet leaving damp stains on the thick carpet. Rifling through her bag, she pulled out her phone, grimacing as she saw the name on the screen.

'It's Valerie,' she called through to Nick.

'What? The dragon lady?'

'Don't say that!' Julia shushed him, as though Valerie could hear their conversation. She looked down at the phone, still flashing in her hand. 'Should I get it?'

'No! It's Friday night and we're away for the weekend. You can get back to her on Monday.'

Julia bit her lip. 'She's not really a nine-to-five, Monday-to-Friday kind of woman.'

'It doesn't matter, just ignore it, she can—'

In the bathroom, Nick groaned as he heard his wife answer the phone. Climbing reluctantly out of the tub, he wrapped a towel around his waist, tucking it in below his belly button, where the dark hair lay in a damp trail.

He shook his head at Julia as he strolled through to the bedroom, and she winced guiltily, turning away.

'Yes, Valerie, absolutely. No, I'm afraid I don't have the details with me right now. No, I... I'm away for the weekend, you see. No, we're in the Lake District, so it's quite a long... Yes, I realise that. I could search through the emails on my phone? See if I have the information on there and...' She caught Nick's eye and he glared at her while she mouthed an apology. 'Oh, I see. Well we won't be back until Sunday evening, so I don't think that... Okay... Yes, I understand... I'll see what I can do. Okay, I'll call you back shortly. Bye Valerie.'

Julia hung up and Nick exploded.

'No, you will not call her back shortly! What did she want anyway?'

Julia pulled a face, feeling caught between Valerie's demands and her husband's desires. 'She can't find the latest version of the guest list, but obviously I don't have it with me. I think I might have something on here…' She trailed off, scrolling through her phone.

Nick marched over and snatched the phone out of her hand. Julia looked up in alarm as he strode across the room to the wardrobe safe, tossing the phone inside and locking it with a combination he didn't reveal.

'Nick!' Julia wailed. 'What are you doing?'

'Taking you for dinner,' he replied calmly. 'Come on, let's get ready.'

'But—'

'It's almost eight o'clock on Friday night on Valentine's weekend. We're in the most beautiful location, in the most gorgeous hotel, and you are *not* going to spend your time working.'

'But what if Debbie rings?'

'If you don't pick up, I'm sure she'll try my number. After all, you did give her it on that endless contact list, along with your parents' details and my parents' details – despite the fact that they live a three-hour drive away – and the number of Jack's doctor, and the nearest out-of-hours surgery, and probably the local vicar too in case he goes all *Exorcist* on her.'

In spite of herself, Julia started to smile.

Nick stepped across, his eyes softer now, as he wrapped his arms around his wife. 'Come on, let's get ready and I'll take you for a lovely dinner.'

Julia let herself be swept up in his embrace, relaxing against his chest as she inhaled the freshly washed scent of him. Although she knew she should be angry with him for taking her phone, it was undeniably sexy to see him behave so masterfully, and it was a relief to know she couldn't speak to Valerie even if she wanted to (which she really didn't).

'Okay,' Julia agreed, kissing him. 'Give me thirty minutes and I'll see what I can do.'

—

'Mmm, this is delicious. How's yours?'

'I don't care how it tastes,' Nick replied, shovelling tender duck breast into his mouth. 'It's just such a novelty to be able to eat a meal without being interrupted by crying or screaming or throwing food. And that's just you on a bad day!'

Julia grinned at his teasing. But she knew exactly what Nick meant. It felt luxurious to be able to linger over dinner without having to get up in the middle of it to see to Jack. Which reminded her...

'I hope Debbie got Jack off to sleep okay.'

'I'm sure he'll be fine. He usually conks out around seven anyway.'

'Yeah, but it might be different if neither of us are there to settle him,' Julia fretted. Whilst she'd initially enjoyed not having her phone, it was now starting to make her anxious. 'I'd feel so much better if I could just drop Debs a quick text...' She looked beseechingly at her husband.

'Okay,' Nick acquiesced, putting down his knife and fork, and handing over his phone. 'Go for it.'

'Thanks, hon.' Julia quickly tapped out a text, then went back to her gnocchi.

'Hey, did I mention that Anthony at work is having a big party for his fortieth? It's the first Saturday in March, and he's hired a function room at some hotel out near Crostwick. It should be a good do.'

'What about Jack?'

'Well we'd have to get a babysitter. Debbie might be free.'

'I don't want to impose. She's already looked after him loads this past couple of months. And if she's not free, there's no one else I'd leave him with.'

'Maybe your parents can come down for the night. We can't stop having lives just because we have a baby. It's been ten months now.'

'What, so at ten months he's old enough to fend for himself while we go out raving?'

'That's not what I meant. But we *are* allowed the occasional night off. Besides, you've done so much for Debbie's wedding that she owes us a few evenings of babysitting.'

Julia nodded, not wanting to get into an argument. 'Okay, I'll ask her.'

They carried on eating in silence as Julia gazed around the hotel restaurant, busy with couples having romantic meals for two. The room was small and cosy, decorated in an olde-worlde style, with dark wooden beams and a roaring open fire.

'Oh, did I tell you what Debbie said the other day? Apparently there's this little girl at nursery – I think she's called Mia – and she turned up wearing a big pink frilly skirt. Jack was obsessed with it and kept following her round, trying to look underneath!'

Nick chuckled as he speared a slice of potato dauphinoise. 'Did he? That's my boy.'

'Hmm, crawling around on his hands and knees, chasing after some piece of skirt? Yeah, just like his dad,' Julia winked. 'You know, he seems to be enjoying nursery so much that I was thinking we should take him to do some other activities – maybe swimming, or baby music? You can even do baby signing! What do you reckon?'

Nick chewed thoughtfully, swallowing before he finally spoke. 'Don't take this the wrong way, but do you think we could talk about something else tonight?'

Julia stared at him in confusion.

'Look, before we had Jack, we used to chat about all kinds of stuff – travelling and careers and which of our friends had got drunk and accidentally slept with one another. Now it's all about what Jack ate today and what consistency his poo was. Not that I don't find that fascinating,' he tried to joke.

But Julia didn't smile. She suddenly felt discomfited, her stomach twisting unhappily.

'Aren't you missing him?' she wondered, staring hard at Nick.

Nick shrugged. 'Yeah, of course. I just don't want us to become one of those couples whose kids leave home one day and the parents find they've got absolutely nothing in common any more. You know?'

Julia nodded, shivering despite the warmth of the open fire.

'Nick,' she began, realising she couldn't put off this conversation any longer. The words were out of her mouth before she'd even thought them through. 'Do you… Do you ever regret having Jack?'

Nick glanced up sharply, taken aback by the question. 'No, of course not. I mean, I'm not going to deny that life's completely different since we've had him, and it's not always been the easiest thing, but I don't regret it. Why, do you?'

'No, absolutely not! I just… Sometimes I get the impression that you're not that interested in him. Like, you're happy to have him around, as long as I do all the work and he doesn't get in your way too much.'

'Oh, we're back to this are we?' Nick groaned. 'You're expecting me to somehow magically look after Jack all day, despite having a full-time job?'

'That's not what I meant at all,' Julia backtracked. 'But even when you are at home, you never seem interested in changing him, or bathing him, or even spending that much time with him. I worry that you're missing out. And that Jack's missing out on Daddy time…' Julia broke off, suddenly close to tears.

Nick heard the crack in her voice, and looked up in surprise. His angry expression instantly dissolved, like a mask being whipped away, and Julia suddenly saw how exhausted and unhappy he looked.

'I don't know what it is,' Nick confessed, his voice barely more than a whisper. 'I just feel so useless when I'm around him.'

'What do you mean?' Julia hardly dared to breathe as Nick spoke. It felt as though a dam had burst and everything was about to come rushing out. 'You're his dad, of course he needs you.'

'It's not that, exactly.' Nick screwed up his face, rubbing his hand tiredly across his forehead as he tried to find the right words. 'When Jack was born, I was elated. It was like nothing I'd ever felt before. I had a son, and my head was full of visions of me teaching him how to ride his bike, and playing football in the park. But he's so tiny still, it's like I don't know what to do with him.

'And you seem to know instinctively,' Nick continued, the words pouring out. 'I watch you and you're so good with him, and he responds to that. During the week, I barely even see him. He goes to bed almost as soon as I get in from work, and I just feel that… Well, it's like I'm not even needed. The two of you can manage just fine, and there's no place for me.'

'Oh, Nick, of course there's a place for you.' Julia's heart ached as she dropped her knife and fork, reaching out across the table to take Nick's hands in hers. 'And I don't mean to take over, I really don't.'

'I know, and I'm not saying that. I just… Be patient with me, okay.' Nick looked up nervously, his dark eyes soft and vulnerable. He smiled hesitantly, and Julia smiled back.

'Whatever you need,' she promised him.

'Well, funny you should mention that,' Nick grinned, leaning back in his chair and throwing aside his knife and fork. The atmosphere changed completely as he looked at Julia, electricity crackling in the air as desire flamed in his eyes. 'What I really need tonight is to spend some time alone with my gorgeous wife. So what do you say we head back to the room, order more champagne on room service, and see where this Valentine's night takes us?'

'Sounds perfect,' Julia grinned, and she meant it.

CHAPTER 20

*'I have great hopes that we shall love each other all
our lives as much as if we had never married at all'*
– Lord Byron

Gill and Mike were sitting in their living room, watching television, as Sam lay on the floor in front of them, playing with his pirate ship. Paige was upstairs, doing her homework, while Kelly was sitting on the far end of the sofa, scrolling through her iPad. Suddenly, she clapped a hand to her mouth, bolting upright.

'Oh, wow!' she exclaimed.

'What?' Gill asked in alarm. Even Sammy looked up from his toys, startled by Kelly's sudden movement.

'I just got my first ever comment on my blog. And it's from America! Look!'

Gill was surprised to see Kelly scramble along the settee and show her iPad to Mike.

'Brilliant, Kel, that's excellent,' he grinned. 'I like the blog name too.'

Kelly looked bashful, but offered a smile in return. She'd gone for 'Kelly's World', the title Mike had suggested.

'Can I see?' Gill asked, leaning across as Kelly shyly proffered the tablet.

The post she'd written was titled 'My Favourite Pieces for the New Season' and was all about '*stylishly managing the transition into spring. Hint: layering is key*'. Kelly had included some of her own items of clothing and photographed them hanging on her wardrobe door, such as her white V-neck Gap T-shirt which could be '*layered with an oversized cardigan and chunky scarf, worn with black skinny jeans and biker boots*'.

She'd asked Mike to take a photo of her wearing '*a classic black polo neck, paired with this printed, calf-length A-line skirt from Topshop and my fave Converse trainers*', and uploaded that too. Gill thought it was a very odd combination, but there was no denying it worked on her daughter.

At the bottom, Kelly had added a handful of her '*dream items*', with pictures of a Burberry trench coat and a Coach bag.

'*Come back next week for my vlog on spring make-up trends*', Kelly had written underneath. Gill had to admit that it looked impressive.

Finally, in the comments section below, someone had written: '*Love your blog, you have awesome style! That skirt looks designer xoxo*'

It was signed: '*Tammy, 14, Kentucky, USA*'

'Hmm, or maybe "*Darren, forty-four, in his bedroom*",' Gill muttered darkly.

Kelly immediately snatched the iPad back from her. 'Why do you have to spoil everything? Why can't you just be happy for me?'

Gill instantly felt bad, seeing how upset her daughter was. 'Kel, I didn't mean—'

But Kelly was already out of the door, running upstairs to her bedroom.

Gill rolled her eyes at Mike, as if to say, *silly teenagers*, but surprisingly he didn't seem to sympathise.

'It was a bit much, Gill,' he said gently. 'She was so excited.'

'I'm only looking out for her. Who knows what freaks are commenting on there. We don't know if that really was fourteen-year-old Tammy from Kentucky.'

'No, and we don't know that it wasn't either. But we've already talked about this. We'll have to monitor as much as we can, but ultimately trust Kelly that she's not going to do anything stupid.'

Gill sat in silence for a moment. She felt put out, but she also had a sneaking suspicion that Mike was right.

'Okay, I'll go up in a bit and apologise,' Gill sighed, wondering when Mike had suddenly become such an expert at dealing with stroppy teenagers.

—

It was a few days later when Gill decided to log on to *Kelly's World*, to see whether there were any more comments on the Spring Pieces post. There was just one – someone with the username *ajhg666td*, who'd written: '*Check the crazy prices at Clothes4U, no need to spend $$$*'. It was clearly spam; she'd have to let Kelly know so that she could delete it.

Kelly had, however, written a new blog post. It was called: 'My mum is getting married, but not to my dad'.

As soon as Gill saw it, she felt an odd sensation in her stomach, as though her guts were twisting into an ever-tightening knot, her whole body on high alert. Taking a deep breath, she tried to slow her racing pulse and calm down enough to take in what she was reading:

Okay, so this blog was originally set up for me to talk about clothes and make-up and stuff, but today I'm feeling quite down so I thought I'd write about one of the big issues in my life. Hope it's not too boring for you, I promise I'll do that make-up vlog at the weekend!

Like the title says, my mum is getting married, but not to my dad. They split up five years ago when I was eight, and it was awful, but I still get to see my dad every couple of weekends so that's okay. Now my mum's met this new guy called Mike. He's okay I suppose, but he's not my dad. He has a really annoying daughter and I have to share a bedroom with her which is so unfair but we don't have enough rooms in our house for me to have my own. She always steals my stuff because she doesn't have any nice stuff of her own and mine's better.

Mum's really into this wedding business, which I think is stupid because she's already done it once. She's too old to wear a big white dress, and I don't see the point if you've done it before. She wants me to a bridesmaid, but I'd better have something cool to wear. I hope I get to choose my own dress.

She's got this woman called Julia to help her plan the wedding, and she's asked me and my brothers and Mike's kids to help out. I don't know how I feel about it all. I want my mum to have a nice wedding day, but it's all so weird. I know my mum and dad won't get back together. They would argue all the time and anyway he's got a new girlfriend called Joanna.

The post ended abruptly, and Gill exhaled shakily, a whole host of emotions running through her. Above all, she felt incredibly guilty that Kelly could pour her heart out online, and say things to a bunch of strangers that she couldn't say to her own mother. Or maybe she *had* tried to say them, and Gill just hadn't listened…

Scrolling down, Gill noticed that there were half a dozen comments beneath the post. With trepidation, she read on:

Stop whining! You're lucky enough to have a Mum and Dad – Emma, Torquay, UK

Weddings are great, so much fun!!! And two families means two sets of presents at Christmas time ☺ ☺ ☺ – Saffron, 15, London / Didcot

How will your dress be like? Maybe you wear black in a protest? – Rock Star Wannabe, Germany

I think your mum sounds awful marrying this Mike that you don't like. She should think about her kids and not herself. I hate my stepdad too, I wish my mum had never married him, now she never spends any time with me – Anonymous

my auntie natalie got married in las vegas. it looked amazeballs, but i wasn't allowed to go. we stayed up really late and watched it on skype – danielle, 12, hull

Gill drank her tea without really being aware of what she was doing, surprised to find that the mug was suddenly empty. Sam was watching cartoons next door, and Gill was vaguely aware that she had to leave soon to drop him at nursery before she went to work. Right now, her head was spinning.

She'd always been aware that Kelly had an issue with her marrying Mike, but they'd never properly talked about it, with Gill burying her head in the sand and hoping it was a phase that Kelly would grow out of once she'd got to know him better. Any time that the subject did come up, it would descend into an argument, and usually ended with Kelly storming out of the room and slamming the door – something she seemed to do on a regular basis.

Gill's life had been so busy since she'd split up with Ian – adjusting to being a single mum, then meeting Mike and taking on this enormous blended family – and she realised that she'd used her hectic schedule as an excuse to avoid sitting down and having a heart-to-heart with her daughter. She saw now that that had been a huge error of judgement on her part. It was heartbreaking that Kelly had felt more able to share her feelings online than with her mum.

Gill read through the post once again, biting her lip as she felt the tears threatening. Her gaze fell on the comments box at the bottom, and without giving herself time to think, she began to type:

I think your mum loves you very much, even though you might not always realise it. Maybe you need to get together, just the two of you, and talk it through. Your happiness is the most important thing in the world to her xxx

She signed it: '*Gill, 44, Norwich*', and quickly hit submit. Then she closed down her laptop, put her mug in the dishwasher, and went to get Sammy.

—

Later that evening, Gill was in the kitchen getting dinner ready when she heard the front door slam. Moments later, Kelly stalked through.

Gill felt strangely nervous, her heart beginning to race. She looked up anxiously, but Kelly was smiling.

'You're so lame, Mum,' she scoffed, rolling her eyes, but Gill knew this was about the best response she could have asked for. Kelly didn't seem angry or upset, and it felt as though something that had been buried for a long time had finally come to the surface.

'Come here,' Gill snuffled, tearing up as she opened her arms.

Feigning reluctance, Kelly walked towards her and let herself be swallowed up in Gill's embrace. 'Are you *crying*, Mum? Jeez, is it the menopause or something? Seriously, don't get snot in my hair, that's gross.'

'You do know I love you, don't you.'

'Yeah, yeah, whatever.' But Kelly was grinning.

'Here, sit down for a moment,' Gill said, indicating the chairs around the kitchen table.

Again, Kelly sighed and acted as though Gill had asked for the impossible. She went over to the fridge and cracked open a can of Diet Coke, sipping it rebelliously and knowing there was no way Gill would tell her off for drinking fizzy pop before dinner. Today, Kelly could have demanded (almost) anything, and Gill would have agreed.

As Kelly sat down, Gill reached across the table and took her daughter's hands in hers.

'I know this isn't the ideal time to discuss everything – I was thinking we should do something, just the two of us. Maybe go get our nails done, or even have a really girly day, with shopping and a nice lunch. What do you think?'

'Sounds cool,' Kelly shrugged.

'But I just want to say how proud I am of the way you've handled this whole situation with Mike. I know it hasn't been easy for you these last few years. There've been a lot of changes and, believe me, I'd rather you hadn't had to experience them. I'd have loved for things to work out with me and your dad – you know, stayed together forever like we planned. But it didn't happen.'

'Yeah, I know,' Kelly nodded, seeming frighteningly grown up. 'You guys were arguing so much, it was better for you to get divorced.'

'And I know that me meeting Mike, and him having kids too, was a massive adjustment for you. The seven of us in this house can feel pretty claustrophobic sometimes, and you've dealt with it brilliantly. The thing is, Kel, life on your own is really hard – those couple of years after I split up with your dad and before I met Mike were a real struggle. You probably don't really remember them clearly, but it was a damned hard slog, and it's so much nicer to have someone to share all that with. And I know you don't always see it, but Mike is one of the good guys. I massively appreciate having him in my life, but I care about you kids more than anything else in the world, and I need to make sure you're okay with it too.'

'I guess,' Kelly said slowly. 'I mean, I want you to be happy and everything. And if Mike's the guy to do that then it's not my place to say anything. It's just sometimes I wish it was how it used to be, and that I didn't have to share you with all these new people. And that I didn't have to share a room with Paige,' she added with feeling.

'I know it's not ideal, but we're all just muddling through as best as we can. It'd mean a lot to me to know that Mike and I have your blessing. And we really do mean it when we say we want you all to be involved in the wedding. It's not just about me and Mike, it's about the whole family.'

'Yeah, I get it,' Kelly nodded. 'Seriously, all this because of that blog post I wrote? I probably should have deleted it.'

'No, I'm glad you didn't. I think this chat's been long overdue, and we'll definitely go and have our girly day soon. But if you ever feel down like that again, you can always come to me – you don't have to put it out there for the whole world.'

'But did you see how many comments I got?' Kelly grinned, her eyes lighting up. 'And when I looked at my stats, two people had viewed my blog from Australia, and even someone in Brazil.'

'That's wonderful,' Gill said, and she meant it. Kelly was growing up, she realised, and there was absolutely nothing she could do to stop it. She was so proud of her daughter, and everything she'd achieved so far. She was a complex, brilliant, beautiful young woman, and just looking at her made Gill's heart swell with love.

The saucepan on the hob began to bubble over, startling Gill out of her reverie as she jumped up to turn down the heat.

'Are we done? Can I go now?' Kelly asked, seeing her opportunity to escape.

'Yes, you can go,' Gill laughed. 'Dinner in about half an hour, yeah? I love you, Kel.'

'Yeah, whatevs,' Kelly called over her shoulder as she walked away. But Gill could hear the smile in her voice.

CHAPTER 21

'Keep your eyes wide open before marriage, and half-shut afterwards' – **Benjamin Franklin**

It was Saturday morning, and Debbie was slowly getting herself ready to face the day. She was curled up on the sofa in her dressing gown, nursing a cup of coffee, whilst on the TV James Martin demonstrated how to cook the perfect pulled pork.

'Bathroom's free,' Stevie called from upstairs.

'Thanks,' Debbie shouted back. She knew she should get up and go for a shower, but it was so nice relaxing against the cushions, with the heating turned up and Scamp curled on the settee beside her. Outside, the first signs of spring were in evidence, as daffodils and crocuses pushed their way up through the earth, but despite the pale sunshine, the weather remained chilly.

Debbie was still sitting in the same place when Stevie jogged downstairs a few minutes later, freshly washed and smelling of shower gel.

'Are you staying in your pyjamas all day?' he wondered, as he bent down to give her a kiss.

'Maybe,' Debbie teased. 'It depends what I feel like. Nah, I'll move in a minute. I was just thinking about what to do today. It's so nice not to have any plans.'

'Mmm hmm,' Stevie replied, a twinkle in his eye that Debbie didn't notice.

'Maybe we should take Scamp for a long walk this afternoon – we could drive out to South Walsham and check on the reception venue while we're there. They might have a wedding on today, so we could see it when it's all decked out.'

'Maybe.' Stevie's tone was non-committal.

'Then I'll batch cook this evening – something like vegetable stew that I can keep in the freezer, and eat with brown rice instead of dumplings.'

'Come on then, chop chop, no time to waste,' Stevie insisted, clapping his hands to chivvy her along.

'What's wrong with you?' Debbie frowned. 'It's the weekend, I'm having a lazy morning.'

'Yes, but you never know what the day might bring, and it's best to be prepared.'

'What's going on?' Debbie was instantly suspicious.

'Nothing.' Stevie was clearly lying, unable to keep a straight face. 'You might want to have a shower and get dressed, that's all I'm saying.'

Debbie broke into a wide smile, wondering what he'd got planned. He looked very pleased with himself, she thought, her excitement growing. Maybe he was going to take her for a romantic lunch at a country pub? Or shopping to choose some sexy new clothes?

'Okay then,' she agreed, playing along, as she made her way up the stairs. She stripped off and stepped into the shower, noticing as she soaped herself how much her body had changed these last few months. The skin on her thighs was tighter, her stomach flatter. Her hipbones and waist were clearly defined, showing off her hourglass shape. Seeing the difference was the biggest motivation she could ask for; proof that all her hard work was paying off, that she was getting ever closer to her target.

Debbie climbed out of the shower, wrapping a towel around her and scooping her hair up into a turban. She padded through to the bedroom and stood thoughtfully in front of her open wardrobe, wondering what to wear. There wasn't a huge choice; her old clothes were far too big for her now. She had a nice pair of jeans, and a new pair of jeggings, or her knee-length cord skirt which looked smart with black tights and boots. It all depended on where they were going.

'Stevie, what do you think I should wear today?' she called down, rifling through the rail and picking out a black fitted jumper which would go nicely with the skirt. 'I don't know where we're going so you'll have to help me out. Stevie?' she called again.

Still no reply.

Frowning, Debbie headed down the stairs. 'Stevie, did you hear me? I was asking what I should wear today 'cos—'

She stopped short, trailing off as she reached the living room. Stevie was slumped on the edge of the sofa, his shoulders hunched, his body language thoroughly miserable. His mood had completely changed from the happy, cheerful state she'd left him in minutes earlier.

'Stevie?' she asked uncertainly.

He looked up, fury blazing in his eyes.

'Stevie, what's the matter?' Debbie repeated, increasingly anxious. 'Has something happened?' She hurried to sit down beside him, their knees touching together. Stevie jumped away as though he'd received an electric shock, but still he didn't speak.

'Stop it, you're scaring me,' Debbie pleaded. She felt suddenly chilly wearing only a towel, goosebumps breaking out along her arms.

Stevie turned to her, his face frighteningly blank.

'Who's Phil?'

Debbie screwed up her face in confusion. 'I don't know. I don't know anyone called Phil.'

'Really? Because he seems to know you.'

Debbie's phone was lying on the coffee table in front of Stevie. He picked it up and tossed it towards her.

Debbie still had no idea what he was talking about, but a very bad feeling was growing in the pit of her stomach. Unlocking her phone, it opened on her text messages. She skimmed over the words hardly able to believe what she was reading:

> *Hey hot stuff, it was gr8 to meet you the other night. U want 2get together tonight 4a repeat? Let's see if I can get that ring off your finger ;) x*

'It's obviously a mistake,' she laughed, relief flooding over her. 'Someone's clearly sent the message to the wrong person.'

But Stevie didn't laugh. 'So why is his number saved in your phone along with his name? Don't lie to me, Debbie, I'm not stupid.'

'But I don't kn—' She broke off suddenly as understanding dawned, her face changing as she realised exactly who was texting her.

'Oh,' Stevie said, his voice heavy with sarcasm. 'So you *do* know him after all.'

'It's not what it looks like,' Debbie burst out, hearing how clichéd that sounded.

'So what is it then?' Stevie rarely lost his temper, but Debbie could see just how angry he was getting. 'Why is some dickhead called Phil texting *my* fiancée and asking her to get together with him for a repeat of the other night?'

Debbie squirmed uncomfortably. When Stevie put it like that, she could see why he might be upset.

'Look, let me explain,' she began calmly. She reached for his hand, but Stevie snatched it away, jumping to his feet and beginning to pace the room. Scamp trotted after him, following every step. Debbie swallowed hard, knowing she had no choice but to tell him the whole story and hope he believed her. 'It was last week. When I went out with Julia and Gill.'

Stevie's hands had tightened into angry fists, exhaling hard through his nose.

'But *nothing happened.* It's all a silly misunderstanding. I'd gone to the bar to get another bottle of prosecco. The bar was busy and this guy next to me started chatting.'

'Good looking, was he?' Stevie asked pointedly.

Debbie flushed red, and Stevie threw her a look of disgust.

'But it wasn't like that! He was just making polite conversation. I guess I was a bit tipsy and started chatting back. I had my phone out – I was actually in the middle of texting *you* – and he asked if he could have my number. I started laughing – I didn't think he was being serious – but he kept asking, and I just kind of… panicked. I didn't want to seem rude, so I… I ended up giving it to him.'

'You didn't want to seem rude?' Stevie was staring at her incredulously.

'I know it sounds pathetic,' Debbie floundered. 'My mind went blank. Then he called my phone so that I had his number, and made me put his name in…' she trailed off, looking guiltily at the phone in her lap. Every admission sounded worse than the last.

'So what does he mean by "*a repeat of last week*"? That sounds like more than polite conversation to me.'

'I don't know! Nothing happened, I swear.'

Stevie was shaking his head. 'Something doesn't add up here. Why didn't you just say no, or give out a fake number? Did you want him to call you, is that what it was?'

'No, not at all! Everything happened so fast, and I was a bit bewildered to be honest. I'm not used to… Well, I didn't quite realise what had happened until it was all over. I didn't know what to do, or say, so I just grabbed my phone and the prosecco and scuttled back to the girls.'

'And then I bet you had a good old laugh about it, didn't you? Telling the girls how you'd just been chatted up.'

'It wasn't like that,' Debbie protested weakly, but Stevie was uncomfortably close to the truth. Then something occurred to her. 'Why were you going through my phone anyway?' she demanded, suddenly taking the moral high ground.

Stevie shook his head in disbelief. 'I wasn't. The text came through and it popped up on the screen. Anyone sending messages to my fiancée that start with "*Hey hot stuff*" kind of catches my attention, you know?'

'Whatever,' Debbie muttered, knowing she was in the wrong, and unable to think of a better response.

Stevie stopped pacing, staring hard at her. 'You've changed, you know that? And I don't just mean physically.'

There was a beat of silence as Debbie took in what he'd just said. 'I know what this is about,' she burst out. 'You're jealous! Jealous that for once another man found me attractive, and you can't handle that.'

'Of course I'm jealous,' Stevie laughed incredulously. 'What man wouldn't be? You think I'm happy that you're getting sex texts from another bloke? You want me to say, "Congratulations Debs, you're looking incredible recently, now get out there and start flirting with other men"?'

'Why can't you be happy for me? You know how hard I've been working, how much effort I've put into trying to lose weight. I reckon you preferred me when I was just a fat blimp hiding in the corner, then you didn't have to worry about anyone else fancying me.'

'Oh, don't be so ridiculous. I've been incredibly supportive to you. I've put up with months of you going on and *on* about how many calories you've eaten, and how you don't want to go for a nice meal anywhere because it's off the diet plan, and you don't want to cuddle up and watch a film because you've got Zumba class instead. I've lived off lentils and salads and *kale* to try and support you and I haven't complained once, because I know how important this is to you. And the first chance you get, you get all dressed up and hand out your phone number to some random guy in a bar. Well thanks Debs, thanks a lot.'

Stevie was breathing heavily, and Debbie looked close to tears. Scamp had curled up on his bed in the corner, and let out a low whine.

Debbie opened her mouth to reply, but at that moment the doorbell rang, the noise seeming to echo in the silence. Scamp jumped up, barking excitedly as he rushed to the front door.

'Oh no, who's that?' Debbie groaned. She really couldn't handle seeing anyone right now.

'That'll be your surprise,' Stevie told her, his eyebrows raised accusingly.

Another wave of shame washed over Debbie. Fifteen minutes earlier, she'd been overwhelmed with excitement about what Stevie had planned for her, and now they were having a blazing argument.

'I can't answer the door, I'm still in my towel.'

Stevie shrugged. 'I thought that was your new thing – wearing skimpy clothes and chatting up strangers. Maybe it'll be the postman, or the delivery guy. You can let your towel slip a little, hand out your number…'

'Sod off,' Debbie shot back, stung by his comments.

The doorbell rang again, three times in succession, and Debbie let out a cry of frustration.

'Go answer it,' Stevie told her. 'It doesn't matter what you're wearing.'

Debbie stomped off down the hallway, clutching her towel tightly around her. Behind the frosted glass, she could make out two shadowy figures, then she heard the sound of familiar giggling. Opening the door just a crack, she peered round to see Julia and Angela standing on the doorstep.

'Surprise!' they grinned.

'What's going on?'

'Let us in and we'll tell you. It's freezing out here!' Julia was wearing a cute bobble hat, and rubbing her hands together to keep them warm.

Debbie stood back as the two women tumbled into the house, fussing over Scamp as he jumped up at them, demanding attention.

'You could have at least made sure she was dressed, Stevie,' Angela chastised him, as she followed Debbie through to the living room.

Stevie smiled tightly. 'We got somewhat… distracted.'

'Ew, I don't want to know!' Angela giggled, not picking up on the strained atmosphere.

'Right, well, I'll leave you ladies to it. Have a good day, Debbie,' Stevie said awkwardly, giving her a formal peck on the cheek. He strode out of the room and they heard the sound of his feet on the stairs, followed by the spare room door slamming shut.

'What's going on?' Julia whispered. She and Angela were looking at one another, panic-stricken.

'We just had a bit of an argument. Bad timing,' Debbie grimaced. 'I'll explain it all later. Anyway, what's going on? Why are you here?'

'Oh, Deb,' Angela was looking at her sympathetically. 'You two never argue! Well don't worry, we're here to whisk you off for the day, and make it all better.'

In spite of herself, Debbie felt a tingle of excitement. 'Why? Where are we going?'

'Well, Ange and I got chatting at nursery,' Julia explained, 'And we thought that as you've been doing so well with the weight loss, you deserved a treat.'

'But not a day off,' Angela added. 'We don't want you to break your diet, and we wanted to do something that would motivate you to keep going so—'

'So we talked to Stevie and we came up with the idea of taking you to a spa,' Julia finished gleefully. 'We've got you a personal training session in the gym, then we can use the pool and the sauna—'

'And we're finishing off with hot stone massages for all of us,' Angela took over, wresting the conversation back from Julia. 'Oh, and in the middle of it all there's a healthy, low calorie yet delicious lunch being prepared for us in the restaurant.'

Debbie's face was a whole mixture of emotions, from excitement and gratitude to confusion and bewilderment.

'But… I'm not even dressed yet!'

'*Exactly*. You've got ten minutes to get some clothes on and dry your hair, or else we're leaving without you,' Julia threatened.

'That sounds amazing, thank you so much!' Debbie beamed at the two of them, throwing her arms around them before bolting for the stairs.

'Oh, and one more thing…'

The sound of Angela's voice stopped Debbie in her tracks, and she turned back round. 'Yeah?'

'Don't forget your swimming cossie!'

CHAPTER 22

'I like everything about marriage but the hours'
– Peter De Vries

'That guy *texted* you?' Angela squealed incredulously.

'And Stevie saw it? Oh no, what a mess,' Julia sighed, not taking her eyes off the road as she drove along the busy country roads.

In the passenger seat beside her, Debbie put her head in her hands and groaned. 'If I ever see that bloke again, I'm going to kill him. Seriously, how arrogant can you be?'

'Let me see,' Angela demanded from the back seat, as Debbie shifted round and handed over her phone.

'"*Let's see if I can get that ring off your finger*",' Angela quoted, making a retching sound. 'Gross. So he knew you were engaged and everything? What a twat.'

'But surely Stevie knows nothing happened,' said Julia, as Debbie shrugged.

'I *hope* so. I think it brought up a whole load of other stuff about me losing weight and him struggling to adjust. I mean, *I'm* struggling to adjust, so I don't know what it's like for Stevie. And I've never really had a lot of male attention, so this is weird – neither of us have had to deal with that before.'

'It's probably making him really insecure,' Angela agreed. 'But that's good! It'll keep him on his toes, make him work a bit harder.'

'But he doesn't need to do that! I love him, just the way he is. He doesn't need to start buying me presents or fulfilling my every whim, because he thinks I'm going to cheat on him if he doesn't.'

'That's so sweet,' Julia cooed. 'Ooh, look, here we are.'

The three women fell silent as Julia hit the indicator and they pulled off the main road, driving through the impressive entrance gates of Ashworth Park. It was a former private country house, now converted into a hotel and spa, with a beautiful neo-classical facade and acres of rolling parkland.

'Oh, it looks amazing,' Debbie breathed.

'Shame we're not staying overnight,' Julia mused. 'But we can always come back. I wouldn't mind checking out their event facilities.'

'Maybe this would be a good venue for your hen do, Debs,' Angela suggested. 'In fact, you should think of today as your practice hen – you know, a trial run at getting drunk and talking about Stevie. Just to make sure you can do it.'

'Thanks very much,' Debbie giggled. 'I'll try my best.'

The spa was in a separate building to the main house, in a conversion of the old stable block, and Julia drove carefully up the long driveway, following signs to the car park.

'Let the games begin,' Angela winked, as the car pulled to a stop and the three women eagerly climbed out.

———

An hour later, Debbie was red, sweaty and in severe amounts of pain.

'I don't know if I can do this,' she panted. Her limbs were pushed to breaking point, and her face was the colour of beet-root, which clashed terribly with the T-shirt she was wearing. It was bright pink and read 'Slimming Down for the Gown!';

Julia and Angela had presented her with it in the changing room.

'Ouch, that hurts! I didn't even know I had muscles there!'

On the treadmills, Julia and Angela were speed-walking as they watched Debbie and giggled unsympathetically. She was currently being put through her paces on the mats in front of them by a very attractive personal trainer called Matt. He had blond hair, and a ridiculously toned body, and right now he was squatting down in front of Debbie, encouraging her to plank.

'Come on, Debs, it's easy,' Angela called out, as Julia unsuccessfully tried to stifle her laughter.

'No… it's… not,' Debbie managed through gritted teeth.

'Careful, Debbie, don't break that line,' Matt warned, placing a hand gently on her back to remind her of the correct posture.

Debbie was face down, raised up a few inches off the floor, her hands clenched together as she supported her weight on her forearms and toes. It looked simple enough, but it felt agonising.

'Give me ten more seconds, Debbie, you're doing so well,' Matt encouraged her.

Debbie couldn't speak; she grunted in reply, sweat dripping from her forehead.

'Eight… nine… nine and a half,' Matt counted with a grin. 'Ten.'

'Urrrgh,' Debbie dropped to the mat with a disturbing noise. 'That… is the hardest thing… I've ever done,' she gasped.

'Seriously, you did a great job,' Matt assured her. 'You've got some really impressive muscle tone and strength. You killed it on the cross-trainer.'

'Thanks,' Debbie replied, slowly getting her breath back. In spite of everything, she did feel proud of herself. She could really tell that her stamina and fitness levels had increased over the past couple of months; now she could jog up the stairs, whereas once it had been an effort, and she actively looked forward to taking the dog for long walks, rather than a short spin round the block.

'And now we'll run through some stretches, so you won't feel too sore tomorrow,' Matt said authoritatively. 'So if you sit up straight, and take your arm across your body…'

He led her through a series of moves, easing out the tired muscles and slowing her heart rate. To Debbie's surprise, she felt energised rather than exhausted, and the ache in her limbs was a satisfying one. Matt had taken her through a tough cardio work-out on the cross-trainer and exercise bike, before toning on the weights, finishing with core work on the mats. Julia and Angela had remained at a safe distance, half-heartedly working out and offering encouragement – with occasional mickey-taking.

When they were finally done, Debbie shook out her hands and feet, her whole body tingling. She knew she looked awful, but she felt fantastic.

'Great work,' Matt grinned, as Julia and Angela came across to join them. 'And good luck with the wedding. That fiancé of yours is a lucky man,' he winked.

Debbie felt the colour rise in her cheeks, making her even redder than she'd been before. Thank goodness Stevie wasn't around to hear Matt's comment, she thought, recalling this morning's argument and feeling guilty all over again. Were Julia and Angela right? Was this something she was going to have to get used to from now on? Debbie had never been one of those girls – the ones who men flirted with, and chatted up, and bought drinks for in the hope of a cheeky snog at the end of the night. She wasn't sure that she wanted to be one of those girls either – she was more than happy with her Stevie.

'Thanks Matt,' she mumbled, scuttling off to the changing rooms, as Julia and Angela followed behind, exchanging knowing looks.

—

'Ohhhh, that feels good,' Debbie groaned, exhaling slowly as she spread a fluffy towel over the wooden slatted benches of the sauna and lay down. The hot, dry air wrapped itself around her, relaxing her weary body.

The three women had the sauna to themselves, and were making the most of it after their busy day. They'd just been in the pool, having a leisurely swim up and down before chilling out in the Jacuzzi. Now they were gossiping in the sauna, and the conversation had turned to weddings.

'So how's it all going?' Angela asked, her head lolling lazily to look across at Debbie. 'Is everything organised?'

'All of the big things are done – the venue, photographer, florist, cake, invitations,' Debbie reeled off. 'All thanks to Julia. She's been brilliant at sorting everything out.'

Julia shrugged modestly. 'It's what I do.'

'I still need to book the entertainment for the evening do. I'm worried I'm leaving it quite late, but we're not sure what we want yet – a DJ or a band or our iPods on shuffle… Then there's all the little bits to do nearer the time, like sorting out the place names and the decorations, and finalising the seating plan.'

'Well, I'll definitely be there,' Angela insisted.

'You'd better be,' Debbie grinned, as she eased herself over to throw some more water onto the coals. It gave a satisfying hiss and an instant hit of heat flooded the sauna. 'And will you be bringing Mitch? Or will you have moved on by then?'

Angela wrinkled her nose. 'Hmm, Mitch might have got the chop by then. But put me down for a plus one. I'll definitely be bringing someone.'

'Even if you have to drag a handsome man off the street?'

'Don't joke about it. I'll probably stop off at the pub on my way to the wedding and see who I like the look of. Ooh, maybe I should ask Matt the personal trainer to go with me?'

'He only had eyes for Debbie,' Julia couldn't resist teasing her, as Debbie looked mortified.

'Change the subject please!' she demanded testily.

Angela laughed, but went along with the request. 'So, Julia, what was your wedding like?' she wondered. 'It must have been spectacular, with all your skills and contacts.'

'Well, it was pretty amazing to me,' Julia remembered, going all misty-eyed. 'But your own wedding day always is. You've got all your family and friends there to see you marry the love of your life, you're wearing a gorgeous dress and then there's an incredible party at the end.'

'Sold,' Debbie giggled. 'I want to do that.'

'But I wasn't doing the events planning back then,' Julia went on, as Angela raised her eyebrows in surprise. It was too hot to move any more than that in the steamy sauna. 'I was a receptionist-slash-PA to the director of a marketing company, back home in Derby. That's where I met my husband, Nick. He was an account manager at the same firm.'

'So how did you get into events?' Angela asked curiously. 'It seems like a dream job, getting to plan weddings and parties all day.'

'It can be. It's great when you're doing the research and creating mood boards and actually delivering the perfect party that the client has asked for. It's less fun when you're standing in a field at six am in the pouring rain, trying to arrange an emergency marquee because the company you used has double booked. Or when someone sneaks a crate of vodka into a sweet sixteen party, and you realise you've got a bunch of drunken teenagers on your hands, all trying to have sex in the toilets and being sick in the flower beds.'

'Wow, do things like that really happen?'

'Yep. I speak from bitter experience on both of those. But once Nick and I were together, it felt a little strange to be working at the same company. I was falling out of love with my job anyway, not convinced it was the right path for me, and then my friend asked me to help out with a surprise party she was planning for her husband. That's when I got the bug. Nick had got a couple of promotions by then, so we were doing okay financially, and we talked about it and decided I'd take six months to try and establish a business. It went from there really.'

'Julia's the best,' Debbie put in loyally.

'Aw, thanks, hon. It makes it so much easier working with lovely brides like you,' Julia beamed. 'You're looking great by the way. I love that swimming cossie on you.'

Debbie was wearing a fifties-style swimsuit with black and white polka dots. She shuffled self-consciously, pulling at the material in an attempt to cover herself. 'Thanks. I've got a long way to go still.'

'You're doing brilliantly. I wish I had a tenth of your will-power. Maybe that way I'd finally get rid of this baby belly.' Julia looked down at her stomach and frowned.

'You're crazy,' Debbie shook her head. 'You look amazing in that bikini. I'd kill to have a figure like yours. Either of you.'

'Of course, you know what the best exercise is if you're trying to lose weight,' Angela smirked. 'A hot and sweaty workout between the sheets.'

'Well I've had no complaints from Stevie,' Debbie confided. 'Honestly, since I've been dropping the pounds I've had so much more energy. And I definitely feel more body confident.'

'Happy to leave the lights on?'

'With the dimmer turned down,' Debbie admitted.

'Lucky you,' Julia grinned. 'It's pretty difficult to find time for all that when you've got a ten-month-old baby. You're constantly exhausted.'

'Your husband's gorgeous, though,' Angela said candidly. 'I saw him when he came to pick up Jack one time. I'd be all over him if he was mine.'

Julia smiled. 'You should have seen me when I was trying to get pregnant with Jack. I wouldn't leave Nick alone! We actually went through a pretty rough time – he said he felt like a sperm donor, and that all I was concerned about was trying to have a baby. He was probably right.'

'I'm sorry,' Angela said awkwardly. 'I wouldn't have said anything if I'd known.'

'No, don't worry,' Julia insisted, thinking that it was quite cathartic to talk about it all. 'Of course, now he's complaining that he's not getting enough.'

'Men,' Angela tutted in solidarity.

'Couldn't live without them…' Debbie added, making everyone laugh.

'I guess they do have their uses,' Angela grinned, her eyes sparkling naughtily. 'Speaking of which, I really should ask for Matt's number. I wouldn't mind a little personal training of my own…'

'You're terrible,' Debbie shook her head, as Angela stuck her tongue out at her.

'Damn, is that the time?' Julia interrupted, glancing at her watch. 'We're going to be late for our massages.'

'All this relaxing is such hard work,' Debbie joked. 'Thanks so much for my amazing day, ladies. I've honestly had a brilliant time.'

'No problem,' Julia smiled back, as she stood up and wrapped her towel around her. 'You absolutely deserve it.'

CHAPTER 23

'I have learned that only two things are necessary to keep one's wife happy. First, let her think she's having her own way. And second, let her have it'
– Lyndon B Johnson

'This is going to be so much fun!' Aimee was grinning excitedly. 'I used to have a Saturday job in a supermarket when I was at college, so it reminds me of that.'

'Except you get to keep everything you scan today,' Julia laughed.

'Well I'll leave you both to start browsing, but don't hesitate to contact me or any other member of staff if you have any questions,' the wedding registry assistant smiled broadly, as she handed over the all-important scan-gun.

Aimee and Julia thanked her, then headed off excitedly to the homeware department, to begin choosing items for Aimee and Jon's wedding gift list. They wandered past bedroom and bathroom accessories, towards crockery and kitchenware.

Julia's gaze darted from one fabulous object to the next, whilst Aimee was beginning to look overwhelmed.

'There's so much choice,' she breathed. 'You don't realise until you actually have to narrow it down to one thing – you know, what colour towels or which pattern on the dinner service.'

'What kind of thing are you looking for? Is there something in particular you need?'

'Not really. Jon already had everything when I moved in – and I mean *everything*. Juicer, bread maker, slow cooker. Whatever the craze, he bought it. Although I'm not sure how often he actually used them…' Aimee smiled affectionately. 'Obviously we have things like bedding and towels, but Valerie says this is a chance to "upgrade" – crystal glassware instead of Ikea, that kind of thing.'

'I'm surprised she didn't come with us today,' Julia couldn't resist saying. 'Valerie usually likes to have an… um… opinion on what's happening.'

'Yeah…' Was it Julia's imagination, or did Aimee look the tiniest bit guilty? 'To be honest, Valerie has this big charity luncheon today at her club. She's been going on about it for weeks. I might have told her that this was the only time we could get an appointment, and that I'd be fine going with you.'

'Really?' Julia looked admiringly at Aimee. The girl had more backbone than she gave her credit for.

'I thought it might be a little… easier… if it was just us.'

The two women smiled at one another in mutual understanding.

'I think you might be right,' Julia nodded. 'And Jon's happy for you to pick on his behalf? I know that choosing items for the gift list is something a lot of couples like to do together.'

'He's fine about it. He's really busy with work, and he said that as I'm going to be running the house – well, it's a flat at the moment, but we're planning to move as soon as the wedding's out of the way – I can choose whatever makes me happy. He really doesn't mind about the colour of the duvet cover, or the style of cutlery, as long as the end result looks good.'

'That sounds very laidback of him.'

'Mmm,' Aimee replied, her tone giving nothing away. 'What do you think of this?' She held up a bone-china gravy boat and stand, with a simple gold design around the base.

'Very nice.'

'Do we even *need* a gravy boat? I think we have one already.'

'Yes, but is it a *Wedgewood* gravy boat?'

'I have absolutely no idea!' Aimee giggled.

'Well we need to start scanning soon otherwise we'll be here all day.'

Aimee stared at the gravy boat once again, then sighed heavily. 'It feels like such a big decision. This gravy boat is the first thing I'm choosing for our married life together. It's almost symbolic.'

'WWVD,' Julia said solemnly.

'Huh?'

'What Would Valerie Do?' Julia spelt out, and the two of them burst out laughing.

'You're right, let's scan it,' Aimee chuckled, as she held the scanner gun up to the barcode and pressed the button. 'Done.'

'So is that what you're going to do after the wedding?' Julia began, remembering what Aimee had said a few moments ago. 'Run the house?' The words sounded old-fashioned even as she said them, as though Aimee would be mistress of a Downton Abbey-style mansion.

'Well we haven't fully discussed…' Aimee trailed off. 'I'd like to do something else as well, something to give me more of a purpose. I thought about going into teaching, but I'm not sure if…' Again, she stopped short, remembering the argument she'd had with Jon after the dinner with Malcolm Huddlestone. 'I know Jon would like to have children fairly soon after we're married, so I guess all my time will be taken up with that.'

'You're not wrong there,' Julia said with feeling. 'Kids completely take over your life. You'll wonder how you ever had so much free time before.'

'How is Jack?' Aimee grinned, recognising that Julia was speaking from experience.

'He's good, thanks,' Julia smiled. 'He's at nursery today.'

'The one where Debbie works?'

'That's the one.'

'Thanks for inviting me the other night, I had a lot of fun. Gill's lovely, and Debbie's hilarious!'

'You're very welcome. I thought you might enjoy it.'

'Yeah, I did. I don't seem to go out as much these days, not since being with Jon. I mean, we do things together, but I hardly see my female friends.' Aimee distractedly zapped a butter dish, then shook her head, as if to clear it. 'I guess that's what happens, right?'

'I suppose. Your priorities change as you get older, and the focus is definitely more on your husband and children than on going out with the girls.'

'But you seem to have a great set-up,' Aimee insisted. 'I know you said the other night that it doesn't always feel that way, and of course nothing's ever going to be perfect, but you've got your husband and son, as well as a fantastic career. It's the best of both worlds.'

'Well, it's pretty hard work,' Julia said lightly, not wanting to disillusion her. 'Like I said, you feel constantly torn – guilty if you're not spending enough time with your child, guilty if you're not concentrating on work, or if you have to cancel a meeting because something's happened at home. But I wouldn't have it any other way. I was going stir-crazy after being in the house 24/7 for six months. Your wedding came at the perfect time.'

'I always imagined being a young mum,' Aimee admitted, as she scanned side plates and cereal bowls. 'But I didn't expect it to be quite so young. I always thought I'd have done something first – you know, seen the world, established a career. Jon's already done all of that.'

'You can still do it after having children,' Julia assured her. 'Plenty of people do.'

'I suppose.'

The two women lapsed into thoughtful silence, concentrating once more on the task at hand.

'I can't believe the price of some of these things,' Aimee marvelled. 'Almost two hundred pounds for a roasting dish! I know they're top of the range, but a lot of my friends can't afford this kind of thing. I feel embarrassed asking for a fifty-pound fruit bowl when I know they've got theirs from Wilko's.'

'As long as you've got a mix of prices on there, they'll find something,' Julia reassured her. 'And if it's what you want, then don't feel guilty.'

'I'm not sure that it *is* what I want, but Valerie was insistent that we registered our gift list here and had all these expensive brands. A lot of Jon's business colleagues are coming to the wedding, and all Valerie's friends are well off, so it's not an issue for them. Honestly, I barely know half the people who are invited!' Aimee tried to make it sound like a joke, but Julia knew there was truth behind the comment.

'It's certainly a very impressive guest list,' Julia commented neutrally. She'd noticed that Jon and Valerie made the majority of the decisions about who to invite, while Aimee's friends and family were relegated to the bottom of the pile.

'Ooh, these are cute,' Aimee said exclaimed, picking up a brightly coloured set of espresso cups. She was poised to scan them when her phone started to ring, and she pulled it out of her bag, making a face as she looked at the screen.

'It's Valerie. Do I have to answer it?' she wondered, reluctantly pressing the green button.

'Aimee? Aimee? Are you there?'

Even though she wasn't on speaker, Julia could clearly hear Valerie's shrill tones on the other end of the line.

'Yes, I'm here, Valerie.'

'Good. I don't have long. I managed to slip out, but I need to get back before the presentations start. Now, how are you getting on with the gift list?'

'Fine. I think we're almost done with kitchenware, so we'll move on to linen and bedding next.'

'Wonderful. Now you won't forget the Le Creuset, will you?'

'No, Valerie, I've got that already.'

'Excellent. And you've put down at least two sizes of casserole dish, haven't you?'

It was all Aimee could do not to roll her eyes. 'Yes, Valerie, I've gone for small for when it's just Jon and me, and large for when we're entertaining.'

'That sounds acceptable. And what colour Denby did you decide on?'

'I actually went for the Jet. I thought it was really unusual and—'

There was a piercing shriek from the other end of the phone; Aimee hastily pulled it away from her ear with a pained expression.

'Aimee, I specifically said Imperial Blue or Regency Green. I told you! Were you not listening to me, or are you just stupid?'

'I…' Aimee stammered, stunned by Valerie's question.

'Aimee? Aimee? Can you hear me?'

'Yes, I can hear you.' Aimee's voice was barely more than a whisper.

'Is Julia there? Put Julia on the line.'

Wordlessly, Aimee handed the phone across. 'She wants to speak to you.'

It was all Julia could do not to pull a face like Aimee had done. Bracing herself, she said breezily, 'Good afternoon, Mrs Cunningham, how are you?'

Valerie ignored the pleasantries. 'Julia, make sure Aimee doesn't get the Jet Denby. I've told her and told her. Honestly, I don't know if she's dizzy or just downright retarded.'

Julia almost dropped the phone in shock. 'Valerie, you can't say that!'

'Oh, one of the PC brigade, are you?' Valerie sniffed disapprovingly. 'Look, I've got to get back to my meeting. I'm worried that Mrs Campbell-White is going to try and make a speech, and I simply must intervene. But make sure Aimee selects a winter *and* a summer duvet, and don't forget the mattress topper.'

'Okay, Valerie, no problem.'

Julia hung up and looked worriedly at Aimee, who seemed utterly shaken.

'How about we take a break?' she suggested kindly. 'We could go and get something from the cafe, have a sit down?'

Aimee nodded mutely, allowing herself to be led away.

———

Over a shared piece of carrot cake and a pot of tea, Aimee seemed to revive.

'So how are you doing?' Julia asked gently. 'I know that getting married is an incredibly stressful time. You'd be completely unlike any other bride I've ever known if you weren't finding it difficult.'

'At least I've got you to help me,' Aimee smiled weakly. 'You're doing all the hard work, I'm doing the fun bits. Well, *supposedly* fun.'

'You must be getting excited,' Julia pressed, trying to inject some enthusiasm into her. 'There's only a few months to go until the big day, and Jon seems like a great catch.'

'He is, I guess,' Aimee said softly, remembering all the reasons why she'd fallen in love with her fiancé. He'd been charming, funny and generous, bowling her over with his zest for life, overwhelming her with the way he'd pursued her. His sheer confidence was mesmerising, his certainty that no one would refuse him anything. Now Aimee wasn't sure whether she'd mistaken that confidence for arrogance; his sexy, dominant streak hiding a more menacing need to control...

'Shame about his mother,' Aimee couldn't resist adding. She raised an eyebrow, that one gesture conveying exactly what she thought of Valerie more perfectly than words ever could.

'I think you're being very patient,' Julia replied tactfully, hiding a smile.

'She's such a nightmare!' Aimee burst out, slamming her hands down on the table so violently that her tea sloshed over into her saucer. 'I don't know how much more I can take of her, I really don't. She's so horrible to me, so rude.'

'Can you speak to Jon about it?' Julia suggested sympathetically. 'He must have noticed the way she speaks to you sometimes. Maybe he can have a word with her, ask her to tone it down a little?'

Aimee shrugged uncertainly. 'I don't know. He seems blind to everything where she's concerned. Mind you, she's the same with him. They have their mutual adoration society going on, where neither can do any wrong in the other's eyes. She's brought him up to believe he's wonderful and he thinks she's amazing in return. Sometimes I even wonder whether there's room for me.'

'Of course there is. Jon loves you, anyone can see that. Valerie will just have to learn to take a back seat.'

'Thanks, Julia,' Aimee smiled. 'Does offering life advice and motivation to the bride-to-be come as part of your package, or do we have to pay extra?'

'I'm very cheap. I can be bought for the price of half a carrot cake,' Julia joked, indicating the plate which they'd scraped clean between them. 'Seriously though, make sure you don't lose your own identity. Jon's got his business, and Valerie has all her committees and charity work. You need something of your own too.'

'A baby?' Aimee suggested ruefully.

'Only if it's right for you. You're still very young, aren't you?'

'Twenty-three.'

'Exactly. Plenty of time to build a career or travel a bit before then. What did you say, you wanted be a teacher? Well, why not? Do some research on the internet, send off for some prospectuses. What's holding you back?'

'I… um… Nothing, I suppose.' Aimee drank the last of her tea thoughtfully, wondering what Jon would say if she turned round and said she wanted to put off having kids for a couple of years. That she wanted to go and study – perhaps do her teacher training – instead. Somehow, she didn't think he'd be supportive.

'Just make sure you do whatever makes you happy,' Julia insisted. 'You only get one life. No point in wasting it.' Personally, she thought that Aimee should run as far away as she could from Jon and his overbearing mother, but it wasn't her place to say. 'Anyway,' she continued brightly, deliberately changing the mood. 'Are you ready to get back out there? Those ironing board covers aren't going to choose themselves you know.'

'And we simply *have* to make sure that stupid girl gets the *right* toilet brush holder, or else I shan't be able to sleep at night,' Aimee parodied, in a perfect imitation of Valerie, as she and Julia burst out laughing.

'Come on, let's go,' Julia grinned.

The two of them were still giggling as they walked away.

CHAPTER 24

'The first time you marry for love, the second for money, and the third for companionship'
– Jackie Kennedy

Breakfast at Gill's house was not dissimilar to feeding time at the zoo, she reflected, as she looked around the messy table at her noisy brood. It was especially true at the weekends, when she encouraged everyone to sit down together and take longer over their meal, without the need to race off to work, or school, or nursery. On Sunday mornings, Gill liked to get her whole blended family around the large table in the small kitchen, where she dished up fried eggs, bacon, beans, sausages and endless rounds of tea and toast.

Of course, it was rarely quiet or harmonious, with all of the kids trying to talk over one other and squabbles breaking out quicker than Gill or Mike could step in to quash them. But to Gill, the weekly sit-down was important, and she hoped it helped introduce a family bond that was sorely lacking at the moment.

'Have you finished with that sausage, Freddy? Then stop prodding it with your fingers and give it to me.'

Freddy dutifully got up from the table and carried his plate across to Gill, washing his sticky hands in the kitchen sink.

'Can we play football today?' he asked beseechingly, looking up at Mike.

'Not today, kiddo. The weather's too bad for that.'

Freddy stood on tiptoe to get a better look out of the window. It was raining heavily; that blustery, grey, depressing March weather that you think will never end and makes you long for summer sun and blue skies.

'How many calories in eggy bread, Mum?' Kelly asked thoughtfully, having just polished off two large pieces.

Gill shot Mike a warning look. Kelly had become increasingly interested in fat content and calories recently, her girlfriends at school apparently preoccupied with diets and 'being skinny'.

'I'm not sure, love. But it's a Sunday treat. Don't worry about it.'

'I don't want to get *fat*,' Kelly said vehemently. 'I mean, it's okay when you're your age, Mum, and you've had loads of kids.'

'Thanks, Kel,' Gill replied, her voice heavy with sarcasm.

Sammy sat quietly, drinking orange squash, while Paige finished her last piece of toast and pushed her plate away. Seeing that everyone had finished, Gill moved in to clear up and wipe down the table, drying it hastily with a tea towel.

'So we can't go outside and play in the garden?' Finlay asked despondently.

'I'm afraid not. *But*,' Gill began, her eyes sparkling. She'd anticipated the wet weather and prepared accordingly. 'I *do* have something fun for you all to do today.'

Paige looked up with interest, as Sammy cried out, 'The zoo! Are we going to the zoo?'

'No, it's not the zoo. But *this*,' she began, indicating the now clean table in front of her, 'is going to be our creative space for today.'

'Is this something *else* to do with the wedding?' Kelly sighed.

'Got it in one, Kel!' Gill hurried out of the kitchen, leaving a room full of inquisitive faces behind her. She returned a few moments later carrying a small cardboard box, and two big carrier bags. The bags were full to bursting, their plastic stretched taut and thin, offering a glimpse of the shiny, sparkly contents.

There was a collective 'Oooh' from the kids, as they sat up excitedly, craning to see what was inside. Kelly feigned disinterest, but Gill noticed that she hadn't moved from her seat, a sure sign that she was intrigued.

'Is it a present?' Sammy asked, as Gill placed the box in the centre of the table.

'Not exactly.' She tipped the carrier bags upside down, and the next moment the table was awash with ribbons, lace, tubes of glitter, coloured pens and pencils, beads and sequins, all prompting more excited cries. It was an explosion of colour and sparkle.

Freddy knelt up on his chair, reaching across the table and pulling out a piece of stiff, white card from the box. 'What's this?' he asked, holding it up.

Finlay snatched it off him, running his finger under the words as he read out loud: 'Mr Michael Marshall and Ms Gillian Skinner request the pleasure of your company to celebrate their marriage—'

'Wedding invitations,' Paige breathed, snatching the invite from Finlay.

'Hey!' he protested, trying to grab it back.

'No need to fight, there's a whole box of them there,' Gill appeased them, reaching in and passing another card to Finlay, before handing one to each of the children for them to look at. They had simple black lettering on plain white card, with no decoration or embellishment.

'Great,' Kelly deadpanned. 'Why are you showing them to us?'

'We need your help,' Mike explained, coming over from where he'd been stacking the dishwasher. '*All* of you.'

'I can help,' Finlay said eagerly. 'What do you need help with?'

Gill sat down at the table, unconsciously picking up a piece of silver ribbon and twirling it between her fingers. 'Well, we thought that as we're a pretty unique family, we needed pretty unique invitations. This is where you guys come in. I've had these invitations printed in the most basic style possible, and I think they look pretty dull right now.'

Kelly nodded her head in agreement, and Gill shot her a look.

'We want all of you to help us decorate them, that's why I've bought all this stuff,' Gill waved her arm, indicating the crafting paraphernalia in front of them. 'There're stickers, and stamps with ink pads, and a heart-shaped hole punch, and all kinds of exciting stuff. Sammy, ask someone to help you if you want to use the scissors. But other than that, you've got free rein to do whatever you want.'

Five bemused faces stared back at her.

'So we're allowed to draw on them?'

'We can put glitter on them?'

'Can we stick bows on them?'

'Yes, yes and yes,' Gill laughed. 'The only rule is no draw-ings of SpongeBob SquarePants, okay?' She looked sternly at the twins, which made them giggle uncontrollably. Both of them were obsessed with the cartoon character, and all of their schoolbooks and notepads were covered with pictures of him. Gill had been livid one day when she'd found a scribbled image of SpongeBob on the hallway wallpaper. Freddy and Finlay had both blamed each other.

'Can I be excused from this?' Kelly drawled. 'I think I'm too old for colouring in pictures of flowers – you know, now I'm not at primary school any more.'

'Yeah, I thought you might say that,' Gill began. She'd fully expected Kelly's objections – was there anything her teenage daughter *didn't* object to these days? boys and clothes seemed to be the only exceptions – and come up with a plan. 'What I really need is someone with extremely neat handwriting to address the envelopes for me. Here,' she continued, handing Kelly a gold pen and a printed list of invitees.

Kelly took them from her, reading through the names with a critical eye.

'Who's Stuart North?'

'Mike's friend from work.'

'Right,' Kelly said, in a tone Gill couldn't quite read, as she continued skimming. 'You're inviting Hayley? I thought you didn't like her?'

'Kelly, she's your godmother. Of course I like her.' Gill's body language indicated otherwise.

'But when she left her husband, you had that big argument where you said she was behaving like a tramp, and she said that you should—'

'Kelly,' Gill cut in sharply.

Kelly stared back with a practised look of innocence, her lips forming the question, 'What?'

'So can we start?' Freddy asked. He'd uncapped a red felt tip pen, and it was poised over the first invite, awaiting Gill's permission.

'Go for it,' she confirmed, grateful for the interruption.

The children were surprisingly tentative at first, as though awed by the gravity of the task they'd been given. Finlay reached for the PVA glue and a tube of silver glitter, as Sammy ripped into a packet of love heart stickers.

'I'm going to draw some doves,' Paige announced, sketching them lightly with a pencil and frowning at what she'd done.

'Haha, they look more like a dogs,' Freddy teased, leaning over to look.

'Shut up! At least I've been more imaginative than scribbling hearts all over it. Oh look, hearts, yawn,' Paige shot back, in a silly, high-pitched voice.

'I think the doves look cool,' Finlay assured her. 'Can I put some glitter on them?'

Paige eyed him suspiciously. 'As long as you're careful.'

Finlay took her warning seriously, his tongue hanging out in concentration as he oh-so-carefully added a neat line of silver sparkle along the doves' wings. After that, he appointed himself Chief Glitterer, adding a touch of sparkle to everyone's decorations.

'What does RSVP mean?' Freddy wondered, as he frowned at the writing on the card.

'It's French,' Kelly informed him, looking up from where she'd been industriously writing names and addresses on the envelopes. 'It means "please reply".'

'That's right, Kel,' Mike chimed in, adding, in a bad French accent, '*Répondez s'il vous plaît.*'

'It's Kelly,' she muttered back, but her voice lacked its usual bite.

'Reppy silly play,' Sammy repeated, making everyone laughed. Pleased with the response, he began parroting it over and over, bouncing his head in time with the words, 'Reppy silly play, reppy silly play.'

'Enough now, Sammy,' Gill groaned, putting her hands over her ears. 'Concentrate on where you're putting those stickers. And try not to put them over the actual writing, darling. Our guests need to see what time the wedding starts.'

Sammy looked down at the invitation in front of him. Realising his mistake, he tried to scratch off the offending sticker with his nails, tearing off the top layer of paper and leaving a messy streak of grey across the middle of the invite.

'Shall we put that to the bottom of the pile?' Gill smiled, tactfully handing him a fresh one from the box. 'Maybe try a new one, hmm?'

Miraculously, everyone seemed to settle down and (relatively) quietly get down to work, drawing and colouring and sticking industriously. Paige picked up the hole punch and made a line of heart-shaped holes across the top of one of the invites, weaving purple ribbon in and out then tying the ends in a bow. Sam ran riot with a flower-shaped stamp and a yellow ink pad, while Finlay wrote 'LOVE' in the border of half a dozen invites using the stencil kit he'd found.

Slowly but surely, a higgledy-piggledy pile of invitations began to build up, every one completely different. Beside them, Kelly's carefully labelled pile of envelopes ran almost as high, and when Freddy began to get fidgety, Gill gave him the job of sticking all of the postage stamps.

'Right way round, please,' Mike's voice boomed, as he peered over Freddy's shoulder to see him putting the stamps on any old how. 'You've turned the Queen upside down! How would you like it if you had to stand on your head all day, hmm? You'd probably be sick,' he chortled.

Freddy began to laugh too, kneeling up on his chair and twisting his body so that his head was hanging upside down.

'Look at me,' he squealed, chuckling even harder. 'I'm an upside down queen!'

Gill burst out laughing, shaking her head as she glanced across at Mike and they caught one another's eye. She knew they were thinking the same thing – how rare these moments of family togetherness were, and how she hoped there'd be many more to come. It was such an unusual occurrence to have everyone sitting down together, the room full of laughter and good humour, with no arguments or bad temper.

By the time the kids had finished, even the envelopes had been decorated, with doodles of wedding bells and bows and rudimentary brides and grooms. When Gill looked at the clock, she was astonished to find that the task had kept everyone occupied for the whole morning. It was now almost one o'clock, and as she glanced out of the window she noticed that the rain had blown itself out; the grey clouds had gone and the sky was brightening.

'Well as you've all worked so hard, how about a treat for lunch? Anyone fancy Al's Diner?' she suggested, naming their local American-style burger bar. There was a chorus of cheers in return.

'Can I get a hotdog?'

'Can I get a peanut butter milkshake?'

'Yes, yes, you can all have what you like – within reason. Now head upstairs and get changed. We can post these on the way,' she added, nodding at the envelopes on the table.

There was a sudden stampede as everyone rushed out of the room to get ready, feet clattering up the stairs and wardrobe doors slamming.

Gill and Mike stared around their bombsite of a kitchen, the remnants of the morning's activities scattered across the table, with pieces of lace and stray sequins on the floor, and everything covered in a fine layer of glitter.

'Well, I think that went pretty well, don't you?' Gill laughed. 'It was a genius idea.'

'And that's why you're marrying me,' Gill grinned, as she leaned in for a kiss.

CHAPTER 25

'In marriage, a man becomes slack and selfish, and
undergoes a fatty degeneration of his moral being'
*– **Robert Louis Stevenson***

'Are you okay to watch Jack today?'

It was Saturday morning, and Julia had just come racing down the stairs into the living room. She was clearly in a hurry.

'Huh?' Nick wandered through, eating a slice of toast. 'What time?'

'In about an hour. I've just had a call from Valerie, and apparently there's been some sort of crisis. She wants me over there asap.'

Nick shook his head. 'No can do. It's Jonny's birthday, remember? He's booked that five-a-side pitch, then we're all off to the pub.'

'Can't you cancel?'

Nick frowned. 'No. We've had it arranged for ages. Besides, they'll be a man down, and you can't have five-a-side with nine players. You'll just have to tell Valerie you can't go.'

'I can't do that, it looks so unprofessional.'

'It's a Saturday. She hasn't given you any notice. She's got to realise that you don't just jump when she snaps her fingers.'

'Unfortunately, Nick, yes I do. That's the industry I'm in.' Julia could feel her frustration growing. 'She's paying me a lot of money, and I need to be available to her for that.'

'So take Jack with you.'

'He's not a handbag I can shove in the corner! Believe me, Valerie is really not the kind of person who is sympathetic to childcare issues.'

'I'm sorry, but I've made plans and I can't change them.'

'I thought you wanted to spend more time with Jack,' Julia shot back. 'You said you were feeling left out – now's your time to bond.'

Nick's face fell, and Julia immediately regretted her flippant comment.

'Oh, it's going to be like that, is it? I open up to you, and you use it against me whenever I don't do what suits you? Thanks, Jules, thanks a lot.'

'I'm sorry,' Julia apologised through gritted teeth. 'I'm just feeling pretty stressed out right now, and I'd appreciate some help.'

'Well I'd love to help, but there's not a lot I can do right now. I can't exactly pull out of Jonny's birthday because I've got to babysit.'

'Newsflash Nick, when it's your child, it's not called babysitting, it's called *parenting*.'

Nick looked guilty but stuck to his guns. 'Can't you give Debbie a call, see if she's free?'

'Fine,' Julia huffed. 'Don't worry about it, I'll sort everything out as usual.' And she stormed out of the room in search of her phone.

———

As Julia pulled into Valerie's sweeping driveway later that day, she was still stewing over the spat she'd had with Nick. Fortunately, Debbie had been good enough to take Jack, and Julia had dropped him off there half an hour earlier, but Nick's dismissive attitude had really riled her. She closed the car door with a satisfying slam, hoping it might help calm her down. It didn't.

Julia jabbed sharply at the doorbell, hearing the now-familiar set of chimes sound inside the house.

A few moments later, Aimee answered, the look on her face making it clear to Julia that Valerie was driving her insane.

'Julia, you're here,' she sighed, in obvious relief. 'Come in. Valerie's just through here,' she explained through clenched teeth, her eyes flagging a warning as she led Julia along the hallway and into the ostentatious living room.

'Julia, thank God you've arrived,' Valerie burst out dramatically when she saw her, one hand flying to her chest in a gesture of relief. 'I have no idea what to do. It's going to be a disaster.'

'What is it? What's happened?' Julia asked in alarm. Had Jonathan had been struck down by some horrible illness? Maybe Aimee's dress had gone missing in transit. Or what if the venue had burnt down?

'Southwark Castle called this morning, and the chef can't source enough fresh asparagus for the starters. Some kind of national shortage apparently. Probably the immigrants aren't picking it quickly enough.'

Julia was almost blasé by now about Valerie's breathtakingly un-PC comments.

'What are we going to do?' Valerie wailed. 'I've got three hundred people expecting an asparagus starter with hollandaise sauce and a poached quail's egg, and I'm not going to be able to give it to them!'

'Did the venue suggest an alternative?' Julia asked, struggling to give Valerie's concerns the gravitas she so clearly expected.

'Stuffed mushroom,' Valerie grimaced, with a curl of her lip that implied it didn't meet her exacting standards.

'And the other choices aren't affected? So guests will have the option of the goose liver pâté, smoked chicken salad, or stuffed mushroom for a starter?'

Valerie nodded. 'It's really not good enough. I expect you to negotiate a substantial discount for this, Julia.'

'I'll see what I can do,' she replied evenly. 'So now we've got that out of the way, what was the big emergency you called me over here for?'

Valerie's forehead creased in confusion. 'What do you mean? The asparagus was the issue, the asparagus!'

'That was it?' The words were out before Julia had a chance to stop them.

'Well, I'm glad you don't seem to think there's a problem.' Valerie's tone changed completely, her voice becoming icy. 'If the unavailability of fresh asparagus spears mere weeks before a wedding for three hundred guests doesn't feature on your radar, then perhaps I misjudged your suitability for this role.'

Julia was too angry to speak. She thought of how she'd argued with Nick that morning, begged Debbie to look after Jack, rushed to get him ready before racing over here on a Saturday lunch time… and all for a shortage of asparagus.

In that moment, Julia realised that Valerie really didn't give a damn about her private life. She fully expected her to be on call 24/7 for her every need, with no consideration for any other plans Julia might have. Then again, she *was* paying a hefty fee for it, Julia reminded herself, forcing herself to count to ten before opening her mouth.

'I'm sorry, Valerie, you were right,' Julia apologised, hating herself as she said the words. 'I just… I expected something different, so I was a little thrown, but I'll get on to Southwark

Castle right away and make sure we're fully covered with other options. I'll make it clear that we expect to see their mistake reflected when we receive the final invoice.'

'Good,' Valerie said, clearly satisfied with Julia's grovelling. 'And while I've got you here…'

Julia's heart sank. She'd been hoping to turn around and go straight back out of the door, to spend the afternoon with Jack and wait for Nick to come home. She had a feeling she owed *him* an apology too.

'…I wanted to go through the running order of the day with you.' Valerie moved across to the sofa, sitting down and taking a pile of papers from the coffee table. 'Aimee, go make us a pot of tea,' she ordered, without looking up.

Aimee and Julia exchanged looks of disbelief. Aimee hesitated for a fraction of a second, as though debating whether or not to refuse Valerie's demand; she appeared to think better of it, and dutifully left the room.

'Now, between you and me,' Valerie continued, leaning in to Julia and lowering her voice. 'I have some serious concerns about Aimee's bridesmaids – not to mention that mother of hers. Oh, she's very sweet,' Valerie added hastily, as she saw Julia's incredulous expression. 'But she's rather… different, to the people Jonathan and I usually socialise with.'

Julia nodded, wondering where Valerie was going with this, but feeling increasingly uneasy.

'As tradition dictates, Aimee will be getting ready at her parents' house on the morning of the wedding, which is all very nice of course but does mean that I won't be there to oversee the proceedings. So, in my absence, Julia, I need you to be my eyes and ears.'

Julia frowned, still not understanding what exactly Valerie wanted.

'I'm sure that Aimee's bridesmaids are all lovely girls – in spite of the fat ankles and ubiquitous tattoos – but I can't help but worry that they're all going to turn up lathered in orange fake tan, with enormous eyelashes and far too much blusher. I also have grave doubts about the mother's ability to dress herself suitably and, to be frank with you, Julia, I don't want any of them lowering the tone on my son's special day.

'So if you could find the time to pop over and ensure that everyone looks… appropriate, I'd very much appreciate it. I'm sure you understand what I mean,' Valerie attempted to smile. She leaned over to touch Julia awkwardly on the arm, as though to emphasise their secret.

'I… Um… That is…' Julia's mouth flapped open and closed, with no idea of what to say. She gaped incredulously at Valerie, but was saved from answering when Aimee came back into the room, carrying a tea tray with a plate of beautifully arranged biscuits. Valerie jumped up, snatching back her hand and hastily flicking through the glossy brochure they'd received from Southwark Castle.

'Julia, your bag's vibrating,' Aimee told her, not picking up on the atmosphere between the two women.

'Thanks,' Julia smiled. She'd left her handbag over by the door and, sensing Valerie's disapproval, was about to ignore the call. But some instinct made her decide to answer it and she crossed the room, pulling out her phone. Debbie's name was flashing on the screen, and Julia instantly felt a pang of trepidation.

'And we really ought to re-think the number of candles,' Valerie was saying. 'Otherwise it'll look more like Irish wake than a wedding, and no one—'

Julia cut her off in mid-flow. 'I'm sorry, I have to take this call. It's my son's childminder.'

She hurried out of the room, hearing Valerie's shocked, 'Well!', as Julia closed the door behind her.

'Hi Debs, what's up,' she said, trying to sound nonchalant despite the fact that some sixth sense was making her incredibly nervous. She fully expected to hear Debbie's cheery tones reassuring her that everything was fine - perhaps Julia had forgotten to pack Raffy and Jack was getting grizzly, or something equally trivial. But Debbie's voice was tight with tension.

'Hey Jules, look I don't want to alarm you, but Jack doesn't seem very well. He's been sleeping since you dropped him off here, and when I went to check on him he'd got a really high temperature – thirty-nine – and a rash.'

'What?' Julia burst out. A wave of sheer terror washed over her, her mind whirling as she imagined all the horrific possibilities of what could be wrong with her baby.

'I called the out-of-hours doctor, and they advised me to bring him into A&E, just as a precaution. I don't have a baby seat, so they're going to send an ambulance. They'll be here any minute so I need to go, but can you meet me there? And can you let Nick know too?'

'Of course, yes, I'll set off straight away,' Julia told her, hanging up. For a second she couldn't think straight. Her hands were shaking, her heart thumping. All she knew was that she had to get to Jack.

She dashed back through to the living room, where Aimee and Valerie looked up in alarm at her anxious expression and wide eyes. 'I'm so sorry, but I'm going to have to leave. My son's been taken ill,' she explained hastily, picking up her bag.

'Oh no, what's wrong?' Aimee asked, clearly concerned, at the same time as Valerie said,

'Julia, children get ill all the time. They're always picking up coughs and colds. You can't simply go running after them at the first sign of a sneeze.'

For once, Julia completely ignored Valerie, speaking directly to Aimee.

'He's…' Julia stopped. Her breathing was coming fast, and there was a lump in her throat making it difficult to speak. 'He's got a temperature and a rash. The doctor's advised taking him to A&E. I'm going straight there now.'

'I'll take you,' Aimee offered, touching Julia lightly on the arm and forcing her to stand still for a moment. 'You're in no state to drive.'

'Well…' Valerie began, looking discomfited. 'This is all very—'

'Thank you,' Julia said quietly, nodding at Aimee. 'That's very kind.'

And the two women rushed out of the door, leaving Valerie alone in the enormous house.

CHAPTER 26

*'Come, let's be a comfortable couple and take care
of each other! How glad we shall be, that we have
somebody we are fond of always, to talk to and sit with'*
– Charles Dickens

Julia rushed into the children's ward, where the A&E receptionist had sent her. She'd had an agonising journey to the hospital, the worst things rushing through her mind, as Aimee drove quickly yet safely through the Saturday afternoon traffic.

'He'll be fine,' Aimee kept telling her calmly.

But Julia didn't reply, staring out of the window and digging her nails into her palm so tightly she almost broke the skin. She'd already called Nick, and he was on his way to the hospital too – they'd meet each other there. She couldn't help but think of the row they'd had this morning, and how they'd parted on bad terms. Now their silly squabble seemed insignificant; the most important thing in the world was that Jack was okay.

'I'm Jack Crawford's mother,' Julia told the paediatric receptionist breathlessly. 'He was brought in by Debbie Barlow.'

The receptionist tapped nonchalantly into her computer, not seeming to appreciate Julia's urgency. 'Yes, he's in examination room three, down the corridor and to the left, the third door along.'

Julia barely waited for her to finish the sentence before she was off and running, with only the vaguest notion of where she was going.

She ground to a halt as she spotted a door marked '3', and she knocked softly, hardly able to stop herself from running straight in.

She heard a movement from inside the room, then the door clicked and Debbie was standing there.

'Julia!'

'Debbie, how is he? What's going on?'

Julia flew into the room, barrelling towards her son who was currently asleep, a drip in the back of his hand. Tears were running freely down her cheeks as she knelt beside him and stroked his forehead, her hands brushing over the baby-soft hair on his head. He looked so tiny and vulnerable in the hospital cot-bed; all she wanted to do was pick him up and hold him to her, but she knew it was impossible.

'What have they said?' she asked, turning away for the first time to look at Debbie.

Debbie's face was grave but calm as she recited the news. 'The doctor's just examined him and he'll be back shortly. They've run some tests, but he did say that he didn't think it was anything serious. We have to wait for the test results to confirm it, but the doctor seemed fairly confident that it wasn't anything major.'

Julia visibly relaxed at this. 'Oh, thank God.' She let her head drop forward, closing her eyes for a second as she took in the news.

Debbie plucked a tissue from the box at the side of the bed. 'Here.'

'Thanks,' Julia said gratefully, wiping her eyes. 'And thank you so much for… everything.' She gestured around her, her voice choked with emotion.

Debbie knew exactly what she meant. 'Don't be ridiculous. Anyone would have done the same thing.' She stepped forward, placing a hand on Julia's shoulder. 'He'll be okay, Jules, I'm sure of it.'

Julia nodded, acknowledging her comment. 'Did the doctor say how long he'd be?'

Debbie shook her head. 'He just said he'd be back as soon as he could. I told him you were on your way.'

'Thanks.'

'What about Nick? Did you manage to get hold of him?'

'Yeah, he should be here any moment. Actually, I'll try and call him now then he can come straight to the right ward.'

Julia stood up from where she'd been crouching beside the bed, taking her hand away from Jack for the first time as she pulled her phone out of her bag. Three missed calls from Nick.

'Would you mind calling him back?' she asked shakily, passing the phone to Debbie. 'I'm in such a state I can't think straight.'

'Sure, no problem,' Debbie agreed. She'd just hit the button to dial Nick's number when there was a sharp rap on the door. Debbie moved to open it and Nick burst in, his face ashen.

'How is he?' he demanded, moving straight to the bed, glancing anxiously between Jack and Julia as he waited for answers.

'Debbie's spoken to the doctor, and he doesn't think it's anything serious. He's run some tests, and he'll be back shortly. That's all we know right now. I only got here a few minutes before you.'

Nick sank down onto a plastic chair by the bed, his head in his hands.

'I should have been there,' he murmured, distraught. 'I should have been looking after him. How selfish was I, insisting on going to play football? What was I thinking?'

'Ssh, it doesn't matter,' Julia insisted, rubbing his back where he was hunched over. 'You didn't know this was going to happen. And Debbie did absolutely the right thing. It was probably even better that he was with her, as she's got her medical training from the nursery. She knows what to look out for in children.'

But Nick was still shaking his head. 'If something happens to him, I'll never forgive myself.'

Julia was facing the exact same fears and guilt herself. What if she'd just said no to Valerie? Told her that family was more important than work on a weekend? But Nick clearly felt even worse than she did, and focusing on him served as a welcome distraction.

Julia crouched down in front of her husband, taking hold of his hand. 'He's going to be fine, I'm sure of it. He's a tough little cookie, just like his dad.'

Nick had his eyes closed, pinching the brow of his nose. He looked utterly beaten.

Then the door opened and Julia jumped to her feet, all three of them looking urgently at the doctor who'd just walked in. He was a tall, tired-looking, middle-aged man, wearing a grey shirt with the sleeves rolled up, and suit trousers. His name tag read: 'Dr Neil Clarke'.

'I'm Julia Crawford, Jack's mother,' she said instantly. 'Is he okay?'

Dr Clarke paused, and in that instant Julia was certain that her heart stopped for a second. She was suspended on a precipice, about to be lifted up or crash to the ground.

'He's going to be fine,' the doctor said.

Nick exhaled loudly and Julia burst into tears, all the pent-up emotions spilling out.

'What happened? What was wrong with him?'

'Jack appears to have a viral infection, but obviously we've taken a blood sample and tested for inflammation, as we wanted to rule out anything more serious like meningitis or pneumonia. We've put him on a drip to stop him getting dehydrated, and given him a very mild dose of liquid paracetamol, to reduce the fever. He's sleeping for now, and I'd advise letting him get as much rest as possible. You'll need to keep a close eye on him for the next few days, but there's no reason why he shouldn't make a full recovery.'

'Oh, thank you so much,' Julia sobbed, trying to get a hold of herself. This last hour had been a real rollercoaster of emotions, and now it was overwhelming relief that swept through her. Nick pulled her to him, hushing her, and Julia clung to him.

'Jules, I'm going to head off now,' Debbie murmured, clearly feeling that she was intruding on the family moment. 'Give me a call later, let me know how he's getting on.'

'Of course. Of course I will,' Julia sniffed. 'Honestly Debbie, I can't thank you enough.'

Debbie shrugged modestly. 'Don't worry about it. As long as he's okay, that's all that matters. Bye Jack,' she whispered, waggling her fingers in his direction. 'Get better soon. See you, Nick.'

'Thanks for everything, Debbie,' Nick said, and she could see the strain of the day etched on his face.

'I'll be back shortly to check on him,' Dr Clarke explained, before leaving the room, Debbie following behind him and quietly closing the door.

Julia leaned down to Jack, taking his tiny hand in hers.

'I don't know what to do, Nick,' she said, gazing pleadingly at her husband. 'What can I do to make him better?' She felt horrifyingly impotent, unable to do anything for her son, when her first instinct was to make whatever was hurting him go away.

'You heard what the doctor said,' Nick reassured her. 'He's going to be fine. We just need to be here for him.'

Julia took a seat on one side of the cot, as Nick sat down on the other, both of them leaning across to stroke Jack's cheek, smooth his hair, hold his hand, as he snuffled and wriggled in his sleep. Outside in the corridor, they could hear footsteps as people passed by, doors slamming shut, nurses shouting. Inside in the room it felt curiously quiet, with nothing but the sound of their breathing, and the regular bleep from the machine that monitored Jack's heart rate.

Julia took a deep breath. 'I wanted to apologise,' she said to Nick. 'For this morning. I don't know what I was even thinking. I should have told Valerie to shove her stupid demands. Do you know what she got me there for? What her so-called "emergency" actually was?' Julia laughed in disbelief. 'The venue couldn't offer the asparagus starter any more, and she needed to have stuffed mushrooms instead.'

Nick shook his head. 'She's crazy. Seriously, Jules, from everything you've told me, that woman is Looney-tunes.'

'I know. Aimee was so sweet – she actually gave me a lift here. We'll need to pick up my car from their house – but I'm *this close*,' Julia held up her thumb and forefinger, an inch of space between them, 'to telling Valerie to just sod off. If it wasn't for Aimee, I'd have resigned from this job weeks ago.'

'Stick with it,' Nick insisted. 'You've put so much hard work into that wedding, and in a matter of weeks it'll all be over. Today was just… really unfortunate. And there's nothing to apologise for. I'm the one who should be apologising. I've been going over and over it in my mind. The whole drive to the hospital,

I couldn't stop thinking that if anything happened to Jack, it would all be my fault.'

Nick leaned in closer to his son, giving his hand a little squeeze, trying to hide the fact that he was welling up once again.

'No, it wouldn't,' Julia insisted. 'Neither of us could have predicted this.'

'But I should have been there. You were right – your job's important and I should have supported you, instead of insisting on going to Jonny's.'

'We'll drive ourselves mad if we keep going on like this, Nick. We can't—'

'I *have* to,' he interrupted. There were things he'd been meaning to say for a while, and now was the time to get everything off his chest. 'I just… You were absolutely right with what you said before. When we had that talk in the Lake District, and you were worried that Jack and I weren't bonding. And it's true. I've really struggled, and I don't know why. But today, ever since you rang, I've literally felt as though a piece of my heart had shattered. There was this huge, gaping hole inside me, and I knew I would have given anything – *anything* – for Jack to be okay again.'

For the first time, Julia let go of Jack's hand and reached across to take Nick's. She didn't speak; she knew it was important to let him talk.

'And now I feel like I've been given a second chance. I absolutely need to make up for lost time, with both of you. I'm so proud that I have a son, and a beautiful wife, and right now I feel like the luckiest man alive.'

For the longest time, the two of them sat in silence, holding hands as they stared down at their son, both lost in their own thoughts. Julia's thumb brushed over her husband's knuckles, rubbing back and forth in a soothing gesture. It was enough; there was nothing that needed to be said.

Then Jack coughed, and both of them sat bolt upright, looking at him in concern. Jack wriggled again, pushing his fists over his head until Julia became alarmed that he'd pull out the drip, and she reached down to gently guide his hands back to his sides. He fell still for a moment, before letting out a little cry. Julia looked at Nick in alarm, but the next moment Jack was opening his eyes, screwing up his face and blinking in confusion.

He looked straight at Julia, then said the word, 'Mama.'

Julia burst into fresh tears, relief and happiness flooding through her, as Nick came round to her side of the cot and the two of them held each other tightly, finally believing that their ordeal was over and Jack was going to be just fine.

CHAPTER 27

'Marriage is like a game of chess except the board is flowing water, the pieces are made of smoke and no move you make will have any effect on the outcome'
– Jerry Seinfeld

Aimee couldn't stay still. She would sit down on the sofa, flick through a magazine, then jump up and move across to the sideboard, making tiny adjustments to the angle of the photo frames, before starting the whole process all over again. She looked up at the oversized clock on the wall, realising that mere minutes had passed since she'd last checked it, and wondering when Jon would be coming home. Surely it couldn't be long now?

Aimee glanced across at the pile of prospectuses on the coffee table, and felt a fresh pang of nerves clutch at her stomach. Her laptop was turned on, the internet open on Norwich University's home page, and Aimee had decided that tonight was the night she was going to have a serious talk with Jon about her teaching ambitions.

She'd been inspired by the chat she'd had with Julia while they were shopping for the gift list, and knew that she couldn't put off the conversation any longer. For the last few weeks, Aimee had been requesting details for various courses, keeping the paperwork in a secret stash at the bottom of her wardrobe where Jon wouldn't find it.

From her investigations, she'd discovered that she could do a three-year English degree, with the teaching qualification forming part of the curriculum. The new term started in September, and the wedding and honeymoon would be over by then, so the timing was perfect. Plus Aimee needed to know that there would be *something* for her to look forward to in the future; something keep her busy while Jon was at work. There were days when she went stir-crazy sitting around in the claustrophobic apartment, trying to keep herself occupied.

Mostly, she needed to be sure that she had Jon's support if she was going to do this, and that was potentially the trickiest part of all.

Aimee exhaled slowly, then walked across to the enormous American-style fridge to pour herself a glass of wine. Jon's apartment was completely open-plan, with the kitchen, living and dining rooms all merging into one. It still looked like the classic bachelor pad, decorated in dark wood and shiny chrome, like something James Bond might choose. Aimee hadn't really made her mark on it yet; she still couldn't help thinking of the flat as 'Jon's' and not 'theirs'.

She'd just taken a sip of the deliciously chilled white wine when she heard the key turn in the lock. Aimee jumped, almost spilling her drink, then told herself not to be so silly.

Jon swept in through the door looking incredibly handsome, and Aimee felt her heart skip a beat. His tie was off, his shirt undone, and he looked gorgeous in a smart navy suit, all dark hair and white teeth and great bone structure.

'Hello, darling.' Jon strode across the room and kissed her. 'You look positively edible.'

Aimee giggled, as he pretended to bite her neck. She was wearing a clinging dress in a flattering shade of royal blue, and she knew he'd love it.

'Mmm, white wine, excellent plan,' Jon grinned. 'Could you pour me a glass? I'm just going to grab a shower and then I'm all yours.'

Relief flooded through Aimee. She loved it when Jon was like this; playful and good-tempered. She could never predict what mood he was going to be in when he came through the door.

'Good day?' she ventured.

A flicker of dark cloud crossed Jon's brow. 'It was okay. This idiot of a supplier completely messed up. He…' There was a flash of anger, then Jon seemed to collect himself. 'Anyway, I won't bore you with that. Besides, I have a surprise for you tonight.'

'A surprise?' Aimee repeated, handing him his glass of wine.

'The Sancerre? Good choice,' Jon praised her, as he took a long swallow.

'So what's the surprise?' Aimee pressed excitedly, unable to help herself.

'I can't tell you,' Jon winked. 'Otherwise it wouldn't be a surprise.'

'Is it to do with the wedding?'

'Might be. Look, let me jump in the shower quickly, and then all will be revealed.'

'Okay.' Aimee caught sight of the brochures sitting on the table and immediately felt nervous. Jon hadn't noticed them yet, and she thought about chickening out altogether – about simply tidying them away and never mentioning the subject.

'There's something I'd like to talk to you about later too,' she blurted out, before she had time to change her mind.

'Great,' Jon swept past, planting a kiss on her head. 'I'll be out soon.'

He disappeared into the bedroom, and Aimee sat down nervously on the sofa, scrolling through the university website. It was full of pictures of young people, just like her, looking earnest in a lecture theatre, or laughing as they sat around in the park with friends, textbooks spread open on the grass around them. That was what she wanted for herself, Aimee realised, with a sudden pang of longing.

True to his word, Jon was back a few minutes later, freshly showered and smelling of expensive aftershave. Aimee was surprised to see him dressed in jeans and a fitted Ralph Lauren sweater, rather than the lounge pants and T-shirt he usually wore round the house.

'Are you ready?' he asked with a grin.

'Ready?'

'To go. My surprise.'

'Oh, I didn't realise it was…' Aimee jumped to her feet, flustered. 'Of course, let me just get my things and… Do I need anything?'

'Just yourself.'

'Great.' Aimee grabbed her bag, noticing the prospectuses. She bit her lip anxiously. 'That thing I wanted to talk to you about—'

'Can we do it on the way?' Jon interrupted. 'I don't want us to be late.'

'Sure,' Aimee agreed, ashamed to admit that she felt relieved, as she closed her laptop and picked up her coat. She followed Jon out to the car and soon they were speeding through the streets, cutting smoothly through the early evening commuter traffic.

'So where are we going?' Aimee asked, excited in spite of herself. She was pleased to note that they were heading in the opposite direction to Valerie's house, so whatever it was, Jonathan's mother wasn't involved.

'You'll see.' Jon's eyes were sparkling. He reached over to rest a hand on her knee, softly stroking her thigh. 'So what was it you wanted to talk to me about?'

'Oh, um…' Aimee hesitated, not really sure if this was the right time or the right setting. It certainly wasn't how she'd imagined having this discussion. 'Well, you know I'd mentioned before about maybe, possibly, doing a teacher training course? Nothing definite, just an idea…'

Jon's hands tightened almost imperceptibly on the steering wheel, and he said nothing. Aimee pressed on, the words tumbling out before she lost her nerve.

'I've been looking online. I actually sent off for some prospectuses, and it turns out that I could do my degree alongside a teaching qualification. It would take three years, so that's quite a long time, but I'm sure it would fly by, and then I'd have so many more options open to me. I could go to university here in Norwich, so I wouldn't need to move away or anything, and term starts in September so well after the wedding. But I'd need to apply quite soon if I wanted to start this year, so…'

She trailed off, leaving the thought open, hoping Jon would jump in and offer his support and agreement.

Instead, there was a long silence. So long, in fact, that Aimee began to wonder whether she'd imagined the last few minutes and never actually said the words at all.

Jon's eyes were focused on the road, his jaw tense. Aimee opened her mouth to say something – anything – to break the uncomfortable silence, but then he finally spoke:

'Aimee, I want you to drop this subject right now.' Jon's voice was low and carefully controlled.

'But Jon, I—'

'I said *no*, Aimee.' Jon yelled so hard that Aimee jumped in fright. 'I don't want to discuss this. Not tonight, not tomorrow night, not *ever*.'

'S-sorry,' Aimee stuttered, her heart racing. She didn't think she'd ever seen him so angry.

'You can be so ungrateful sometimes, you know that?'

Aimee blinked in astonishment.

'I've gone to a lot of trouble to plan this surprise for you, but did you even consider that, hmm? No. No, you didn't. I just don't understand you sometimes, Aimee. Did you intentionally want to ruin tonight for me?'

'N-no. No, of course not. I just—'

'You just what?' Jon spat back, his voice like ice.

Aimee swallowed. 'Nothing,' she said quietly. She bowed her head, her hands clasped in her lap, wondering how this had all gone so badly wrong. Jon was right, she realised. This was completely the wrong moment to bring up the subject of her studying. He'd been so excited about the surprise he'd organised, and she'd spoilt everything, wittering on about herself.

'Sorry,' she repeated.

Jon said nothing, and they didn't speak until they pulled into the car park on the outskirts of town. He turned off the engine and exhaled loudly, turning to Aimee and taking her hands in his.

'You get me so riled up sometimes, you know that? You get to me like no one else does. I was so looking forward to tonight, to arranging this for you, and then I felt as though you weren't interested, that you didn't appreciate what I'd done.'

'I know, I know, it was totally thoughtless of me,' Aimee agreed, hugely relieved that he didn't seem to be angry any more. 'I really am sorry.'

Jon leaned across, kissing her softly. 'I love you so much, Aimee, you know that don't you?'

Aimee nodded, kissing him back gratefully.

'So do you want to see your surprise?'

Aimee nodded again, looking at her surroundings more closely. They were facing a one-storey, whitewashed building, with small, high windows and peeling paint. It looked pretty run-down, if Aimee was being entirely honest. She couldn't imagine what on earth could be inside.

'Where are we?' she wondered.

'You'll see.'

They held hands as they walked towards the building together. Jon pushed open the door, leading Aimee through into a narrow corridor, with noticeboards on the wall and a small changing area off to one side. From somewhere in the building, Aimee could hear music playing. She frowned at Jon, but he simply smiled back. He walked confidently to wherever they were going, and it was clear he'd been here before.

As they passed through a set of double doors, Jon stopped, indicating that Aimee should go ahead. She stepped into a large, empty room, with a sleek wooden floor. Mirrors ran along the full length of one side, with a barre attached at waist height. It looked like a dance studio.

'Hi, you must be Aimee.'

She jumped as the man approached; she hadn't noticed him in the corner. He was wearing black sweatpants and a tight black T-shirt, and he smiled as he shook hands with her.

'I'm Alex. Good to see you again, Jon,' he added, turning to her fiancé.

'I still don't understand what's happening,' Aimee confessed.

Jon simply grinned, as he took her in his arms and began swaying her in time to the music. As it reached the chorus, Aimee suddenly recognised the song – 'It Had to Be You', by Frank Sinatra.

'Welcome to your first dance, Mrs Cunningham,' Jon murmured in her ear, as they moved across the floor. 'I thought it might help to get a little professional training in first.'

'Really?' Aimee squealed. 'This is our first dance?'

'Yes, darling,' Jon nodded, delighted by her enthusiasm. 'It's what you wanted, isn't it?'

'It's absolutely perfect,' Aimee beamed, squeezing him tightly. She'd dreamed of having this song for her first dance; it meant so much to her. Her father was a huge Frank Sinatra fan, and she'd grown up watching him and Pauline dance around the living room to Frank's crooning. Incredibly, it had been playing in the hotel bar on her first date with Jonathan, which Aimee had seen as a positive omen.

'So, no "Blue Danube"?' she added tentatively, gazing up at him. That had been Valerie's preference for their first dance, and Aimee had been terrified that she was going to insist upon the classical piece.

'No, of course not,' Jon confirmed. 'It's our wedding day, right? Mother understands that. We've got to do whatever makes *us* happy.'

Aimee felt giddy with delight right then, as he said the words she'd been longing to hear. It was *their* wedding, and *they* were calling the shots – not Valerie. Jonathan had just confirmed it.

And it was so romantic and thoughtful of him to organise this dance lesson, Aimee thought dreamily, as Alex got to work, guiding them round the dance floor. When Jon fumbled his steps, he laughed as though he didn't have a care in the world.

Aimee adored him when he was like this – fun, caring, spontaneous. It reminded her why she'd fallen in love with him, and right now she felt like the luckiest girl in the world.

Alex showed them a basic routine, incorporating a few flourishes that they would never have managed on their own. They messed up frequently, giggling like naughty children when they got it wrong, but out of the mistakes a solid routine was slowly emerging.

'Excellent, beautiful,' Alex called out, as they finally managed a tricky reverse pivot, pulling it off with flair.

'I'd forgotten what a good dancer you are,' Aimee grinned up at Jon, her eyes sparkling naughtily. They'd gone clubbing a lot in the early days of their relationship, back when everything was casual and carefree. Lately, since he'd taken over the business, Jon never seemed to have the time or the energy.

'The horizontal tango is my speciality,' he winked, raising his eyebrows flirtatiously as Aimee burst out laughing.

He span her around and she giggled delightedly, the steps coming far more naturally than they had half an hour ago. Aimee imagined them dancing like this on their wedding day, with all their friends and family watching, celebrating the special occasion. For the first time in a long time, she felt genuinely happy, able to put all of the doubts and worries out of her mind and simply look forward to becoming Mrs Jon Cunningham.

CHAPTER 28

'Of course, I do have a slight advantage over the rest of you. It helps in a pinch to be able to remind your bride that you gave up a throne for her' – **Edward VIII**

It was morning playtime at Two Trees Nursery. The May sunshine streamed in through the windows, as the children pulled out trucks and dollhouses and teddy bears, some sitting down on the floor to carefully to do a jigsaw, whilst others raced around playing a giddy game of make believe.

Debbie and Angela kept a careful eye on their charges, occasionally intervening in a dispute over who'd picked up the racing car first, or stepping in to help one of the toddlers find the right piece for the shape-sorter.

'Are you okay?' Angela asked, as Debbie listlessly scooped up some discarded Stickle Bricks and dropped them in their tub.

Debbie shrugged. 'I'm just feeling a bit down.'

'Why? It's almost the weekend, and you're getting married in less than a month. You should be walking on air.'

'Yeah, I know.'

'You and Stevie haven't had another row, have you?' Angela looked at Debbie's left hand, then gasped in shock. 'You're not wearing your engagement ring!'

'Don't panic, I'm getting it re-sized, that's all. I've lost so much weight that it's too loose now.'

'Oh, I see. So everything's okay with you two?'

Debbie managed a smile. 'Yeah, Stevie's been great. We're finally over all that stupid texting business.'

She thought back to the rollercoaster of emotions they'd been through over the last couple of weeks; how a still-furious Stevie had given her the silent treatment when she'd returned from her spa day with Julia and Angela, much to her frustration. When he'd finally started to thaw, Debbie had picked an argument over his lack of trust in her, and the row had started all over again.

But Debbie's frightening experience with baby Jack had thrown everything into sharp relief, and their silly argument had been forgotten, with Stevie back to his usual, caring, supportive self. The following evening, when Stevie returned home with an enormous bouquet of red roses and a hangdog expression, they'd made up in the best way possible…

'Then what's the matter?' Angela pressed, not noticing how Debbie's cheeks flushed at the memory. 'I hate seeing you like this. You're usually so full of life.'

'Are you sure you're not getting me confused with someone else?' Debbie joked lamely. But Angela didn't laugh, staring intently at Debbie in an attempt to make her crack. It worked. 'Okay, I'm feeling pretty rubbish because I haven't hit my target weight,' Debbie sighed heavily. 'I've got this last half stone to shift, and nothing seems to be working.'

'Debs, you don't *need* to lose any more weight. You're literally half the woman you used to be. You've done incredibly well, and you look amazing.'

But Debbie wasn't listening. 'I just don't know what else to do,' she wailed. 'I've been exercising every day, and all I've been eating is homemade vegetable juice and quinoa salad, but nothing seems to work!'

'Vegetable juice and quinoa?' Angela shuddered. 'I'm not surprised your body's protesting. Seriously, Debs, you don't want to go too far. It's becoming an obsession.'

'You don't understand,' Debbie insisted. 'I've got my final dress fitting next week, and I'm desperate to be a size ten. That's what I've dreamed about, ever since I started this weight loss thing months ago. I'm so close and I'm going to fail. There's no way I can lose half a stone by then.'

'You are *not* a failure,' Angela insisted. 'So what if you're a few pounds off your target weight? You've already lost almost four stone.'

'The thing is – hang on…' Debbie stepped away for a moment, helping Sammy to put together sections of the train track he was playing with. When she came back over, Angela noticed her guilty expression.

'What? What were you going to say?'

'There's another reason I wanted to get to a size ten. Something I haven't told you.'

'What?' Angela demanded, clearly intrigued.

'You remember months ago, when I first started my diet, and you suggested I should have some kind of reward system. Treat myself every time I lost half a stone.'

Angela nodded. 'Yeah – we went to get pedicures, and you bought that gorgeous dress from River Island.'

'Which is now too big for me,' Debbie interjected.

Angela raised her eyebrows in an *I told you so* gesture.

'Well there was one other thing I planned to do when I reached my target weight.' Debbie hesitated, steeling herself for the big confession. 'I decided to—'

The door opened and Julia burst in, carrying Jack in her arms. As soon as he saw the other children, he strained to get away from her, so she stood him down on the floor where he swayed uncertainly for a moment before plopping onto all fours and crawling across the play area to join a group of kids playing with a toy kitchen.

'Oh, he's so nearly walking,' Angela squealed.

'Yeah, I know. He'll walk if you hold his hands, or if there's furniture to grab onto, but he hasn't quite got the confidence to do it by himself. He keeps going back to hands and knees,' Julia said ruefully, watching him hold onto the edge of the kitchen unit to haul himself upright.

'He'll get there,' Angela asserted confidently. 'They always do. Looks like he might have ambitions to be a chef too,' she chuckled, as he grabbed a saucepan and placed a plastic banana inside, stirring it with a wooden spoon.

'You can tell he gets his cooking skills from me,' Julia joked. 'I really have to stop feeding him boiled bananas for tea.'

'So is he okay now?' Angela asked in concern. 'Debbie told me what happened.'

'Seems to be,' Julia said, as she watched him playing. 'Fighting fit and raring to go. It was pretty scary though. I've genuinely never experienced terror like that. It was horrible. But the hospital staff were absolutely brilliant – as was Debbie,' she grinned at her.

Debbie shrugged modestly. 'Anyone would have done the same.'

'Maybe not,' Julia disagreed. 'I honestly couldn't have left him in better hands. Nick and I can't thank you enough.'

'How long is Jack with us for today?' Angela asked.

'I'll be back for him about four. Obviously I don't want to let him out of my sight after everything that happened, but life goes on, I suppose. The big wedding I'm doing is just a few weeks away now and there's so much left to do. It doesn't help that the groom's mother keeps changing her mind every few minutes about what she wants.'

'The groom's mother? Isn't it supposed to be the bride?'

'You'd think so, wouldn't you? The bride's lovely, but she's barely getting a say in her own wedding. Ooh, that reminds me, I need to speak to you later, Debs, about the flower arrangements for the church.'

'Sure,' Debbie nodded.

Julia stared at her for a moment. 'Is everything okay?'

'Oh, don't even go there,' Angela groaned. 'Debbie's on a downer because she hasn't lost enough weight.'

Julia's expression was incredulous. 'Debbie, you're tiny! You're smaller than me now.'

'Yeah, but she's not a size ten,' Angela cut in sarcastically. 'And that's the Holy Grail, apparently.'

'It's not that, it's… Oh, never mind,' Debbie's tone was defensive.

'What were you going to say, anyway?' Angela remembered. 'This special thing that you can *only* be a size ten for.'

Debbie gave her a withering look. 'It's all right for you. You've always been a skinny minny.'

'Stop avoiding the question,' Angela shot back.

Julia leaned in, sensing gossip. 'Ooh, tell me too!'

Debbie's gaze darted between the two women, wondering whether there was any way she could get out of telling them her plan. She realised that there wasn't – Angela was never going to let this drop – so she took a deep breath, gearing up for the big confession.

'Okay, so I decided that when I finally got down to a Perfect Ten I was going to…' She lowered her voice to a whisper, conscious of the children nearby. 'That I was going to do a sexy photo shoot for Stevie. You know, all dressed up in lingerie, with gorgeous hair and make-up, so I could do some naughty pictures. Nothing too outrageous, obviously,' she added hastily. 'I'd be keeping it classy. But the idea was to give him the photos as a wedding present. That's why I've booked tomorrow off work.'

Both Julia and Angela gasped. 'Debs, that's an incredible idea!'

'You *have* to do it.'

'How can I do it when I look like *this*?' Debbie protested. 'When I planned it, the idea was that I'd be a slim and sexy size ten, not dumpy and squidgy, with these flabby love handles and chunky thighs that won't seem to get any slimmer.' She jabbed at them in frustration.

'Are you serious?' Julia burst out.

'I think you've got that body dysmorpha-whatsit,' Angela added. 'Honestly, there's not an ounce of squidge on you, Debs. You're so toned from all that exercise you've been doing, but you've still got these massive boobs and curves in all the right places that'll look incredible in the photos. Seriously, Stevie won't know what's hit him.'

'He'll *love* it,' Julia added. 'What man wouldn't?'

But Debbie wasn't convinced. 'I've decided to cancel it,' she insisted. 'I'm gutted, but there's no way I can go through with it if I'm feeling like this. I just don't have the confidence.'

'No, you can't cancel!'

'Do you want one of us to come with you?'

Debbie shook her head fiercely. 'No. I don't want anyone seeing me when I look like this.'

She bent down to help Luke tie his shoelace, and Julia and Angela conferred in hurried whispers.

'We've got to make sure she does it.'

'We can't let her back out.'

Julia looked at her watch anxiously. 'I really need to get going, but whatever you do don't let her cancel. She'll regret it if she does.'

'I won't. Even if I have to kidnap her and drive her there myself, I'll do it.' Angela started laughing. 'Can you imagine me trying to wrestle her into a push-up bra and stockings while she's trying to fight me off?'

'Now *that* would make a funny photo shoot,' Julia giggled. 'I'll see you later, okay Debbie?' Julia called across. 'And promise me you won't cancel.'

Debbie muttered something unintelligible as Julia said bye to Angela and headed out of the door.

Angela was called away to help Mia go to the toilet, and then it was snack time for everyone. It wasn't until the children were occupied with their activity later that morning , and Debbie and Angela could go on their break, that they finally got chance to talk.

'You know you really should do the photo shoot,' Angela insisted. The two women were sitting in the kitchen, where Angela was tucking into a KitKat whilst Debbie was nibbling at an apple. 'You have to. I think you'll regret it if you don't.'

'I'll see,' Debbie offered. 'I suppose I can always go for the shoot and if the pictures look awful, I never have to tell Stevie about them.'

'They won't though,' Angela smiled. 'Seriously Debbie, I don't think you've realised how much you've blossomed. You need to appreciate how far you've come, instead of beating yourself up about the last little bit.'

'Thanks, Ang,' Debbie smiled warmly at her friend. 'I think it's all the wedding stress. Everything's so close now, and I want it to be perfect.'

'It will be, because you're marrying Stevie and that's all that matters. No one cares if the napkins aren't folded into swans, or if you've got cava instead of champagne. We all want to see you happy. Both of you.'

'You'd better stop soon or else I think I might cry,' Debbie sniffed, half-laughing at the same time.

'And I need you to do me one other favour.'

Debbie looked at her suspiciously. 'What?'

'Eat a stick of this KitKat. It's not going to kill you.' Angela held it out tantalisingly.

Debbie stared at it, feeling unexpectedly nervous. It was like facing down an enemy she'd been avoiding for months and now the confrontation was finally happening. She experienced a stab of panic, convinced that if she gave in and ate the chocolate, it would instantly undo all her hard work over the past few months, the fat suddenly bubbling up and splurging out over the top of her size twelve jeans.

'Ange, I—'

'EAT. ME,' Angela demanded, putting on Dalek-type voice as she jabbed the chocolate in Debbie's direction.

In spite of everything, Debbie started to giggle. She suddenly realised how ridiculously she was behaving, and that everything Angela and Julia had said to her was true. She'd done incredibly well, she'd lost nearly four stone, and she looked and felt like a different woman.

'Give it here,' she chuckled, grabbing the KitKat from Angela and biting it in half. 'You know what? I bloody deserve it!'

CHAPTER 29

*'When a man opens a car door for his wife it's either
a new car or a new wife'*
– Prince Philip, Duke of Edinburgh

'Jon, they're my best friends! You can't just stick them at the back of the reception like naughty children.'

'Oh, so you want me to stick the MD of Maison Furniture there instead, where he'll feel incredibly unimportant and probably won't renew his contract with us? If they were your true friends, they'd understand the reasons for this.'

'*I* don't understand the reasons, so how can you expect my friends to?'

Jon's eyes blazed in fury as he gripped the steering wheel tightly, the sleek white Porsche hurtling along the country lanes at a speed that terrified Aimee.

'I've explained to you before, Mother and I have a lot of very influential people coming to this wedding. It's a great opportunity for me to make some new contacts and consolidate existing ones.'

'It's our *wedding*, not a networking event,' Aimee yelled in exasperation. She was close to crying now, her face flushed with annoyance.

'It's my business that keeps a roof over our heads, and pays for all those nice trinkets you love. I didn't see you complaining last week when I took you to The Fat Goose for a surprise dinner, or when I bought you that Coach handbag you'd been eyeing up for ages.'

It was a low blow, and one that only increased the lump in Aimee's throat. *I don't love the material things, I love* you, she wanted to retort. But for some reason the words wouldn't come.

'Your contacts might be important to you, but my friends are important to *me*,' Aimee told him. Her voice cracked on the final word, tears finally spilling over and racing down her cheeks, ruining the make-up she'd so carefully applied that morning.

Jon glanced across at her and rolled his eyes. Instead of being moved by her tears, he seemed irritated instead.

'Oh, not the waterworks again. That's all you seem to do at the moment. You can't get your own way just by crying all the time you know.'

'I'm crying because I'm *upset*,' Aimee shot back furiously, astounded by his coldness. 'I can't believe you'd bring up the seating plan again, today, of all days. My make-up's ruined now…'

They were still rowing as they pulled into the driveway of Southwark Castle, the magnificent location they'd chosen as their wedding venue, and the location for today's pre-wedding photo shoot.

Jon killed the engine, and the two of them sat without speaking, the only sound being little snuffles from Aimee as she tried to stop the tears. Jon was grinding his teeth, his jaw working furiously, in a clear sign that he was angry.

Ever the peacemaker, Aimee leant towards him, placing a hand on his knee. 'Jon—'

'Don't,' he hissed, his face contorted with rage. 'I don't know if you realise how angry you get me, Aimee.' He slammed his hands against the steering wheel using the full force of his body weight, and Aimee jumped in shock.

When he finally turned to her, Jon seemed to have regained control of himself, but his voice was like ice. 'We need to go now. Katherine will be waiting for us. Please try to conduct yourself with some dignity, and don't you dare do anything to embarrass me.'

Meekly, Aimee climbed out of the Porsche, following behind Jon as he strode across the car park to the glorious stately home. His strides were long, and Aimee had to hurry to keep up.

They walked up the imposing steps and into the opulent entrance hall. Aimee was too distracted to notice just how beautiful it was, with its sweeping marble staircase and enormous gilt-framed mirrors, antique oil paintings and exquisite fresh flower displays. There were leather armchairs and velvet upholstered sofas in a formal seating area to the left, and Aimee spotted their photographer, Katherine Connor, seated beside a low table, scrolling through her phone.

Jon made his way over to her, greeting her with a warm smile. There was no trace of the earlier temper he'd displayed; he was all charm and good humour.

'Katherine, good to see you again,' he said, as she stood up and the two of them shook hands. Katherine was a slim, blonde woman in her early forties, smartly dressed in black trousers and a loose-fitting shirt. She'd won the prestigious Wedding Photographer of the Year title at the recent Wedding Industry Awards, and Valerie was adamant that no one else would do for her only son's wedding. 'And you remember my fiancée, Aimee.'

He stood aside to let Aimee through, and she registered the look on Katherine's face as she took in Aimee's pink, swollen eyes.

'Is everything okay?' she asked in concern.

'Oh, fine,' Aimee laughed a little too loudly. 'I just... I had something in my eye. Both eyes. My, um... contact lens slipped,' she lied.

Katherine nodded slowly. 'Right. Do you have any eye drops or solution with you? It's just, it's not going to look great on camera.'

Aimee's cheeks flushed. 'Oh, I see. Well I'm fine now. I'm sure that by the time we're set up, it'll all be okay.'

'Great,' Katherine smiled brightly, happy to change the subject. 'I've already spoken to the concierge to let them know we're here, and I thought we might start with some exterior shots. It's such a nice day outside, and the grounds here are beautiful, so we might as well make the most of them.'

'Fine with us,' Jon chuckled. 'You're the professional.'

Katherine picked up her camera bag, hitching it onto her shoulder and making her way to the rear of the house. Jon threw his arm around Aimee's shoulder, guiding her in the same direction. His touch felt heavy and smothering, and Aimee wanted to shrug it off, but she didn't dare. Instead she walked silently by her fiancé's side, wiping her eyes and hoping that the puffiness would begin to subside.

Jon leant across to murmur in her ear. Aimee expected an apology and was stunned by the words that came out: 'Sort yourself out, darling, you look a mess.'

'Everything okay?' Katherine asked, turning to look at them over her shoulder as they emerged into the formal gardens at the back of the castle, the sunshine beaming down.

'Fine,' Jon called out.

'Great. Now I did a little recce of the place earlier, and I've found a couple of really nice locations to shoot in. Here, for example,' Katherine smiled, as they rounded a corner and she waved her hand with a flourish, indicating a pretty little kitchen garden. It was laid out in a traditional style, neatly divided by low walls into separate areas for basil, parsley, borage, mint and lavender, and the smell was pungent and delicious. In the centre was a small stone temple, comprising four ornately carved pillars and a domed roof. The folly was just wide enough to fit a bench inside, and from there, the view over the well-kept grounds was exquisite.

'I thought we'd start with some pictures of you two sitting on the bench first,' Katherine suggested, motioning that they should go ahead. 'These are just test shots to get you feeling comfortable, and I'm looking for something very casual and relaxed.'

Jon led Aimee up the steps and over to the bench. The two of them sat down side by side, Aimee leaving a small space between them and instinctively crossing her legs and arms. Jon put his arm around her shoulder and moved closer, attempting to close the gap, as Aimee smoothed down the strappy floral summer dress she was wearing.

Katherine quickly fired off a couple of shots then checked the screen on her camera. She frowned and changed position, squinting up at the sunlight.

'Aimee, could you try and look a little more relaxed? Just let your arms sit naturally, and lean in to Jon maybe.'

Aimee swallowed. Her throat felt dry, and she wished she'd remembered to bring her bottle of water from the car. Dutifully, she did as Katherine had suggested, leaning awkwardly towards her fiancé. She uncrossed her hands and, unsure what to do with them, rested them in her lap like a school photo.

Katherine continued to snap away, calling out directions as she went. 'How about you put your hand on Jon's knee, Aimee? And cuddle into him a little? Anyone would think you didn't want to marry him!' Katherine tried to joke, but the comment fell flat, the atmosphere becoming more awkward than ever.

Aimee winced as she felt Jon's hand grip tighter on her shoulder, his fingers digging into her flesh. 'Ouch! You're hurting me,' she squealed, jumping away from him.

'Sorry, darling,' Jon replied smoothly. 'I didn't realise.'

Aimee stared back at him, her brow furrowed, trying to work out whether he'd done it on purpose. She stroked the tender spot at the top of her arm where a red mark was already beginning to appear and shivered, noticing her skin was covered in goosebumps. Although the day was warm, they were shaded beneath the roof of the temple, and the air was much chillier.

Katherine was scrolling through the pictures on her camera, biting her lip anxiously. 'I'm just wondering whether we should try a different location. The photos aren't coming out too great here and… I think it's the light,' she finished tactfully. 'There's a beautiful area down by the river, in the Great Meadow. Why don't we head there?'

'Sure,' Jon agreed easily.

They stepped down from the temple, Aimee's wedge heels clacking on the stone.

'Why don't you two go ahead?' Katherine suggested. 'I'll hang back, and if you two hold hands I'll get some great shots from behind as you walk through the long grass.'

It was the last thing that Aimee felt like doing, but it was as though she was strapped in on a rollercoaster that was about to plummet, and there was no way she could back out now. At least if the photographs were from behind, they wouldn't show her puffy eyes or unhappy expression; she half-suspected that was why Katherine had suggested it.

Aimee took the hand Jon was offering, noticing how cold his skin felt, how his large hand seemed to dwarf her tiny one, swallowing it up and devouring it. Neither of them spoke, taking long strides across the meadow until they were well ahead of Katherine. Jon glanced back over his shoulder, making sure she was out of earshot.

'What the hell's going on with you today, Aimee?'

'I don't know! I'm just upset, that's all.'

'You're not *still* going on about that bloody seating plan are you? For Christ's sake, get over it. You're like a child, sulking when you can't get your own way.'

Aimee laughed in disbelief. In her opinion, her fiancé was the one behaving like a child. He'd been so spoilt and coddled by his mother that he wasn't used to anyone saying no to him – and he didn't like it when anyone did, Aimee was beginning to realise.

'You seem to be going out of your way to ruin this shoot today. Do you have any idea how much it cost? No, you don't, because you're not the one paying for it, are you? Maybe you'd make a bit more of an effort if it was coming out of your pocket, but as usual you're just content to live off me and do exactly as you please.'

'That's not true,' Aimee protested, but she felt a wave of guilt wash over her nonetheless. She *hadn't* thought about how much this was costing. She knew a session like this wouldn't come cheap, especially with one of the leading photographers in the industry, and it was true that she'd been wallowing in her own unhappiness, refusing to make an effort. Perhaps Jon was right. Perhaps it *was* all her fault.

'I'm sorry,' she mumbled, her cheeks growing hot. 'I didn't think—'

'No, you didn't,' Jon cut her off sharply. 'You never do. You're just a selfish little bitch.'

Fresh tears sprang into Aimee's eyes, and she gasped in shock. It was at that moment that she heard a voice behind her, calling, 'Mr Cunningham, Miss Nicholls.'

Aimee half-turned, trying to keep her face hidden behind her hair, and saw a pretty young waitress dressed in a black skirt and white blouse approaching them, carrying two glasses of champagne on a silver tray.

Katherine was walking up behind the waitress, still clicking away with the camera.

To Aimee, the whole situation felt unreal. She forced herself to plaster a bright smile onto her face, even though inside she wanted to crumble.

'Compliments of the management,' smiled the woman, whose name tag read 'Marta'. 'We want to say thank you so much for holding your wedding here at Southwark Castle, and please let us know if we can be of any assistance to you.'

'What a lovely gesture, thank you, Marta,' Jon smiled, taking a flute of champagne. Aimee reached for the other and noticed her hands were shaking.

'How about a photo of the two of you celebrating?' smiled Katherine. 'If you could gaze into each other's eyes and clink glasses…' She held up her camera expectantly.

Aimee swallowed. As Jon raised his glass, she brought hers up to meet it, but somehow mistimed it, smashing the flutes together in an explosion of bubbles and broken glass.

'I'm sorry,' Aimee gasped. 'I'm not feeling well, and—'

'Look at the bloody state of me,' Jon roared. His shirt and trousers were soaked through, his shoes covered in shards of glass. 'This is my best suit and it cost me an absolute fortune! Not to mention the dry cleaning it'll need.'

'I'll pay for the dry cleaning!' Aimee yelled back, wondering why once again everything came down to money. She looked down to see her finger was bleeding, red drops staining her dress. Jon didn't appear to notice.

'I'll clean everything up,' Marta said anxiously, bending down and carefully piling the remains of the flutes onto her tray. 'Don't worry about it.'

'I'm so sorry,' Aimee apologised once again. 'I just—' she broke off as she saw Jon staring at her accusingly, and was suddenly overwhelmed by the need to escape. 'I'm sorry,' she repeated, before taking off across the meadow and back towards the main house.

'Aimee, where are you going? Get back here this instant, you little idiot. Aimee!'

As Jon sprinted after her, Katherine and Marta looked at one another in astonishment.

'This behaviour is normal?' Marta tried to joke, as Katherine raised an eyebrow.

'I've seen a lot of nervous brides-to-be, but never one quite like that.'

'Miss Nicholls, she did not seem very happy,' Marta remarked astutely.

'No,' Katherine replied, shading her eyes from the sun as she watched Aimee reach the castle and bolt inside, as though she'd found sanctuary. 'No, she really didn't.'

CHAPTER 30

'An archaeologist is the best husband a woman can have. The older she gets, the more interested he is in her' – **Agatha Christie**

Debbie stared at her reflection in the mirror and wondered what on earth she was doing. Her heart was pounding, her chest rapidly rising and falling like a bird, and she could see the look of terror in her eyes. Now that the big day was finally here, she didn't know whether or not she could go through with it. It had taken months of hard work, not to mention all the support she'd had from Julia and Angela, and now Debbie was *this close* to chickening out.

'Everything okay?' smiled Sasha, the make-up artist, as she swirled a subtle peach blusher over Debbie's newly prominent cheekbones.

Debbie swallowed. 'Fine.' Her mouth felt dry, and she coughed to clear her throat.

'Don't worry, it's natural to be nervous,' Sasha assured her. 'You wouldn't believe how many women I've seen sat in this chair, racked with doubt about whether or not they've made the right decision. But by the end of the day you'll be floating on air, I promise you.'

Debbie didn't reply. She continued to stare straight ahead, barely recognising the woman looking back at her. It wasn't just the weight loss, although that was substantial; she was literally half the woman she used to be. She'd had her hair professionally styled so that it hung in soft, tumbling waves, zhooshed up with volume at the crown in true glamour-girl style. Her make-up, too, had been expertly applied by Sasha, who'd given her smoky, kohl-lined, come-to-bed eyes and a glossy, rosebud pout.

One final dusting with powder, and Sasha declared, 'Okay, that's it, we're all finished here. You look gorgeous, Debbie. Now go and knock 'em dead!'

Debbie stood up, wobbling precariously on her high heels. Her thin silk robe was wrapped around her, belted tightly to emphasise her slender waist, and beneath it she wore nothing but a black lacy bra and matching panties, sheer stockings and a suspender belt. The look was classic, glamorous and – Debbie hoped – incredibly sexy.

Tentatively, she made her way through the open doorway to the next room, carefully stepping over a bunch of cables stuck to the floor with gaffer tape. One side of the studio looked like an ordinary bedroom, with exposed red-brick walls and a beautiful four-poster bed covered with a mink-coloured faux-fur throw, a crystal chandelier hanging from the ceiling. The other side was full of photographic equipment: a camera mounted on a tripod, dazzling studio lights and a giant silver reflector.

Debbie heard a low wolf-whistle, and felt the colour rise in her cheeks.

'Debbie, my love, you're a vision,' Marcus, the photographer told her, as Debbie batted away his compliments. 'That fiancé of yours isn't going to be able to believe his eyes.'

'I'm really nervous,' she confessed, as she took a deep breath then exhaled slowly, trying to slow her racing pulse.

'Don't be,' Marcus insisted. 'You and me are the dream team, I can just feel it.'

Marcus Henry was a short, slim man in his early fifties, with the beginnings of a pot belly, and a thick shock of grey-blond hair. He was dressed in black trousers and a close-fitting black T-shirt, paired with circular black-rimmed glasses. Debbie had liked him immediately when she'd spoken to him on the phone a few weeks ago, and was pleased to find that he was just as warm and witty in person.

Marcus' studio was out near Dereham, and Debbie had taken the day off work to drive over there especially for her long-awaited boudoir shoot. *This* was the promise she'd made to herself all those months ago, when Stevie had tried to take a naughty snap of her on his phone and she'd been too self-conscious to let him. Well now she was going to more than make amends for that, with a gorgeous, glamorous keepsake for her and her husband-to-be.

'Right, my love, we'll just do a few warm-up piccies while we get the lighting and the settings right, so if you wouldn't mind stepping this way.' Marcus offered his arm which Debbie clung onto gratefully, as he guided her across the set to where a white voile curtain was hanging from a high rail.

'That's perfect, right there,' he assured her, as he moved back to the camera.

'What do you want me to do?' Debbie asked, feeling silly.

'Don't you worry about a thing, just concentrate on looking gorgeous. Turn so that your back's facing the camera, and look at me over your left shoulder.'

'Like this?'

'Exactly like that. Turn your shoulder out a little bit, so we can see that fabulous neckline… Perfect.' Marcus ran through a series of test shots, checking the results as they popped up on the large computer screen sat on his desk, and making little adjustments to the strength of the lights, or the angle of the reflectors.

'Are they okay?' Debbie fretted. When she'd first booked the shoot, she'd been convinced that by now she'd be a skinny size ten, but as she hadn't quite hit her target weight, she was concerned about what the pictures might look like.

'Absolutely gorgeous. Trust me. Right, we're going to do this bit by bit so that you feel comfortable,' Marcus began. He'd been a photographer for many years now, starting off with weddings and moving into portraiture when he had enough money to buy his own studio. He'd purchased the run-down old farm building over a decade ago, transforming it into a bright, welcoming work space, and he found he was increasingly specialising in boudoir shoots as the concept became more fashionable.

Marcus' easygoing, no-nonsense manner – not to mention the fact that he had absolutely zero sexual interest in the women he was photographing – meant he'd acquired an excellent word-of-mouth reputation, and it was important to him that his customers thoroughly enjoyed the experience of being photographed, without feeling pressured in any way.

'Just loosen your robe ever so slightly and give your shoulders a little wiggle.'

Debbie did as she was told, giggling nervously as the robe slid down to reveal the bare skin beneath.

'Exactly like that. Now look straight down the lens at me...' Click. 'Close your eyes for a second. Now open and...' Click. 'Drop your chin a little. Relax your mouth...' Click, click, click.

Debbie followed Marcus' directions, laughing at the jokes he made and gradually becoming more relaxed, the robe slipping further as her confidence grew.

'Imagine your man – what's his name? Stevie, yes, that's it. Imagine Stevie watching you and you're trying to seduce him. Give me those sexy eyes... Yes! That's it, that naughty little twinkle right there, you saucy minx.'

Debbie burst out laughing, and Marcus quickly snapped away, getting glorious shots of Debbie looking happy and carefree, her head thrown back as her hair tumbled over her naked shoulders.

'You take direction perfectly, you should have been an actress,' he flattered her, as Debbie grinned.

She was hugely enjoying herself, her self-assurance blossoming with every click of the camera. When Marcus finally announced that it was time to take a break whilst they set up for the next set of pictures, Debbie was surprised to find how disappointed she felt.

Sasha dashed in to retouch Debbie's make-up, applying a slightly darker lip colour, and adding a deep chocolate brown to her eyelids. 'You're doing brilliantly,' she insisted. 'Are you enjoying yourself?'

'It's fantastic,' Debbie replied truthfully, her eyes sparkling as the adrenaline raced through her body, giving her a natural high. 'Everyone should do it. It's such an incredible feeling.'

'It's empowering, isn't it?' Sasha agreed. 'To stand in front of the camera and feel gorgeous and say to everyone, "This is my body and I am proud of it!"'

'Yeah, it is,' Debbie nodded thoughtfully, realising that she agreed with Sasha. She *was* proud of her body, and all the hard work she'd put into its transformation. Okay, so she might not have reached the magical size ten, but what she *had* achieved was immense. Not only had she lost weight, but she was now fitter, stronger, healthier. She didn't get out of breath when running up the stairs or walking Scamp and, to her surprise, she'd found herself looking forward to her weekly Zumba classes, feeling sluggish and lethargic if she had to miss a session. Not to mention the way all that extra energy had been spicing things up in the bedroom…

'The pictures look amazing by the way,' Marcus called through, from where he was shifting equipment across the studio.

'Oh, can I see?' Debbie pleaded.

'Not until we're finished. But you're going to love them, I promise. Now Sasha, are you nearly done with our Debbie, as it's time for her to give the public what they want.'

Sasha spritzed Debbie's hair with spray, and declared that they were good to go.

'All right, Mr DeMille, I'm ready for my close-up,' Debbie purred as she tottered back through to the studio, making Marcus roar with laughter.

This time the pictures were being taken with Debbie positioned on the bed. After a moment's hesitation, she removed her robe, lying on her stomach on top of the luxuriously soft faux-fur throw.

'Now this is entirely your call,' Marcus said, as he fussed around, arranging the throw so it draped flatteringly round her body. 'We can go with or without the bra. Obviously it will be tastefully done – you're on your stomach, so we won't see anything, but it just means your bra straps aren't in shot, and it gives the illusion that you're in the altogether.'

Debbie thought about it for a moment, then decided not to think too hard.

'I'll take it off,' she agreed recklessly.

'That's my girl,' Marcus cheered, modestly averting his eyes as Debbie reached round behind her to unhook her bra. 'Now cross your arms in front of you to make sure everything's covered, and push yourself up ever so slightly on your elbows to elongate your neck, just like that. Now look straight at the camera... Gorgeous!'

For the first time in a very long time, Debbie actually believed that she *was* gorgeous. She certainly felt like it – sexy and strong and womanly. What did it matter if she hadn't hit her target weight, she told herself, as she posed and pouted for Marcus' lens. She hadn't had a body like this for years! Probably not since she was in her mid-teens, almost a decade ago. Stevie was going to explode with excitement when he saw these pictures.

'And that's a wrap,' Marcus announced finally, as he and Sasha broke into a round of applause, Sasha helping Debbie discreetly back into her robe and picking up her discarded bra.

Debbie stood uncertainly for a second, wondering what to do now that it was all over. She'd been so confident up there, in her own little bubble, and now it was over she felt lost.

Marcus was over by the computer, scrolling through the pictures. 'Would you like to see?' he asked, his eyes twinkling behind his glasses.

'Yes, please!' Debbie squealed, running over as quickly as she could in the enormous heels. 'Oh my,' she gasped, clapping a hand to her mouth. She almost welled up as she gazed at image after image of her displayed on the screen in tiny thumbnails. The pictures were elegant and tasteful, and Marcus had taken many of them in black and white, or sepia, giving them a classic feel.

Marcus clicked on one particular shot, enlarging it; Debbie's chin was resting lightly on one hand, her hair curling softly around her face, as her other arm covered her breasts, revealing creamy skin and just a hint of cleavage. Her eyes were clear and sparkling, her mouth full and glossy. She looked stunning.

'Do you like them?' Marcus asked softly.

Debbie simply nodded, unable to speak. She couldn't stop staring at the pictures. 'I never knew I could look like that,' she managed finally.

'Of course you can,' Marcus gave her a little squeeze. 'It's *you*. That's what you look like, and don't you forget it.'

Debbie smiled in disbelief. 'I love them,' she said quietly.

'I'll edit them down to the best ones, then send them over to you,' Marcus explained. 'There'll be around a hundred and fifty by the time I've finished, then you can choose your favourites and I'll retouch them.'

'Retouch?' Debbie repeated uncertainly.

'Nothing major. I'm certainly not going to be Photoshopping you until you're unrecognisable. It's what I like to call "improving on perfection". I can get rid of any little blemishes, make sure your skin tone's even, that kind of thing. But to be honest, there's very little that needs doing in this case.'

Debbie was glowing with pride, unable to take her eyes off the screen. She couldn't wait for Stevie to see the pictures.

'You're pleased with them then?' Marcus asked smugly, knowing what her answer would be.

'Oh yes,' she gushed, finally tearing her gaze away from the photos and smiling at Marcus. 'You're a miracle worker. I'm going to recommend you to everyone I know!'

'Well that calls for a celebration,' Marcus smiled. 'I'll finish up here while you get dressed, then I'll get Sasha to pop a bottle of fizz and we can all have a cheeky drink.'

'Deal,' Debbie grinned happily.

CHAPTER 31

'There's only one way to have a happy marriage and
as soon as I learn what it is I'll get married again'
*– **Clint Eastwood***

'So are you feeling excited about today?' Julia asked, as she stepped onto the escalator in the department store.

'I guess,' Kelly shrugged, trying to play it cool, but Julia could tell she was looking forward to it. There'd been none of the usual attitude or sarcasm, and she'd even made an effort to be nice to Paige, letting her borrow her phone when hers had run out of battery.

'How about you, Paige?'

'Yeah, definitely,' Paige grinned, showing off the braces she'd recently had fitted. At first she'd been devastated that she'd have them for the wedding, but Mike and Gill had reassured her that she still looked gorgeous and it would all be worth it in the end. 'I was looking online last night, and there's this one I really like that's purple with spaghetti straps.'

'What have I let myself in for?' Mike groaned, shaking his head as the girls laughed.

As Kelly and Paige were to be Gill's only bridesmaids, they'd asked if they could pick their own dresses and surprise Gill on the day. Gill had initially been hesitant, worrying about what they might choose, but Mike had offered to take both girls shopping. As back up for him, and to cast an expert eye over the proceedings, Gill had asked whether Julia might like to go along too, and Julia had readily agreed. Nick had immediately said he would look after Jack, and the two of them had plans to go to the park for the afternoon, to play on the swings and then feed the ducks at the pond.

'I thought we could look at ordinary dresses first,' Julia suggested. 'Before we head to the bridal department. You can often get bridesmaid dresses that are just as nice from high street shops, and that makes it a bit cheaper so we can spend more money on the reception.'

'Cool,' Paige agreed, as they stepped off at the womenswear floor where the branded concessions were.

Julia could see the panic in Mike's eyes, as he took in the clusters of teenage girls, the posses of mothers and daughters all fervently browsing the rails. Pop music was blaring and the labels had their summer ranges out, all soda pop colours and sparkle, denim shorts and crop tops.

'Wow, those shoes are awesome,' Paige exclaimed, gravitating towards a pair of incredibly high floral-print wedges.

'Let's try and stick to dresses,' said Julia. 'We can do accessories later, once we know what we're pairing them with.'

Kelly, meanwhile, had picked out a loose-fitting white jumpsuit, and was holding it up thoughtfully. 'This is so cool,' she mused. 'Maybe we should get something like this, instead of a traditional dress. It would look really chic with some chunky jewellery, or even a big floppy hat. Very Bianca Jagger.'

'How do you even know about Bianca Jagger?' Mike wondered incredulously. 'She was way before your time.'

'Duh, she's, like, a style icon,' Kelly retorted. 'She was on my "Top Ten Wedding Dresses" feature on my blog, between Kate Moss and Grace Kelly.'

Mike raised an eyebrow, exchanging glances with Julia. 'I think your mum would prefer it if you stuck with something traditional,' he advised. 'A pretty dress in a normal colour that's not too revealing.'

'Snoozeville,' Kelly murmured, putting the jumpsuit back.

'What about this?' Paige was pointing at a pale lemon maxi dress, with a white lace trim around the hem and neckline.

'Now that's more like it,' Mike nodded approvingly. 'As long as the neckline doesn't come down too low.'

'*Daaaad*,' Paige rolled her eyes.

'What do you think, Kel?' Julia asked. 'Should I get a couple of these to try?'

'Mmm hmm,' Kelly said distantly, as she picked up a knee-length, strapless, bright coral dress with a tulip skirt. 'This might look cute.'

'Yeah, I like that,' Paige agreed immediately.

Julia looked across at Mike, both of them surprised at how amenable the two girls were being.

Twenty minutes later, and the small group had armfuls of dresses which they carried over to the changing rooms.

'Do we have to wear the same one?' Kelly wondered, eyeing some of Paige's choices with a critical eye.

Julia turned to Mike, who shrugged. 'I don't know. You'd have to check with your mum, but probably not. I'm sure she'd want you to feel relaxed and happy in whatever you choose.'

The answer seemed to satisfy Kelly, who disappeared into a cubicle to get ready. Mike sat outside on a pink chair shaped like a giant shoe, looking somewhat self-conscious.

'I'll go in and help the girls get ready,' Julia offered. 'Then we'll come and show you the ones that we like.'

'Fine with me,' Mike nodded, doing his best to look inconspicuous as a group of giggling teens surged past.

A few minutes later, both girls emerged excitedly with Julia, eager to show off their outfits.

'Well, what do you think, Dad?' Paige twirled around, the ice-blue A-line dress flaring out as she span.

Mike sucked in his lips, his forehead wrinkling. For a moment, he looked overwhelmed, as though it had suddenly hit him that his little girl was growing up. Paige was almost a teenager now, and she'd been through a lot in the past few years, with her mum leaving, and Mike struggling with being a single parent. It had been a massive readjustment for them all when he'd moved in with Gill and her family, but his daughter was turning into a wonderful young woman and she was making him proud.

But all he said was, 'Yeah, it's nice.'

'Dad, you're useless! What about Kelly's dress?'

Kelly looked at him with something akin to shyness, and Mike was taken aback once again. It was an entirely new phenomenon to have Kelly wanting his approval.

'That's very nice too,' he said, which for Mike passed as overwhelming enthusiasm. 'You both look very grown up.'

'Hey, do you mind taking a photo?' Kelly asked, handing him her phone. 'I might do a bridesmaid feature on my blog.'

'No problem,' Mike said casually.

She struck a pose outside the entrance to the changing rooms, one hand on her hip to show off the bell-sleeved, boho-style mini dress.

'Cool,' she said, after Mike had taken a couple of different shots. 'And now get one of me and Paige.'

'Am I going to be on your blog?' Paige squealed, sounding awed, as she moved in beside Kelly for the photo.

'Maybe. I haven't quite decided yet.'

The two girls disappeared back into the changing room to try on outfit number two, and this time Julia stayed outside with Mike.

'They seem to be getting on really well,' she remarked.

Mike shook his head in disbelief. 'I've genuinely never seen them like this. They're usually at one another's throats. I daren't say anything in case I jinx it, but long may it last.'

'They're both lovely girls. A real credit to you and Gill.'

'I don't think either of them have had the easiest time, but they're both doing well. Hopefully now we're getting married, they'll finally have some stability.'

'You're such a sweetheart,' Julia smiled, seeing that he was getting choked up. 'Gill's lucky to have you.'

'*I'm* the lucky one,' Mike insisted. 'I was a bit of a mess before Gill came along. She's sorted me out good and proper. And she's amazing with Sammy. I think he completely considers her to be his mum now. He doesn't even remember Tina.'

'Do you ever think that—' Julia began, but broke off as Kelly and Paige appeared once more, beaming from ear to ear. 'Oh, you both look gorgeous,' she gushed.

The two of them were wearing the coral-pink strapless tulip dress that Kelly had picked out and, although they were different heights and had different colouring, the dress miraculously seemed to suit them both. It was absolutely perfect for them; fresh and young, but formal enough for a wedding.

'Photo, photo,' Kelly called, as she and Paige instinctively put their arms around one another, grinning as Mike took another round of pictures.

They each had three more dresses to try, all of which were photographed for posterity (and Kelly's blog) before it came to crunch time.

'Have you made a final decision, or do you want to go elsewhere?' Julia asked them.

Kelly looked at Paige, biting her lip.

'If you both like different ones, that's fine,' Mike told them. 'We've already got Freddy and Finlay, so we don't need another set of twins.'

Paige giggled. 'You say first,' she told Kelly.

'No, let's say together.'

'Okay then, after three. One… two… three…'

'The coral one!' both girls burst out in unison, before clasping hands delightedly.

'Well, that was a lot easier than I expected,' Mike remarked, reaching into his pocket for his wallet.

'You ought to come shopping with us more often,' Paige told him.

'Especially if you're paying,' Kelly added cheekily, and for once Mike didn't mind a bit.

—

The foursome were wandering down the street, Kelly and Paige clutching their carrier bags and browsing in the shop windows. As they passed The Body Shop, Paige suddenly clapped a hand over her mouth.

'I totally forgot. It's Stacey's sleepover tonight and I need to get her a present,' she panicked, looking up at Mike.

'Come on then. Do you want to get her something from here?'

'Maybe,' Paige looked torn. 'Although I wouldn't mind looking in the Apple Store, to see if I can get her a cool phone cover. Or maybe I could get her something from Pandora…?'

'Fine, let's go,' Mike sighed, no doubt thinking of the battering his credit card was taking today.

'All of us?' Kelly asked, pulling a face. Julia heard the defiant tone in her voice, and knew that her positivity had been too good to last.

'We won't be long, will we?' Mike asked, looking at Paige for confirmation. 'Then we can all head home, or look for shoes, or whatever it is you girls want to do.'

'Well I don't want to trek from shop to shop while Paige makes up her mind about what to buy her lame friend,' Kelly retorted. 'Maybe there's some paint drying somewhere that I could go watch instead.'

Mike looked torn, but then Julia had an idea.

'Why don't you and Paige go and look for the present?' she suggested to Mike. 'And I don't mind going somewhere with Kelly – wherever she wants to go – then we can meet up with you a bit later.'

'Really? That'd be great,' Mike looked relieved. 'Is that okay with you, Kel?'

'Sure,' she shrugged. 'Anything as long as it's not shopping for Stacey. I'll see you later.'

Julia waved goodbye, and the two of them walked on. 'So where do you fancy going?'

'Dunno.' Kelly was suddenly back to the taciturn teenager.

'We could go to Miss Selfridge, or Office, or Accessorize?' Julia began naming shops in the immediate vicinity, but Kelly didn't jump at any of them. 'Or there's a Häagen-Dazs cafe nearby,' Julia suggested, with a sudden burst of inspiration. 'We could go get ice cream?'

Kelly's face brightened. 'Yeah! They're supposed to do amazing frozen yoghurt in there. And it's fat free.'

'Then let's go.'

Five minutes later, the pair of them were sitting in a bur-gundy-coloured booth, two cardboard tubs of dessert in front of them.

'Yum, this is amazing,' Julia groaned, as she licked the salted caramel ice cream off her plastic spoon. 'Are you sure you don't want to try some?'

'I'm fine,' Kelly insisted, tucking into her frozen yoghurt. She'd opted for coconut flavour, with a topping of fresh straw-berries. 'I want to make sure I can still fit into the dress for the wedding.'

'I don't think you've got anything to worry about there,' Ju-lia assured her, thinking of her own body issues when she was Kelly's age, and how she'd trade anything to have her thirty-three-year-old, baby-ravaged body back to how it was in her teenage years. 'So how are you feeling about the wedding?' she asked casually. 'You didn't seem too keen on the idea the first time I met you.'

Kelly raised an eyebrow. 'It's up to Mum, I guess. It's her life. She has to do what she wants.'

'Well the plans for the reception are coming along brilliantly. You've been such a great help, sending me everyone's suggestions and finding suppliers. I'd never have known where to hire those giant letters, or that sweetie cart, if it wasn't for you.'

'No probs. It's been kind of fun, actually.'

'I'm glad. And your blog sounds like it's going really well.'

Kelly's face lit up. 'Yeah, I love it. I wish I could do it all the time, like, as a job. I've been thinking I might like to have a career where I can write, or maybe something to do with fashion, like a stylist. But some people make careers out of blogs you know.'

Julia nodded. 'So do you think you're going to write about today?'

'Uh huh. I'm going to do a feature on bridesmaid fashion – cool styles that you can wear after the wedding too. I don't think I'm going to put *this* on there though,' Kelly nodded at the bag by her feet. 'Because if Mum reads it I don't want her to see what we've actually decided on.'

'I think Paige was pretty excited about being featured on your blog.'

Kelly rolled her eyes. 'She's such a loser.' But the comment was said with affection, Julia noticed.

'I reckon she really looks up to you.'

'Maybe,' Kelly acknowledged. 'She's not as annoying as she used to be. It's just kind of weird, y'know, to suddenly have a sister who's only a few months younger than me. And Sammy too. He's cute, I guess, but it means Mum's really busy all the time, running around after so many kids. I just kind of do my own thing.'

'I'm sure she's always got time to talk to you, if you need her.'

'Yeah, I suppose. It's cool talking to you though, 'cos you're younger, and you listen to what I say.'

'Well… thanks…' Julia grinned, feeling an irrational surge of pride and pleasure that Kelly thought she was cool.

'Mum doesn't always understand about stuff. Like, with my blog, she was convinced I was going to run off with some paedophile or something. I mean, I'm not stupid. Weirdly Mike was the one who talked her round. He's all right sometimes. He's not my dad, obviously, but sometimes he can be funny and he makes Mum happy.'

'I think he seems like a really nice guy,' Julia told her. 'And you know, if you ever want to chat about anything, you can always call me or email me. You've got my number, right?'

Kelly nodded. 'It's on the bottom of your emails.'

'You know, I actually have a really good feeling about this wedding,' Julia grinned, as she finished her ice cream and pushed the tub away with a contented sigh. 'You guys have all come up with such brilliant ideas, I think your mum's going to be blown away.'

'Maybe I should become an events planner too,' Kelly suggested, with a cheeky grin.

'Don't do it, you'll put me out of business!' Julia laughed. She noticed Kelly's empty tub, and reached for her bag. 'All finished?'

'Yep.'

'Then let's go and find Mike and Paige, see how they're getting on.'

'Sure.' Kelly stood up, picking up the carrier bag with her bridesmaid dress. 'And thanks for the chat. It was really nice talking to you.'

'Any time,' Julia replied. And she meant it.

CHAPTER 32

*'If you want to sacrifice the admiration of many men
for the criticism of one, go ahead, get married'*
– Katharine Hepburn

'And the winner is...' Aimee let the moment hang, her eyes darting between the two groups of expectant women. In front of her, her two best friends, Rachel and Charlie, had been decked out as 'brides', swathed in yards of white toilet roll with pillowcase veils, pieces of tinfoil fashioned into a shiny wedding rings and dazzling hair decorations.

Rachel's team had opted for a classic dress style with a fitted bodice and layer after layer of trailing toilet paper skirt; Charlie had taken a risk and gone modern, with loo roll tightly bound on her body and stopping mid-thigh, a dramatic toilet paper flower on one shoulder and a contrasting belt made from tinfoil.

'Charlotte,' Aimee announced gleefully, as the group on her left broke out into squeals and cries, hugging each other.

To her right, Rachel slumped dejectedly, slowly peeling off sheets of toilet paper from around her waist and letting them flutter to the floor. 'I knew I should've been more daring,' she sighed.

Aimee went across to give her a conciliatory hug. 'Sorry,' she apologised. 'I just liked the drama of Charlie's. It's so completely different to what I'm having.'

'Never mind. I'll forgive you.'

Tara and Katie, two girls Aimee had worked with at the pub where she'd met Jon, emerged from the kitchen. 'Food is served,' Tara grinned, balancing a pizza in each hand and carefully putting them down on the coffee table, as Katie followed with fries and onion rings.

'Will someone give me a hand with the nachos?' she called out, returning moments later with an enormous bowl of corn chips covered in melted cheese and jalapeños, smothered in guacamole and sour cream.

'Mmm, this looks amazing, ladies,' Aimee sighed happily, as she took in the array of fast food in front of her, whilst Tara topped up her wine glass with chilled rosé. There were a dozen women altogether, and they all piled onto the sofa, or sprawled out on the carpet, helping themselves to gooey slices of margarita pizza and dough balls drenched in garlic butter. *Clueless* was playing on the TV in the background, but no one was watching, as the conversation became louder and ever more raucous.

It was Aimee's hen do, and she and her friends had hired a cottage for the weekend in the beautiful Suffolk countryside. It was cosy and modern, with wooden floors and Ikea furniture, and her friends had decorated it liberally with bright pink 'Hen Party' balloons and banners. The kitchen was filled with dozens of carrier bags brimming with snacks and alcohol, whilst Charlie had made cupcakes, decorated with 'B-R-I-D-E-T-O-B-E-X-X-X' in pink icing, one for each guest.

The women had started arriving in the early afternoon, and since then they'd been catching up and gossiping, drinking and playing party games. It was exactly what Aimee wanted. She'd decided against a night on the town, where she was forced to wear L plates and fairy wings; nor did she want to make everyone pay a small fortune for a weekend in Barcelona or Amsterdam. Instead, she wanted to relax and have fun with her closest friends, in a grown-up version of the slumber parties they used to have at school.

'While we're eating,' Rachel announced, waving her pizza in the air in an effort to get everyone's attention, 'We're going to play a fun little game called "How Well Do You Know Your Hen?" There'll be a series of questions all about Aimee, and we'll see who knows the most about her.'

Aimee cringed, wondering what Rachel had in store for her, as the others hooted with laughter, and Charlie gave her a sly wink.

'So,' Rachel shouted over the noise, as she consulted the list she'd scribbled earlier that week. 'Who was Aimee's first kiss?'

'I know this!' Ellie, who'd been friends with Aimee since primary school, screeched excitedly. 'It was Ricky Gillingham, and it was the Year Nine school disco. They had a cheeky snog to Daniel Bedingfield.'

There were cheers and catcalls, as Aimee burst into giggles. 'Ah, Ricky Gillingham. I didn't even fancy him, I just wanted a snog because everyone else was getting one!'

'He looked like Wayne Rooney,' Ellie cackled.

'No, he didn't!' Aimee squealed. 'If you squinted, he looked a bit like a dark-haired Justin Timberlake.'

'If you squinted and all the lights were turned off, then maybe,' Ellie scoffed.

'Okay, okay, next question,' Rachel pressed on, as everyone looked up expectantly. 'What is Aimee's bra size?'

Half a dozen voices yelled back, '34B!'

'Hardly worth bothering with,' Aimee chuckled.

'You know what they say,' Charlie yelled. 'Any more than a mouthful's a waste!'

'Charlie!' Aimee exclaimed, laughing as she threw a cushion at her.

'Where are Aimee and Jon going on their honeymoon?' Rachel called out. 'And a bonus point if you can name all the countries.'

'I don't even think *I* can name all the countries,' Aimee giggled, at the same time as Tara shouted:

'Caribbean cruise!'

'Lucky cow,' Katie grinned, but it was said with affection.

'…Barbados, St Lucia, Antigua, Jamaica, St Kitts…' Ellie was attempting to list all the destinations.

'And we start off in Miami,' Aimee couldn't resist adding.

'All right, all right, don't rub it in!'

'Moving swiftly on… What is Aimee's favourite sexual position?' Rachel grinned, to another round of whoops and giggles, as Aimee flushed bright red, burying her face behind her hands.

'Girl on top?' guessed Tara.

'Doggy style?'

'Reverse cowgirl?'

'Ha ha, I bet Jon loves missionary, doesn't he?' Ellie teased.

'Yeah, come on Aimee, tell us what Jon's really like in bed.'

'Someone pour her another glass of wine!'

'I bet he's really uptight. Or is he totally wild between the sheets?'

'Is he into some kinky Christian Grey stuff?'

'Does he have to ring his mother and ask for permission before he ejaculates?'

'Charlie!' Rachel screeched, flinging another cushion her way.

The girls fell about with laughter, half-horrified and half-hysterical.

'Charlie, I can't believe you said that,' Aimee exclaimed, her face still beetroot red.

'Sorry,' Charlie grinned. But her eyes were sparkling, and she didn't look the least bit sorry.

'She'd never give him permission anyway,' Aimee couldn't resist saying, making her friends scream with outrage, a few of them breaking into applause.

'Oh, it's just so good to have the old Aimee back,' Charlie sighed, as she crawled across the floor and threw her arms around Aimee, squeezing her tightly. 'Even if it is just for a night. You're so much fun when you're like this.'

'Yeah, we never seem to see you any more,' Rachel added, piling on the guilt.

'I miss you guys too,' Aimee said sadly, realising that she genuinely did. 'I've just been so busy with the wedding and everything.'

'I thought you had a wedding planner?' Tara interjected, as she scraped the last of the cheese from the bottom of the nacho bowl.

'Yeah, but I still have to make the decisions.'

'I thought his mother was making all the decisions.'

'Not all of them,' Aimee shot back, getting defensive.

The room fell silent for a moment, the only sound coming from the movie playing in the background, where Cher and Dionne were giving Tai her makeover.

'So where's Jon going on his stag?' Katie asked casually, changing the subject.

'He's not sure if he's going to have one,' Aimee explained. 'He's been really busy with work, you see, and as it's getting so close to the wedding he doesn't know if there'll be time to organise it—'

'And he doesn't have any friends which makes it harder,' Charlie quipped, and there was a ripple of uncomfortable laughter.

Aimee swallowed hard, a tight feeling in her chest. 'Char, that's my fiancé.'

'Yeah, I know but he's…' Charlie trailed off, realising she probably shouldn't say what she was about to.

'He's what?' Aimee demanded, tears springing into her eyes. She didn't know if it was the stress of the wedding, or whether she'd had too much to drink, but she'd ended up in the middle of an argument with one of her best friends. Her heart was beating fast as she stared Charlotte down, daring her to answer.

The silence was shattered by Aimee's phone ringing. Everyone looked across to see the picture of Jon light up as the phone jangled away.

'I'd better take this,' Aimee said quietly, as she reached for it.

'No, you're on your hen do! No male contact allowed.' Tara tried to lighten the mood, but somehow the joke fell flat.

Aimee shrugged, her expression resigned, as she picked up her phone and ran upstairs to the bedroom she was sharing with Rachel. She sank down onto the floral duvet cover, and swiped to answer the call.

'Hey, baby,' she greeted Jon softly.

'Hey,' he sounded instantly relieved. 'Is everything okay?'

'Yeah, sure, why wouldn't it be?'

'No reason. I just wanted to make sure you weren't in A&E having your stomach pumped by now. I know these kind of nights can get pretty outrageous.'

As if on cue, a gale of laughter wafted up from the living room.

Aimee smiled sadly. 'I'm just having fun with the girls. We're eating pizza, watching films, that kind of thing.'

'Right, well, don't let them lead you astray. I know what they're like.'

It was an innocuous-sounding comment, but for some reason it grated on Aimee. 'What's that supposed to mean? What are they like?'

'Oh, you know.' Jon's voice had that airy, judgemental tone that Aimee had found increasingly irritating in recent weeks. 'Well, that Tara, for example. She's sleeping with a different man every week, isn't she? She'll get herself a reputation, and that's not the kind of person I want my fiancée associated with. And that ginger one, Catherine, she—'

'Her name's *Charlotte*, Jon. Charlotte! She's one of my best friends, and she's going to be my bridesmaid, and you can't even get her bloody name right.'

'Calm down, Aimee, it was just a slip of the tongue—'

'Rachel,' Aimee burst out. 'My best friend and maid of honour—'

'Well of course I know Rachel,' Jon blustered.

'What's her boyfriend's name?'

There was silence on the other end of the line.

'My best friend's boyfriend, Jon. They've been together for five years now. What's his name?'

'Aimee, I don't know what you're trying to prove, but it's late and—'

'You don't know it, do you?' Aimee exploded, weeks of pent-up frustration finally spilling out.

'It merely slipped my mind, that's all and—'

'Why don't we ever socialise with them? We never go out with my friends.'

'That's not true!'

'We went bowling once with Rachel and Charlie, at that big multiplex with the cinema and the Nando's. You said, and forgive me if I don't get the phrasing quite right, that they must be "mentally deficient if that's what they consider a good night out".'

'You see Aimee, this is exactly how you behave when you're around those girls, and that's exactly what I don't like. You become bolshy and vulgar, and it's really not very attractive.'

'What you mean,' Aimee's voice was getting louder with each word, 'is that you don't like it when *I* have an opinion. When I say what I think and it's different to what *you* want me to think. When I'm not just some perfect little fiancée who stays at home to cook your meals and dress prettily for you and have sex whenever you want it, and you don't even care whether or not *I* have a good time.'

There was silence on the other end of the line. Aimee was breathing heavily. She had a sneaking suspicion that she'd gone too far, but it actually felt good. Cathartic.

She jumped as the door flew open and Rachel bounced in yelling, 'Tell Jon to get off the phone, you're going to miss the stripper!'

She shut up as soon as she saw Aimee's face.

'So there's a stripper, is there?' Jon's voice was like ice.

'She's joking, Jon,' Aimee said wearily.

'Hilarious. Well, this seems like the right time to say goodnight.'

'Jon—'

'I'll speak to you tomorrow, Aimee.' The line went dead.

The phone slipped from Aimee's hand onto the bed, a solitary tear rolling down her cheek.

Rachel looked horrified. She stepped into the room, closing the door behind her. 'Are you okay, hon?'

'Yeah,' Aimee sniffed. The tears were falling faster now, and she wiped them ineffectually with the back of her hand. 'Just a stupid argument. I think I'm a bit drunk.'

'You're supposed to be drunk. It's your hen do. *He's* not supposed to be a dickhead about it.'

'He wasn't.' Aimee automatically leapt to his defence. 'It was me, I was just…'

'Why do you always do that? Why do you always stick up for him when he's being an arsehole?'

'You don't understand. He can be so sweet and so caring. You just don't see that side of him.'

'No, I don't. And I never see *you* any more either.'

'I know. But once the wedding's out of the way I'll have more time and—'

'No, you won't. Then he'll have you in his clutches and he'll never let you out again.'

It was meant to be a joke, but Aimee began to cry harder. 'Please don't be mad at me, Rach. I can take anything but you being mad at me.'

Rachel reached across for a hug, and Aimee clung to her. 'I'm just so stressed out by this whole wedding thing. There's so much to plan and his mother is such a nightmare and I feel I'm stuck in the middle trying to keep everyone happy and I don't know how much more I can take. Jon and I seem to be arguing constantly, about every little thing. It should be the happiest time of my life and I just feel… I'm so miserable,' Aimee confessed.

'Oh Aimee,' Rachel sighed, stroking her hair. They sat in silence for a few moments, both of them lost in their own thoughts. Aimee couldn't help but remember back to the disastrous photo shoot the other week. She'd never seen Jon like that before. Oh, she'd seen him angry, but never in such a rage. She knew he was under a lot of pressure, with his business and the impending wedding, but surely the two of them needed to work together, not against one another, if they were going to get through this with their sanity intact.

The atmosphere since that day had been awful. Aimee was walking on eggshells around her fiancé – the slightest provocation set him off on another furious rant. Aimee had been losing weight with all the stress; she was worried that her wedding dress was going to hang off her unflatteringly and—

'You know something, Aims?' Rachel began to speak, cutting into Aimee's thoughts, as she eventually plucked up the courage to say what was on her mind. 'You don't have to do this. If you don't want to marry him, you really don't have to.'

'I *do* want to marry him,' Aimee protested weakly.

'No one would think badly of you if you changed your mind. This is the rest of your life, and you've got to be a hundred percent certain that you're making the right decision.'

'Of course I am. I love him,' Aimee replied. But her words sounded less than convincing. She wasn't even sure whether she believed them herself.

CHAPTER 33

*'By all means marry. If you get a good wife you will
become happy, and if you get a bad one you will
become a philosopher'* – **Socrates**

Debbie stood in the living room of the house she shared with Stevie, looking around as though it was the first time she'd ever visited. It was neat and tidy, with all the usual clutter put away in the cupboards, magazines in the rack and DVDs in their cases. She'd spent the day vacuuming and dusting, scrubbing and cleaning, and now the place gleamed.

In front of her was a small travel suitcase, and stacked up in the hallway were half a dozen carrier bags containing the overflow that wouldn't fit in her case, as well as a garment bag hanging from the picture rail. Scamp jumped up at her, demanding attention, sensing that something was happening.

'Have you got everything, then?' Stevie asked, turning off the television and coming over to her.

Debbie nodded, not trusting herself to speak. If she did, she might cry.

'I guess this is it then,' Stevie said, his tone serious. 'I guess it's goodbye.'

'Only 'til tomorrow!' Debbie burst into nervous laughter, relieving the tension.

'You promise you'll be there?'

'Of course I will! Nothing can stop me from becoming your wife.' Debbie leaned in towards her fiancé, and the two of them kissed tenderly.

She was about to drive to her parents' house, to spend the night in her childhood bedroom, and respect the tradition of not seeing the groom the night before the wedding. It was the oddest feeling, knowing that the next time she set eyes on Stevie, it would be the biggest day of her life, and she would be about to make her vows in front of all their friends and family.

'And don't let Olly keep you up late or get you drunk,' Debbie warned him firmly.

Olly was Stevie's best man, and he was coming round to spend the night with him. She was somewhat concerned about the quantities of whisky that might be drunk that evening, and would cheerfully throttle Stevie – and Olly – if he turned up at the church with a hangover.

'Of course not. We're just going to watch some telly, maybe have a cheeky Scotch for luck – a toast to the bride's health and all that,' Stevie grinned naughtily. 'Then get an early night. Big day tomorrow.'

'Don't I know it,' Debbie giggled. Then she became serious again. 'I love you, Stevie. I really do.'

'I love you too, Debs,' Stevie murmured, and Debbie heard the catch in his voice. 'So much. I can't believe you're going to be my wife.'

'Mrs Stephen Reid. Debbie Reid. Deborah Reid,' Debbie sang, trying the words out for size.

The moment was interrupted by Scamp, whimpering by her feet. Debbie picked him up, burying her face in his fur as he tried to lick her face. 'Oh, Scamp, I'm going to miss you too. I wish you could be there.'

'He'd be an excellent ring bearer.'

'Probably better than Olly,' Debbie quipped. 'Shame the vicar won't allow dogs in the church. And you've got all the arrangements sorted for him?'

'Yeah, I'll take him round to Cath's in the morning,' Stevie nodded, referring to their next-door neighbour. 'She'll keep him tomorrow, then Mum'll pick him up and take him to hers the following day.'

'While we're in Greece,' Debbie whooped. 'I really can't wait! I don't know what I'm more excited about – the wedding or the honeymoon.'

They'd booked the perfect hotel in Santorini, high up on the rocky cliffs in a little whitewashed village, with incredible views over the stunning cerulean sea. Their room had its own private balcony, and a winding set of stone steps would take them down to the narrow strip of beach below.

'I can't wait to see you in a bikini,' Stevie growled, his hands roaming over the newly slender curves of his fiancée.

'Wait until you see me on the wedding night,' Debbie winked. 'Which reminds me,' she continued, pulling away from Stevie's increasingly amorous advances. 'I left you a present upstairs on the bed.'

'Ooh, saucy. Have you bought us matching underwear?'

'Damn, I should have thought of that. They never mention that in the bridal magazines.'

'They're missing out. I look amazing in white lace panties,' Stevie joked. 'But seriously, what did you get me? Can I go open it?'

'Wait until I've gone,' Debbie instructed him. 'And *don't* open it in front of Olly.'

'Intriguing.' Stevie's eyes were sparkling. 'I guess it's a good job I got something for you too.'

'You got me a present?' Debbie squealed excitedly.

'It's tradition, I believe,' Stevie smirked, reaching into his pocket and pulling out a blue velvet jewellery box.

'Is it a car?' Debbie teased. 'That convertible Audi I've been looking at?'

'Yeah. I got one of those special TARDIS boxes,' Stevie shot back. 'Go on then. Open it.'

Biting her lip, Debbie gently opened the box. Inside was a pair of vintage diamond drop earrings that perfectly matched her engagement ring.

'Something new,' Stevie murmured, as Debbie gasped.

'How on earth did you afford these? We've been putting every spare penny into the wedding.'

'Well, you know, I've been eating baked beans for lunch, only washing my pants once a week. These little savings add up.'

Debbie threw her arms around him. 'I don't care if you robbed a bank, I'm just glad you did. They're absolutely perfect.'

'Like you.' Stevie kissed her gently on the nose. 'You're always perfect to me, Debs, you know that. Whether you're a size ten or a size twenty, you're always you. And you're all I want.'

Debbie gazed up at him, her gorgeous, funny, caring fiancé, and knew without a doubt that she wanted to spend the rest of her life with him.

—

'Try to get some sleep tonight. I know you're excited for tomorrow, but you'll need it.'

'Don't worry, I'm counting on adrenaline to get me through,' Debbie grinned.

'Do you want me to bring you anything? A hot drink? A snack? You hardly ate anything tonight, and I don't want you overdoing it on this diet of yours,' Debbie's mother, Kathleen, looked at her in concern. She was a larger lady – Debbie had inherited her build from her mother – and she wore oversized, tortoiseshell glasses. Kathleen had the same thick, dark hair as her daughter, but hers was shot through with strands of grey.

'I'm fine, Mum. I just wasn't very hungry.'

'That'll be the nerves.'

The two of them were sitting in Debbie's old childhood bedroom, where the posters of Leonardo DiCaprio and Johnny Depp had long since been taken down. The previously lilac walls had been repainted in a neutral shade of buttercream, and Debbie's old single bed had been replaced with a double, complete with a brown and cream checked duvet cover that Debbie would have hated as a teenager. Now that the room was largely used for guests, Kathleen's tastes had taken priority over Debbie's.

'I'm not nervous. Just excited.'

'He's a good lad, is Stevie. You know your dad and I really like him.'

'Thanks, Mum, that means a lot.'

'And you're going to look so beautiful tomorrow.' Kathleen stroked her daughter's hair tenderly, trying not to get emotional. Seeing Debbie all tucked up, as she sat on the bed beside her, reminded Kathleen of so many childhood moments. But this time it was different. This time it was the eve of Debbie's wedding, the last time she would ever be here as Miss Barlow and a single woman.

'You too,' Debbie smiled. Her mother had bought a lovely dress, in royal blue silk, with a matching bolero jacket and co-ordinating hat. It was the most expensive outfit she'd owned in a very long time.

Kathleen waved away her comments. 'Oh, I'll do, I suppose. But I honestly can't believe how different you look. You've changed so much these last few months. Promise me you won't overdo it though, I don't want you disappearing.'

'There's no fear of that,' Debbie laughed. 'Anyway, I'm planning to stuff myself on honeymoon. I can't wait for all that yummy food – the olives and the calamari and the roast lamb.' Debbie's mouth was watering just thinking about it. 'Oh, that reminds me, did you tell the caterers that Jenny's vegetarian?'

'Yes, don't worry. Oh, and Julia said she'll talk to the venue about serving the wedding cake with the coffees. I spoke to her earlier, and she's got a meeting about another wedding tonight, but she's going down to the Tythe Barn first thing tomorrow to oversee all the set-up, so you don't have to worry about anything.'

'Brilliant. Julia's so lovely, I'm so lucky to have found her. Have you heard from Sasha?'

Debbie had hired the same make-up artist who'd created her look for the boudoir shoot to style her for the wedding.

'Yeah, she's coming over at nine tomorrow, the same time as Graham the photographer. Sasha will sort out the bridesmaids out first, then you'll be done around eleven thirty. The car will be here at one for you and your dad, and I'll get a lift with your Auntie Jean.'

Debbie settled back against her pillows and sighed happily. The wedding that she'd dreamt about for so long was finally coming together, and it was going to be perfect, she could just feel it.

'Thanks so much for all your help, Mum.'

'Don't be daft, that's what I'm here for.'

Kathleen bent over and kissed Debbie on the forehead, like she used to when she was a child, softly smoothing down her hair. Then she stood up, heading for the door. 'I'll see you in the morning. I'll get the Buck's Fizz and croissants ready.'

Debbie grinned. 'Thanks Mum, love you.'

'Love you too.'

Kathleen turned off the light, gently closing the door behind her and padding quietly down the stairs.

Left alone in her old room, Debbie's mind was spinning. As her eyes slowly adjusted to the darkness, she could pick out the outline of objects in the gloom, both familiar and different at the same time. There was the same old dressing table she'd had since she was a child, but it had now been moved over by the window. The wardrobe was new, and the free-standing mirror had been replaced by one on the wall, casting unexpected shadows across the carpet.

Debbie thought back to when she'd lain here as a teenager, wondering what life held for her and dreaming of marrying Duncan from Blue. Okay, so she might not be about to become Mrs James, but somehow that didn't seem to matter. She was incredibly happy to be getting hitched to Stevie Reid instead. She was so excited to spend the rest of her life with him, whatever that might bring, and she genuinely fell more in love with him every day. She wanted to have children with him, make memories with him, and grow old with him.

Debbie's brain was finally starting to wind down, her body beginning to relax, when her phone beeped on the bedside table. She was instantly wide awake again and lunged for it, hoping it might be Stevie. Instead, it was Angela:

Hey bride2b, can't wait for tmw, its gonna be a blast! I'll be round about 8.30, get the champagne on ice!!! Xxx

Debbie texted back:

Lol, thanks, just gone to bed but too excited to sleep. I'm getting married tomorrow!!!!! Don't worry, mum's putting on a spread in the morn, all the croissants u can eat. Luv u bridesmaid xxx

Her phone beeped again, almost instantly, and Debbie opened the text thinking it would be Angela again. She flushed with pleasure when she realised it was from Stevie:

Hey darling, not sure if this is allowed, but just wanted to say how much I love u &I can't wait for tomoro. Olly finally in bed so just opened my pres. You look amazing! Seriously amazing! When did you get them done? Can't wait to ravish you tomoro night wifey ;) xxxxx

In the darkness, Debbie grinned to herself. She thought the photos looked pretty amazing too, even if she did say so herself. Marcus had done a brilliant job with the sultry lighting and stylish setting, and Debbie had had her favourite shots made into a book, which is what she'd given to Stevie, all tied up with a big red bow.

Thanks babe, thrilled u like them. I can keep secrets too ;) Can't wait for that ravishing but we've got to get married 1st! See u tomorrow fiance (last time I can call u that!!) Love u with all my heart xxxxx

Debbie set her phone back down, realising that now she'd heard from Stevie, she suddenly felt much calmer. She wriggled down beneath the duvet, snuggling into the pillow and closing her eyes. She fell asleep within minutes, a smile on her face, knowing that when she woke up in a few hours' time, it would finally be her wedding day.

CHAPTER 34

'Never marry for money. Ye'll borrow it cheaper'
– Scottish proverb

Aimee's head was swimming. Someone handed her a glass of champagne and she gratefully accepted it, answering the same questions over and over again with the same answers and a polite smile.

'So just over a week to go until the big day, are you excited?'

'Do you realise how lucky you are, marrying into the Cunningham family?'

'You must be so grateful to Valerie for everything she's done.'

Aimee nodded, trying her best to sound sincere. 'Yes, Jon and I couldn't have managed without her.'

'Valerie really does have impeccable taste,' gushed the Vice President of the Horticultural Society – or was it the Heraldry Society? Aimee couldn't remember, and she'd completely forgotten the woman's name. 'I'm sure it's going to be such a wonderful occasion. I know how much hard work Valerie's put into this wedding. She even left the AGM early because she wanted to accompany Jon to his appointment at the tailor's. Isn't that sweet?'

'She's been wonderful,' Aimee lied, glancing across to where Valerie was schmoozing the local MP. 'If you'll excuse me, I need to phone my parents. I can't think where they are.'

With a sigh of relief, Aimee extricated herself from the throng of people and bolted through the French doors out into the back garden. It was a deliciously warm summer's evening, the sun only now beginning its descent in the hazy sky. The birds were still singing, as bees buzzed lazily from one brightly coloured flower to the next. But Aimee was far too stressed to appreciate how pretty the scene was.

She'd been summoned to Valerie's house, supposedly to go through the final arrangements with Julia, but Valerie had turned the occasion into some sort of pre-wedding drinks party, inviting everyone from the registrar to the local Master of the Hunt. Guests were spilling through from the living room to the dining room, where tray after tray of canapés had been laid out, and the champagne was flowing like water.

The only people who were missing were the ones Aimee wanted there most of all – her mum and dad. Aimee had asked them to arrive for seven o'clock, and it was now almost eight. It was so unlike her parents to be late; they'd never been to Valerie's before, and she wondered if they'd got lost trying to find the house. Both her parents' mobiles were going straight to voice-mail, whilst their home number just rang and rang.

'Aimee, what are you doing out here? Everyone's looking for you.'

Jon stepped out onto the terrace, looking handsome and stylish in stone-coloured chinos and a pale blue Ralph Lauren shirt.

Aimee laughed humourlessly. 'I doubt it. I don't know any of them.'

'And you won't get to know any of them unless you go back in there and talk to them, instead of hiding out here. They'll all be at the wedding next week, so it'd be nice if you'd make an effort.'

'I was calling my parents,' Aimee shot back, holding up her phone as though that constituted proof.

'Yes, I was wondering where they were.' There was a clear note of disapproval in his voice.

'I'm worried. They're never late to things, and neither of them are picking up their phones.'

'It's probably just Friday night traffic. You know how busy it can get when everyone's leaving work.'

'At eight pm?'

'Well maybe their car's broken down. That old banger was on its last legs anyway,' Jon smirked.

'Look, would you do me a favour?' Aimee asked, trying to ignore her fiancé's spiteful comments. 'Could you just pop out the front, see if you can see anything? They might be driving up and down the road, not sure which house it is.'

Jon sighed. 'I'm sure they'll be fine, Aimee. Don't they have a sat nav or something? Or are they incapable of reading door numbers?'

'The house is set back from the road, it's impossible to see the sign. Please Jon, just to set my mind at rest.'

'This is supposed to be *our* party. There are people in there I want to talk to. I don't want to spend my time running up and down the street on a wild goose chase.'

'Fine, I'll go myself,' Aimee snapped, pushing past him. He reached out to grab her arm, his fingertips digging in with surprising force. She pulled away angrily, her hand instinctively cradling the skin where he'd held her.

'How about we give it ten more minutes,' Jon suggested, his tone softer now. 'If they're still not here, I'll come and look with you, okay?'

Aimee hesitated. 'Okay,' she finally relented, letting herself be led back inside.

The first thing she heard was Valerie's loud, grating voice, rising above the babble. 'Well of course there'll be a string quartet playing during the wedding breakfast. And Aimee was keen to have a disc jockey for the evening party, but I really didn't think that was suitable, so now we're having a vintage band, which sounds rather fun…'

Aimee picked up another glass of champagne, and took a large gulp. She wasn't a big drinker, but getting heavily intoxicated seemed massively appealing right now.

She drifted through the crowd of people, making occasional small talk about her upcoming nuptials, but mostly being ignored. She felt strangely detached from everything; she could overhear everyone discussing *her* wedding, but these people were strangers to her.

The actual wedding day was going to be nothing like she'd envisaged either. Valerie had had her way on almost every issue, no matter how much Julia had tried to get Aimee involved. The dress was the one thing Aimee had stood firm on – and the one thing Valerie wasn't paying for, so couldn't control. She'd finally decided on a very simple off-the-shoulder sheath dress in shantung silk. It was plain and unadorned, nothing like the old-fashioned, fussy lace creations that Valerie kept encouraging her to try.

The rest of the wedding, however, was hallmarked with Valerie's preferences throughout, from her choice of minimal white orchid centrepieces (Aimee would have preferred romantic displays of dusky pink peonies and cream roses with baby's breath), to the choice of music, with Valerie insisting on Handel's *Water Music* for the signing of the register, not the Ed Sheeran song that Aimee wanted.

She picked up a goat's cheese canapé, popped it in her mouth and strolled over to Julia, who was sitting at one end of the enormous polished oak table, surrounded by pieces of paper. Like Aimee, she'd been told that tonight was about finalising the wedding details, but since the party had kicked off she felt like a spare part.

Julia smiled when she saw her, glad to see a friendly face. 'How are you doing?'

'Oh, you know…' Aimee replied, raising her eyebrows meaningfully. 'You?'

'About the same.' The two women laughed; a shared moment of understanding amidst all of the madness.

'Would you like a glass of champagne?' Aimee asked, noticing that Julia had a tumbler of water in front of her.

'I don't think I'm allowed.' A hint of a smile played across Julia's face. 'Someone tried to give me one earlier, and I was swiftly told that I was here to do a job, not to take advantage of the free alcohol.'

Aimee's mouth fell open in shock.

'Valerie said that?'

Julia gave a half-nod, aware of being overheard.

'I can't believe it. You'd think the way that woman goes on about manners that she'd have some of her own. Here, take this one.' Aimee pushed her flute across the table.

'Better not,' Julia said ruefully. 'I'm fine with my tap water, thanks. Hey, I'm glad you came over. I've been meaning to ask you, is this right?' She span one of the sheets of A3 paper around for Aimee to see. It showed a floor plan of the reception room, with circles and boxes representing the tables and guests. 'The bridesmaids have been taken off the top table, and are now…' Julia trailed off, pointing to the bottom of the plan, where the furthest tables were crammed between the fire exit and the toilets.

Aimee's eyes narrowed, her lips tightening in fury. 'No, that's not right. I thought we'd agreed at the last meeting that Rachel, Charlie and Tara were going there,' she jabbed at the paper. 'And Jon's cousins would be on a table with their parents.'

'I had a call from Valerie yesterday,' Julia said carefully, watching Aimee's face. 'And she asked me to change it back again, saying this was final. I assumed you'd agreed.'

'No, I hadn't.' Aimee felt another white-hot burst of anger surge through her. It was most unlike her to get so het-up, but it was something she'd been feeling more and more lately. 'Honestly, she's a bloody witch that woman. They're my best friends. They deserve to be on the top table, far more than her stuck-up relatives that she hardly ever sees.'

'Is everything okay?' Jonathan came over, looking concerned. He tried to top up Aimee's champagne glass, but she waved him away.

'Why have my friends been moved again?' she demanded.

Jon let out an irritated sigh. 'Are you *still* going on about that? I thought you'd worked it all out.'

'So did I, but apparently your mother's decided to change it again.'

Jon stared at her coldly. 'I don't appreciate your tone, Aimee. I don't think you realise quite how much time – and money – my mother's putting into this wedding.'

'Well I never asked her to,' Aimee hissed back, a lump forming in her throat. 'I'd have happily got married in some tiny venue, just the two of us with a handful of guests and none of this crazy hoopla.'

Jon took hold of her hands, trying to pacify her. 'Look, after the wedding, it *will* be just the two of us. We'll have this big celebration next week, and then everything will get back to normal. Just me and you.'

Aimee stared at him, finally comprehending something she should have realised a long time ago. 'It won't be though, will it?' she said quietly. 'It won't ever be just me and you.'

Jon opened his mouth to reply, when Valerie's voice rang out across the room, slicing through the buzz of conversation like a knife blade.

'Jonathan, darling, do come and speak to Hetty, you've hardly said two words to her all night. She's going through a tough time right now because her daughter's just split up with her fiancé. You remember Annabel, don't you? Pretty girl, works in PR for an equestrian company. Very bright and very well connected, apparently.'

Jon obediently trotted off, all thoughts of comforting Aimee forgotten. Julia gave her a sympathetic look.

'If I make it to the wedding without strangling that woman, it'll be a bloody miracle,' Aimee swore heatedly.

'I wouldn't blame you if you did.' It was an unprofessional comment and Julia knew it, but right now she felt bad for Aimee.

Her remark raised a smile at least, and Aimee felt grateful to have an ally in this room full of strangers. She looked across at Valerie, her hand possessively on Jon's arm, as he chatted to a middle-aged woman in a lilac skirt-suit with stiff, lacquered hair and an equally stiff expression.

'I just wish he had some backbone,' Aimee sighed, suddenly feeling the need to vent her frustration. 'He never stands up to her. Even if he took my side, just once, but he never does. I thought things would be different when we're married, but now I'm not sure they will…'

Aimee trailed off, staring unseeingly into the distance. Her mobile began to ring and she jumped, startled out of her reverie, before mouthing an apology to Julia and racing outside.

'Mum, finally! Is everything okay?'

'Yes, of course it is, I was about to ask you the same question. We've got half a dozen missed calls from you. I said to your dad I hope everything's okay.'

'Where are you?' The line wasn't great, but Aimee could hear people talking noisily in the background.

'Oh, we're at The George,' Pauline chuckled. 'Thought we'd treat ourselves to a night at the pub. They do a lovely scampi and chips.'

Aimee frowned in confusion. 'But why aren't you here? At Valerie's?'

There was a beat of silence on the other end. 'I thought that had been changed to tomorrow.'

'No, Mum, it's tonight. Why would you think that?'

'Because Valerie called us this afternoon and said it had been changed to tomorrow,' Pauline explained patiently. 'As we'd been planning to go out anyway, we thought we'd come to the pub. Has it changed back again?'

'Yeah, sort of…' Slowly, Aimee began to realise what had happened. She could feel her blood beginning to pump harder, anger pulsing through her veins. Trying to keep her voice calm for Pauline's sake, she said, 'Look, don't worry about it, Mum. I'll call you back later. Love you.'

'Love you too.'

Aimee clicked to end the call, her heart pounding furiously as adrenaline raced through her body. And then something snapped. Like an angry bull let loose, she stormed into the house and pushed through the tight press of people, making a beeline for Valerie.

CHAPTER 35

*'Marriage is a fine institution. But I'm not ready
for an institution'* – **Mae West**

'Why did you call my mum and tell her tonight had been changed to tomorrow?' Aimee's eyes were blazing, her breath coming in short, angry bursts.

Valerie turned to her calmly, giving a tinkling little laugh that made Aimee want to throttle her on the spot. 'I don't know what you're talking about, Aimee. Of course I didn't.'

Aimee stared at her in disbelief. 'You did. You're lying,' she said baldly.

For the first time, Valerie looked ruffled, her composure slipping. Some of the guests had stopped their conversations and were turning to look, trying to work out what the commotion was about.

'I'm so sorry,' Valerie apologised to the couple she was speaking to, and Aimee suddenly recognised them as Malcolm and Janette Huddlestone. Then Valerie turned back to her son's fiancée, and her tone became steely. 'Do calm down, Aimee. You're making rather a show of yourself.'

Jon came rushing over, concern etched on his face. 'What's happening?'

'Your mother called my parents today and told them tonight had been moved to tomorrow. That's why they're not here.'

Jonathan turned to Valerie. 'Is this true?'

'No, of course it's not. I expect they just got confused.' Valerie's face was the picture of innocence.

'There you are. It all sounds like a misunderstanding. Aimee, I think you owe Mother an apology.'

Aimee's jaw dropped in amazement. She felt as though she was trapped in a nightmare; the room had fallen silent, with everyone craning their necks to watch the spectacle.

'You're not going to believe her, are you?' Aimee burst out. 'It's obvious that she's lying. She didn't want my parents here so she called them and changed the date, in the same way she keeps moving my friends to the back of the reception, and in the same way that she keeps trying to exclude me from my own wedding because she doesn't actually want me to marry you. The reality is that she wants to keep you all to herself, and no one will ever be good enough for her precious son – especially not me!'

Aimee was breathing hard after her outburst. The tension in the room was palpable, every eye trained on the three of them to see what would happen next. Aimee gazed pleadingly at Jon, willing him to man up and take her side, to see the truth about his mother just this once.

Jon swallowed hard, shaking his head as though he couldn't believe what he was hearing. When he spoke, his words were slow and careful, as though talking to a skittish horse. 'Aimee, I don't know what's wrong with you right now. I'm willing to put it down to the stress of the wedding, but you simply can't say things like that. I need you to apologise to Mother right now.'

Aimee stared at the two of them – Valerie with a triumphant smirk on her face, Jonathan with a protective arm around his mother. His eyes were cold, his expression detached. Aimee realised that she didn't know him any more. He wasn't the man she'd fallen in love with, and he certainly wasn't the man she wanted as her husband.

In that moment, Aimee knew exactly what she had to do.

'Jon, could I speak to you for a moment? In private,' Aimee added, fighting to keep her voice steady.

She expected Jonathan to refuse, but he must have heard something in her voice to convince him she was deadly serious.

'Of course,' he replied tightly. 'Let's go through to the study.'

'Jonathan!' Valerie protested, almost stamping her foot in annoyance like a petulant child. 'I need you *here*, to greet your guests. You can't go running off around the house with…' she trailed off, looking Aimee up and down as though she was something Valerie had found on the bottom of her shoe.

'I'll be back shortly, Mother.' The tension in Jon's voice was clear. 'I'm sure you can keep everyone occupied until then.'

Aimee couldn't help but find it ironic that this was the first time she'd ever seen Jon go against his mother's wishes. And it was too little, too late.

'Very well. I suppose it's a good idea to take her away, and let her calm down a little.' Valerie's tone was icy, but for once, Aimee genuinely didn't care. It was almost over, and in a few moments' time, she'd never have to worry about Valerie ever again.

Fighting the urge to stick two fingers up at her, Aimee followed Jon out of the room as he led her to the study. The room was on the other side of the vast house, and Aimee half-wondered whether he'd chosen it deliberately, so that their guests couldn't hear if she started screaming and shouting.

As they walked in silence, Aimee looked around, as though seeing everything for the first time. The house was undoubtedly impressive and tastefully decorated, but there was something almost cold and clinical about it. It was like being in a stately home, or a museum, where everything was for show, and there were no personal touches.

As she passed the enormous painting of a horse and hounds scene, Aimee slipped the heavy engagement ring off her left hand, balling it tightly in her fist, feeling the jagged edges press into her skin. She felt better almost instantly – lighter, freer, as though a huge weight had been lifted from her shoulders.

Jonathan closed the study door behind them. It was a beautiful room, with row after row of leather-bound books on solid oak shelves, and a large photograph of Nigel Cunningham on the polished wooden desk. But Aimee didn't notice any of that. She stretched out her hand to Jon, the engagement ring sitting on her upturned palm.

'Here,' she said softly. 'Take it.'

Jon stared back at her incredulously. 'Aimee, what are you saying?'

'It's over, Jon.' She felt a huge rush of emotions as she looked at him. Sadness, mixed with relief, mixed with anger and grief. But the overwhelming feeling was a certainty that she was doing the right thing. She wished she'd done it a long time ago.

'What do you mean, it's over? Calm down, you're not thinking straight. That incident with Mother was just a misunderstanding. I'll speak to her about it, we can sort this out…'

Aimee shook her head ruefully. 'I think we're past that. I'm sorry, Jon, but we're done.'

She stepped forward, placing the ring on the desk next to a stack of papers. Sunlight streamed in through the mullioned windows, reflecting off the ruby in a thousand splintered fragments.

Aimee wasn't sorry to let it go; she'd never really liked it. The ring was too big, too brash, too ostentatious. It had never been right for her – just like her fiancé.

Jonathan looked at it in disbelief, unable to comprehend how she could simply cast aside an expensive family heirloom. Something seemed to jolt inside him at that moment, a realisation that Aimee was serious.

'Sweetheart, please,' he began, stepping towards her and instinctively taking hold of her hands. His expression was pained, beads of sweat gathering on his forehead that were caused by more than the warm summer evening and the stuffy study they were standing in. When he spoke, there was desperation in his voice.

'There's a roomful of people out there. A houseful. There are all Mother's friends from the club, and my business acquaintances, and half the local council…' Jonathan was growing paler with every guest he recalled. 'Please don't do this to me today,' he begged. 'We can talk about it later – I'll give you whatever you want. Just go through with tonight and don't make a scene.'

He was genuinely afraid, Aimee realised – a coward at heart, and terrified of his mother's reaction if he messed up her special night. Aimee felt bad for him – but not bad enough to step back into that throng of pretentious, judgemental people who'd made her feel so unwelcome.

'I'm sorry,' she said again. 'I can't do it. Look, tell them anything you like, I don't mind. Tell them I was ill and I had to go home. Tell them I've gone to pick up my parents and then make up something else later, whatever you want to say. But I can't go back in there, Jon.'

She stared up at him, willing him to understand. Memories came flooding back to her, as she remembered the good times (despite everything, there had been many), mingled with huge sadness and uncertainty about where her life was going to go. Jon had been all she'd known for almost three years now. She'd intended to marry this man, have his children and grow old with him. It would take some adjusting to accept that wasn't going to happen.

They were still holding hands, and Aimee squeezed his fingers affectionately, taking in his face for the last time. He was undoubtedly a good-looking man, with those brooding dark looks, model-like bone structure, and smooth, freshly shaven skin.

As she gently pulled her hands away from his, she saw his face harden, his eyes grow cold.

'You ungrateful little bitch,' Jon spat, his outburst coming out of nowhere.

'What? Jon, I—'

'After everything I've done for you, you won't do this one thing for me?'

'It's not like that, you—'

'You've leeched off me for three years now, haven't you? You've bled me dry and now you're off to find some other sucker, is that it?'

Tears sprang into Aimee's eyes, and she blinked them back furiously. She wasn't going to cry for him, not now. He'd made her cry enough times in the past, and she was damned if he was going to do it again. She shook her head, bitterly refuting the accusations.

'That's not true. I don't have to listen to this.' She made a move towards the door, but Jon grabbed her, his fingers digging in painfully in the way he'd done so many times before. She'd always wondered whether or not it was accidental, but Aimee understood now that it was about power and control, like so many of his actions.

'You *do* have to listen,' Jon hissed, and she felt flecks of spittle land on her cheeks. 'I've put a roof over your head, paid for all your meals, even the clothes you're wearing now were bought by me.'

With a sickening jolt, Aimee realised that was true. She looked down at the pretty chiffon summer dress from Karen Millen and felt nauseous, hating herself. Never again, she vowed. Giving up her job had been an enormous mistake; she never wanted to lose her independence like that.

'I'm sorry,' she gabbled, seemingly incapable of saying anything else today. 'I'll pay you back, I'll pay it all back.'

'Pay it back? With what? You don't have any money, and neither do your parents with their measly little house and clapped-out car. Mother was right all along – you were never good enough for me.'

His grip was tightening with every word, and Aimee winced in pain, genuinely frightened.

'Jon, you're hurting me,' she cried, sounding terrified.

Jonathan didn't seem to hear, his eyes blazing as he continued to rant maniacally. 'You're just a common little slag, out for whatever she can get, and I fell for it like—'

Aimee shoved him as hard as she could and he lost his balance, falling hard against the desk. The jolt stopped him in his tracks, and Aimee seized her opportunity, making a bolt for the door. She pulled it open, then stopped abruptly in the doorway, turning back to look at her ex-fiancé. He was slumped against the desk, his head bowed, looking utterly dejected.

'I never meant to hurt you, or for us to end up like this,' Aimee told him. He raised his eyes to look at her, his expression beaten. 'I did love you, Jon, you know that. But I can't marry you.'

With that, Aimee turned on her heel, walking for the final time along the plush cream carpet to the enormous front door. She could hear the sound of chattering and laughter drifting through from the back of the house, and felt nothing but relief that she no longer had to deal with those people.

Collecting her handbag from the entrance hall, she pulled out her car keys and realised that the gleaming Mercedes had been yet another (unwanted) gift from Jonathan. There was no way she could drive home in it. She left the key on the side table and pulled out her phone to text Julia:

Meet me outside the front gates asap!!

Aimee didn't want to hang around on Valerie's property any longer than she had to. She marched sharply across the gravel driveway and out through the imposing gates. Moments later, Julia arrived, confusion written across her face as she spotted Aimee.

'What happened? Is everything okay?'

Aimee held up her empty left hand. 'I think you might be out of a job.'

Julia's eyes widened in shock. 'Are you being serious?'

Aimee nodded, suddenly feeling close to tears once again, but this time it was for an entirely different reason. 'I told him I couldn't marry him.'

'Oh, Aimee,' Julia sighed, instinctively hugging her. 'How did he take it?'

'As you'd imagine. Shock, anger… Overall I think he was more sorry about being embarrassed in front of his guests and disappointing his mother, than any genuine sadness about splitting up with me.'

'Well for what it's worth, I think you did the right thing.'

'Really?'

'I'd have jacked in this job ages ago if it wasn't for you. Jon and Valerie are a total nightmare!'

'Why didn't you tell me earlier?' Aimee wondered.

'As a wedding planner, it's really not my place to try and stop the wedding. It's kind of counterproductive,' Julia smiled. 'Seriously though, are you okay?'

'I will be,' Aimee nodded.

'If there's anything you need, anything at all, just let me know.'

'Um… there is one thing…' Aimee began. Julia looked at her expectantly. 'A lift to my parents' house. I just gave Jon the keys for the Mercedes. Symbolic, but not very practical.'

Julia burst into laughter. 'Absolutely,' she grinned. 'It would be my pleasure. Come on, Runaway Bride. Let's get you out of here.'

CHAPTER 36

'My most brilliant achievement was my ability to persuade my wife to marry me' – **Winston Churchill**

The first strains of Wagner's 'Bridal Chorus' creaked into life on the organ in the old country church, and the expectant congregation turned around in their seats, every eye focused on the ornate door through which the bride would make her entrance.

Outside, on a brilliant, summer, sun-dappled afternoon, a beautiful young woman stood beside her father, aware that these were her final few moments as Miss Deborah Barlow. In approximately thirty minutes' time, she would be Mrs Stephen Reid, and the happiest woman on earth.

But this was no fantasy, from which Debbie would shake herself free in a few moments to discover the disappointment of being in her scruffy old bedroom. This was actually happening. It was her wedding day, and everything was even better than she'd dreamed.

The weather was beautiful – not too hot, in a way that would make the guests swelter uncomfortably, and the bride perspire, in a distinctly un-bridal fashion, but with warm rays of sunshine that caressed her bare shoulders.

Debbie was standing outside St Anne's, the same parish church in which she'd been christened as a baby, in which she'd gone to midnight mass as a child, and which she'd recently re-discovered with Stevie, making a point of getting to properly know Father David before he bound the two of them in holy matrimony.

On the pavement that ran past the church, a small crowd had gathered to watch and share in the happiness of the occasion. It didn't matter that they were strangers – there was something pure and joyful about a beautiful bride in her gown on her wedding day.

'Not long now,' Angela winked.

Debbie grinned back, as Angela fussed around her, making tiny adjustments to ensure that she looked perfect. She smoothed down a hair, where it had escaped from the intricate low bun at the nape of Debbie's neck, and brushed away the tiniest speck of mascara from the corner of her eye.

'Thanks Ange. I would hug you, but…' Debbie gestured at her dress; crisp and white and certainly not made for spontaneous hugs – not at this stage of the day.

'I understand. And you look absolutely stunning, Debs, you really do.'

For once, Debbie believed it. She'd finally made it into her perfect wedding dress. Okay, so it might not have been a size ten, but the size twelve gown fit her to perfection, emphasising her newly slender figure and trim waist. It was an A-line cut in ivory satin, with a jewelled belt and a corset back, a chapel-length train trailing behind her. She'd paired it with a simple, pencil-edged veil, and in her bouquet were sweet-smelling, pale pink roses, cream hydrangeas, freesias and lisianthus. It was everything she'd ever wanted.

Debbie's father, Norman, turned to her, his face a mixture of nerves and pride and awe. He held out his arm for his daughter to take. 'I think it's time.'

Debbie felt a sharp pang of nerves, and then it was as though all of her anxieties melted away, dissipating through her body, and leaving her perfectly calm, perfectly serene. She linked her arm through her father's and took a deep breath as they stepped through the stone archway into the church.

It took a second for Debbie's eyes to adjust to the dimness of the interior after the brightness outside. When they did, she saw the familiar old church looking more beautiful than she'd ever known it. The florist – a friend of Julia's called Linda, who ran a flower shop in the city centre – had done an incredible job of decorating it. Garlands of ivy were looped along the window frames, decorated with white orchids and spray roses, while posies hung from the end of every pew, illuminated by thin shafts of light piercing through the stained glass windows.

As Debbie advanced down the aisle, the pipe organ ringing out in celebration, she passed her friends and relatives, all dressed up in their finery. She grinned at Gill, nodded at her friend, Alex, unable to keep the smile off her face. There was cousin Wendy in her big hat, and Auntie Jean crying into a handkerchief.

Following behind her, all of Debbie's bridesmaids were wearing her favourite shade of peach, but in different styles to fit their very different figures. Her two nieces, as flower girls, wore white with a peach sash, and carried baskets of peach and white petals.

Debbie was vaguely aware of the photographer walking a few steps ahead, trying and failing to be unobtrusive as he snapped the pictures that would form the basis of her memories, and which she hoped in years to come she would share with her children and grandchildren.

And right there, at the end of the aisle, was Stevie. He looked more handsome than she'd ever seen him, in his grey morning suit, with a cream-coloured waistcoat and peach tie. He couldn't take his eyes off her; the expression on his face was pure love, and Debbie felt a lump rise in her throat, willing herself not to cry. She knew it was all pomp and ceremony and tradition, but right now she couldn't think of anything more incredible than two people making vows to love and cherish each other for the rest of their lives.

As she finally reached her very-soon-to-be-husband, Debbie slipped her arm out from her father's, and he and Stevie shook hands. From that moment on, it was as though no one else existed. Debbie and Stevie gazed at one another, mesmerised, as though surprised to suddenly find themselves all dressed up and about to get married.

'You look beautiful,' Stevie whispered.

For what was possibly the first time in her life, Debbie *felt* beautiful. And it was nothing to do with her size or shape or even the dress she was wearing. She felt radiant, buoyed up by the love in the room.

'I love you,' Debbie whispered back.

They squeezed one another's hands in a gesture of affection and reassurance, then turned to Father David. He was in his seventies and grey-haired, thin and a little stooped, but he'd known Debbie's family for decades.

'Dearly beloved, we are gathered here today to join this man and this woman in holy matrimony…'

Time seemed to fly. Debbie was vaguely aware of the photographer snapping away, capturing their special day forever, and she felt grateful as the ceremony seemed to pass in a blur and she knew there was no way she would remember it all. Then the vows had been said, the rings exchanged, and the vicar was giving Stevie permission to kiss his new bride.

Spontaneous applause broke out in the church, as Stevie gave her a tentative peck, then swept her backwards, movie-style, in his arms, as Debbie giggled joyfully and held him tightly, kissing him back for all she was worth.

—

'You did such a good job,' Gill smiled, her hand in Mike's as she came over to greet Julia. They were standing outside in the churchyard, as Debbie and Stevie assembled for photos with their friends and family, still smiling in wonder and delight at the novelty of being husband and wife.

'Hopefully the reception will go without a hitch, too,' Julia replied, as she accepted a glass of champagne from a passing waiter. The Tythe Barn – Debbie and Stevie's chosen reception venue – was a short way down the road, close enough for most of the guests to walk, and the staff had agreed to serve drinks in the field surrounding the church immediately after the ceremony.

'I can't wait to see what ours is going to be like,' Gill grinned, giving Mike's arm a squeeze. He looked a little uncomfortable in his smart suit, but Gill looked wonderful in the blue and white china-pattern dress she was wearing.

'I've no idea what those kids of ours will have come up with,' Mike said, shaking his head worriedly.

'You'll enjoy it, I promise you. They've done you proud.' Julia assured them.

Gill and Mike still didn't know what their wedding reception would involve. They'd decided on a small registry office ceremony, with the children and close friends in attendance, but the reception was entirely out of their hands, planned by the kids and brought to fruition by Julia. The only thing Gill knew was that Sammy had extended an invitation to his favourite nursery assistant, Debbie, hence why Gill and Mike had been invited to Debbie's wedding.

'Doesn't she look beautiful,' Gill sighed, looking across to where Debbie was laughing joyously as a group of her friends covered her in confetti and the photographer snapped away. The fitted gown followed every movement of her figure as she walked, perfectly showing off her new shape.

'She looks like a different woman,' Julia remarked. 'She's completely transformed from the Debbie I met last year.'

'I wish I'd had the willpower to do that,' Gill said wistfully. 'But with five kids, dieting's the last thing on my mind.'

'You don't need to diet,' Mike said, sounding outraged, as he pulled her to him, squeezing her waist. 'You're perfect just as you are.'

'Aw, thanks.' Gill kissed him. 'You're not so bad yourself. Do you know, I think I might marry you.'

They nuzzled again, and Julia decided to let them have their moment. 'I'll catch up with you two later. I'll go and give my congratulations to the other pair of lovebirds.'

Julia headed off across the churchyard, her fuchsia chiffon dress swishing around her tanned legs. There were so many happy couples here today, she thought with a pang. It seemed silly, as she'd attended dozens of weddings with her job, but it still made her feel strange not to have Nick by her side on such a happy occasion. She was really missing him today, she realised, wondering when she'd suddenly got so sentimental.

This past year since Jack had been born had been the most turbulent of Julia's life – nothing could have prepared her for the upheaval that perfect little bundle would bring to both of their lives, or how much she could feel love for a brand new person. She simply couldn't imagine her life without him now.

But neither had she expected just how exhausted, anxious, and at times completely overwhelmed, she would feel. The feelings of failure she'd experienced in the early days, when she didn't know how to stop Jack from crying, or even how to work the bottle steriliser, had severely knocked her confidence. Parenthood had been a massive learning curve, and she knew there were so many times when she'd been worried and irritable, taking her mood out on Nick or failing to see his side. But as they'd celebrated Jack's first birthday a few weeks ago, they'd both been happy and loving, open with each other about how far they'd come and what still needed to be done in their relationship.

Julia had promised Nick that once these weddings were out of the way, she'd find a babysitter for Jack and whisk her husband away to a hotel for the night, to show him exactly what he'd been missing out on recently.

'Julia!'

She turned to see Angela waving at her, and the two women embraced. 'You look gorgeous, Ang. That colour really suits you. And wasn't it a lovely ceremony?'

'I was tearing up all the way through,' Angela confessed. 'Just knowing how hard Debbie's worked to look like that, and it was all totally worth it. She looked so gorgeous. And speaking of gorgeous… have you met my date for the day?'

Julia shook her head, then her mouth fell open in shock as Angela turned and grabbed the hand of a hot, blond guy. 'You remember Matt, don't you?'

'Matt!' Julia exclaimed, recalling the personal trainer from Debbie's spa day. 'Of course I do! How are you?'

'Pretty good thanks,' he grinned, gazing adoringly at Angela.

'So how long have you two been… I mean when did you… How…?'

'He got my email from the receptionist at the hotel, from when we made the booking,' Angela grinned, her eyes sparkling. 'How cool is that?'

'I owe that girl a drink,' Matt beamed, clearly smitten, as he wrapped his arm around Angela's shoulder.

'We've been together almost three months,' Angela explained. 'Which is something of a record for me.'

'Who knows, we might be needing your services soon,' Matt winked at Julia, as Angela looked shocked, then giggled delightedly.

Julia heard a commotion behind her, and turned to see Debbie gliding across the churchyard towards them.

'Julia, I've been so busy I haven't had a chance to talk to you,' Debbie said breathlessly.

'Oh, don't worry about it, today will be a whirlwind. You look beautiful, by the way.'

'Thank you,' Debbie smiled radiantly. She really was glowing, emanating pure happiness. 'It feels amazing. Look!' she cried, holding up her hand to show them the shiny new wedding band nestling below her engagement ring.

'You're married!' Julia exclaimed, swept up in Debbie's enthusiasm.

'And I couldn't have done it without you.'

Julia waved away the praise. 'Of course you could. But I was happy to help. You deserve to have a fantastic day.'

'Can we have the bride and groom with the bridesmaids over here please,' the photographer shouted. Debbie glanced across, seeing everyone beginning to gather for the photo.

'I'd better go,' she said apologetically to Julia, grabbing Angela and pulling her reluctantly away from Matt. 'But we'll catch up later, at the reception?'

'Of course,' Julia promised, as Debbie turned to go, her expression one of pure bliss, her veil billowing out behind her, caught by the gentle summer breeze.

CHAPTER 37

*'The absolute yearning of one human body for
another particular body and its indifference to
substitutes is one of life's major mysteries'*
– Iris Murdoch

'What's that Jack? What is it? It's a giraffe, isn't it? Can you say
"giraffe"?'

'Af,' Jack managed, staring up in wonder at the long-legged,
long-necked creature in front of him. He hugged his toy giraffe,
Raffy, close, watching in fascination as the real giraffe silently
chewed on a leaf it had plucked from the trees, its long lashes
sweeping up and down as it blinked.

'Clever boy!' Julia exclaimed. 'Giraffe, that's right. Did you
hear that, Nick?' She swung round excitedly to face her husband.

'Yes, I heard,' he smiled indulgently, amused by Julia's enthusiasm. 'I've always said that boy's a genius. He clearly takes after
his dad.'

Julia rolled her eyes, but she was laughing.

'Do you want to take a closer look, Jacky-boy?' Nick wondered, bending down to unclip Jack from his pushchair and
hoisting him up onto his shoulders, holding him to keep him
stable.

Jack's chubby legs clung tightly around Nick's neck, grasping him in a virtual headlock.

'Af af af!' Jack screeched, pointing up at the giraffe which suddenly seemed much closer and larger than it had from buggy level.

It was a glorious Saturday in mid-June, so the animal park was packed, with families milling all around, enjoying the fine weather. The two giraffes were the star attraction, and were the most exotic creatures the small zoo held.

'So where next?' Nick wondered, as he swung Jack back down again, squinting up at the nearby signpost. 'We could go to the reptile house, or the farmyard, or the aquarium?'

'Let's wander this way and see where it takes us,' Julia suggested, pointing at a winding path that led off into the trees.

'Okay, you're the boss.'

They set off, Julia doing her best to push the cumbersome buggy over the uneven ground.

'Do you want me to take over?' Nick offered.

'No, I'm fine thanks,' Julia insisted. 'It's good exercise for me.'

'Not that you need it. You're looking amazing lately,' Nick growled, giving her a cheeky pat on the bottom. 'Very sexy.'

Julia flushed, glancing around in case anyone had seen. 'I can't wait to get back to Zumba classes once this last wedding's out of the way. I've had no time for anything recently.'

'Don't I know it,' Nick teased. 'So you've just got Gill's wedding next week?'

'Yep, just one more to go. And Debbie gets back from her honeymoon tomorrow. I can't wait to hear all about it. She posted some pictures on Facebook and it looked amazing.'

'So does that mean we get our babysitter back?' Nick grinned. 'Then we can make the most of your free time.'

'Hmm…' Julia replied, deciding that now wasn't the best moment to tell Nick about the email she'd received that morning. Debbie's uncle was the Director of the Norfolk Museum of Antiquities, and he'd got chatting to Julia at the wedding, asking for her card. According to the email, he was very interested in hiring her to plan the museum's one hundredth anniversary celebrations…

'I hope Aimee's okay,' Julia chattered on, changing the subject. 'I texted her this morning, but I haven't had a reply yet.'

The reason Julia had a rare Saturday free to spend with her husband and son was because today should have been Jon and Aimee's wedding day. Julia couldn't even begin to imagine what Aimee was going through; as much as their split was undoubtedly for the best, she knew that Aimee would be finding today incredibly difficult.

'Have you had any response from the dragon lady?' Nick wondered, referring to Valerie.

Julia shook her head. 'No. I think I'm going to have to get a lawyer involved. I really didn't want that to happen, but I don't see what choice I have. I can't afford to lose all that money.'

Despite the fact that the wedding had been cancelled, Valerie still owed Julia for all of the work she'd done to date. But when Julia had submitted her invoice, she'd received a very impolite phone call from Valerie telling her exactly where she could shove it. The fact remained that Julia had spent weeks working on the wedding, and Valerie was contractually obliged to pay her for all the hours and expenses she'd accrued up until then.

'Anyway, let's not talk about that now,' Julia went on. 'I want to have fun today, not think about anything bad.'

'Fair enough,' Nick nodded, a mysterious twinkle in his eye. 'Although I might have a cunning plan to get the old battleaxe to pay up… Leave it with me for now.'

'Okay,' Julia giggled, wondering what on earth he had in mind. 'Oh look, Nick, this is beautiful. Don't you think this would make a good picnic spot?'

They'd emerged at the top of a low hill, with grassland spreading into the distance, and a large duck pond just in front of them. Beside the pond were a dozen picnic tables, already occupied by harassed parents and excited children, and an ice cream van parked up nearby was doing a roaring trade.

'Looks good to me,' Nick grinned, as Julia came to a stop and Nick began unpacking the buggy, shaking out the picnic rug and spreading it on the ground.

Julia unclipped Jack and sat him down, passing him his toy cars to play with, while Nick opened the containers of food, arranging them on the chequered blanket.

'Mmm, this is lovely,' Julia sighed, stretching out her bare legs and turning her face up to the sun. She was wearing denim shorts and a white T-shirt, a straw trilby perched jauntily on her head.

'We should definitely do this more often,' Nick declared, as he tucked into a mini pork pie.

'Oh, I meant to mention, we're both invited to Gill's reception next week. Obviously I'll be there anyway, in a professional capacity, but they've asked if you'd like to come along as well, as a guest in the evening.'

'Is that the one that the kids are organising?'

'I'm helping them!' Julia retorted indignantly, as she peeled open a yoghurt and began feeding Jack. 'But yeah, they've come up with the ideas and they've done a brilliant job. I can't wait for you to see it.'

'Do I even know Gill?'

'I think you might have met her once or twice at nursery. But like I said, it's just for the evening reception, and the kids want as many people as possible to create a party atmosphere.'

'Right, so I'm just there to make up numbers,' Nick teased. 'What about Jack?'

'We can take him with us. Debbie's invited too, so she won't be around to babysit,' Julia joked. 'We can just stick him in his buggy when he's ready to sleep. There'll be loads of other children there too, so it should be a fun night.'

'Sounds good,' Nick agreed amiably.

There was a sudden commotion down by the water, as a flock of ducks came in to land, quacking loudly and causing excitement amongst the children at the water's edge.

Jack turned his head to watch, pointing at them agitatedly, and making a noise that clearly indicated he wanted to go see what all the fuss was about.

'Do you want to go see the duckies, hey, Jacky-boy?' Julia fussed, as she cleaned his sticky face and hands with a baby wipe. 'You want to go visit the quack quacks?'

'I'll take him if you like,' Nick offered. 'You've hardly had a chance to eat anything.'

'Okay, thanks,' Julia said appreciatively. 'Here, take these crusts with you.'

She passed them across as Nick got to his feet and helped Jack up, holding his hand as they slowly toddled off across the grass towards the pond.

Julia smiled as she watched them, unconsciously checking out Nick's body in his shorts and slim-fit T-shirt. He looked so strong and manly; it was incredibly sweet to see him playing the doting father as he strolled along with Jack.

Watching the pair of them, Julia couldn't help but reflect on everything they'd gone through since Jack had been born. It had been a real rollercoaster of ups and downs, and she knew that Nick, especially, had struggled to adjust. But since Jack's time in hospital he'd been as good as his word, really making an effort to spend quality time with his son. He'd started coming home from work earlier, and it seemed as though he'd barely seen his friends for weeks, genuinely preferring to hang out with Jack and Julia.

Now, whenever Julia needed to work, Nick was always available to look after his son. The other week, when Jack had fallen over on the patio and scraped his knee, it had been Nick, not Julia, he'd wanted to comfort him. It was a strange sensation for Julia, but she understood that her little boy was growing up. One day, he wouldn't need her at all, she realised with a pang of sadness.

In the distance, the sun was shining off the water, so bright that it cast Nick and Jack in silhouette. A cluster of eager ducks flocked around them, fighting for the bread crusts, and she could hear Jack laughing, that delightful, joyful, childish giggle, so free and unselfconscious that it made her heart soar. And Julia knew that moments like these were the stuff life was made of; memories like these would be cherished forever.

CHAPTER 38

'Marriage is a three ring circus: engagement ring,
wedding ring and suffering' – **Unknown**

Gill's house was usually chaotic, but she'd never seen anything like the mayhem that reigned on the morning of her wedding.

Mike had spent the night at the home of his best man, Dennis, so Gill was in charge of getting all five children prepped and ready. Of course, she wasn't entirely alone; Julia was rushing around ensuring everything ran smoothly and to schedule, while Gill's mother, Dee, was also helping out, shepherding the kids to where they needed to be and doing her best to keep them all entertained.

What seemed like dozens of people had passed through the house that morning, a veritable convoy streaming in and out as the florist dropped off the bouquet and the buttonholes, the postman delivered a flurry of cards, the neighbours popped in to say congratulations, and good luck, and generally bask in the party atmosphere. The kettle was constantly boiling, with Dee making endless rounds of tea and coffee, hand-washing the cups to ensure they didn't run out.

Right now, Gill was sitting in her bedroom – otherwise known as wedding HQ – in her dressing gown, watching as Paige had her hair styled and make-up applied by Jenny, a friend of Gill's from the local beauty salon. Sammy was giddier than Gill had ever seen him, bouncing up and down on her bed, clutching a Ben 10 figure which he was waving in the air. She'd given up trying to stop him, and was now just hoping that he wore himself out and kept quiet for the ceremony. She was ashamed to admit that she'd left the twins to play on their PS3, something that was never usually allowed on a Saturday morning, but it kept them occupied and out of the way.

'What time is it?' Gill asked for the hundredth time that morning, turning to Julia.

'Eleven twenty. Just over three hours until we need to leave. Don't worry, everything's on schedule,' Julia smiled, consulting her notebook. 'Have you heard from Mike yet?'

'Yeah, he texted earlier. He's got the easy job,' Gill grumbled. 'A nice lie-in, followed by a cheeky nip of Scotch to calm the nerves, and a chilled morning getting ready at Dennis'. He doesn't have to deal with all this drama,' she continued, as Sammy's shrieking reached fever pitch and he threw himself down on the pillows.

'Well all you have to do is worry about getting to the ceremony on time and looking spectacular,' Julia assured her. 'The reception's all taken care of.'

Paige overheard Julia's comment and squealed gleefully. 'Don't give anything away,' she warned.

'I won't,' Julia smiled, putting a finger to her lips.

Paige grinned back, mimicking Julia's gesture, then looked over at Gill. 'I can't wait for you to see it.'

'Me neither,' Gill replied. 'I'm honestly clueless about what you've got planned. I'm really looking forward to the surprise.'

'All done,' Jenny called out, causing Paige to jump up in excitement, turning back and forth in front of the dressing table mirror to admire her reflection. Her hair was pulled back in a sleek French plait, accessorised with a sparkling headband. She was wearing pale coral lip gloss, with a touch of light brown eye shadow and clear mascara, emphasising how young and fresh she looked.

'Gorgeous,' Gill proclaimed, as Paige beamed.

'Can I put my dress on now?' she begged, as Gill shook her head. The kids were still in their pyjamas, and Gill didn't want them putting on their smart clothes until the last possible moment.

'No, not yet, I don't think my nerves could stand it. One spill or tear and it'll be ruined. Let's wait a while, okay?'

'Okay,' Paige huffed, but nothing could ruin her good mood today, and her smile was quickly back on her face.

'Could you do me a favour if you're not busy? Could you go and grab Kel and let her know Jenny's ready for her.'

'Sure,' Paige said obligingly. 'Come on, Sammy,' she added, reaching out a hand for her little brother. 'Let's go get Kelly.'

'Hiiiii-Yaaaa!' Sam let out a terrifying cry as he leapt off the bed with a karate kick, sprinting out of the door ahead of Paige.

'Peace at last,' Gill sighed, sinking back in her chair and closing her eyes for a blissful second. 'Not that it'll last.'

'You deserve a medal,' Julia joked.

'Well, it was sweet of Paige to take Sam with her. I don't know where he gets his energy from. Ooh, do you know, I could murder a cup of tea.'

'No champagne this morning?'

Gill shook her head. 'I need to keep my wits about me with this lot. I don't want to be half-cut before the ceremony!'

'Well I'll pop down and get you one if you like.'

'I would love that, thanks Julia.'

'Can I get one for you, Jenny?' Julia addressed the hair and make-up stylist.

'That'd be lovely, thank you. Milk, no sugar. Oh, and if you see Kelly send her this way. I'm aware the timings are tight, so I need to get started on her as soon as possible.'

'Hmm,' Julia frowned, looking at her watch. 'Good point.' She jogged downstairs and into the kitchen, spotting Paige and Sammy outside in the garden. 'Paige,' Julia called, as she stepped out of the back door. 'Did you tell Kelly that Jenny's ready for her?'

Paige shook her head. 'I haven't seen her yet. We're looking for her out here.'

'Okay, thanks. You haven't seen Kelly, have you?' Julia asked Dee, as she dropped three teabags into three mugs.

'No, not for about half an hour. Do you want me to make the teas and bring them up?'

'Could you? Thanks,' Julia said gratefully, heading back up the stairs. Gill and Jenny looked up expectantly as she entered the room. 'Look. I don't want to alarm anyone unnecessarily, but no one's seen Kelly for a while. I'm not sure where she's got to.'

Gill frowned. 'Isn't she in her room?'

'Apparently not – Paige said she'd checked there.'

'Well she has to be here somewhere,' Gill said, sounding exasperated.

Dee arrived in the doorway carrying the drinks, Paige and Sammy running up behind her.

'Kelly's gone,' Paige announced dramatically.

'Gone,' Sammy echoed.

'What do you mean? She can't be gone,' Gill retorted.

Paige shrugged. 'We checked. She's not in her room and she's not in the bathroom or the living room. We checked all upstairs and downstairs, and she's not outside either. We even looked in the garage.'

'We saw a spider,' Sammy piped up.

'Oh, this is ridiculous,' Gill tutted, reaching for her phone and calling Kelly's number. 'I told her not to wander off. She knows how important today is and—' Gill broke off, listening intently. 'Voicemail,' she mouthed at Julia. 'Hi Kelly, it's Mum. I'm not sure where you've got to, but if you've popped to the shop or something, can you get back here as soon as possible? It's kind of an important day. Love you.'

Gill hung up, looking around at the sea of worried faces staring back at her.

'What now?' Julia wondered, her eyes full of concern.

Gill raised an eyebrow. 'Now? Now we wait.'

———

An hour later, all hell had broken loose.

Kelly was officially missing. No one had heard from her since she'd left the house that morning, and no one knew where she was. Dee and Jenny were out combing the nearby streets, checking with neighbours and local shops, but there'd been no sightings.

Gill was growing hysterical and Julia was doing her best to keep her calm.

'What if she's run off with someone she's met on the internet?' Gill panicked. 'I knew we should never have let her write that blog, I told Mike, but he insisted…'

'She won't have done,' Julia assured her. 'She's far too sensible for that, you know she is.'

'Do I?' Gill looked at her uncertainly. The fact remained that Kelly had gone, and no one knew why.

'There's nothing missing from her room, is there?' Julia pointed out. 'She hasn't taken a bag, or a change of clothes.'

'I think we need to call the police,' Gill declared, pacing up and down her room, too on edge to stay still. 'We've waited too long already, we have to—' She was interrupted by her phone ringing, and she pounced on it. It was Mike.

'Have you heard anything?' she demanded.

'No. I take it that means you haven't either?'

'I think we need to call the police, Mike. Anything could have happened to her.'

At the other end of the phone, Mike sighed heavily. 'You're probably right. How long's it been now?'

'Nearly two hours!' Gill wailed. 'She could be anywhere by now. With anyone!'

'I'll call the registry office,' Mike said softly. 'Explain that we might not make it.'

'Oh, Mike,' Gill murmured.

'Kelly's the priority right now,' Mike replied, and Gill felt a wave of love and affection for this caring, big-hearted man.

'Thank you,' she whispered. 'I'll call you as soon as I have an update.'

Gill hung up, closing her eyes for a moment and exhaling deeply.

'Are you okay?' Julia asked gently, placing a hand on her arm.

Gill swallowed. 'I'm calling the police.' She dialled the number, biting her lip anxiously, then raised the phone to her ear. One ring, two rings, three—

Gill inhaled sharply; her eyes widened in alarm, her whole body going rigid.

'What is it?' Julia demanded, panicked by Gill's behaviour.

'I know where she is,' Gill burst out. 'I know! She's–' Gill broke off, and ran out of the house.

—

'Kelly!'

Gill was exhausted, gasping for breath as she stumbled through the park, shouting her daughter's name. It was a busy, sunny, Saturday lunch time, and scores of children were playing on the swings, shrieking as they whooshed down the slide, scrambling over the climbing frame. Their parents stood guard, closely watching their charges; a few of them looked over in Gill's direction, disapproval written across their faces.

But Gill didn't pay any attention to them. She veered away from the children's playground, following the path that led behind the tennis courts and down towards the stream. It was somewhere round here, she was sure of it…

'Kelly?' Gill called again.

This part of the park was deserted, overrun with thick undergrowth, bathed in shadow where the sun didn't penetrate. There used to be a statue around here, Gill knew; it had long since crumbled and decayed, but the pedestal was still there, thick ivy wreathed around its base. It made for a surprisingly comfortable seat, covered by the sweeping branches of the trees and hidden from view of any passers-by on the path. But if you cut through the bushes and knew exactly where to look…

'There you are,' Gill said softly, all the pent-up anger and anxiety dissipating the second she saw Kelly. The only thing she cared about was that her daughter was safe.

Kelly was sitting curled up on the plinth, her knees tucked into her chest, her skinny arms wrapped around her legs.

As soon as she saw Gill, she burst into tears. 'I'm sorry, Mum. I'm so, so sorry.'

'What's going on, Kel?' Gill asked, coming to sit beside her, wrapping her arms around her shoulders and squeezing her tightly. It felt so good to hold her again, to stroke her hair and smell the distinctive scent of shampoo and body spray and cocoa butter.

'I don't know.' Kelly was crying and hiccoughing. 'I just needed to get away. I just left, and I came here, to get some peace. Everything was so crazy this morning, so many people coming and going. I felt overwhelmed, like I was going to have a panic attack or something.'

'You should have told me,' Gill chastised her gently. 'We've been worried sick, Kelly. You could have texted.'

Kelly held up her phone. 'Dead. No battery.'

Gill didn't speak for a moment, letting Kelly cry as she gently rubbed her back.

'What's all this really about?' Gill asked eventually. 'I know you've had your issues with Mike, but I thought you were okay with us getting married.'

'Everything's going to change,' Kelly sobbed.

'What do you mean? Nothing's going to change.'

'Yes, it will. I already feel like I've lost my dad, now I'm going to lose you too.'

'What do you mean? Of course you're not going to lose me, I promise you, Kel. And you can see Ian as often as you want.'

'But he's always busy with his new girlfriend, and now you've got Mike. I didn't feel like there was a place for me,' Kelly explained. 'I thought the best thing for me was to get out of the way. I didn't expect you to come looking like this and kick up a fuss. I thought you'd go and get married and I'd catch up with you later or something.'

Gill almost laughed out loud. 'Of course we wouldn't do that. How could I get married without my beautiful, precious daughter by my side?'

Kelly shrugged, wiping her eyes on the back of her hand. Her eyes were red and puffy, tear tracks streaking down her cheeks.

'Look, Mike and I have said all along that we want you to be involved, and we meant it. The wedding's about all of us. And from what I've heard from Julia, you've been doing a terrific job.'

Kelly managed a half-smile. 'It's been kind of fun, I guess. But this morning it didn't feel like that.'

Gill opened her mouth to reply, but then her phone started to ring. 'It's Mike. He's been so worried,' she told Kelly. 'I found her,' she said immediately, hearing Mike's exclamation of relief on the other end. 'Yeah, she's okay, I'll explain later… Yeah, we're heading back soon… I'm really not sure. What did the registrar say? … Okay, well we'll just have to see what happens… Yeah, I know. I know. I'll keep you updated, okay? … Love you too.'

'What time is it?' Kelly asked immediately, as Gill hung up.

'Almost two. Why?'

'But the ceremony's supposed to start at three!'

'I know,' Gill said ruefully. 'I can't imagine what distracted me.'

Kelly pulled away, staring at Gill as though seeing her for the first time. 'Mum, you're wearing your dressing gown.'

Gill looked down at herself, then burst out laughing. 'Not quite a wedding dress, is it?'

But Kelly didn't laugh. She sat bolt upright, then scrambled down from the plinth. 'Shit, Mum, we've got to go.'

'Kelly, language!'

'Never mind about that now.' Kelly reached for Gill's hand, urgently tugging her off the seat. 'Come on, hurry up! We've got a wedding to get to.'

CHAPTER 39

'I first learned the concepts of non-violence in my marriage' – **Mahatma Gandhi**

'Can you see them?' Paige was standing anxiously at the edge of the field, peering as far down the road as she could, and listening for the telltale growl of an engine.

Beside her, Julia shook her head. 'They can't be far off though.'

'I'm so excited,' Paige squealed. 'I can't wait to see what they think of everything.'

At her feet, Sam clamoured to be picked up. He looked absolutely adorable in a grey three-piece suit with a blue tie, a replica of what Mike had worn for the wedding. Paige bent down and lifted him onto her hip, murmuring, 'Can you see Daddy coming in the big car?'

Sam squinted into the distance, one hand thrown over his eyes to shield them from the sun. 'I can see them, I can see them!' he yelled excitedly, kicking his legs as Paige winced in pain.

'Are you sure, Sammy? I don't think…' she trailed off, as the cream-coloured vintage Rolls-Royce purred into view. It was a glorious vehicle, with red leather seats, polished wooden runners, and the traditional white ribbon running from the wing mirrors to the silver Spirit of Ecstasy on the front.

'There they are! They're here!' Paige shouted, spinning round and beckoning for the others to join her. Freddy and Finlay sprinted across the field, their formerly pristine white shirts already covered in grass stains. Kelly followed more sedately, and Julia watched as she picked her way over the grass in her wedge heels.

She certainly looked wonderful, in the coral tulip dress which she'd accessorised with a chunky turquoise necklace. Jenny had done a fantastic job in the limited time available, applying a light covering of make-up to Kelly's youthful skin, and quickly styling her hair into a glamorous up-do, held in place with a sparkly hairclip.

Julia gave Kelly a reassuring smile as she came to stand beside her, and Kelly smiled back, looking happy and relaxed.

'Everything okay now?' Julia murmured.

Kelly nodded. 'Yeah. I feel so bad about earlier.'

'No harm done. Everything worked out okay in the end,' Julia assured her. She still didn't know exactly what had happened, or how Gill had known where to find Kelly, but right now that didn't seem to matter.

Moments later, the Rolls pulled to a stop at the side of the road and the besuited chauffeur got out, opening the door for his passengers to exit. Mike climbed out first, looking happy and proud, then held out his hand to help Gill. As soon as she emerged from the car, a chorus of cheers and applause erupted from the crowd gathered in the field. Gill clapped a hand over her mouth, looking utterly shocked as she saw everyone, tears springing into her eyes.

'Did you organise this?' she demanded, looking down at the children.

Freddy and Finlay were nodding enthusiastically, as Paige put in, 'Julia helped of course.'

'Ah, but you guys did most of it,' Julia demurred. 'You came up with all the ideas.'

'It looks incredible,' Gill breathed, dabbing at the corners of her eyes and feeling overwhelmed.

The kids had gone for a 'Funfair and Festival' theme, hiring a field in the Norfolk countryside, and going all out to fill it with as many fun things as they could find.

There were stilt walkers, jugglers and a magician, a coconut shy and a croquet pitch. There was apple bobbing and a tin can alley, and even a red London bus where guests could go and relax. A three-piece harmony group with guitars and a saxophone were strolling amongst the guests, singing 'Crazy Little Thing Called Love' and encouraging everyone to join in.

'Come and look,' Paige told Gill shyly, taking her by the hand and pulling her forwards. 'Oh, and you'll need these first.' She handed Gill and Mike a small silver bucket each, full of gold tokens. 'These are what you need for the food and games,' Paige explained, adding in a whisper, 'Everyone got some, but you two got the most.'

Gill let herself be led across the field, as the children gabbled away excitedly. The afternoon was magical, with a hot sun high in a blue sky painted with fluffy cotton-wool clouds. Gill looked beautiful in a simple cream shift dress with three-quarter-length sleeves, a pair of sparkly sandals on her feet and a cream fascinator in her cropped purple hair. In the end, she'd deliberately steered away from an over-the-top white gown, wanting something low-key for the registry office ceremony.

'It's unbelievable,' she commented to Mike, as they made their way over the grass, taking everything in.

'And to think it nearly didn't happen,' Mike whispered back, as Gill shushed him with a pointed glance at Kelly.

Kelly, however, was happily oblivious, busy showing them the Pimm's stall and the slushy stand, the beer and wine tent and the ice cream stall. There were half a dozen different food options, with a burger van, a hotdog stand, pizzas, a salad bar, and even a hog roast.

'There is *no way* I'm getting on that,' Gill giggled, as she saw the bucking bronco the kids had hired.

'You can go on the bouncy castle instead,' grinned Paige.

'I can't believe how many people are here,' Mike marvelled. There were close to a hundred and fifty people milling around the field right now, enjoying the fine weather and lounging around on picnic blankets and bales of hay.

'We added to the guest list a little bit,' Paige confessed with a grin.

'We invited all our friends, and all their parents too,' Freddy explained. 'And we've got *a lot* of friends.'

'We wanted it to be the best party EVER,' Finlay shouted, jumping into the air to emphasise his point.

'I'm sure it will be,' Gill assured him, pulling the twins to her and squeezing them tightly, as she began to tear up once again.

'What are those?' Mike asked suspiciously, looking at the cream-coloured domes in the far corner of the field.

'They're tents, Dad,' Paige told him with a giggle. 'Duh!'

'We're going to camp!' Finlay squealed, still bouncing up and down despite Gill's grip on him.

'We blew the hotel budget on the party,' Kelly explained. 'Did you know that for the same price as a night for two in a five-star hotel suite, you can hire three tipis and a yurt?'

'No,' Mike laughed. 'No, I didn't know that, Kelly.'

'And we've got midnight snacks,' Sam cried. 'And onesies.'

'Sssh, Sammy, don't spoil the surprises!'

'I hope you're planning to take lots of photos,' Mike said to Kelly.

'Of course.' She rummaged in the clutch bag that accessorised her bridesmaid outfit and pulled out a digital camera. 'I've taken loads already... but I don't have one of all of us.' She turned around, spotting Julia who was standing nearby talking to Debbie and Stevie. 'Hey Jules, would you mind taking a photo?'

Julia smiled at Kelly's familiarity, and excused herself from the conversation. 'Of course not. Okay everyone, huddle together. Big smiles and... say cheese.'

Julia clicked the button and captured the image; a beautiful, happy family with beaming smiles and not a care in the world.

———

'Well I never thought I'd spend my wedding night in a tent,' Gill giggled, as she wriggled round and cuddled up to Mike.

'I never thought I'd spend it in a separate sleeping bag from my new wife,' Mike replied. 'Bit of a passion killer.'

'Are you saying I don't look hot in my onesie?'

'You look hot in anything, wifey,' Mike replied, earning him a kiss from Gill.

They'd finally crawled into bed at gone midnight, finding that 'Just Married' onesies had been left on their sleeping bags, along with chocolates and a bottle of champagne. Surprisingly, there were more than twenty tents dotted around the field; many of their guests had taken it as the perfect opportunity to have a camping adventure with the kids, and it meant they didn't have to worry about driving home after the party.

The night had gone off without a hitch, with everyone enjoying themselves enormously, as a local band called the Rascals played a medley of hits, covering everything from The Beatles to Bruno Mars. Gill and Mike had slow-danced to a live rendition of 'Let's Stay Together', as the guests formed a circle around them, whooping and whistling. After that, there'd been no stopping everyone, the women kicking off their heels and dancing barefoot in the grass as the revelry got underway.

'So d'you reckon we can consummate this marriage?' Mike asked cheekily, moving closer. 'Or do you reckon the kids have put too many obstacles in our way? You know – onesie, sleeping bag, thin canvas tent with all our friends and family surrounding us?'

'Well, when you put it like that...' Gill laughed. 'There's always the honeymoon.'

Somewhat miraculously, they'd managed to arrange a long weekend to Sorrento, on the Italian coast. Kelly and the twins were going to stay with their father for a few days, whilst Mike's mum would stay on after the wedding to look after Paige and Sammy.

'I'm not sure I can wait until then,' Mike growled, rolling over and making a grab for Gill, who squealed hysterically, laughing as Mike unzipped her sleeping bag. Suddenly, she shushed him frantically, pushing him away.

'What is it?' he whispered, as Gill sat bolt upright, listening intently.

They heard the sound of the tent zip being undone, and Gill gripped Mike's arm tightly.

'What if it's an axe murderer?'

'Murdering newlyweds in the Norfolk countryside? Ow, you're cutting off my blood supply, Gill!' The two of them fell silent, hearts racing. 'Who's there?' Mike called out gruffly.

'Sam,' came the forlorn reply, as Gill and Mike burst out laughing.

'Sammy, what's the matter?' Gill called, as she fumbled with the torch and turned it on to see Sam standing there in his Bob the Builder pyjamas and bright red Wellington boots.

'Scared. I want to sleep in your tent,' he whispered, sucking on his thumb for comfort.

'Come on then,' Gill sighed, as she and Mike moved aside to make some space in the middle, and Sam wriggled his way between them.

'I think we might be waiting until the honeymoon after all,' Mike quipped.

Gill gave him a resigned look, then switched the torch off, plunging them into darkness. She'd barely lain back down when she heard the tent being unzipped once again; this time it was Paige.

'Dad, have you seen Sammy?' she demanded urgently. 'I've lost him. One minute he was next to me, and then the next—'

'Yes, he's here with us,' Mike told her, turning the torch back on.

'Oh,' Paige chuckled as she saw the three of them. Sam snuggled up to Gill, patting the space beside him for Paige to join them. As she crawled in beside Mike, he and Gill exchanged weary glances, all thoughts of romance pushed firmly to one side.

It wasn't long before they heard the twins giggling and whispering outside, then two heads appeared in the tent's entrance.

'We heard voices,' Finlay explained.

'And we wanted to join in,' added Freddy, as he launched himself into the middle of the group, landing heavily on Mike's stomach.

Moments later, the six of them were blinded by a brilliant flash. When Gill's eyes adjusted, she saw Kelly kneeling inside the tent, a smile on her face and her camera in her hand.

'Come on in, then,' Gill laughed. 'Why not? The more the merrier.'

Somehow, all five children managed to find space in the tiny tent, crammed in between Gill and Mike, all cuddled up and cosy. It might not have been the most conventional way to spend her wedding night, Gill reflected, but for her it was perfect. She had her family around her, the man she loved beside her, and she wouldn't have had it any other way.

———

The moon was full and bright in the dark night sky as Nick and Julia drove home along the deserted country roads. Jack was fast asleep in his car seat, snoring gently; he'd passed out hours ago, tucked warmly beneath a blanket as he snoozed in his pushchair.

Julia felt relaxed and contented, her feet aching from all the dancing, her head a little fuzzy from the champagne. She leant across to where Nick was driving, resting a hand lovingly on his knee.

'It was a good night, wasn't it?' she murmured.

'Almost as good as our wedding… But not quite.'

'Our wedding was amazing, wasn't it?' Julia sighed, remembering how much fun they'd had.

'It was the second best day of my life – after Jack's birth.'

'Hmm, Jack's birth was kind of mixed emotions for me. Utterly amazing to have Jack, but the most painful experience of my life by a mile.'

'I'm sure you were exaggerating,' Nick teased, as he dodged a playful poke from Julia. She let her hand settle back on his knee, running her fingertips teasingly along his thigh.

'Do you think we've changed?' Nick asked thoughtfully, after a pause. 'You know, since we got married.'

'Yeah, I'm sure we have,' Julia replied, surprised by Nick's reflective mood. 'But that's life, isn't it? All of these experiences change you, but as long as you're on the same page, you come through them stronger than ever.'

'Good. I hoped you'd say that,' Nick smiled, taking one hand off the steering wheel and lacing his fingers through his wife's. 'I might not always say it, and it might get lost in all the everyday rubbish, but I do love you, Jules. More than ever.'

'I love you too,' Julia told him, before letting out an enormous yawn.

Nick laughed. 'Don't worry, Cinderella. We might not get back before the clock strikes midnight, but we'll be home soon.'

'I can think of one or two things I'd like to do when we get there,' Julia winked suggestively.

Nick looked at her in surprise. 'Really? Is that a promise?'

'Absolutely.'

'Then I'd better put my foot down!'

Nick pressed the accelerator and the car leapt forward with a growl, speeding through the quiet night to ferry its precious cargo safely home.

EPILOGUE

*'A good marriage is like a casserole, only those
responsible for it really know what goes in it'* –
Unknown

Three months later...

Aimee was sitting at a window table in Mimi's Cafe, a stack
of books piled in front of her beside a forgotten cup of coffee.
She was oblivious to the rest of the world, absorbed in a copy
of *Great Expectations* by Charles Dickens. She turned the pages
eagerly, her head full of the marshes of Kent, the adventures of
Pip and the cruelties of Estella.

It was Saturday and, in just two days' time, Aimee's degree
course would start at the University of Norwich. She was both
excited and terrified in equal measure – excited to start her new
life and begin doing what she'd dreamed about for so many
months now, but terrified in case she couldn't handle it. She'd be
attending lectures with eighteen- and nineteen-year-olds, fresh
out of college, or just back from their gap year travels; Aimee
hadn't studied for more than five years now, and wasn't sure if
she could still remember how.

She'd spent the last few weeks trying to prepare herself, burying herself in literature as she ploughed through the recom-

mended reading list, devouring Shakespeare and the Brontës and even attempting Chaucer.

Her newly found studiousness wasn't the only change taking place in Aimee's life recently. After that fateful evening at Valerie's house, she'd moved back in with her parents – something Pauline was delighted about. She'd signed up with a temp agency and got some summertime admin work, so she finally had a (small) income once again, and was saving every penny she could.

And, of course, she'd put in her university application. She was worried she'd be too late for the September start, but she'd been thrilled to be accepted to study English Literature alongside QTS training. It meant that, in three years' time, she'd be a qualified teacher, Aimee realised, thinking what a different path her life would have taken if she'd become Mrs Jonathan Cunningham.

Looking back on her relationship with Jon, Aimee couldn't understand what on earth had possessed her to put up with him for as long as she had. Even when the warning signs had become too obvious to ignore, Aimee had stumbled on, naively believing that everything might work out in the end. A desire to please everyone – her parents, her fiancé, and his awful mother – meant that she'd suppressed her feelings of unhappiness and frustration, her own personality gradually subsumed by Jon's until she was nothing more than an extension of him and what he wanted.

Since their break-up, Aimee had blossomed. She'd reconnected with her old friends, and they'd met for dinner, gone for drinks and danced the night away, having fun the way women her age were supposed to. She'd rediscovered the little things that she loved, simple pleasures like watching *EastEnders* or reading gossip magazines – things that Jon would never have approved of. Aimee could see now how she'd deferred to him on every decision, from what she should wear to what she should eat for dinner that evening. It was frightening how much control he'd had over her.

Aimee had seen Jon only once since she'd broken off their engagement, when she'd gone round to his flat to collect her things. Jon had been civil, but cold, and he was clearly still hurting badly, however much he tried to hide it. Aimee suspected it was the blow to his ego that had hit him hardest.

She'd made the decision to only take the things that she'd bought herself, and it was almost embarrassing how very few possessions that amounted to. She'd left behind a whole rail of clothes, a dozen boxes of jewellery, endless DVDs and books, not to mention her beloved iPad. There was no doubt that Jon had been extremely generous towards her, but if Aimee was going to move on, she needed to leave all that behind.

The two of them hadn't been in touch since and Aimee didn't expect them to be. Their worlds were too different; there was little chance of them salvaging a friendship from their disastrous failed relationship, and they both knew it.

'Aimee!'

Aimee's head snapped up as she heard someone call her name, and she looked up to see Julia and Debbie standing there.

'Hello, you two,' she beamed, closing her book as she stood up to give them both a hug.

'It's so good to see you,' Julia exclaimed, as she slid into the chair beside her. 'You look fabulous.'

'Thanks,' Aimee grinned. She'd acquired a tan over the summer, and she'd let her hair grow out, the blonde waves already below her shoulder blades. She was dressing far more casually these days too, now that Jon didn't dictate her wardrobe, relaxing comfortably in cropped jeans and a loose, striped T-shirt.

'Ooh, *Great Expectations*,' Debbie said, sounding awestruck as she noticed Aimee's choice of reading material. 'Very impressive.'

'Yes, well, I'm a student now,' Aimee explained, looking bashful. 'Well, almost. I start on Monday.'

'I'm so proud of you for doing that,' Julia gushed. 'It's great to see you following your dreams.'

'Well I'm definitely a lot happier now,' Aimee replied, and Julia knew that she was referring to more than just her decision to study.

'Has anyone heard from Gill?' Debbie wondered.

'Yeah, she should be along soon. I think she was dropping Sammy at a friend's birthday party. She never stops!'

'I can't wait to see her,' Debbie sighed. 'I can't believe we haven't had a chance for a proper catch-up before now.'

'I know. The time just flies,' Julia agreed. 'Can you believe it's almost a year ago since we were first sitting here, brainstorming ideas for your wedding? It seems like ages ago.'

'And now I've been married for three whole months,' Debbie laughed, her eyes widening as the waitress put down a tall glass of hot chocolate in front of her, liberally topped with whipped cream. 'Ooh, that looks delicious, thank you.'

'Wow!' Julia exclaimed, as she poured herself a cup of tea. 'Looks like you've eased up on the diet since the wedding.'

Debbie giggled guiltily. 'This is a one-off treat, okay? It's a special occasion! But I'm definitely not obsessively calorie counting like I was before. I'm still trying to keep an eye on what I eat and not let it run out of control, and so far it seems to be working. I have put on a bit of weight,' she admitted. 'But I'm staying pretty stable at a size fourteen, and that's good enough for me.'

'Well you look great,' Julia assured her. 'Positively glowing.'

'Thanks,' Debbie grinned. 'I came off the diet as soon as we got on honeymoon. There was no way I could resist all that gorgeous Greek food – that delicious bread with houmous and tzatziki, the enormous salads with feta cheese drenched in olive oil. Not to mention all the meat and moussaka and… mmm…' Debbie finished happily, practically dribbling at the memory.

'Sounds like someone had a good honeymoon,' Aimee teased.

'We did other things apart from eat!' Debbie retorted.

'I bet you did,' Julia shot back, which set Debbie off blushing.

'I meant cultural things and… oh never mind, get your minds out of the gutter!'

They all laughed, as the door swung open and Gill rushed in, wearing her usual harassed expression.

'Sorry, I'm late,' she called, as she threw herself into the empty seat. 'Bit of an emergency. No one bothered telling me until the last minute that Sammy's party was fancy dress so I had to improvise – we wrapped him in tinfoil and told everyone he was a spaceman. Could I get a latte?' she asked the waitress, who was dropping off a plate of scones with jam and cream at their table.

'Mmm, they look incredible,' Aimee sighed, reaching for one, as the others followed suit. 'By the way, Julia, I've been meaning to ask – did you have any trouble with Valerie after… well, you know.'

Julia rolled her eyes. 'Oh, she was a nightmare, as you'd expect. Obviously everything was a little bit awkward, but when I sent her my final invoice, she refused to pay a penny!'

'No!' Aimee stared at her in shock.

'She said that she'd hired me to organise a wedding, and as there was no wedding she didn't see why she should pay me anything.'

'Oh, Jules, I'm so sorry…'

'What about all the work you'd done up until then?' Debbie cut in, looking horrified.

'Exactly. It all got a bit nasty, really. I had to hire a solicitor, and Valerie was still ignoring the situation, insisting she didn't owe me anything. I was dreading having to take her to court.'

'You should have told me,' Aimee insisted, as Julia shook her head.

'There was no point getting you involved. Believe me, you were best off out of there.'

'But I thought she had tons of money,' Debbie spoke up.

'She does,' Aimee agreed. 'I can't believe she refused to pay. She knew how much work you'd done, Jules.'

'Well, anyway, the whole thing was ridiculous and it was getting really stressful. I was at the end of my tether, when Nick had a brilliant idea.'

'Ooh, what?'

Julia grinned. 'He suggested we write letters to certain prominent people, who just happened to be Valerie's friends. So I sent one to the local MP – you know, Nigel Bowles – and another to Mary Moorhouse, who's the President of the Norfolk Chamber of Commerce, and who'd originally recommended me to Valerie. I explained that I'd taken Valerie on as a client as I understood that they were friends, but unfortunately I wasn't able to get any response from Valerie with regards to settling my invoice, and it was now extremely overdue. Could she be of any assistance?'

'Oh, she'd have hated that,' Aimee squealed, her eyes sparkling.

'What happened?' Debbie asked breathlessly.

Julia let out a wicked cackle. 'The money landed in my bank account the next day.'

Gill was shaking her head, looking disgusted. 'It just shows you, doesn't it? Honestly, the cheek of the woman.'

'I think it's brilliant,' Debbie grinned. 'It just shows you how much she cares about her reputation.'

'That's pretty much the only thing she does care about,' Aimee muttered under her breath, thinking once again what a lucky escape she'd had.

'Anyway, let's change the subject,' Julia said brightly, turning to Gill and asking, 'So how's married life treating you?'

Gill smiled enigmatically. 'Well on the surface, nothing's really changed – everything in our house is still just as manic as ever. But I think the difference is that there's this feeling of security, which is lovely, really.'

'Aw, that's so sweet,' Debbie sighed.

'And what about Kelly?' Julia asked hesitantly. 'Is everything okay with her?'

'Seems to be, fingers crossed. She's been making such an effort recently, getting on with Mike and Paige, helping out around the house. She's really happy doing her blog, and she's getting lot of hits, or whatever you call them. I just wish she'd spend as much time on her schoolwork, but you can't have everything I suppose. Although she's getting top marks in English.'

'She's a great kid,' Julia smiled. 'I'm so pleased she's doing well.'

'Funnily enough, Paige has been talking about becoming an events planner,' Gill laughed. 'When it was Sammy's birthday, she insisted on picking a colour theme, and buying matching paper plates and napkins.'

'Tell her not to do it,' Julia laughed. 'Tell her to get a proper job instead, this one's too stressful!'

'Have you got much on at the moment?' Debbie wondered.

'Yeah, it's been pretty hectic. I've had quite a few corporate events over the summer, which are always good fun as they have such large budgets, and now I'm starting to get lots of enquiries about Christmas parties, so I'm scheduling those in. But business is going well, Nick seems happy, and Jack's amazing.' Her face softened as she spoke about him. 'He's a real little character.'

'How about you?' Gill turned to Debbie. 'Any babies on the horizon?'

'What do you mean? I've already got Scamp, he's my baby,' she chuckled. 'To be honest, we have talked about it and… well, watch this space,' she grinned.

The women chattered on, discussing love and life and children, and their fears and hopes for the future. They knew that life wasn't always easy, that it would throw up challenges for all of them, but there would be moments of real happiness and joy too. The past year had only reinforced what was most important to all of them and, with family, friends and love in their lives, they were lucky enough to be blessed with everything they needed.

LETTER FROM SOPHIE

Hello, lovely readers, and a massive thank you for reading *The Girl's Guide to Getting Hitched* – I hope you liked it!

I'm currently planning my own wedding, so taking on three fictional weddings at the same time was so much fun! It meant I got to vicariously experience all different styles of wedding, and for the last few months I've been immersed in a world of handsome grooms, diamond rings and beautiful white dresses – what could be better!?

If you'd like to find out more about what I'm up to, or even just say hello, you can find me on Twitter and Facebook. Do pop by for a chat!

To keep right up-to-date with the latest news on my new releases just sign up using the link below:

www.bookouture.com/sophie-hart

And finally, if you enjoyed *The Girl's Guide to Getting Hitched* and would like to tell others about it, I'd be very grateful if you could write a review. It really does make such a difference, and a great one can make an author's day!

With very best wishes,

Sophie x

🐦 @Cafe_Crumb

f ngbclub

THE GIRL'S GUIDE TO FALLING IN LOVE

A refreshingly open and **uplifting romantic comedy about friendship and love.** Sometimes you need to step out of your comfort zone in order to give a relationship a good dose of TLC…

Annie Hall helps couples put the fizz back into their relationships. It's a shame her own love life is non-existent. When Jamie who works next door catches her eye, she can't ignore the spark of chemistry.

Most men would jump at the chance to skive off work for an afternoon quickie with their gorgeous wife, but Nick knows Julia is after only one thing – a baby. Sex shouldn't be a chore. Can Annie help Julia see that?

Newly engaged Zoe and Simon can't keep their hands off each other. They've decided to take a vow of celibacy until their wedding night. Will Annie help them stick to it?

Ray and Linda have been married for over thirty years but she's more interested in the family business than spending time with him. Can Annie convince Linda to rediscover her passion for Ray after all this time?

While Annie begins to work her magic with the three couples, she soon discovers that she'll need to take some of her own advice if she's going to let a new man into her life.

Note: previously published as 'A Girl's Guide to the Birds and the Bees'.

'A charming, feel-good novel… **packed full of friendship, romance and was simply a really warm read** – the equivalent of an uplifting day spent catching up with old friends with lots of laughs and smiles.' *Reviewed the Book*

Lightning Source UK Ltd.
Milton Keynes UK
UKOW06f0822070617

302831UK00022B/542/P